BLOOD TIES

BLOOD TIES

NICHOLAS GUILD

A TOM DOHERTY ASSOCIATES BOOK

NEW YORK

BLOOD TIES

Copyright © 2015 by Nicholas Guild

A Forge Book
Published by Tom Doherty Associates, LLC
175 Fifth Avenue
New York, NY 10010

www.tor-forge.com

Forge® is a registered trademark of Tom Doherty Associates, LLC.

The Library of Congress Cataloging-in-Publication Data is available upon request.

ISBN 978-0-7653-7845-3 (hardcover)
ISBN 978-1-4668-6160-2 (e-book)

Forge books may be purchased for educational, business, or promotional use. For information on bulk purchases, please contact the Macmillan Corporate and Premium Sales Department at 1-800-221-7945, extension 5442, or write to specialmarkets@macmillan.com.

First Edition: May 2015

Printed in the United States of America

0 9 8 7 6 5 4 3 2 1

This book is for Thia,
who knows all the reasons why.

BLOOD TIES

1

The rain had stopped just before dawn, but up on the coast high-way the air was still laden with heavy mist, enough to dissolve the flashers on the police cruisers into pulses of smeary red light. A couple of uniformed officers Ellen didn't recognize were already put-ting up yellow tape to keep onlookers at a distance. The morning traffic was light, but word got around, even on a weekend. In twenty minutes they would have their hands full.

The site was a lookout point with space for about ten cars. She saw three black-and-whites and a dented powder-blue Chevy, which presumably belonged to the man who had phoned in the report, which meant that Ellen's partner Sam hadn't yet made it up from Daly City.

Even before she had put her Toyota into park, a cop was leaning over the door.

"You'll have to move on, Miss. This is a police inquiry."

Without so much as glancing at him, she opened the door and, as she stepped outside, took out her badge case and lapped it over the breast pocket of her worn tweed jacket. Standing there, she was al-most as tall as he was.

"I'm Ridley," she answered.

The dispatchers did this to her every time, as if the gag would never wear thin. They would radio the scene, *Inspector Ridley will be there in twenty minutes,* and never use her first name.

Two years ago, during her early days on the homicide squad, she would have made an issue of it. She would have looked the man straight in the face, daring him to smile or say a word, daring him to look beyond the badge to the slender woman with short reddish-brown hair who appeared perfectly ready to break both his knees. But somewhere along the line she had made her peace with what the other women detectives referred to as the Nancy Drew syndrome. You can't reform the world.

So she directed her attention to a group of four men drinking coffee out of Styrofoam cups. All of them were cops except one, who looked ancient and was wearing a green Army coat he had probably owned since Korea.

"Is that the guy who found her?"

"Yeah."

"Anybody question him yet?"

"No. We were waiting for you."

Ellen nodded, as if acknowledging a neutral fact, but she was pleased. During her three years in uniform she had had it drilled into her that the officers who got there first were supposed to protect the crime scene, identify and detain any witnesses, and keep their mouths shut, but not everyone followed procedure.

As she approached, the three uniforms faded back and left her alone with the man in the Army coat, who smiled at her until he saw the badge. He had a weathered face, and the fingernails of the hand that held the coffee cup were discolored by decades of cigarette smoke.

"You went fishing this morning?" she asked.

He nodded. "Down just before sunrise. That's the best time."

His eyes glittered with excitement, but that was natural enough. Half an hour ago he had found a dead body, so the adrenaline was still rushing. He had had time to stop being scared and now he was just enjoying himself.

But he had been scared enough then. His khaki trousers were covered with fresh mud, as if he had scrambled back up that bluff on his hands and knees.

Ellen looked over to where the land seemed to end abruptly in a few tufts of dry grass. It was a good sixty feet to the beach and almost a straight drop. She would not have liked climbing around there in the dark.

"You know, you're not supposed to do that." She tried to keep it from sounding like a threat. "The tide can come in here pretty fast. Every couple of years it catches somebody before they can get back on the trail, and the body washes up in Half Moon Bay."

"Don't worry about me," he said, happy to show off a little. "I've lived in the Bay Area for forty years. I know this coast, every inch of it."

"So when was the last time you fished this stretch?"

"Two weekends ago. Yeah—last Sunday I was a couple of miles further south."

"And you went down this morning in the dark? When did you find the body?"

"Right away. I had my flashlight with me, and she was hard to miss."

He laughed nervously, making it sound like the punch line of a dirty joke, like whoever was lying down there dead was somehow the guilty one. Ellen decided she didn't like the fisherman very much. She would leave him to Sam, who would manage to convey the impression that the police regarded him as a leading suspect. That would ruin his day.

"Thank you," she said, glancing away. "Someone will be along shortly to take your full statement."

"Will I have to go downtown?"

Ellen smiled at him, perhaps a trifle maliciously. "Oh yes. You'll get to know us all real well."

And now it was time to pay her respects.

Sam said you got used to it, but she was beginning to wonder. Death still had not lost its power to humble her. Even if the corpse was a drug mule, shot in a dispute with management and left in some alley off Mission Street, she could never quite overcome the feeling that she was intruding on a private tragedy, that she was out of place. That it was none of her business.

"You're not being rude," Sam had told her once, when she was a fresh transfer from Juvenile Division and he had only just stopped expecting her to sick up. "They're dead. They won't mind. Stop worrying about their modesty. If it makes you feel better, just remember that you're the last person who's ever going to do them a favor. You're going to catch whoever killed them."

The grass at the edge of the bluff waved forlornly in the ocean breeze. The path down to the beach was just wide enough for one person and the night's rain had churned the gravelly ground into mud.

The victim was about fifteen feet from the top, head down, snagged on the bushes so that her left arm fell across the path as if she were trying to arrest her fall. Except for her bikini-style red panties and a pair of red satin heels, she was naked. Her face was turned away and her short, dishwater blond hair was matted and dirty, almost as if she were wearing a cap. There were no obvious wounds, but she was lying facedown so there wouldn't be.

Ellen, standing on the edge, forced herself not to look away. It was the terrible helplessness of the dead that got to her. This woman, who-ever she was, could not so much as put up a hand to ward off the disrespectful attention of strangers. She had been stripped not only of her life but of her dignity as a human being and had not even the power to protest. Somehow that fact made what was happening to her now almost as bad as death itself. It was as if they had all be-come accomplices in a murder of her soul.

"I think the shoes add a nice touch, don't you? I always like a vil-lain with a sense of humor."

She hadn't noticed Sam coming up behind her. He took off his hat to push back a tangle of steel gray hair. The hat was canvas, putty col-ored and brand-new, the only thing he was wearing that didn't look as if it had come out of the Goodwill bag, and he put it back on his head with appropriate delicacy. Sam, who had a reputation for being the best homicide detective in the state, had been on Homicide for fourteen years and Ellen's partner since she had come on the squad.

"He's teasing us," Ellen said, with just the faintest trace of resent-ment. "He wanted her found quickly, and he wanted us to know it. He didn't just throw her out of the trunk of his car."

"If he had, those bushes wouldn't have held her. The crabs would be having her for breakfast. I think he carried her down there."

"Probably. And the rain last night took care of any fiber evidence."

"He's a clever bastard." Sam lit a cigarette, an unfiltered Camel, and took a drag so deep he gave the impression he had been holding his breath.

"What do you make of the panties?" she asked. "Why did he leave them on?"

"Good question. But I don't suppose we'll find out until we can ask him." He took the cigarette out of his mouth and frowned slightly, as if faced with an unpleasant choice. "You want to go down there and do the honors?"

"Aren't you coming?"

He shook his head and smiled. "She's all yours, Ellie. I can wait until she's on the table. Have you had a word with whoever found her?"

"Only just. I left him for you."

This made Sam laugh. "I'll see if I can't smarten up his attitude a little," he said.

The path to the beach was treacherous. She had to watch her feet every step or the rain-slick, sandy earth would slip away under her shoes and take her with it. Ellen could see why someone going down here in the dark might make it almost to the body before noticing it.

And that, apparently, was what had happened to their fisherman, because his flashlight, coated with mud, was lying not five feet from where the dead woman's hand reached out onto the path. His big surf-casting rod was hung up in some bushes nearby. He must have had himself quite a shock.

"Steady, girl," she told herself, just under her breath, so that no one except she could hear. "Stay below zero."

She had learned she had to distance herself from the normal human responses. Disgust, anger and pity just got in the way. She was there to observe. That was it. And it was the only part of her job she really hated. But it was what she owed to the dead.

There were beads of rainwater all over the woman's skin. It was obvious there was no evidence here beyond the body itself, but Ellen still was careful not to disturb the scene. Holding on to some bushes, she went off the path to get lower down to have a peek at the face.

Nobody's looks were improved by a night out in the rain, especially if they were dead to begin with, and Ellen had the impression this lady might have been someone who cared about appearances. There were still traces of makeup on her face, and from the way it was holding up it didn't seem to be the kind you picked up at Kmart. There was a thin gold chain around her neck that looked like it might be worth something.

She was a small woman, with the light bones of someone destined to stay slender. Her eyes were open. There was no expression in them, but there never was. Ellen didn't see any obvious wounds or ligature marks around her throat.

She found herself staring at the arm stretched out into the path, and then she realized why. There was a band on the wrist where the rainwater seemed to be beading differently. Ellen took a pair of latex gloves out of her jacket pocket and put them on. Then she reached out to touch the skin. It felt sticky. The murderer had probably used duct tape to bind his victim's arms together. In a week they would probably identify the brand, which probably wouldn't bring them any closer to catching the son of a bitch but at least would provide one more homely detail to add to their impression of him.

"You'll have to pardon me, Inspector Ridley."

Ellen looked up and saw Allen Shaw, MD, Chief of Forensic Pathology for the City and County of San Francisco, standing almost directly above her. He was wearing a clear rain slicker over his brown suit and holding a black medical bag in his left hand.

She was surprised to see him because Dr. Shaw was not known to be a particularly zealous public servant. It was unusual to find him out this early on a Sunday morning, attending to a routine suspicious death. He had assistants for that sort of thing.

"All yours, Doc," Ellen said, releasing her hold on the victim's wrist and stepping a pace back down the slope.

"Much obliged."

Dr. Shaw frowned at her and crouched beside the body. He was a heavyset man in his early sixties, so that was a laborious process. He opened his bag, pulled on a pair of latex gloves and took out a fingerprint kit.

"You'll oblige me even further if you'll stick around long enough to take these up to my truck," he said as he began inking the fingers of the dead woman's hand. "I'll hardly be a moment."

The coroner's van was parked just at the edge of the bluff, and a middle-aged woman in a white lab coat was standing in front of the open rear door. She almost snatched the fingerprint card out of Ellen's hand.

Sam was still talking to the fisherman. When he finished he glanced in her direction and Ellen nodded toward her car.

"I think we've got a situation here," she told him. "Shaw's down there. The first thing he did was take prints. They're being faxed in right now."

"Since when can't they wait to print her at the morgue?"

"My point exactly. You check the missing persons sheets lately? I don't happen to recall seeing Reese Witherspoon's name on the list."

Sam appeared not to have heard. He was staring out at the highway, where cars were crawling past and a group of about thirty on-lookers had already gathered beyond the yellow police tape.

Some were just passersby, and some, the Fans, had probably heard a report over their shortwaves and come running. Their cars were curbed across the highway, pulled up on the muddy shoulder.

They looked the usual sort: mostly male, mostly young to midthirties, mostly giving the impression they had nothing better to do with their lives than be flies on the wall at every murder investigation since the Stone Age. They would hang around until the body was brought up, or until somebody got annoyed and went over to start handing out parking tickets.

Ellen glanced at them and then almost as quickly looked away.

"What do you think, Ellie? Did Our Boy get the door prize this time? You suppose maybe he killed somebody the world might miss?"

"Where's the photographer, Sam?"

"Say what?" He looked at her as if she had just lapsed into Norwegian. "He came with Shaw, so I guess he's down with our mystery guest."

"I think I'll go tell him to take some shots of the crowd."

"Why? You see a familiar face?"

"I don't know."

"Woman's intuition?" He smiled, as if he had decided to indulge her in a whim, and then he turned to look back toward the trail down to the beach. "I'll see if I can scare him up."

"And tell him not to announce himself, pretty please. Some people are camera shy."

"I think he probably knows that, Ellie."

As soon as she was alone, Ellen started to feel bored and then apprehensive. She glanced at the gray dawn sky and it occurred to her that she should probably phone Mindy Epstein, her roommate during their last two years in college, whom she was supposed to be meeting for lunch today to hear the details of her second divorce. Mindy was probably asleep in the arms of some new gentleman friend—Mindy had no gift for abstinence.

Ellen's parents had almost certainly gone out somewhere last night, probably until the small hours. They had a wide circle of friends and belonged to a number of clubs, and her mother was fervently sociable.

It was a Sunday morning and, except for fishermen, murder victims and cops, everyone was home in their beds. Even Gwendolyn was doubtless still asleep in her cage, dreaming of lamb chop bones.

Which constituted one more reason to resent the perpetrator, who had already started out on the wrong foot by leaving his victim on what amounted to a cliff face, where there was no room for a proper workup of the scene and where a nasty night could reasonably be expected to have scrubbed everything squeaky clean.

Ellen's taste in homicides ran to dimly lit walkups, where the bedroom carpet was matted with fiber evidence and the light switch was always smudgy with fingerprints. It all might end up as nothing, but it gave you hope and something to do, and you didn't have to stand around thinking about how clever this particular nut job was beginning to seem and how if you caught him at all it would probably be just dumb luck.

Ellen was reasonably sure he had killed at least twice before. There were at present two uncleared homicides of women, both apparently random and both what might best be described as recreational murders—someone's idea of fun—but there was nothing specific in their methods or physical circumstances to connect them. Nothing except a certain polish to both performances.

The first victim was three months ago, a seventeen-year-old hooker, but already beginning to be known to the vice squad, who worked the downtown hotels and had turned up in a bathtub at the Marriott. Somebody had stuffed the muzzle of a .22-caliber pistol about four inches up her rectum and then fired off two rounds, hollow points that disintegrated without hitting anything vital but had torn her insides apart so that she bled to death in seconds. No evidence of sexual assault and, needless to say, nobody heard the shots, nobody saw anything, there were no prints and no trace of the weapon, and the room hadn't been rented in three days. A "Do Not Disturb" sign was found hanging from the bathroom doorknob.

The murderer, who thereafter was referred to by Sam as "Our Boy," couldn't have gotten off to a worse start because, as it happened, the victim was known to Ellen.

Four years before, while she was still in her first year with juvie, Ellen had arrested a thirteen-year-old named Rita Blandish for shoplifting at a gourmet food shop in North Beach. It was the second time in less than a week the manager had caught her at it, so he detained Rita in his office and called the police.

She was a dark-haired little thing, vaguely pretty and still on the innocent side of puberty, and she was clearly terrified. She sat on the chair beside the manager's desk, tears running down her face and her eyes wide with dread.

While her partner sat with the manager and filled out the complaint form, Ellen took Rita outside to their car.

Once she had the girl in the rear passenger compartment, which was as secure as any jail cell, Ellen climbed into the front passenger seat and twisted around to look at her prisoner through the clear plastic barrier.

"What did you steal?"

Immediately Rita began shaking her head, so fast she might have given herself whiplash.

"I didn't steal anything," she almost shouted. "I was gonna pay for it."

Ellen made a sound that was just short of an exasperated laugh.

"You know, you're not going to do yourself any good by lying, so let me rephrase the question. What did you steal?"

"Two cans of tuna fish."

Instantly Rita began to cry again, and Ellen was left to wonder why any little girl who hadn't even had her first period yet would steal tuna fish. Candy, yes. Something fancy and expensive, sure. But not tuna fish.

She couldn't help herself. Ellen felt sorry for the little tyke.

"You know, it isn't going to be that bad," she said. "How old are you?"

"Thirteen last August."

And here it was October. As old as that.

"Well, nobody's going to assume that you're a career criminal at thirteen. Have you ever been arrested before?"

"No."

"Then you'll probably only get a little probation. And when you turn eighteen your juvenile records are sealed. It isn't going to follow you through life.

"So, why tuna fish?"

"What?"

"Why did you steal tuna fish?"

Her question seemed to perplex Rita—not the question itself but why anyone would need to ask.

"You can go a long time on a can of tuna fish," she said.

• • •

A little investigating cleared up the mystery of why the nutritional value of tuna fish might be important. While Rita was enjoying her first dinner at the Juvenile Detention Center, Ellen drove over to the address Rita had listed as home. It was a down-at-heel apartment building in the Mission District, and Ellen had to phone the owner, whose number was conveniently listed in the entranceway above the mailboxes, before she could get into Number 105.

There were the usual signs of recent human habitation—dishes in the kitchen sink, a sweater lying across the back of a chair in the only bedroom, et cetera—but the clothes closet contained only what one assumed was Rita's meager wardrobe and the bathroom had been pretty well cleaned out. There was an empty box of Playtex tampons in the wastepaper basket, but no other sign that the apartment was inhabited by a woman old enough to be Rita's mother, and evidence of any male presence was completely absent.

The refrigerator and the kitchen cabinets were almost empty of food, which explained why Rita had been stealing tuna fish.

At thirteen years old she had been left to fend for herself. What choice did she have except to steal?

"Mom took off," was the way Rita explained things, the next morning. She didn't seem to regard it as anything like an unusual occurrence, so perhaps it had happened before.

"When did she do that?"

"Eight or nine days ago. I'm not sure. It was a Friday."

"Where did she go?"

The only answer was a shrug.

"What about your father?"

But Rita just looked at her blankly, then said, "Mom had a lot of men friends."

In the end Ellen talked the gourmet-food-store manager into dropping the charges, and Rita was classified as an abandoned child. She was put into foster care.

Nothing was ever again heard of her mother.

Thereafter, Ellen kept a loose watch on little Rita, and it turned out to be a sensible precaution. At its worst, foster care was little more than a racket, and Rita's first such home was pretty bad. Ellen got her out of that, and her second placement seemed to be a little better. At least, Rita wasn't complaining.

There was some trouble along the way, usually with boys or what passed among adolescents for recreational drugs. And then, the previous year, Rita simply disappeared.

• • •

And now she had turned up again, dead for probably a little less than twenty-four hours, crouched naked in a bathtub at the Marriot Hotel with a wide smear of dried blood trailing down the inside of her left leg from her anus.

Her face was turned to the right, as if the killer had twisted her head around, perhaps for the pleasure of watching her death agony. Ellen had recognized her at once.

It was too much. Ellen simply stood up and walked out of the room. When Sam followed her, he found her sitting on the corner of one of the twin beds, sobbing.

"Are you all right?" he asked.

It was a fair length of time before Ellen was able to answer him.

"No, I'm not all right," she said, her voice ragged. "I knew that girl from juvie." Her shoulders hunched in a despairing shrug. "Sam, if ever there was a kid who didn't get the breaks, it was her."

Sam gave her about two minutes to settle down, and then he shook his head.

"We all get cases like that," he said, wistfully. "I remember once . . ." And then his voice trailed off, as if whatever memory he was on the point of relating had suddenly engulfed him.

When he spoke again, his voice was almost grim.

"Ellie, very few people deserve to get murdered, but we're homicide detectives, not social workers. Injustice is our stock-in-trade. Now get back in there and tell me what you see."

Ellen got up from the bed and did as she was told. She would be fine, she thought. Or at least okay.

But she promised herself that Rita Blandish would have her revenge.

• • •

Then, last month, a man in North Beach had taken his car out of the garage, noticed a bad smell and opened the trunk. There he found the body of a woman who had lived directly across the street, a saleswoman named Kathy Hudson with no known boyfriends, reported missing by her mother the week before. Her throat had been cut, very carefully, so that it took a while for her to die. There was minimal blood in the trunk, indicating she had been killed elsewhere, and the man who owned the car had just that afternoon returned from a two-week vacation in the Philippines. No suspects, no leads, no useful physical evidence.

Like everyone else, murderers sharpened their skills with practice, and both of these crimes were what Sam described as "quality work," not the kind of slapdash performance you see in your garden-variety sex slaying. The odds of two such virtuosos operating in the same city at the same time were not very good.

Ellen wasn't alone in making the link, but at present the department was treating the two homicides as unrelated. The department did not want to admit even the possibility that there was a serial killer at large in the Bay Area because the news media would go straight overboard with it and that wouldn't be good for public morale.

Homicide—the Holy Grail of police work. It offered a panoramic view of all that was darkest in human character. Greed, lust and madness, in every possible permutation. From time to time it occurred to Ellen to wonder if she wasn't a little mad herself to be so committed to it.

Only her father understood. "Sometimes I almost envy you," he had told her once. "Working with children, I hardly ever see the aberration played out to its logical extremity. I haven't dealt with a full-blown sociopath since I was a resident."

"I'm only interested in catching them, Daddy," she had told him. "I don't try to understand them."

But he had smiled and said, "Oh yes, you do."

And now Mommy wanted him to give up his practice so that he would have more time to partner her at bridge. What she didn't understand—what she could not see, no matter how or how often Ellen explained it to her—was that if she succeeded in badgering him into retirement he would die of boredom. He would never live to collect Social Security.

Each of them, father and daughter, needed their work to keep life real.

It was twenty minutes before the photographer came up from shooting the body. He was carrying a video camera in a shoulder sling, so that it was pressed between his chest and his right arm. He was very good. He faced the road and then turned his body to pan the crowd that had collected behind the police tape. He did it twice, looking up at the sky over their heads like a man trying to decide whether it would rain again. They never noticed.

"How do you want 'em?" he asked, coming up next to her. "Stills or the movie?"

"Can I get both?"

The photographer shrugged. He was a short, compact man with a blond crew cut and a face suggesting that life had run out of surprises. He wore soiled jeans and a torn gray T-shirt. He looked about thirty-five.

"You can have anything you want. You'll get the disk this afternoon, but the stills won't be before Tuesday. Shaw wants to do the post right away, so I'll be busy with that. Sorry."

"The movie will be fine for starters. Thanks."

"Don't mention it."

He took a stick of Juicy Fruit out of his pocket, peeled away the tinfoil, folded the gum in half and stuck it in his mouth, all without even glancing at Ellen.

"I hate this fucking job," he said, and strolled away.

Sam came up to the top of the footpath and lit another cigarette. He had to step aside almost at once for a couple of young men in blue coveralls carrying either end of a stretcher. Strapped to it was a red blanket partially covering a dark gray body bag. The bag looked almost as if it were empty. The rear doors of the coroner's van opened seemingly of their own will and the two men got the stretcher inside and pulled the doors shut behind them.

"Show's over. We can go home now," Sam announced. He didn't look happy.

"Is it Our Boy?"

"Oh yes. She was opened up in one stroke, breastbone to crotch.

Then most of her insides were taken out, leaving her hollow as a gourd. Shaw won't know for sure until he checks the free histamine levels, but he doesn't think the injuries were postmortem. 'Our Boy' cut her to pieces while she was still alive."

2

Sam drove their fisherman downtown for detailed questioning, and Ellen, on the perfectly reasonable assumption that for the time being the case belonged to Evidence and the coroner's office, went home to her apartment to look after her domestic responsibilities.

She was hardly inside the door when Sam phoned. Fingerprint identification had scored a direct hit. The victim's name was Sally Wilkes, a twenty-three-year-old cocktail waitress from the Western Addition, whose death was important to the larger world only because she had recently filed a paternity suit against one George Feldstein, whose mother just happened to be the newly elected mayor of San Francisco.

So the first priority of the police department, in the few hours before the newspapers learned that the dead body found along the Coast Highway came with a name, was to confirm that neither Her Honor nor young George had been personally involved in disemboweling the poor girl. Other, more senior inspectors were engaged in the delicate business of establishing that all important persons had alibis which held up.

"We get to toss her apartment," Sam announced. "I've still got a little to clear up here, so I'll pick you up in about an hour."

"Sure."

Against an inside wall of Ellen's living room there was a wire cage, about five feet high by three feet wide. The interior was crowded with ramps and platforms, and suspended like a hammock from the ceiling was a piece of heavy red cloth, about the size of a pocket handkerchief. There were various other objects inside, among them a shoe box half full of Ping-Pong balls.

Ellen opened the cage door, about a foot square. With her finger-tips she touched the red cloth, making it sway slightly.

"Wake up, baby. Mommy's home."

Instantly Gwendolyn, all fifteen inches of her, skittered weightlessly over Ellen's hand and up her arm, and then draped herself around the back of her neck like a fur collar—in one of her rare flashes of wit, Ellen's mother had once referred to Gwendolyn as "that animated fashion accessory." Gwendolyn then occupied herself with a detailed inspection of Ellen's left ear.

Apparently oblivious to these attentions, Ellen went into the kitchen.

"Would you like some breakfast?" she asked, getting a sandwich bag full of cut-up chicken out of the refrigerator.

She sat down at the kitchen table and fed Gwendolyn pieces out of the bag as Gwendolyn clung to the lapel of her jacket, watching her every movement with small black eyes that glittered in her bandit's mask.

In was easy to overfeed her, so after a few minutes Ellen closed the bag.

"Want to go play, baby?"

Forty minutes later, with Gwendolyn asleep in her lap, Ellen heard her cell phone ring.

"Five minutes?" Sam asked.

"I'll be outside."

. . .

"A nice neighborhood for a gin slinger," Sam observed as he pulled in by the curb at the very end of Sutter Street.

And it was. The houses were Victorian and well kept up, some with ground-floor garages in a city where space and parking were always at a premium. It was home to the comfortable middle class, not a neighborhood where people expected to get murdered, at least not the way Sally had been.

They walked back half a block until they came to the right street number. There was an open stairway leading to the second floor and two mailboxes bolted to the stucco beside the front door, which suggested that the house had been divided into two apartments. The name on the outside mailbox was "Wilkes."

"What do you say we go wake the people downstairs and ask them for a key?"

Behind Sam's back, Ellen grinned with mischief.

Sam took off his hat with one hand and ran the other around the inside of the rim, as if adjusting its fit, and then carefully replaced it. Then he studied the front of the house, shaking his head.

"Show a little consideration, girl. It's Sunday morning."

"Then I guess we'll just have to break in."

"That's the idea."

By the time they reached the top of the stairway Sam had extracted from his billfold a thin iron rod, about six inches long with a slight curve at one end, which he held out to Ellen as if soliciting her admiration.

"Time for your master's examination."

"Sam, you're my teacher and hero," she said, accepting the lock pick.

They were on the other side of the door within fifteen seconds.

The air in the apartment had that dead, still quality of unoccupied space.

Sam took a pair of latex gloves from his jacket pocket and glanced around as he slipped them over his huge hands. He was peering into the kitchen, the entrance to which was almost directly opposite the front door. There was a half-empty glass of some dark liquid on the drain board.

"I don't see any other dirty dishes," Ellen said. She went into the kitchen, which was really only a corridor between the entry and the narrow L of the living room, which included a dining table. Standing beside the sink, she bent over the glass to smell its contents. "Root beer, if memory serves. Otherwise the place looks pretty clean. Maybe she was just in a hurry."

"Or maybe she wasn't the one who was thirsty. I don't see any lipstick on the rim, do you? Bag the glass and mark it down for prints and saliva. Let's hope whoever drank from it was a secreter."

"You think he could have grabbed her here? In her own apartment?"

"It's possible." The crow's feet around Sam's eyes deepened as his face took on a suspicious cast. "Something about this place doesn't smell right."

Ellen dutifully put on her own gloves, took a plastic bag out of her pocket, scribbled a note on the paper label affixed to the top of the bag, then put two fingers into the glass so she could pick it up without touching the outside and slipped it into the bag without spilling a drop. Then she set the glass back down on the drain board.

They went into the living room, where there was a painting over the sofa, a seascape of the type sold at Costco for $49.95. There was also a television set on a metal stand and, in front of the sofa, a coffee table. In an ashtray on the coffee table was a brass key, about an inch and a half long.

"I'm taking bets that fits the front door," Ellen said. "Nobody leaves their house key lying around in their living room, and why isn't it on a ring? He's playing with us again."

"What do you mean '*again*'? He's never stopped."

They hadn't gotten very far down the hallway to the bedroom before Sam's remark about the place not smelling right suddenly took on a ghastly aptness. Every homicide inspector in the world knew that odor and, with the discrimination of a connoisseur, could sniff it out from any other shade of putrefaction.

Ellen noticed it first and stopped just in front of the bedroom door, which was standing ajar no more than half an inch.

"It smells like about twenty-four hours." She looked back at her partner and raised her eyebrows in a silent appeal to his judgment.

"I make it less. Twelve to eighteen, no more."

There was no point in arguing. Sam's nose was as good as any bloodhound's.

"But I know what you mean," he went on, shaking his head. "It's a little odd—a shade too pungent."

Without touching the knob, Ellen pushed open the door, expecting to find a bloodbath inside.

There was an unmade double bed, a night table with a tiny, elaborately feminine lamp, still switched on, a stereo system in one corner, a chest of drawers with another television set resting on top. The folding doors to the closet stood open and clothes and underwear littered the floor. The room was a mess, but there were no signs of violence.

"It's coming from there," Sam said, pointing to the bathroom door, which, like the door to the bedroom, was just slightly ajar.

Ellen was closer. The room was tiled in lime green, right up to the ceiling. It was very hot in there. There was a small sink, a toilet and a bathtub with a pink plastic shower curtain drawn closed. She used the barrel of a ballpoint pen to move the curtain aside.

Collected around the drain of the bathtub were viscera—lungs, liver, intestines, the whole show, by now almost black with clotted blood. Presumably all this had once belonged to Sally Wilkes. Her heart lay at the center of the twisted mass, as if on display.

Ellen could feel her own heart pounding in her ears, and the sweat was breaking out under her clothes. Nothing in two years with Homicide had prepared her for this.

But she had to keep it from Sam. For Sam she had to be the Ice Queen, or she was in the wrong business.

He came in for his own look. She glanced at him quickly, but his face displayed no particular emotion. He might have been checking the mail.

"So that's why," Sam announced casually. "No body, just guts." He raised his eyes to the light in the ceiling. "And just to make it extra nice for everybody, he left the heat lamp on to speed up the process of decay."

Suddenly he gave Ellen a wary, sideways glance. "Are you okay, girl?"

"Sure. Fine." She showed him a fast, insincere smile.

Suddenly she felt as if she were ready to start sobbing.

"Okay then. Now tell me what you see."

She was back to being a detective, which somehow made it less terrible.

"She wasn't killed here," Ellen said, surprised and relieved that her voice didn't sound shaky. "There'd have to be blood all over the place."

"Unless he washed the walls down."

"No." Ellen ran a gloved finger over the tile and showed her partner the faint traces of dust she had picked up from the grout. "Nobody's done this bathroom in a week."

"You still think he grabbed her here?"

"No." In the crowded bathroom, Sam allowed himself a slight shrug. "He wouldn't do that and then come back. Think of the risks. He grabbed her somewhere else. He had to have supposed she wouldn't be missed for a while, not until well after she was dead. He killed her, took the key from her handbag and let himself in.

"But our masters knew enough to worry that the next stray corpse might be hers. Who filed the missing persons report?"

Sam looked at his watch, as if knowing the right time would help him remember.

"Her lawyer. Sally missed an appointment. So when he couldn't reach her within the prescribed twenty-four hours, he phoned in a missing persons report. He probably also got to thinking it wouldn't be bad publicity."

They both stared down at the mess in the tub.

"Well, the killer didn't bring all that back here in his pocket," Sam continued. "What do you suppose a full set of guts weighs? Twenty pounds? Maybe thirty? I suggest we look around for a garbage bag."

They found it in the toilet. All they had to do was lift the lid. The sides of the bowl were smeared with blood.

"I suppose prints would be too much to hope for."

"Probably."

Sam made an impatient gesture with his left hand.

"Enough is enough," he said. "Let's go back to the car and phone it in. Let Forensics take this place apart and, besides, I could use some fresh air."

Outside it was still Sunday morning. Their footfalls were reassuringly noisy on the wooden stairway. Across the street a lawn sprinkler was running.

Ellen stayed outside while Sam got in the car to use the phone, which reminded her that she had to phone Mindy to tell her she couldn't make it for lunch. Mindy would understand. Mindy was a lawyer in the district attorney's office, so she had broken a few lunch dates herself.

Listening to the sound of the lawn sprinkler, Ellen wondered why anyone would water their lawn when it had rained last night, and then it occurred to her that the system was probably controlled by a timer. The people who owned the house might even still be asleep, unaware that their sprinkler was running, or that it had rained last night or that their neighbor had been disemboweled. When they found out they would feel a thrill of fear and talk about it for a month, but it wouldn't really touch them. Murder only existed in the newspapers.

The art of modern living was not to care.

Only, she didn't want to learn to be that hard. In civilians it was just a species of emotional shallowness, but for cops it was an occupational disease. She didn't want to become one of those for whom it was all just an intellectual game, who could look at a corpse like it was a gum wrapper someone had dropped on the sidewalk. Sally Wilkes might not have been every mother's dream, but that didn't entitle anybody to cut her up like a chicken. Sally Wilkes needed an avenger.

That was stupid. Ellen knew it was stupid and still felt it and was ashamed of feeling it, but she had felt that way ever since finding Rita Blandish in a hotel bathtub. This particular series of murders had slowly evolved into her personal crusade, which was not only stupid but unprofessional. Ellen realized she was a little off the rails on this one, but it didn't seem to matter. It came down to her gut feeling that it would be impossible for her to remain icily objective and still contrive to be a human being.

Maybe after they caught their killer she would be entitled to feel any way she wanted. Maybe.

She watched Sam through the windshield as he talked on the car phone, wondering if he really was unmoved by the sight of a woman's insides lying at the bottom of her bathtub, knowing she would never find out.

Finally he hung up and came outside again, slamming the driver's side door with a trace more force than was absolutely required. He leaned against the hood and watched the sprinkler running on the other side of the street. Then, after maybe thirty seconds, he lit a cigarette.

"Our man has made his first mistake," he said finally. "The autopsy is still going on, but the word is they recovered semen samples from Sally Wilkes' body."

"It wasn't a mistake."

"It wasn't a mistake? We can type him now. If we ever catch him, his DNA will buy him the Needle."

"We were meant to find it, Sam. It was raining last night, remember? And she was wearing her panties. Which do you think is more likely, that our killer wanted to be sure the rain wouldn't give her a douche or that he was concerned for her modesty?"

Sam pursed his lips slightly, which meant that he saw her point. "By that logic, then the glass in the kitchen was left behind deliberately.

And if it yields a usable saliva sample, it'll match up with the se-men."

"That's right. And if the panties didn't do the job, he's given us a backup. He wants us to have his DNA."

"And the glass will check clean for prints."

"He knows what he's doing, Sam."

"Then he's very weird, even for a guy who likes to carve up wait-resses."

"Yes, he's very weird."

.   .   .

The discovery of Sally Wilkes' internal organs meant virtually a sec-ond autopsy. And because their villain seemed to have such a won-derful sense of fun, Forensics would even have to cross-check tissue samples to make sure they really were Sally Wilkes' internal organs and not some other lucky girl's. It would be the middle of the week before the reports were ready, and in the meantime the investigation would have to subsist on such tidbits as Dr. Shaw felt inclined to dis-pense through his subordinates.

While they waited for the evidence team to show up Ellen had a chat with the elderly couple who lived downstairs and, as expected, owned the duplex. They hadn't heard anything, and they hadn't seen any strangers around. They didn't seem to like their tenant very much and didn't seem surprised when they were told she had been found dead that morning.

What really offended them was hearing that the apartment would be sealed.

"Was she killed up there?"

"We don't think so," Ellen replied, hoping she wouldn't have to tell them about what was in the upstairs bathtub. "But we have rea-son to believe the murderer may have been on the premises, so it's a possible crime scene."

"Well, how long will it have to be empty?"

"Hard to say. A few months at least."

"It's the last time we ever rent to a single," the woman said, clutch-ing her bathrobe around her as she sat on the sofa in her living room, glaring at her husband as if he were somehow responsible. They were probably in their seventies, but both of them looked frail and bleached out. Even their eyes seemed colorless. "Singles are worse than people with young kids."

Outside, technicians from Evidence were busy unloading a blue van and preparing for their assault on the walkup.

"We can go now," Sam announced, his face as empty of expression as a dish towel. "As you know, I'm allergic to fingerprint dust."

• • •

Since it was Sunday, and also Sam's turn to buy, they had lunch out of the vending machines on the third floor of police headquarters. Ellen had a bag of corn chips and coffee. Sam was the only person she knew who was actually prepared to eat the sandwiches.

"What is it today?"

Sam spread open one corner of the sandwich and looked inside, shaking his head. "The label says salami, but I'm not certain."

"Tell you what, if I volunteer to do some phoning around, will you write the sheets?"

"Sure. Give me your notes on the guy who found her."

The arrangement in Homicide was that partners had adjoining desks and one computer, each little constellation changing owners from shift to shift. The computer was always on the junior partner's side.

You filled out form sheets. There was an arrest sheet, an interrogation sheet, a search sheet, a properties sheet. It was endless. Ellen always did the sheets. She was the junior partner and she could type.

Meanwhile Sam checked in with the Men's Club, that vast network of drinking buddies and guys in this or that department who owed him favors or just liked to gossip about whatever case or semipublic scandal was on at the moment. Ellen had her own list of contacts, but it was nothing compared with Sam's. There was hardly anything in Official San Francisco that Sam either didn't know or couldn't find out about. All he needed was to shut himself up in the lieutenant's deserted office and get on the phone.

Just shy of an hour later he came back into the duty room, closing the lieutenant's glass door behind him.

"Word is the mayor's boy is clear," he said, falling heavily into his chair. "Sally Wilkes died between four and six yesterday afternoon, and young George spent all day yesterday on a charter boat out on

Monterey Bay with about two dozen of his most intimate friends. Afterwards they had a long and boozy dinner together. The party broke up about an hour before Sally was discovered."

"Well now, isn't that a relief."

"Not for us. Her Honor still wants the board cleared with all possible dispatch. She isn't going to be happy until somebody is sitting in a cage for this, somebody she doesn't know and never heard of. I don't suppose I can blame her."

"What else did you find out?"

"You were right about that drinking glass."

"The one from the apartment?"

Sam nodded. "It was clean of prints."

"What about the saliva?"

"They won't know until tomorrow."

"What else? I know that look, Sam. It means you're saving the best for last."

"Shaw doesn't think our victim was raped."

From the tone of his voice he could have been announcing the weather. Of course, nothing surprised Sam, not even impossibilities.

"You mean he thinks it was consensual?"

"I mean he thinks there was no sex. At least, nothing that you or I would describe as sex."

"How the hell could Shaw know something like that?"

Sam leaned back in his chair and clasped his hands behind the back of his neck. Then he raised his shoulders in a theatrical shrug.

"The guy's probably done three or four hundred rape murders in his time. God alone knows how many semen samples he's swabbed up in the last twenty years. I guess he knows the difference. Besides, it was stated as an impression, not a fact. Shaw thinks the semen was introduced into her vagina after death, and by some means other than the customary blunt instrument. In plain English, Our Boy didn't screw Sally Wilkes."

3

The shift ended at four o'clock, and Sam went home to his wife and their three dachshunds in Daly City. It was about a quarter after four by the time Ellen finished her case notes and climbed into the elevator. When the doors opened on the ground floor she almost bumped into the photographer who had worked the crime scene that morning.

"Looks like I nearly missed you," he said, holding out to her a padded shipping envelope about half an inch thick. "The video, remember? I promised I'd get it to you this afternoon."

"Yes, thanks." Ellen accepted the package and noticed warily that the man had changed into a pair of clean slacks and a tan sport coat over a blue dress shirt. She also thought she detected a whiff of lime aftershave.

"Listen, if you're off work maybe you'd feel like some dinner . . ."

He smiled hopefully, but Ellen shook her head.

"I can't, sorry. I've got my folks coming in. In fact I'm already late."

"Oh, well, another time then."

"Yes, fine. Another time."

He went with her as far as the police garage in the basement. His name, as it turned out, was Ken, and he seemed like a nice guy. He even waved to her as she drove off.

"Why the hell did I do that?" she asked herself, out loud, as she waited in her Toyota for the light to change on Market Street. "Why the hell . . . ?"

Because her folks weren't coming in. Her folks were an hour down the Peninsula, in Atherton, and, aside from her father's furtive visits to have lunch with his little girl, they only came up to use their season tickets to the symphony. About four times a year they would all get together around the family dinner table for a couple of hours so

Ellen and her mother could misunderstand each other, but tonight wasn't one of those occasions.

So why, might one ask, hadn't she taken Ken up on his offer of hot food and maybe a few laughs? He wasn't bad looking, not precisely Johnny Depp but not bad. He even displayed symptoms of being a nice guy. Just dinner and a few laughs and, maybe, if they struck a few sparks . . . After all, this wasn't high school. He didn't have to be the love of her life. How long had it been since she'd done anything like that?

Too long. She couldn't remember exactly, which in itself was a bad sign.

There were times when she felt the job was swallowing her whole. Sam had warned her. Even Daddy had warned her. "The work becomes a substitute for life, even an escape from life. Life is full of complicated choices. By comparison, the work is simple. And it doesn't matter what the work is—psychiatry, catching murderers, writing advertising copy. It becomes a place to hide that we call "dedication.""

●　●　●

Ellen's apartment was over a hardware store near the Embarcadero. She had lived there ever since joining the force. It was convenient and it was cheap. However, the one time her parents had come to visit her they had left their Mercedes parked out on the street and had come out to find it stolen.

"Just explain to me why you have to live in a neighborhood like this," her mother had asked her as they sat downtown in the waiting room at Grand Theft Auto, watching her father fill out the report forms.

"It's what I can afford."

"But it's so *dangerous*! You could be raped. You could be killed!"

"Mother, I'm a trained police officer. I carry a gun and I know how to use it. Believe me, I can look after myself."

"Your father is so worried about you. He'd be so happy if you'd just let him buy you one of those lovely apartments near Telegraph Hill . . ."

Silence.

And of course he would have been. Her parents were far from poor and they loved her. Just a nod and she could have found herself sitting in a two-bedroom palace with a view of Alcatraz.

But she had paid her own tab ever since graduating from college, and she meant to keep it that way.

As much as anything, it was a question of personal integrity, almost a gift she had given herself. Other, quite ordinary people managed to get through life without being umbilically connected to rich relatives in Atherton. Sam, for instance, hadn't inherited anything from his parents except a taste for olives in his lasagna. Being able to get by on one's own practically defined being a grown-up.

By contrast, Ellen's mother had never stopped being her father's little girl. Even in ordinary conversation with her own daughter, she still referred to him as "Daddy"—not "your grandfather," but "Daddy," since the day she was born her guardian and protector, her shelter against the storms of life. She remained his little girl, even now, eleven years after his death. After all, that was what wills and trust funds were for.

Thank you, no. Ellen loved her parents, but she didn't want to depend on them.

So she lived over a hardware store near the Embarcadero.

Actually, she liked her apartment. It was convenient and roomy and the landlord, who was the owner of the hardware store and the handy type, would come on an hour's notice to fix her garbage disposal. She liked the Chinese family who lived next door, whose children, to the intense embarrassment of their grandmother, were always after her to tell them stories about her cases—most of the time she made up the stories; the kids, two boys, ages eight and ten and very well behaved, could hardly imagine a crime more sinister than jaywalking.

She liked everything about where she lived except, sometimes, every now and then, the fact that she lived there alone.

It was hard to have a normal love life if you were a cop. Stockbrokers and corporate lawyers, regular guys of any description, resented the hours and the commitment. They just didn't understand what it was like, and they didn't want to understand. Ellen had learned that lesson the hard way.

She had had three serious relationships since graduating from college, and each had floundered over the intractable problems of reconciling police work with the demands of what most men seemed to regard as the necessary conditions of private life. The last disaster, and the worst, had been Brad the hedge fund manager.

Everyone's first impression of Brad was that he was like the hero of a paperback romance novel, and, well, with a name like "Brad" how could he be anything else? He was handsome, intelligent and rich. His conversation could be immensely entertaining. He knew everything there was to know about wine and food and where to buy his clothes. He was one of the Beautiful People. Ellen's mother was crazy about him.

They met on a neighbor's tennis court in Atherton, where they had both grown up in perfect ignorance of one another. For once Ellen had Sunday off and, feeling guilty about her parents, she had gone home to play the suburban princess.

Ellen's efforts at physical fitness were restricted to three visits a week to the police gym. She didn't play tennis—tennis was too obviously patrician, so she had spent her adolescence resolutely refusing to learn—but Daddy did. Brad was some sort of cousin of the neighbor's, down for the weekend.

It was an unequal struggle. In three sets Daddy never scored a point, but Brad was enough of a sportsman not to gloat. Ellen sat on the sidelines, wearing an enormous pair of sunglasses and admiring Brad's perfect tan.

Then Daddy and the neighbor played, and Brad sat down with Ellen to drink iced tea. He was no end of charming and seemed less impressed with himself than perhaps he had a right to be. Somewhere in the conversation he asked her for a date. They would meet for dinner in the city the following Wednesday.

It got off to a rocky start. She and Sam had been working a very messy domestic murder since about one in the afternoon, and she didn't have Brad's cell phone number. She showed up at the bar at Ernie's almost three quarters of an hour late. There hadn't even been time to change.

"I'm sorry," she said. "Things got a little hectic at work."

He glanced at her tan corduroy jacket, which was not too bad but probably not up to corporate standards, and asked her what she did.

"I'm a homicide detective."

By then Ellen had been on the squad for two months, and she still felt as if she had received an Academy Award. Probably she had expected Brad to be impressed. He wasn't.

"Well, I hope then you remembered to wash your hands," was all he said.

But Brad was the type who could make a quick recovery and the rest of the meal went much better. They talked about growing up in Atherton and discovered they had friends in common. Ellen felt very much at ease with him.

Probably she should have known better. She should have finished her dinner, given up on Brad, and gone home to feed Gwendolyn. Instead they made another date, and then another, and after the third she decided he was a really nice guy who made her feel like she might genuinely matter to him, so she went back with him to his three-bedroom apartment on Russian Hill and climbed into his bed.

Brad was very good at sex, if a bit of a technician. Most of the time she was too busy enjoying herself to notice, but sometimes he left her wondering if he hadn't taken a course in the subject at Harvard Business School.

Their relationship lasted for a little over a year and a half, although they never actually moved in together. And that was probably just as well. He seemed such a catch, but the distance between the places where they each lived their lives was emotional as much as geographical.

Brad cared nothing about justice or unraveling the little mysteries of hatred, jealousy and fear that controlled so many people's lives. If something didn't net you an income in the high six figures or wasn't "amusing"—one of his favorite words—he didn't want anything to do with it.

Sam met him once, briefly and quite by chance when she and Brad were on a date and she took the summons to an apparent drug murder in the Mission District. He wasn't happy about it, but Brad drove her all the way across town to where the uniforms were already putting up their barriers to keep the foot traffic away.

It was an interesting moment.

The crime scene was an alley off Dolores Street, and they pulled up in Brad's BMW. Ellen took her badge case out of her purse and hung it over the neckline of her black cocktail dress. The uniforms seemed to find this hysterical and Brad was embarrassed.

Sam stepped out of the alley, took one look at Ellen and said, in a perfectly expressionless voice, "Sorry to spoil your evening. Our guest of honor is Freddy Hines—you remember him?"

Under the circumstances, with Brad at her elbow, Ellen didn't want to talk about Freddy Hines, whom they had dragged in for questioning the week before in connection with another murder. So she retreated into introductions, and Sam shook hands with her beau.

"Do you want me to wait?" Brad volunteered.

Sam answered for her. "This could take a while," he said. "I'll see that she gets home."

Two minutes later, Brad was gone.

As they walked back to where Mr. Hines was lying tangled up with the garbage cans, Sam explained to her one or two curious details of the case, such as the fact that their Freddy had been shot in both knees before getting the back of his head blown out.

"Somebody didn't like him," was Ellen's comment. "I suppose our perp must have used a silencer."

"It seems likely."

Sam never mentioned Brad, then or later, which could have meant anything or nothing. Ellen had been partnered with him for only about four months, so perhaps he felt some delicacy about commenting on her boyfriends.

Brad was more forthcoming.

"What a specimen," he said on a subsequent occasion. "He looks like he should be working as a longshoreman."

"Sam is the best homicide detective I've ever seen or ever heard about."

There was no response, but apparently Brad didn't regard that as much of a distinction.

Police work was neither highly paid nor "amusing," you see. It might be a lifetime high point for somebody like Sam, but Ellen was part of the gentry. Therefore he tended to regard her job as some sort of neurotic obsession or, at best, a hobby.

Also, she couldn't control her time. Since the West Coast was three hours behind New York, Brad was in his office from five A.M. to two

P.M., Monday through Friday, and the weekends were consecrated to the Good Life.

"Have lunch with me on Tuesday. There are some people I want you to meet."

"I'm working Tuesday. If I'm lucky, lunch will come out of a vending machine."

"Call in sick—what can it matter?"

"It does matter. And if I called in sick every time you wanted me to, they'd fire me."

Apparently, from his silence, that didn't strike him as an adequate reason.

There were lots of good times, so Ellen tended to regard her lover as basically a decent sort of man with a few blind spots. By the beginning of their second year together this description was starting to seem a little shopworn.

The breakup came over a trip to the Florida Keys—lots of sunshine, lots of beachfront, lots of people with serious money. But at the last moment Ellen found herself working a triple homicide, a prostitute and her two children killed by her boyfriend. She couldn't tear herself away.

After that, Brad stopped calling. She had tried calling him a few times, but all he had to do was glance at the digital readout on his cell phone to know it was her. He just didn't answer or respond to her messages. And she was damned it she was going to camp out on his doorstep.

That had been four months ago.

At first it had been simply a numbing shock. She couldn't believe it. They had seemed to strike such a chord together. And then Ellen had begun to see all the reasons why it hadn't worked—why, probably, it could never have worked.

It was the job, and it wasn't the job. She could have been a high school teacher or the Wolf of Wall Street, and it wouldn't have made any difference. It was the commitment Brad couldn't handle. If she had been more committed to him and to the relationship, if she had been prepared to get married and spend the rest of her life sending his suits to the cleaners, then he probably would have been satisfied. Brad was the center of his own life and he couldn't understand why she wasn't content to make him the center of hers.

All right, that made it somewhat easier. She was a martyr to her job and he was a narcissistic prick. But she still missed him, particularly in the small hours of the morning, if something happened to wake her and she found herself alone. And she was still in mourning for him—as was evidenced by the fact that she had turned down dinner and maybe a little fumbling around with Ken the police photographer.

It was past time for getting on with her life.

Thus the question became what sort of man would not be a mistake.

One point Ellen had settled with herself early on was that the last thing she needed was another cop sharing her electric blanket. She didn't want a man who stared out at the world through such deeply cynical eyes. She didn't know how Sam's wife stood it.

. . .

By seven-thirty she had eaten her dinner—lamb chops because Gwendolyn liked chewing on the bones—and she had watched the evening news.

Ellen was beginning to worry about Gwendolyn. Gwendolyn was seven years old, which was close to the average life expectancy of a ferret, and Ellen had the impression that she was beginning to slow down. Even a year ago her evening entertainment would have been forty-five minutes of turning the apartment into chaos, but now, after twenty minutes with her yarn ball, she was ready to call it a night. She was presently asleep on a sofa pillow.

After the day's events, the prospect of finding Gwendolyn dead in her cage one morning filled Ellen with dread.

She decided she needed a distraction. Finally her eyes came to rest on the video disk that was lying on top of her purse on the coffee table.

"Okay. What the hell. Sherlock Holmes every minute of the day."

It was only about ninety seconds long. Just a crowd of men standing behind the police tape, like tramps waiting for a free lunch. She watched it through and saw nothing to interest her, so she clicked it back to the beginning and watched it again. Then she watched it again.

It wasn't until the fourth time around that she saw him. He was tall and slender, better looking than the others, with a sharp-featured, intelligent face. Light brown hair, a tan Windbreaker, trousers that might have been dark green or brown.

But his gaze was fixed on the camera lens. Nobody was fooling anybody. He knew he was being filmed, and he didn't give a damn. You could read it in his eyes.

Those eyes seemed to look straight through you.

4

The next morning Ellen brought the disk with her to Homicide and, when Sam came in, played it for him.

"Tell me if I'm crazy. . . ."

"You're crazy."

"Right. But does anything strike you about any of these guys?"

Sam watched the disk through again and then shrugged.

"Did I miss something? Does one of them have a sign around his neck, 'Stop Me Before I Kill Again'? What are you getting at, Ellie?"

Ellen clicked the disk back to the beginning and then played it over, hitting the freeze frame button in the middle of the second pass over the crowd.

"Him," she said. "The one in the middle, in the tan jacket." She tapped on the TV screen with her fingernail to show the person she meant. "See the way he looks into the camera?"

"So what? Maybe he's got a letch for the cameraman. Girl, this is San Francisco."

"He knows he's being photographed."

"All right—he knows. Maybe he's just smarter than the rest of the innocent bystanders. That doesn't make him guilty of anything."

"I've seen him before. The car trunk in North Beach, remember?"

"Maybe he's a homicide groupie. Anyway, the car trunk thing wasn't our case."

"So? I heard it on my police band and thought I'd drop by."

"It was your day off. Are you nuts?"

"If he's a groupie, you must have seen him before—you never forget a face, Sam. Is this guy somebody you know?

Sam reached over and, with an impatient stab of his finger, hit the power button on the TV set. The image of the young man in the tan Windbreaker imploded into a tiny dot of light, and then flickered out.

"Our Boy is turning into an obsession, Ellie. Get a life. Go out and find yourself a new boyfriend or something. You've got to stop this shit."

"Have you ever seen this guy?" Ellen answered, ignoring the advice.

"No, never."

"And how many murders have we worked since then? How long has it been? Six weeks? And you've never seen this particular specimen behind the barricades?"

"You need a vacation, Ellie. Come home to Daly City with me tonight and let Millie feed you some of her lasagna. Afterwards we'll have a little three-handed canasta and play with the dogs."

"Let's find out who he is, Sam."

It was not very difficult. Murderers loved to admire their own handiwork so, as a matter of routine at every homicide that attracted a crowd, one of the uniformed officers would be assigned to walk around and write down the license plate numbers of all the cars in the immediate area. If a suspect turned up, his car plates were checked against the lists, and if the numbers matched, it at least established his presence at the scene. Also it provided the sort of corroborating evidence that made an interrogator's life so much easier: *What were you doing at Van Ness and Stockton at three o'clock in the afternoon on the twenty-sixth? You think we don't know you had your car parked around the corner from where David Thomas got his head blown off?* More than one man had been put on death row that way.

And so, to cut down on computer time, they compared the plate numbers from the Sally Wilkes scene with those from the North Beach killing. They found three matches. They would start with those. They ran the numbers over the hookup with the DMV, checking the photographs on the driver's licenses. Two of them Sam recognized at once as well established members of the Fan Club. The third was the man in the tan Windbreaker.

"Stephen Tregear, six twenty-one North Point Street."

"So the guy isn't broke." Sam lit his tenth cigarette of the morning and exhaled a cloud of smoke that seemed to stand as a comment on life's many injustices. "Apartments that close to the Wharf go for a nice nickel. I imagine you want to run a check on him."

"It wouldn't hurt."

But a search of the department database came up empty. Stephen Tregear, it seemed, had never been arrested or questioned by the police, had never been mentioned in any filed report, had never even received a parking ticket. He seemed to be a model citizen.

Which should have ended it—it ended it for Sam.

"So file his name," he said, "and we'll see if he turns up again sometime."

"Let's dig around a little."

"Why?" Sam held up his hands, as if to prove he had washed them. "You have nothing on this guy except you don't like the way he looked at the camera. For the rest, he's Mr. Clean."

"He's too clean."

"Just so you know, Ellie, there actually are people out there who go through their whole lives without so much as incurring a library fine. He isn't any guiltier because we don't have a folder on him."

"I think we should run him, give him the full treatment. We'll find something."

"Ellie—sweetheart—give it a rest. What have you got in mind? The Bureau? His service records? A search like that costs money, and what are we going to tell the lieutenant when he asks us why?"

"He won't ask if we come up with something."

"And if we don't? Forget it. The answer is no."

Sam was right. He was usually right. His was the received wisdom of the department and Ellen went back to her paperwork without even a grumble of rebellion.

By eleven o'clock a preliminary report on the glass found in Sally Wilkes' kitchen had made it upstairs to Sam's desk. He handed it to Ellen almost as if disappointed.

"I don't suppose we could have asked for more," he said. "They came up with good saliva residue, and Our Boy is definitely a secreter, so the next step is to see if the DNA in the saliva is a match with the semen."

"And no prints."

Sam raised one shoulder and smiled, as if to say, *What did you think?* "He's arrogant, but he isn't stupid."

"You think he's still playing with us."

"Oh sure. He'd love for us to spend a couple of hundred hours of very expensive lab time trying to find a cross match. He knows we won't find it, and he doesn't expect we'll catch him."

"None of them ever expect that."

"And some of them are right."

Two or three times a year the department had to requisition a new swivel chair for Sam. He was a big man—he had played football in high school—and he was hard on the furniture. He didn't so much sit down as throw himself into a chair, and he would lean back in it until, eventually, the bearings would wear out or a leg would come loose or some other catastrophe would befall it and it would have to be taken out with the trash. The lieutenant received regular complaints from Accounting, but he never mentioned them to Sam because he, like everyone else, had come to realize that such casualties were necessary. Chairs were the innocent victims that got caught in the cross fire of Sam's career-long war against the bad guys.

At that moment he had his feet up on the desk, and the chair was cradled under him at precisely the angle to put maximum stress on the back legs. It was a posture that suggested the darkest pessimism.

"This guy is beginning to spook you."

Sam didn't take offense. At first he didn't even seem to hear.

"Could be," he said finally. "I keep thinking about Sally Wilkes' guts, spread out like that in the bathtub. He didn't kill her there—as you pointed out, you can't disembowel someone without making a hell of a mess, and the place was spotless. For another, we're going to find out that she was alive and conscious when he did it, probably without even a gag to keep her from screaming. The screaming is likely the part he enjoys most, and she would have awakened the whole neighborhood. No, he killed her in some secret place of his own and then carted her insides back in a garbage bag and left them for us to find.

"Which, incidentally, leaves Mr. Tregear out. He's got an apartment on Fisherman's Wharf, remember? Crowds, neighbors—not the sort of place where you can really enjoy yourself the way Our Boy does."

"If he's rich enough to live on North Point, he can afford a dungeon someplace."

"Possible, but not likely." Sam made a small gesture with his hand to suggest how little he thought of the idea. "Face it, Ellie. This humorist isn't some pathetic weirdo who cuts up girls because his mommy used to threaten to snip off his dick with the pruning shears. This isn't about sex with him, or even anger. It's about winning. He's a game player. So far he's making all the right moves."

"And he's laughing at us."

"Looks like it."

Sam took his feet down, and the front legs of his chair hit the floor with a snap that should have shattered them like glass. He stood up and then settled again on the corner of Ellie's desk.

"Play the disk again," he said. They watched it through twice more, each time freezing on the man in the tan Windbreaker.

"Maybe he's made his first mistake."

Ellen felt a disappointment that was like grief when Sam shook his head.

"Maybe, but this isn't it. That isn't him, Ellie. Haven't you figured it out yet? He knows our methods. He knows all about how we go after sick fucks who butcher cocktail waitresses and leave them out in the rain. If we ever do catch him, it won't be because he fell into our laps."

• • •

When her shift ended Ellen went home and played with Gwendolyn until the poor baby curled up in her lap and went to sleep. By then it was five, time to start thinking about dinner, and Ellen didn't feel like cooking.

Mindy Epstein was probably going to be sleeping on the sofa tonight, since that was what she had done after leaving her first husband. She had phoned and said her suitcases were in the trunk of her car. Perhaps Mindy would feel like dinner out.

She dialed Mindy at her office and they decided on a restaurant by Fisherman's Wharf where you could get scallops and pasta and a bottle of halfway decent wine and still pay the rent.

"It was too domestic," Mindy announced, describing the collapse of her second marriage. "He had this house over in Tiburon. . . ."

"I know. I've been there."

"Really? You're sure?" She seemed momentarily taken by surprise. "Remind me. When was that?"

"Seven months ago. Right after the honeymoon."

"Oh, yeah."

They were about three-quarters down on a bottle of Chardonnay, so perhaps it wasn't so surprising that Mindy was a little vague on the details. But she was clear enough on the main point—the house in Tiburon was the *casus belli*.

"I think Stewie saw our relationship from the point of view of property management. He wanted someone on the premises to deal with the lawn service guys and make sure the cleaning lady didn't get into the liquor cabinet. Tiburon, for God's sake. Do you have any idea how long the commute time is from Tiburon to Bryant Street on a Monday morning? I might have gotten used to that, but I'm an assistant district attorney and he wants to play Ozzie and Harriet."

"So you dumped him."

"Damn right."

Mindy nodded emphatically. She was a small, dark-haired woman given to quick, rather startled movements, and she did most things emphatically. She was just the same in a courtroom, which was one reason she was such an effective prosecutor and most of the defense lawyers in San Francisco were scared to death of her.

"I just packed my bag and walked out. He can keep his house and his alimony checks. The manager of my old apartment building on Fell Street has promised they'll have a vacancy at the end of this month. Once my mother gets over the shock, it'll be like the whole thing never happened."

"Is she taking it hard?"

"You can imagine."

Yes, actually, Ellen could imagine. On the one occasion she had met Mindy's parents, when they had come all the way out to California to visit their daughter, they had been invited down to Atherton for dinner with the roommate's family. Mrs. Epstein and Mrs. Ridley had discovered they were kindred souls.

"I told Mom I'd probably be ready to settle down by the time I got to my fifth husband, but that didn't seem to console her."

Mindy refilled her wineglass, which killed the bottle. She took a sip and smiled in a way that suggested she had at last come to the interesting part of her narrative.

"And now let me tell you about my new squeeze."

. . .

They walked out of the restaurant about five to seven, and Ellen gave Mindy the key to her apartment.

"I just have a quick errand to run," she said.

Five minutes later she was parked on North Point, across the street from Number 621. The idea had been forming in her mind all during dinner. She just wanted a quick look at Stephen Tregear's premises.

It was almost the end of spring, when the evenings lingered forever and the light seemed less to diminish than simply to clarify.

Just as Sam had predicted, it was a very nice building. Each unit was a town house, brick with bowed windows and a front door painted Delft blue. The rent payments couldn't have been less than five thousand a month.

That was about as much as she was likely to find out.

"What am I doing here?" she asked herself. "What is this supposed to accomplish?"

Nothing. That was the only possible answer—nothing. He wasn't likely to come out and volunteer a confession and, short of that, she couldn't go calling on him. She had no probable cause, so she could have looked through his apartment door and seen bloody handprints all over the walls, and they wouldn't have been admissible as evidence. She had no warrant and no grounds to apply for a warrant. She had nothing.

She had nothing, and she was sitting in her car, across the street from a suspect's apartment, because she didn't want to go home to a sleeping ferret. She envied Mindy the chaotic drama of her personal life and she wanted a little excitement. Well, she wasn't going to find it on North Point Street.

"I'm out of here."

Her hand was actually on the ignition key when the door to Tregear's apartment opened and a man in a tan Windbreaker stepped out onto the street. It was him, big as life.

He closed the door behind him and started to walk down North Point in long strides. Suddenly he crossed the street. Then he turned a corner and was gone.

It was irresistible. He was practically begging her to follow him.

She hardly expected that he would lead her to an unmarked grave in the middle of Ghirardelli Square, but the thing was still irresistible.

Ellen had never tailed anyone before, but she knew it was a team sport—on the sidewalk, you needed at least five people to shag someone for any distance. Thus she knew she had a better chance if she followed him in her car than if she started off on foot. Careful, she thought to herself. He knows you by sight. She felt reasonably confident that Tregear hadn't noticed her yet.

She drove up to the intersection and slowed. The sidewalks weren't crowded, so she had no trouble spotting him. He had cut across to the other side, so it was a safe bet he was heading toward Fisherman's Wharf.

In San Francisco the tourist season never ended so the Wharf was always mobbed, particularly in the evening, when the restaurants were serving dinner. The closer you got, the bigger the crowds and the more the streets belonged to them. She would have to leave the car.

She crossed the intersection, drove two more blocks and pulled over to the curb.

On the bay side of Jefferson she took up her station behind a rack of T-shirts under the awning of a tourist shop and waited, scanning the sidewalks, with a good view in all four directions, almost hoping that Tregear had only gone out for a pack of gum and the sports pages and was by now safely back in his apartment.

Assuming the guy was a serious suspect, she had no business doing this; if he spotted her it would only complicate the investigation. The problem was, she couldn't help herself.

She just had to get inside his head a little. She wanted a sense of him, something to go with the way those eyes had focused in on the camera—fearless, almost amused. The joker who takes the trouble to have his victim found wearing a pair of red satin heels.

Besides, he wasn't going to spot her. Why should he? He had no reason to believe he wasn't absolutely in the clear and, until a few hours ago, he had been. He was clever, but he wasn't a mind reader.

And, anyway, he wasn't going to spot her because she had probably missed him. If he was going anywhere on the Wharf he would have to pass this intersection. It had probably been seven or eight minutes since she had seen him coming out of his front door, so where the hell was he?

Childishly, she was disappointed, as if she had been stood up by a date. She had felt something, an excitement, and now it was gone. She didn't have a lover to go home to, but she had had Tregear—briefly—her very own quasi suspect. But not now.

And then, there he was, strolling up the street toward her, with all the careless self-possession of a man with nothing on his mind or conscience. Ellen stood perfectly still, hardly breathing, as he passed by on the sidewalk, close enough that she could almost have reached out and touched him. He never glanced at her.

Aside from a fleeting glimpse of the man on disk, this was the first chance Ellen had to take a good look at him, and she had no trouble understanding how women might be willing to put themselves in his power. He was not handsome in any conventional way, but he was attractive. He had a small, rather thin mouth, but his face, which was angular and hard and appeared a trifle sunburned, was dominated by his eyes. His eyes, for those few seconds at least, were far from cruel. Deep set and shaded beneath heavy eyebrows, they were somewhere between blue and gray and seemed to suggest that they had seen too much. What they reflected back to the world was something almost like compassion.

And, God, he was a treat to watch. His every movement was graceful, so that he made crossing the street look like something out of a Fred Astaire movie. The man was elegant—there was no other word for it.

It wasn't until he had passed, as she was looking at his back, that she observed he had a newspaper tucked under his right arm.

She counted to thirty before she came out onto the sidewalk. He was three-quarters of a block away, almost lost to sight in the evening foot traffic. She didn't begin to follow until he had crossed the street.

He made it easy for her and went to the Cannery, which was a big, open structure with lots of corners and enormous cement pillars to hide behind. He couldn't have been nicer about it—he took a table out on the patio, crossed his legs and opened the newspaper. With the sports pages open in front of him like a sail, he seemed to think he had the universe to himself. It was several seconds before the waiter could attract his attention to take his order.

"Your usual?"

On the second floor, lurking around in the impenetrable early evening shadow, Ellen was too far away to hear the words, but that was
what it looked like. Without even pausing for an answer, the waiter
set a cup down on the table and produced a silver coffeepot from
somewhere behind his apron. No cream, no sugar. No little plate of
chocolate-covered cookies. That was that. He seemed to enjoy a comfortable understanding with Tregear, as if what a man liked to drink
over his *Chronicle* was the true index of his character. If only he knew.

Not that Ellen was feeling particularly smug about it. Looking
down from her hiding place at the man with his newspaper and his
neat coffee, she was forced to admit to herself that Stephen Tregear
was a highly unusual suspect.

How many murderers had she processed in her two years on Homicide? Maybe thirty or thirty-five. As a rule they were not very complicated types. As a rule they were stupid, astonished to be under
arrest. Astonished at the fuss everybody was making just because they
had knifed some guy over a twenty-dollar gambling debt. The more
intelligent ones, the career bad guys, that distinct minority who could
figure out for themselves that homicide was not classified as a misde-
meanor, were usually remarkable only for what was missing from their
interior furnishings—principally any sense at all that, aside from their
own, human life had value.

Killing was simply a way of tidying things up, an exercise in problem solving. As Stalin put it: no man, no problem. Murderers, in Inspector Ridley's experience, were guilty first and foremost of a lack
of imagination.

But the man who had eviscerated Sally Wilkes while she was still
alive was neither a fool nor an emotionally blunted drug dealer just
looking after his customer base. Our Boy was an enthusiastic student
of pain and death, a perfectionist, a technician and an artist, laughing at his critics and audience, the SFPD. He was a book written in a
language only he understood, a permanent enigma. He was a monster, a beast that should have been born with scales and claws.

And right now, if hunches meant anything, he was sitting in the
patio of the Cannery, drinking a cup of black coffee and reading the
basketball scores. A nice fellow, a favorite customer. His human face
was his disguise.

The sunlight was fading. The outside floodlights popped on with a little electronic crinkle of sound, which somehow threw Ellen's hiding place into deeper shadow.

This is where I live, she thought. In shadow.

In her head she kept replaying Mindy's reaction to her turning down Ken the photographer's dinner invitation.

"Are you out of your mind?" she had almost shouted. "Why the hell did you do that?"

"I don't know."

And that had been the truth—she didn't know. And then she had mumbled some excuse about not being big on casual sex.

"Well, great. We're over thirty and you want to play the dewy virgin." And then she had cocked her head to one side, looking at Ellen through narrowed eyes. "You're not still pining for Brad, are you?"

"No—maybe. I don't know."

"What are you going to do, be like the Indian widows and throw yourself on the funeral pyre? Brad wasn't worth it. And casual sex is better than no sex at all. Any day."

And now, instead of being tucked up in bed with Ken or anybody else, she was watching a man read the sports pages.

For twenty minutes Tregear had been hidden behind that newspaper. Then, all at once, he closed his paper, folded it neatly and stood up. He shelled out five bills on the table—no wonder the waiter liked him—and started up the steps that led to Beach Street.

Ellen left the building by another direction. She took her time, and spotted him again within a block.

She had more or less decided she would let him go now. The fit had passed off, and she realized she wasn't going to gain anything by following him back to his doorstep. She was parked on Beach, not a block away, so she would wait until he was out of sight and then she would go home to a little television and a long evening of contemplating her assorted sins.

When Tregear drew even with her car he seemed to slow a trifle. Right in front of her bumper he stepped off the sidewalk and, before crossing to the other side of the street, he lifted the driver side windshield wiper and slid the newspaper underneath it. Then he walked away, without ever looking back.

The son of a bitch had made her. He had been toying with her the whole time. Even while she was still sitting in her car, trying to decide what she should do about him, he had spotted her. It was one of the most humiliating moments of her life.

The newspaper was folded to show two columns of print from the second page. The article was headlined: BODY DISCOVERED NEAR COAST ROAD.

5

Inspector Sergeant Sam Tyler did not look convinced.

"This is the guy," Ellen said to him, not for the first time. "Don't look at me that way, Sam. Stephen Tregear is not some innocent civilian. He's in this up to his belt buckle."

"You followed Mr. Tregear . . ."

"Will you stop calling him that?"

Sam paused for a second, subjected her to his best deadpan stare, and then started over, as if she hadn't uttered a syllable.

"You followed Mr. Tregear from his place of residence to the patio of the Cannery, where he feloniously drank a cup of coffee. He spotted you, which somehow I have no trouble believing, and, just because he didn't want you to imagine you were invisible, he decided to let you know he knew you were there. Very humbling I'm sure, but doubtless good for the soul."

"He's teasing us, Sam. He's having his little joke. Remember what you said, 'a villain with a sense of humor'?"

"Sticking a newspaper under your windshield wiper doesn't qualify as much of a joke—not really up to Our Boy's standards. However, if it would make you feel better, I suppose we could arrest Mr. Tregear for littering."

They were sitting in Sam's car. It was eight-fifteen in the morning and he had just picked her up for work. When she didn't answer immediately, he opened the paper bag that was on the seat beside him and brought out a Styrofoam cup with a plastic lid. He handled it gently, with the tips of his fingers, since the coffee was still hot.

Ellen took it from him, cracked open the little tab on the lid and took a tentative sip.

"Where did you buy this stuff?" she asked. "It's even worse than usual."

"You want me to bring it all the way from Daly City? If you'd find yourself an apartment in a decent neighborhood, instead of this slum, then just maybe I could find a place nearby that sells decent coffee."

"We have to take life as it comes to us, Sam."

He didn't reply. He just extracted his coffee from the paper bag, drained off about an inch, and put the cup in a plastic holder attached to his dashboard. Then he shifted out of park and they were rolling.

"You know what you've done, don't you?" he said, once they had crested the hill and Market Street was in sight. "You've tipped him. Now he knows we're looking at him as a suspect, so he's going to be very careful. It was a mistake. You shouldn't have gone anywhere near him."

"You've got it backwards, Sam. He tipped us."

This answer seemed to focus him morosely on his driving. For two blocks, through heavy morning traffic, the very stripes on the crosswalks were the objects of his dark and unpitying concentration. In perfect silence, he glowered as if he wanted to arrest every pedestrian in sight.

"Sometimes I think you have too much imagination to be a cop," he said at last, without looking at her. "Twenty years have taught me one thing, which is that the best way is to put off reaching a conclusion for as long as possible. Just let the evidence gather, and it will lead you to your suspect. You're doing just the opposite. You have a hunch about Mr. Tregear, and you're torturing perfectly neutral facts into supporting evidence. This is going to come to grief, Ellie. Even if Tregear is Jack the Ripper, it'll end badly."

"Sam, could we just take a look at this guy?"

"Ellie . . ."

"Come on, Sam. Just give it a day or two. It's not like we have any other hot leads."

. . .

Lieutenant Commander Hal Roland parked across the street from the San Francisco Police Department. He picked up his hat from the seat beside him and, before he locked the car, took his uniform coat from the hook above the rear door. As he almost always did lately, he looked at the gold stripes on the sleeve—thick, thin, thick—and experienced a faint twinge of anguish.

He was due for promotion. In another two months, if everything proceeded on schedule, that middle stripe would widen out to catch up with the other two, and it was about goddamned time.

Until recently, Roland had had few anxieties about his career or much of anything else. He was a Navy recruiting poster boy, athletic and trim, with the sunny smile that comes with excellent fitness reports from adoring superiors. He had finished in the top ten percent of his class at Annapolis, having been gifted with the kind of practical intelligence the brass likes to see in an ambitious and promising junior officer. His private life, like his personnel file, was without blemish. He was happily married with twin girls. Everyone liked him, which even his posting to the Shore Patrol hadn't changed. He was that contradiction in terms, a popular cop.

And then one fine day he had been assigned as Stephen Tregear's case officer.

For starters, Tregear was a civilian. Granted, he worked for the Navy, but as a private contractor, so why was he the Shore Patrol's responsibility? Naval Intelligence, yes—and Roland had more than a suspicion that the spooks kept themselves very well informed about Tregear's movements and associations—but it was not normally part of the Shore Patrol's duties to babysit the errant geniuses of Special Projects.

And then there was the man himself. It gave Roland the fidgets just to be in the same room with him.

Roland had read the files. Stephen Tregear, having lied about his age, had joined the Navy at sixteen. He had risen to the rank of seaman first class. He had never even finished high school, and yet out of the blue, God knows how or where he had picked it up, his Standard Interservice Aptitude Test scores revealed he possessed a knowledge of mathematics and probability theory that would have been considered astonishing in an MIT graduate. His IQ was not even considered measurable.

The Navy had taught him computers and, after a while, had put him to work in Codes and Ciphers, where apparently he had performed wonderfully. The Navy had offered to send him to school so he could qualify for a commission, but he had declined. He regularly refused promotion. Still, at the end of his tour, Tregear had reenlisted for another four years. He seemed at home, a career man albeit rather a strange one.

And then, at the beginning of his second tour, the whole world changed. There had been an arrest. A chief warrant officer had been selling code manuals to the Chinese for some eight years, and the Navy suddenly found itself without any secrets. The enemy had everything they needed to read Navy cipher like it was the Sunday funnies. But four weeks after the indictment Tregear came up with what amounted to a version of the old-fashioned book code but was virtually unbreakable because the referent was itself encoded and, anyway, changed randomly, sometimes even from line to line in the same message.

Overnight, he was the indispensable man. He held the whole apparatus of naval security in the palm of his hand.

The brass couldn't do enough for him. Anything he wanted was just fine. He still wouldn't take a promotion, but lieutenants and above answered to him like they were messenger boys. His commanding officer had only one standing order: keep Seaman Tregear happy and working.

Then, halfway through his third tour, he put in for separation. Even more astonishing, the Navy agreed. He was mustered out and entered into a murky arrangement with the Department of Defense, the details of which were classified.

Roland had a theory that Tregear had given the brass an ultimatum—either let me out, in which case I will continue to do whatever it is I do for you, except as a civilian, or I stop doing it. You can set me to swabbing decks for the next two years, or you can send me to the brig, but you can't make me do what you want done on any terms except my own.

But that was just a theory. Two things that Roland did know for certain were 1) the powers that be considered Tregear indispensable, and 2) it was in the terms of his contract with the Department of Defense that he was subject to surveillance and could not leave the United States without the Navy's permission.

Otherwise, he was free to come and go as he pleased. He worked at home, and home had been a lot of different places in the eight years since he had taken off his uniform.

Fine. Lots of people liked to travel. But a normal human being with

complete freedom of movement didn't spend six months in Spartan-
burg, South Carolina, then pay out the lease on his apartment to move
to Wichita, in the middle of winter. Then some dog hole in New
Mexico, then Chicago, then half a dozen places nobody ever went if
he weren't born there or didn't have to, then Seattle for six months,
then San Francisco.

Also fine. The world was filled with very bright people, and a lot of
them were reasonably weird, but Roland had always figured he could
handle anyone. That was what he was good at, handling people. Tregear, however, was a little different.

It wasn't that he wasn't a nice guy. He seemed to be a very nice
guy. It was that he insisted on playing by his own rules and he made
the lives of his babysitters miserable—because, of course, the Navy
wasn't going to let him just wander around loose.

There was a story, unconfirmed but probably true, that one team
of watchers in Seattle got tired of the way he kept disappearing on
them and put a signaling device on his car. The next day Tregear went
for a ride, and everything worked precisely according to plan. For
about twenty minutes. He was headed south on Highway 5. The team
was about three-quarters of a mile behind him. Then all at once, the
signal shifted. Tregear's car was on Highway 90, halfway to Mercer
Island. Except that was impossible, because the intersection with
Highway 90 was three exits north of them. They turned around and
went back, and found the car in a parking lot. The signaling device
was precisely where they had put it. They never figured out how he
did that.

And there was something about the way he looked at you. Roland had been his case officer for two months, and in that time he
had met personally with the man twice. On both occasions Tregear
had been scrupulously polite, but you had the feeling he could see
into your brain. Every word you said, every smile, every gesture, was
analyzed and understood. He seemed to know exactly what it meant,
what it was intended to mean and what it was hiding. It was like being naked—no, that wasn't quite right. It was like being transparent.

You couldn't control Tregear. You couldn't charm him, and you
couldn't do without him. And he got you into situations like this. Situations that could easily backfire and end up as nasty little addenda
to otherwise exemplary fitness reports.

Roland slid his arms into the sleeves of his uniform coat and locked the car. Now he had to make a ticklish decision. All the way from Treasure Island, where, even after the naval base had been decommissioned, the Navy still maintained a nondescript field office, he had been weighing his choices, but now he had to come down one way or the other. He was here to make a complaint, yet he had no jurisdiction in the matter and he had no desire to antagonize the SFPD.

God knows he didn't want to be here, but Tregear had phoned him at home at seven-fifteen that morning and insisted.

"Take care of it, Hal," he had said. "I have enough grief with you guys. I don't need SF Homicide added in. I don't know what they want with me, but you get them off my back."

And, since Tregear himself had all kinds of ways of punishing innocent lieutenant commanders up for promotion, Roland had decided the discreet and sensible thing to do was to have a word with the local law. He was less afraid of them.

So whom should he talk to? Where would that word do the least harm and still satisfy Tregear?

How would he, Hal Roland, USN, feel if the SFPD came to him on similar business? The natural thing for them to do would be to see the shift commander, the man in charge. But if then the shift commander came and unloaded it all on him, he would resent that. If there was a problem with one of the Shore Patrolmen, it was more diplomatic to take it up with the man's immediate superior.

So the smart thing to do, the tactful and career-protecting thing, was to proceed laterally and drop in on the offending officer's lieutenant.

Homicide was on the third floor.

You got off the elevator and you walked down a corridor that was like the Steinhart Aquarium. There were rooms on either side, like fish tanks, into which you could peer through huge plate glass windows—even at this hour of the morning there were people in there, hopeless-looking and stranded, stuck to their chairs like mollusks to a rock.

The duty room was a larger, less tidy version of the one on Treasure Island, furnished more or less at random with desks and metal chairs, a few computer terminals and a coffeemaker on its own wooden table near the door to the lieutenant's office. It had to be the lieutenant's office because that was what was written on the door—LIEUTENANT.

"Is he free?" Roland asked, pointing to the door and addressing his question to any one of the five men who happened to be lounging around the room. They looked him over, or rather his uniform, as if he had arrived in a space suit. "Is he in his office?"

"Yeah, he's in there. Do you have an appointment?"

"Are you his social secretary?"

The man leaned back in his chair and allowed himself a few syllables of good-natured laughter. He was in his forties, bald with a small black mustache that ran over his upper lip like a caterpillar. He wasn't wearing a coat and his shirt, which was rolled up over thick forearms, was a pale mint green. There was nothing on his desk except a telephone, a newspaper and a black straw hat with a wide, colorful band. The man could have been a bartender or a racing tout as easily as a cop. Roland didn't like him.

"Yeah, Captain. I'm his social secretary. Go on in. He'll be glad to see you."

With a wave of his arm he dismissed Roland from existence.

Roland tapped twice on the frosted glass and opened the door.

"And who might you be?"

Roland took his identity card from his inside jacket pocket and placed it on the desk. The lieutenant picked it up and read it carefully, glanced at the back, which was blank, and put it back down. He didn't return it. He kept it right there on his blotter, as if he were considering adding it to his collection.

Then he looked up at Roland, then back down at the card, which included a small photograph, then at Roland again.

"So sit down. Name's Hempel. What can I do for you?"

Roland accepted the invitation, removing his hat and smiling his best all-American-boy smile. "I'm almost embarrassed to mention it," he said. "You have an Officer Ridley on your shift, an Ellen Ridley?"

"Yeah, sure. So what's the problem?"

Lieutenant Hempel's face, which was narrow to begin with, seemed to close even tighter at the suggestion that the Shore Patrol might have the gall to come into his jurisdiction and claim to be *embarrassed* about one of his officers. The tips of his long fingers went up to run caressingly along his jawline as he considered the affront.

"I wonder if you could tell me what cases she's currently working on."

"I might, if I knew why you want to know."

Apparently Hempel had played these games before. Roland stopped smiling—it wasn't working anyway—and drew himself up straight in his chair. It was his way of acknowledging defeat.

"It's really not a jurisdictional thing," he began. "Within the city limits, criminal investigations that don't involve service personnel are, as a rule, strictly none of our business, and we like to keep it that way. There are, however, a few civilians living in San Francisco in whom, for security reasons, we take an interest. These people are assets to the Navy, and we like to keep them out of harm's way, if we can. If you like, we're babysitters."

"And Inspector Ridley has stumbled over one of your babies?"

"Yes. He tells me she accessed his DMV records yesterday morning, and then last night she followed him. We need to know why."

For a long moment Lieutenant Hempel appeared not to be listening, and then, very slowly, his gaze swung around to Roland and his eyebrows went up about two millimeters.

"She accessed his DMV records? How the hell would he know that? Did she tell him?"

"No. There was no contact. But he knows. I haven't a clue how, but take my word for it. He knows. By now he probably knows Inspector Ridley's high school grade average. There are no secrets from this man."

"Who is he? Houdini?"

"In reverse, yes. He doesn't break out—he breaks in. He's a computer security specialist and a cryptographer. That's what he does for the Navy."

"Then maybe Ridley's on to something." The lieutenant smiled faintly. "He must be keeping a pretty careful watch if he knows that Ridley looked up his driver's license."

"Not necessarily. I wouldn't be surprised if he's got all his records flagged. If anybody anywhere does a search on him, he gets a readout on his screen."

"He can do that?"

"He can do that. The Navy's working assumption is that he can do just about anything he wants. That's why I'm here. Anything that touches him is automatically a security issue."

Roland allowed himself a few beats of silence, just to let it all sink in, and then he leaned forward a little in his chair, his face a mask of polite insistence.

"Now, can you tell me what Officer Ridley's interest might be?"

"What's his name?"

"Stephen Tregear."

Hempel wrote it down on a notepad on his desk. It wasn't really something he needed to remember. He was stalling, taking those few seconds to make up his mind about something.

"You familiar with the Sally Wilkes case? Ridley's working that."

"Was that the woman they found sliced up by the Coast Road?"

"Yeah."

"Tregear is a suspect?"

"Not that she's mentioned to me."

"It's fantastic." Roland actually laughed, although he couldn't have said why. "I know this man. He's not the type. Believe me, he is not the type."

"Is there a type?"

Was there? And, upon reflection, what did anybody know about Steve Tregear's inner life? Perhaps it wasn't so very safe to defend him.

"He's under routine surveillance," Roland lied. He knew the one thing the Navy would want above all else was for their wunderkind to be protected. They wouldn't care if he cut up half a dozen prom queens a week. "If he were engaged in any kind of criminal activity, we'd know about it."

"Would you?" Lieutenant Hempel actually seemed to want that confirmed. "Then he doesn't have anything to worry about."

"Pull Ridley off."

"Why? As a professional courtesy?"

"Yes." Roland ignored the dig. "She's wasting her time. We'll investigate. The Navy owns him—we don't have to worry about his civil rights. If there's anything, we'll find it. You'll get a complete report."

"Oh. That's very comforting."

Lieutenant Hempel, Homicide, crouched slightly in his chair, giving the impression he was getting ready to spring. He smiled faintly. The smile might have been intended to be reassuring, but its effect was precisely the reverse.

Hempel looked at the ID card again, as if he wanted to make sure he was talking to the right person, and then handed it back to Roland.

"Your Mr. Tregear sounds like a clever guy," he said. "He's important to you, but you let him run around loose. Why? Because he doesn't give you a choice?"

Roland wasn't aware that his face betrayed anything, but Hempel nodded.

"I thought so. I think the main reason you're here is that you don't want to piss off your whiz kid. Well, we're a little different. We've got a homicide to solve, and we don't care how Mr. Tregear feels about it."

"He's not involved. I can guarantee that."

"Can you? From what I've heard from you, he's smart enough to get around the Shore Patrol—and don't tell me you watch him all the time, because the Navy has a budget just like the SFPD, and I know what full-time surveillance costs. At best, you keep a loose watch, now and again, when you have the personnel."

Hempel stood up and held out his hand, making Roland scramble to rise and take it.

"It's been nice talking to you, Commander," he said, smiling his wintry smile. "We're not giving your Mr. Tregear a free pass, but I'll tell you what we will do—we'll give him a very close look. That way, provided he's clean, we'll be out of his life as quickly as possible. I'll see to it that you receive a copy of Inspector Ridley's report."

And that was that.

• • •

Stephen Tregear was sitting on the left side of the sofa in his living room, his cell phone resting on the coffee table, within easy reach. He was waiting for Hal Roland's call.

The living room was sparsely furnished. Against the opposite wall there was one chair and above it hung a print of one of Renoir's river parties left in a closet by the previous tenant, nothing else. The truth was that Tregear hardly ever used this room. He never entertained. He ate in the kitchen and worked in a spare bedroom. Once a week he came to dust the living room and to vacuum the carpet, which for the rest was undisturbed by his footprints. Tregear spent most of his time by himself, but here, in this room, which bore almost no trace of his life, he truly felt alone. Here he felt like Robinson Crusoe.

Today he didn't mind. It seemed appropriate. He hadn't thought it out—hadn't thought about it at all—but here he was, waiting to hear if Roland had played his part as expected.

He discovered that he wasn't frightened, which surprised him a little and made him worry that perhaps he was becoming arrogant. If you guess right too many times you begin to confuse probability with certainty, to underestimate difficulties, and that was a weakness. Tregear was afraid of weakness.

He was also afraid of indifference. He was frightened of not being frightened because he needed, above all else, to stay alert. Indifference was a natural consequence of weariness, either physical or emotional, and he couldn't afford to grow weary. He was involved in something that he preferred to think of as a game because games were abstract things with rules which were at once absolute and arbitrary. Spades were higher than hearts. A pawn could go forward two spaces with its first move but after that only one. Seven was a winner only on the first roll of the dice.

The rules of this game were not of his choosing, but he was bound by them. The game had absorbed his whole attention until there was almost nothing outside it. He had not won yet, but neither had he lost. One loss and the game was over, and with it his life. He needed to concentrate, so that he would make no mistakes.

Right now, the correct move was for Hal Roland to give the police a little prod. Nothing big, just enough to annoy Inspector Ellen Ridley into prodding back. Tregear hoped that Hal could tell him something more about her, so he could have some sense of whether his instinct had been correct.

He knew she was intelligent. She had graduated from Berkeley with honors and from the San Francisco Police Academy with the best record of any cadet in the last ten years. She was on the fast track within the department. They expected great things from her.

Well, so did he.

Tregear's cellular service package with Pacific Bell included caller

ID, and the number on his display screen indicated that Roland was phoning from his office at Treasure Island.

"Yes, Hal."

"I told them you're a government asset and a model citizen, so they'll get finished with you as quickly and unobtrusively as they can. You haven't been carving up hookers in your spare time, have you, Steve? Hah, ha!"

"Is that what they think, that I'm the Zodiac?" Tregear didn't laugh out loud, but he allowed himself a smile. What could be more perfect?

"I'm sure it's only routine. Just be your sweet, cooperative self and they'll see for themselves what a choirboy you are and leave you alone. Promise me you'll be good? Come on, pal—for the Navy."

Naturally Hal would invoke the Navy. He was ever the team player.

"The Navy is supposed to protect me from things like this, Hal. You messed up."

"It's murder, Steve. Mur-der. They seem to think you're involved. San Francisco Homicide isn't a branch of the Department of Defense. What did you expect?"

"Did you talk to Ellen Ridley?"

"No. I talked to her lieutenant."

Of course, he would. Hal was a politician.

"Fine, Hal. Then I guess I'll have to take care of it myself. Just try to stay out of the way."

Tregear pressed the "end" button, cutting Roland off in mid-syllable. He had nothing against Roland, but the man had no aesthetic sense at all. Roland could never appreciate this. *They seem to think you're involved.* It was delicious.

6

"So. Who is this guy Tregear and why are you following him around like a bitch in heat?"

Sam and Ellen, who had been summoned into their lieutenant's office almost the instant they walked into the building, exchanged a perplexed glance. Sam even managed a faint shrug, as if to say, *Well, I didn't tell him.*

The lieutenant waited. Obviously he wasn't feeling collegial. He hadn't even asked them to sit down.

"Am I going to get an answer here, or what?"

When he was unhappy, Hempel's face had a way of narrowing down until it resembled the blade of an ax. Today he was not happy.

"Has he filed a complaint?" Ellen asked blandly.

"A complaint? As in an *official* complaint?" Hempel shook his head, almost as if it grieved him to have to deny it. "No. There was no official complaint. But this morning I received a friendly little visit from a lieutenant commander in the Shore Patrol. And the lieutenant commander told me you accessed Tregear's DMV files yesterday and that—Sam, you'll love this—our Girl Scout here followed him around Fisherman's Wharf last night. Ellen, what were you thinking about?"

"She wanted a closer look at him," Sam answered, discreetly saving his partner the trouble. "So what? It isn't a violation of anyone's civil rights if Inspector Ridley decides to hang around the Cannery for a little while. She was off duty."

Apparently having decided he'd had enough of this nonsense, Sam dropped heavily into a chair. You could almost hear the legs buckling.

"How did the sailor boy know about the DMV search?" Ellen asked, still standing in the doorway.

Sam was in the middle of lighting a cigarette and seemed not to have heard, but Hempel actually grinned.

While she waited for an answer, Ellen sat down in the one remaining chair.

"Tregear told him."

"And how did Tregear know?"

"That's what he does for the Navy. He's a computer whiz. According to Lieutenant Commander Roland, USN, he's just about a national treasure.

"Now. I'll ask again: What is your interest in this guy?"

Sam, having taken a long drag on his unfiltered Camel, and having found it to his liking, reached across and touched Ellen on the arm, which was his way of telling her to shut up and let him do the talking.

"It was a hunch," he said, as if he expected this answer to be completely satisfactory.

"A hunch?" Hempel actually shook his head in disbelief. "A hunch, you say? Excuse me, is this the SFPD or the back lot at Paramount? Sam, Bulldog Drummond has hunches. Policemen work the evidence."

Sam made a dismissive little gesture with his right hand, dropping cigarette ash on the lieutenant's floor.

"Normally I'd agree with you, but Ellie didn't like the look of Mr. Tregear and she talked me into spending a few hours on him." He glanced at Ellen and smiled faintly, then turned his attention back to Hempel. "Would you care to hear the results?"

Without waiting for an answer, he took a notebook out of his inside jacket pocket and flipped it open with his thumb. This was pure theater, as Ellen knew perfectly well, because Sam hadn't had a pen in his hand all day.

"You remember the hooker they found in a bathtub at the Marriott? Mr. Tregear signed his current lease exactly four days later, so he was probably in town for the occasion. Further, we have him in the Fan Club for both the Hudson and the Wilkes killings. He pays his rent with checks drawn on a Seattle bank, so we phoned the Seattle police. They know all about him. He's listed as a person of interest in a string of very polished homicides there, although he was never even questioned. The guy seems to have a 'Don't Touch' sign hanging around his neck. Convenient if your hobby happens to be cutting up women."

Sam closed his notebook and restored it to his inside jacket pocket. He stubbed out his cigarette and lit a fresh one. He looked bored.

For about ten seconds Hempel seemed to consider the matter, and then his eyes narrowed.

"My question is, do you have probable cause?"

"No. Just an interesting series of coincidences."

"Then either put together a case against this citizen or forget about him. I give you three days."

• • •

"You lied to the lieutenant about the Seattle police, Sam. I'm ashamed of you. That was very naughty."

Sam never raised his eyes from the menu, which he was studying like the signed confession of an ax murderer. The interview with Hempel had delayed his lunch.

"By now he won't remember whether it was Seattle or Spokane or Topeka. I once partnered with him for two years—he's not one for follow-up."

"Still, you took a chance to cover for me. Thanks."

This was ignored. Sam glanced up, but only to search for the waitress. Only when he had ordered a bacon cheeseburger, medium, with steak fries, did his mind return to business.

"We've got three days, Ellie. How do we build a case against Tregear in three days?"

"We could go ask him if he'd like to volunteer a semen sample."

"Very funny. Hilarious."

They were in a diner about half a block from the police department, and many of the other patrons were cops. With an expression of envy, Sam watched them eating.

"However, we could pay him a visit," he said. "If only to apologize. A social call, as it were. It would get us in the door."

"Hempel would have a stroke."

"No, he wouldn't. How could he object? It's good public relations."

The waitress arrived with their orders, restoring Sam to a more philosophical temper. Ellen let him finish about a third of his hamburger before asking the inevitable question.

"Are you by any chance serious?"

"Yes."

"Then let's do it."

She seemed ready to rise from the table in that instant, but Sam shook his head.

"Don't you dare. The first rule of good police work is never question a suspect on an empty stomach."

An hour and ten minutes later they were parked directly in front of Stephen Tregear's door. They got out of the car and Sam rang the bell. Within fifteen seconds the door swung open and their suspect was before them, dressed in a blue, long-sleeved sweatshirt and a pair of tan shorts. He didn't appear at all surprised to see them.

"Mr. Tregear, this is Inspector Ellen Ridley and I'm Inspector Samuel Tyler."

"Inspector *Sergeant* Samuel Tyler." Tregear corrected him, even as Sam was reaching to produce his badge. He smiled pleasantly, as if to affirm that he had intended a courtesy. And then his attention shifted to Ellen. "Would you care to come in?"

A short hallway led to the front room, which had the rather sterile atmosphere of a place reserved for company that never came. Tregear directed them to the sofa but remained standing.

"Can I offer you anything?" he asked, the perfect host. "Coffee? Tea? Lemonade?"

"No, nothing. We've just had lunch."

Sam smiled. He had a gift for interrogation, and he was downshifting to the proper gear. On occasions like this he could fall in with the mood of his subject and charm him half to death. At other times he could be ferocious.

Tregear seemed to take the bait and sat down on a leather chair that looked as if it had just been delivered.

"We're sorry to trouble you, Mr. Tregear. Our office has already received a visit from the Navy and we realize that you're an important and busy man, but we're investigating a homicide. We just have a few points to clear up and then we'll be out of your life."

"So soon?"

With marvelous self-control, Sam ignored the interruption.

"Do you own a shortwave radio, Mr. Tregear?"

"Set to the police frequencies? No."

He let his gaze settle on Ellen in a way that suggested he had already lost interest in the conversation, and then he smiled and his eyes softened.

Then he turned back to Sam.

"But I have software that can achieve the same effect with greater precision. It involves voice printouts and code classifications, along with street mapping."

"And are you interested in police calls, Mr. Tregear?"

"As a general rule, no."

"But there are exceptions?"

"Yes. There are exceptions."

Even sitting in his chair, hardly moving, Tregear seemed to possess the natural elegance of a dancer. Then he raised his left hand and touched his face, just beside the eyebrow. There was something graceful in the gesture, all the more so for its apparent unconsciousness.

"There have been three homicides in this city that interest me."

He seemed to disappear inside himself, and then, when Sam was almost ready to ask the inevitable next question, Tregear shook his head slightly and frowned.

"Actually two," he said, almost to himself. "I haven't made up my mind about the third."

"Which three—or two?" Ellen asked. She glanced at Sam, offering a mute apology.

Tregear looked at her again, but this time he didn't smile. He seemed disappointed.

"You know which three."

"But tell us anyway." Sam's voice was not so much urgent as encouraging, so that he seemed to be inviting the man to unburden his soul. "Which three?"

Tregear made a weary gesture, as if to say, *Oh, all right!*

"The prostitute at the Marriott three months ago, then the woman who was found dead in a neighbor's car trunk, then this latest."

"The woman on the coast road?"

"Yes."

"But you haven't decided about her yet?"

"No." Tregear shook his head, suggesting that the quest was futile. "I don't know enough about her yet."

"When will you know?"

"When you file the autopsy protocol."

It was the only time Ellen could recall when Sam appeared to have been caught totally off guard. He had been about to say something, but the words seemed to have vanished from his mind. He was stunned.

"You have access to police files?" Ellen asked, if only to give her partner time to recover.

"Yes. Through your computer system."

"But now that we know, we should be able to lock you out."

"That doesn't follow."

There was absolutely nothing of triumph in Tregear's manner. He seemed to be explaining a commonplace.

"In any database system that can be accessed from the outside, there are always multiple ways in. In computer parlance they're called 'back doors.' At present the SFPD uses a two-hundred-and-fifty-six-bit encryption system, with access codes that are changed weekly, but if you restructure the system I'll be back inside within an hour. Computer security is an illusion."

"Hacking the police system is a felony."

This seemed to amuse him.

"You'd have to prove your case in open court, and the evidence I would offer in my own defense would compromise so many security systems that the Department of Defense will never allow me to testify. Thus, since I can't be permitted to give evidence, I can't be tried."

"But your life could be made very unpleasant. Police attention is always disagreeable."

"Are your threatening me, Inspector Ridley?" He shook his head yet again. He seemed on the verge of laughter. "I am of sufficient value to the Navy that they don't really care what else I do. They just want to keep me happy and working. If someone were to get in the way of that, they wouldn't take a very forgiving attitude."

"Then perhaps you could tell us about your interest in these homicide cases."

It was Sam who spoke, having recovered his poise. Tregear only glanced at him, and then seemed to dismiss him from existence.

"I'm not ready to answer that yet," he said, to Ellen. "It's not a question of what I can tell you, but of what you can tell me."

"Then what can we tell you?"

"Everything that you know, or guess, about the Wilkes killing."

Ellen turned to Sam, who merely shrugged.

"First we should find out what he knows," he said, exactly as if they were alone in the room. Then he turned to Tregear and smiled, not very nicely. "You claim to be able to read our minds—tell us what's in the department files about the first two murders."

It was an impressive performance. For more than an hour, Tregear fed back to them everything on record about those two cases. The autopsy reports, the house-to-house interviews, the physical evidence gathered at the scenes, even the name and Social Security number of the cleaning woman who had discovered Rita Blandish at the Marriott. There were no mistakes and there were no additions. There was nothing to suggest that he knew anything more than the police about these murders, or any less.

Ellen listened in awed fascination. She had been over the case files several times but, inevitably, some of the details had grown blurry in her mind. Tregear, apparently, did not suffer from any such intellectual weaknesses. His command of detail was perfect.

But what impressed her even more were his powers of organization and analysis. There were no digressions. He could have been reading from a script. And his critiques of some of the lab work were both pitiless and brilliant.

"I was surprised and disappointed to find that your forensics people offered no opinion as to whether the Hudson woman's throat was cut from right to left or left to right. All they had to do was examine the wound under magnification—20X would have done it—and they would have been able to see in which direction the fraying occurred."

"And that would have told us exactly what, Mr. Tregear? Whether the killer was right- or left-handed?"

"Only if we assume he was standing behind her when he cut, Inspector Tyler. Of course, if he had her tied faceup on a table, for instance, in which case he could have been standing on either side, then it would tell us nothing."

"And do you have an opinion, Mr. Tregear? Which is he, right- or left-handed?"

"An opinion, Inspector Tyler? No."

"Or, since you're obviously a man who chooses his words with care, you know it for a fact?"

For a moment Tregear appeared to be studying Sam's expression, as if seeking some clue to his intentions. Or, more probably, he had already made up his mind on that point, and he was simply enjoying himself. Ellen fancied there was the faintest trace of a smile on his face.

"Your killer is left-handed," he said at last.

"And you know this for a fact?"

"Yes."

"And you're left-handed yourself. That's interesting."

Sam was sitting on the right-hand side of the sofa, and he shifted his weight so that he was leaning a little more heavily on the armrest. He appeared to be measuring Tregear for his shroud.

"You conclude this from the fact that I wear my wristwatch on the right," Tregear answered, holding that arm up for inspection. There was something almost pitying in his voice. "Feel free to inspect my left hand. There's a writer's bump on the middle finger, so you're correct in your assumption. It's an infirmity I share with from five to fifteen percent of the population—I've often wondered why that particular statistic isn't more precise."

Sam didn't look happy. Perhaps he was beginning to realize that he was out of his depth with this guy. But like a good cop he went straight ahead.

"I wonder if you'd care to share with us how you know this particular bad guy is left-handed."

Tregear shook his head.

"No. I'm not ready yet, which means that you're not ready yet. But I'll give you something else."

"I can hardly wait."

It was clear that Sam didn't enjoy being toyed with, but Ellen had the impression that that was not what was going on. Tregear was serious.

"I'm sure it's obvious to you," he said finally, "that this particular murderer has had a lot of practice. He isn't making his debut in San Francisco. Can we agree on that?"

Sam nodded, with effort. "For purposes of this discussion, yes."

"Then I can offer you something," Tregear announced, as if genuinely pleased. "Talk to the Seattle police about four unsolved murders that occurred between June and November of last year. Then call a Sergeant Carton at Boise Homicide, about a case that's still on the books from last April. Needless to say, there are others, but those will give you a taste.

"And now you can do something for me." Tregear addressed this to Ellen. "Tell me about the Wilkes killing."

Ellen glanced at Sam, who looked as if his lunch was beginning to disagree with him, and then turned back to Tregear with what she hoped was a modest, slightly embarrassed smile.

"I wonder if I could use your bathroom."

It took a brief moment for the request to register, and then Tregear instantly switched back to the perfect host.

"Certainly." He halfway rose out of his chair, as if he thought he might be required to lead her by the hand. "Up the stairs. First doorway on your left."

As she exited the room, she wondered if Tregear was watching her. And then she wondered what her wondering might mean.

It was the cleanest bathroom in living memory, which was a disappointment. There was nothing on the sink except a dispenser of liquid soap—no comb, no brush, no electric razor. The medicine cabinet was just as barren.

Ellen had the sinking feeling that this was probably the guest bathroom.

Then she noticed the towels. They weren't folded as if they had just come from the linen closet. She touched the face towel and it was still slightly damp.

This was Tregear's bathroom. He was just a clean freak.

There was a shower stall. Lots of people preferred a shower stall to a bathtub. Maybe the only thing Tregear did in this room was use the shower.

The shower drain was covered with a plastic cap. She took out the jackknife she always carried and pried the cap out.

Praise be to God, there were a few strands of hair sticking to the inside.

Ellen extracted an evidence bag and one plastic glove from her pocket. By the time she had put the glove on, used her finger to scoop out the hair strands, put both the glove and the hair in the evidence bag and then put the bag back in her pocket and replaced the drain cap, she had been in the bathroom for about a minute and a half.

She was almost ready to leave and go back downstairs when she remembered she had forgotten to flush the toilet. She worked the handle and then made a leisurely production out of washing her hands. Men always assumed that it took women forever to pee, so when her hands were clean she inspected her face and hair in the mirror.

She didn't like her expression. It was cold and cynical. This is what I do, she thought to herself. I steal hair out of people's drains. I pry into their lives.

When she got back to the living room, there was complete silence. Ellen had the impression there had been what her mother would have called a "scene." Sam looked angry and Tregear looked uncomfortable, as if he had just witnessed a display of bad manners he was too polite to acknowledge.

Sam stood up. "We'd better be going now."

The only exchange of pleasantries at the door occurred when Tregear took her hand and smiled the kindest, warmest smile Ellen had ever seen.

"It was a pleasure to meet you," he said.

They were in the car and had already slipped into the flow of traffic before Ellen could bring herself to speak.

"So what happened while I was gone?" she asked.

"I told him I'd check with Seattle and Boise and that if his information turned out to be useful we might have another chat." Sam was clenching the steering wheel as if he hated it. "But if that freak thinks I'm going to share any information with him, he really is crazy."

Then he looked at her and grinned, almost savagely.

"I think your little hunch might just pan out, Ellie. I think this might be Our Boy."

Ellen didn't answer. In theory she agreed. Tregear was the leading contender. He even fit the psychological profile, another narcissistic game player, a smart son of a bitch who thought the rest of the human race existed solely for his amusement. Another Brad, if you will.

Except that this guy was even smarter than Brad, and Brad expressed his contempt of women—or, at least, of her—by dumping them without even the courtesy of a good-bye, which was a step or two up from cutting their guts out while they were still alive to enjoy it.

"Didn't you just love the way he played with us?" Sam shook his head and, as he changed lanes, almost sideswiped a little old lady in a white Buick. "He thinks he's so smart. He thinks he can come this close to the fire and not get burned, the arrogant prick. Well, his arrogance will be his undoing. I'll enjoy putting the cuffs on this one."

In that moment Ellen decided she wouldn't tell Sam about the hair samples.

7

Tregear saw off his visitors, locked the door behind them and went upstairs to the guest bathroom.

There was a bathroom immediately across the hall from his bedroom, but it didn't have a shower stall, which he preferred to washing himself while he stood in a bathtub screened by a plastic curtain decorated with blue waves and mermaids. He liked to be able to see out, just in case he should have forgotten to lock the door.

Thus he always showered in the guest bathroom. Otherwise, he used the one next to his bedroom.

He wasn't absolutely sure that Ellen Ridley had had some devious purpose in visiting his bathroom, but he preferred to know these things.

The inside of the sink was wet and there was a droplet of liquid soap clinging to the nozzle of the dispenser, so she had washed her hands. But the toilet seat was still up. How many women would think to put the toilet seat back up? So the odds were good that she had flushed the toilet without actually using it.

And thus it followed that she had been up to something.

The room contained only the toilet, the sink, which she had used, a medicine cabinet, which contained nothing except a bottle of rubbing alcohol and three boxes of bandages, and a shower. Tregear opened the shower door.

There was nothing obvious, so he got down on his hands and knees for a closer look.

Sure enough, he found a tiny scratch in the metal rim of the drain. It sparkled under the light, so it was new. Inspector Ridley had been here ahead of him.

Tregear pried off the drain cap, but there didn't seem to be anything remarkable about the drain. Then he turned the cap over and had a look at the inside.

There were two strands of his hair just under the top, but the sides, where he knew from experience that hair would be more likely to collect, were perfectly clean—just as if someone had scoured all the way around with her finger.

Now, who could that have been?

He popped the drain cap back into place, closed the shower door and went back downstairs to his kitchen to make himself a cup of tea. When it was ready, he took it with him into the living room and sat down on the leather chair. As he drank the tea, he stared at the left side of the sofa, where Inspector Ridley had been sitting not twenty minutes earlier. He seemed to be trying to conjure her up out of the thin air, and perhaps he was.

"Sneaky girl," he said, without anger, in a voice that was just audible. "Now why did you do that?"

The obvious answer had of course occurred to him, but he almost dismissed it out of hand as too wildly improbable. What could she possibly want with a few strands of his hair except a DNA sample? But, once she had it, it would be useless unless she had another sample, taken from a crime scene, to which she could match it.

There had been no suspect DNA recovered from the bathroom at the Marriott and none from the car trunk in which Kathy Hudson had been found. So far, the autopsy findings on Sally Wilkes hadn't been posted, but Tregear would have been prepared to bet very serious money none had been found there either.

He wondered if she had any plans to tell her partner about the hair samples.

Of course both of them thought that he was their killer, an idea he had made no attempt to discourage, but they had nothing tangible that connected him with any of these murders. They had only the information he had given them and Inspector Ridley's tenuous hunch.

Tregear was in love with Inspector Ridley's hunches. The instant he first saw her, up on Skyline Boulevard when she got that photographer to film him, he had sensed that she was not a by-the-book type.

In the slightly more than twenty-four hours since she had pulled up his DMV records, Tregear had learned a good deal about her, and a streak of rebellion ran through the details of her life like a flaw through a diamond. The child of money, she was a working cop who gave every indication of living on her police salary. The performance records written by her immediate superiors were generally glowing, shadowed only here and there with oblique references to a less than perfect respect for authority and proper procedure: "Patrolwoman Ridley certainly merits promotion to Assistant Inspector, where her independence of mind will find more scope." "Inspector Ridley's first year in Juvenile Offenders has been generally satisfactory, even exemplary. Like so many of our better officers at the beginning of their careers, she has at times exhibited an understandable degree of impatience with the workings of the juvenile justice system." There was even a complaint, which the judge had dismissed out of hand, from a drug-addicted father whom she had threatened with mayhem if he didn't stop abusing his daughter.

Alas, so things went. There was justice, which dwelt in Heaven, and then there was the law, in this case represented by the San Francisco Police Department. And Inspector Ellen Ridley seemed to feel the tension between them as a kind of private travail. Thus, impatient of constraint, she had ignored the rules and followed her nose to Fisherman's Wharf, hoping to pick up the scent of a murderer.

Well, good for her.

But could it be that now, as she and Inspector Sergeant Tyler drove away together, perhaps she was just a shade less confident? Tregear was not much given to vanity about his effect on women, but he was observant—he could read the signs. And he had detected a chord of sympathy in Ellen Ridley which, under happier circumstances, might have emboldened him to ask her if she might care to share a few glasses of wine with him.

At least, he felt permitted to suspect, she would not be utterly crushed to discover that Sally Wilkes had been murdered by somebody else.

And that, probably, was the best he could hope for.

Still, she was a pretty woman—prettier at close range than she had appeared to be up on the coast road—and it was a pleasure to remember her. He liked her hair. It was an unusual color, a mix of red and brown which couldn't possibly have come out of a bottle. It was almost a pity she wore it so short, but it framed her face and somehow emphasized the delicacy of her features. She had beautiful, clear skin and a mouth that just hinted at a streak of sensuality in her nature. And her eyes, large and light brown, were lovely.

But today was probably as close to her as he would ever manage.

As he sat alone in his living room, holding an empty teacup, Tregear was forced to admit to himself that there were times when he found the circumstances of his life utterly depressing.

8

Ellen soothed her conscience with the reflection that she couldn't have told Sam anyway. Sam had his pension to think about. She had illegally gathered evidence, and she had no business involving him in that.

Besides, he was obsessive about proper procedure. Yesterday she had followed Tregear along a couple of blocks of public sidewalk, and Sam had given her one of his copyrighted lectures. What would he have said if he knew she was carrying strands of Tregear's hair around in her coat pocket? He wouldn't have understood.

And, truth to tell, she wasn't sure she understood herself. The hair samples would not be admissible evidence and, if it ever got out how she had obtained them, any subsequent case against Tregear stood a good chance of being thrown out. Ellen was perfectly aware that during the last twenty-four or so hours she had not been behaving like a model detective.

Their shift was nearly over. They drove back to the station and Ellen found two manila folders on her desk. The first was thicker and contained about twenty high-definition photographs of the crowd at Sally Wilkes' discovery site. The detail was much better than in the video. Ellen was at last able to determine that the trousers Tregear had been wearing were olive green.

In five of the photos his face was particularly clear, and one of them Ellen would have liked to pin up on her refrigerator. Probably it had been taken before he noticed the camera, and his expression reflected an anguish Ellen had sensed in him but never actually seen. It was impossible to look at that face and believe Stephen Tregear was a murderer.

He was something, this guy. He wasn't amazingly handsome, but he made your average heartthrob movie star look like a troglodyte.

His face radiated intelligence, as if no secret could be hidden from him, and somehow that was way sexier than sculpted eyebrows.

After about five minutes, she put the photos back in their envelope. After all, this was a murder investigation.

The other envelope contained, providentially, the DNA report on the semen recovered at autopsy from Sally Wilkes.

While Sam was in the men's room, she took the report over to the Xerox machine and copied it, all five pages.

When Sam came back, he threw himself into his chair and lit a cigarette.

"Girl, I don't know what you've got in mind for the contents of that envelope, but just don't sell it to *The National Enquirer.*"

Then he laughed.

After Sam had driven her home, and she was alone in her apartment, she threw a frozen lasagna into the microwave, poured herself a glass of Pinot Grigio, and sat down to read the report. For all that she was able to understand it, it might as well have been written in cuneiform.

With some obscure idea of eventually going to law school, Ellen had majored in philosophy. The physical sciences were not among her strengths and the report, with its references to VNTR assays and SNPs, was completely unintelligible to her. Even the graphs, which looked like finger paint smears, meant nothing.

Okay. In any case, she could hardly turn her purloined hair samples over to the police lab; she would need an outside expert.

And that meant she would have to beg a favor from Daddy.

Fortunately, tomorrow was her day off; she could postpone her visit home for another twelve or thirteen hours.

• • •

The next morning Ellen was up at five. Her father's office hours didn't start until ten, and so he never left the house before nine-forty. She could be in Atherton by seven, which would give her plenty of time to work on him.

The section of Atherton where her parents lived was enclosed by a brick wall and was home to some of the wealthiest people in the San Francisco Bay Area. Both her mother and father had inherited money, and her father had a lucrative practice—many of his patients were the children of neighbors—but even between them they didn't have quite enough money to really fit in. Thus, their social position was ambiguous. They were popular, particularly Ellen's father, but Dr. Ridley was someone you hired by the hour. It was all very distressing.

Ellen had gone to private schools, and her grades and SAT scores would easily have qualified her for Stanford, but she chose instead to attend the University of California at Berkeley. Over the summers she worked at a Dairy Queen in Redwood City. To her mother, all of this was incomprehensible.

The truth was that, somewhere in her middle teens, Ellen had discovered she found her parents' world claustrophobic. The ideal was to go to the right college so you could graduate into the right sort of job and live in a seven-bedroom house in the right sort of neighborhood. Life was supposed to be an orderly progression from success to success, without risk or uncertainty. It was a prison without the bars.

Escape had become her dream, her one consolation for all the proms and tea parties and weekends at Big Sur she had been forced to endure. She hated the boys she met in Atherton because all they could think about was getting into her pants and where they would go to college. It was an atmosphere as pointlessly competitive as a dog race.

And then, four weeks after graduation from college, she told her parents she had applied to the police academy in San Francisco. For the better part of a month her mother couldn't look at her daughter without dabbing at her eyes with an embroidered handkerchief. Even to this day, their relationship was only a kind of armistice.

Her father was more tolerant.

"Daddy, I just want a success that hasn't been handed to me. Is that so difficult to understand?"

Then he said something for which she would always love him.

"I'm proud of the ambition, if nothing else," he told her. "If this is what you want, then fine." And then he glanced away for a few seconds before going on. "I've never regretted the way my own life has worked out, but once or twice it has occurred to me that perhaps it was all just a little too inevitable. All of us wonder where some other path might have taken us."

"Except Mommy."

This made him smile. "Yes, except perhaps Mommy."

Mommy, they both understood, had no doubts, and her disappointment was not very well concealed. She probably wondered if perhaps her daughter wasn't a lesbian.

It sometimes occurred to Ellen that her mother might have made an easier adjustment if she had had other children, but Ellen's had been a difficult birth and afterward Mrs. Ridley had been advised not to risk any further pregnancies, with the result that all of her aspirations and fears had settled upon her daughter.

Thus Ellen always dreaded coming home. And this morning, at seven-fifteen, while she parked her four-year-old Toyota in the driveway, she couldn't quite stifle an irrational terror that she might never escape again.

They were still at breakfast. Preston Ridley, MD, was dressed in a pair of tobacco-colored corduroys and a blue broadcloth shirt. His wife, Tracy, was wearing a housecoat. Underneath there was a bra, panties and a slip, and her makeup was perfect and her blond hair exquisitely highlighted. The housecoat would be replaced by a dress around noon, when she would meet one of her friends for lunch and then go shopping.

Her mother, even in her early fifties, was a stunningly attractive woman, but Ellen had always been grateful that she took more after her father—in appearance and in other things.

Preston and Tracy. One could imagine their parents searching the *Social Register* for those names. It had been an act of mercy for them to name their daughter and only child Ellen.

"Ellen—this is a surprise."

Her father, from the fact that he always sat facing the kitchen door, was the first to see her. He actually got out of his chair and came over to give her a kiss. Her mother merely turned her head and her eyes took on that wide, moist look that was the hallmark of her dread.

That's what it was, Ellen had finally decided. Her mother was profoundly afraid of the world outside her cocoon of wealth, and this was precisely the world her daughter had embraced. God alone knew what horrors she imagined threatening her child.

"Daddy, I need to talk to you."

Without a word, he put his arm across her shoulders and guided her out through the dining room, then through the living room, then up the stairs of his study.

What does he expect? she found herself wondering. *That I'm in debt? That I'm pregnant?*

The study walls were lined with books—most of which, to his credit, Dr. Ridley had actually read. He sat down behind his desk, which meant that the interview was being regarded as an official act. Suddenly she felt like one of his patients.

There was only one other chair in the room, reserved for penitents. Ellen had no choice but to occupy it.

"What's the problem?" he asked, looking grave. Yes, this was exactly how he talked to the twelve-year-old boys who had been caught peeking at their sisters.

On a certain level, Ellen was looking forward to his disappointment.

"I need a DNA test run, Daddy. I need it off the books, like it never happened, and I need it fast. It's about a case, but I can't take it to the police lab."

"Is it illegal?"

"No."

And that was the truth. Perhaps—probably—it had been illegal for her to scoop out the hair in Stephen Tregear's drain, but there was nothing illegal about some lab technician running a test on samples about which he was blissfully ignorant.

"You have friends at Stanford Medical, Daddy. I need this."

"I'll make a call." He took a long look at his watch, not to determine the time but to call attention to it. "But it's a little early." And then, "Is everything okay with you? You seem a trifle harried."

Ellen sighed, without meaning to. "It's this job. Did you read about the woman found along the coast road? I'm the case officer."

"And?" Her father raised his eyebrows in expectation.

"And we've got a serial killer operating in San Francisco. And, so far, he's smarter than we are. This guy is a virtuoso."

"'On Murder Considered as One of the Fine Arts'?" When Ellen looked perplexed, Dr. Ridley smiled. "It's an essay by De Quincey. Early nineteenth century."

"Yes, well, something like that. He's laughing at us."

"He won't be laughing when you catch him." He shook his head. "Still, I'd love to interview him, although, unless he turns out to be twelve years old, I probably won't get the chance."

"You'll be retired," his daughter said archly. "You'll be too busy playing golf."

It was one of their little private jokes. Golf was a game Dr. Ridley had dutifully learned but did not much care for. In fact, it bored him. He said he couldn't quite see the point.

"There'd be other things to do besides golf," he answered, with perhaps less than perfect conviction. "I could catch up on my reading. I've been in private practice for nearly thirty years now. Your mother thinks I'm getting too old for it. She thinks the stress is beginning to tell."

Ellen made a disdainful little grunt.

"The translation of which is, after a full day of patients, you don't necessarily want to go to the club for dinner and bridge. You'd rather stay home and relax with De Quincey.

"You're only fifty-seven, Daddy. You're too young to die of boredom."

Dr. Ridley laughed. "You've always had such a charming way of putting things, Ellie. Now let's go down and have a cup of coffee with your mother."

He raised his eyes to his daughter and tilted his head slightly, as if to say, *Would it kill you?*

No, it wouldn't kill her. Daddy was a sweetie and her mother's only sin was the uncritical assumption that "decent" and "rich" were synonyms. So they went back to the kitchen and Ellen fetched a mug down from the cupboard and poured herself some coffee.

As soon as she took her seat at the breakfast table, she knew from the way her mother looked at her, her lips slightly pursed, that she had committed a breach of decorum. It was the mug. Nice people drank coffee out of cups, but you picked up bad habits in a police squad room.

Nice people. Her mother's world was not sufficiently narrow that she didn't feel the need to constrict it further with a set of rules that were positively Victorian—or perhaps these only applied to her daughter.

Ellen found it possible to pity her, and to wonder what had rendered her so frightened of life. Of course, she would never know.

The next hour was excruciating. Within five minutes her mother had expressed the wish that Ellen would let her father buy her a new car. Something "good," which probably meant that she would be prepared to compromise on a BMW.

"So it can be stolen, like your Mercedes? I'm better off with a car no self-respecting thief would touch."

But Mommy was one of those women for whom it was a fixed conviction that all her little girl really needed was some guidance so, as she not so subtly tried to goad her daughter back to safety, the conversation followed an inevitable trajectory. First her car, then the horrors of her apartment, then her love life—or lack thereof.

"Mommy, I'm a homicide detective. I don't meet very many nice men."

After which Ellen avenged herself by hinting at what she had found in Sally Wilkes' bathtub.

"I think I'll make that phone call now," her father announced suddenly.

He came back from his study holding a slip of paper on which was written, *Chun Hei Kim, Building A, Rm 322.*

"She's a leading authority, Ellen. So be nice. She'll see you at nine o'clock, and for a rush job she'll want five hundred dollars. In cash. Would you like me to write you a check?"

Ellen managed a tight smile. "I can swing it, Daddy."

• • •

It was eight-thirty, but Palo Alto was only about ten minutes away, so even with a stop at the Bank of America, Ellen arrived at the Stanford Medical School in plenty of time.

Dr. Kim turned out to be a smiling, agreeable middle-aged woman with a heavy Korean accent. She showed Ellen into her office, which was clean and sparse. There was nothing on the desk except a blotter pad and a single pencil. One suspected that Dr. Kim didn't spend much time there.

Ellen gave her the evidence bag and the DNA report from the police lab. Then she placed on the table an envelope containing ten fifty-dollar bills. She didn't offer it. She merely set it down.

"Your father tells me you are a policewoman," Dr. Kim said, as if this might represent a problem. "Does this relate to your work, or is it a private matter?"

"It relates to my work, but nothing you do for me today will be introduced into evidence. I won't ask you for a written report, merely a conclusion. I need to know if the hair and the semen are a match."

"And for this you are prepared to pay five hundred dollars of your own money. I won't inquire why. Come back around noon and I'll tell you what I have found."

"Thank you."

• • •

Ellen had three hours to kill, so she went to the Stanford Mall, conveniently just across a little bridge from the university, and found a Starbucks. She ordered a caramel frappuccino, which she imagined would be disgusting and therefore would not tempt her to drink it quickly. That was the whole idea, to waste time.

She used a spoon to eat the whipped cream with the caramel drizzles. She picked it apart as carefully as she would have a pile of garbage she suspected might contain body parts.

She was glad Sam wasn't there to watch her with her caramel frappuccino. She would never hear the end of it.

Actually, it wasn't bad. This discovery worried her, since she had the impression that every time she came home she started reverting to type—the mall rat with frosted hair and a standing appointment to have her nails done. The little rich girl.

And for this you are prepared to pay five hundred dollars of your own money. Wasn't that reverting to type? Sam would say so.

"It's a job. It's not a personal crusade," he had told her once. "Don't get emotionally involved. And when you go home, forget about it."

But she was home, and she couldn't forget about it.

She was shelling out almost three days' pay to find out if Stephen Tregear was a murderer, and she had no clue what she wanted the answer to be. If it was a match she would focus on him until she put him on death row. But, God, what a waste.

Yesterday she had been convincing herself that Stephen Tregear was nothing more than Ted Bundy on steroids, a particularly brilliant example of the charming, personable sociopath that was almost a cliché of abnormal psychology. She had interpreted his attitude toward Sam as subtle mockery. Now she was no longer so sure.

When will you know?

When you file the autopsy protocol.

Had it been merely an act, or was he really waiting for information? And what would their murderer learn from the autopsy of Sally Wilkes that he didn't already know?

If we ever do catch him, it won't be because he fell into our laps. Sam's very words.

And Stephen Tregear had fallen into their laps.

Ellen had listened with rapt attention to his astonishing disquisition on their files and, if he had made a mistake and had any information beyond them, she hadn't caught it. His knowledge of those three homicides was precisely congruent with the police records. Would a man who was capable of such exquisite intellectual discipline be reckless enough—assuming he was guilty—to expose himself like that to the detectives working the case? Why would he? Vanity?

It didn't seem likely. Stephen Tregear gave the impression of being in perfect control of himself.

What a waste, if he was guilty.

Even so, if he was she promised herself she would burn him.

She finished her frappuccino in about twenty minutes and decided, what the hell, she would go shopping for something to spruce up her wardrobe.

• • •

At two minutes before twelve, she was back tapping on the door to Dr. Kim's office.

"Please, come in."

This time the desk was covered with papers. The state of Ellen's nerves reminded her of exam day at Berkeley.

She sat down in front of the desk, forcing herself to appear calm. "Is it a match?" she asked. "Yes or no?"

Dr. Kim smiled. "It is more complicated than yes or no. But it is not a match."

Ellen didn't move. She might as well have been made of stone. But as she analyzed her reactions she found that she was relieved. Stephen

Tregear wasn't a murderer. She felt as if a weight had been lifted from her shoulders.

"Okay," she said. "Then it was a blind alley."

"No."

Dr. Kim shook her head. It was obvious that she was enjoying this, but in the way someone enjoys giving a birthday present.

"As I said, it is more complicated than yes or no. There is a relationship between the samples, but it is not identity. It is a criminal case we are dealing with here?"

"Yes. Murder."

"Then I think you are very close to a solution. The semen sample is from the murderer?"

"Yes."

"Then all you need to do is ask the donor of the hair samples, and he will be able to tell you who committed the crime."

"I don't follow you."

"The relationship between the two samples is familial. They are both male and, based on experience, I would hazard a guess that they are not more than one generation apart. Beyond that, it's conjectural."

9

On the drive back to San Francisco, Ellen was perplexed and angry—what kind of game was this guy playing with them?

She worked the evidence every way she could. Had Tregear planted the semen sample to implicate someone else? How do you get a semen sample, particularly from a close relative? Were the hair samples planted? How could he have known that Ellen would raid his shower drain? This wasn't an Agatha Christie novel; this was real life.

The conclusion was inescapable. Tregear was not the murderer, but he knew the identity of the murderer.

How could she tell all this to Sam? She couldn't.

She was half-tempted to say to hell with it and drive to the airport to catch a plane for Aruba. She needed two weeks of lying on the sand, listening to her suntan oil sizzle. She needed to get plastered on piña coladas. She needed to find some big, strong beach bum she could climb all over. She needed to be just about anywhere but where she was, doing what she was doing, the problem being that life just didn't work that way.

In the end, the decision made itself. At one forty-five in the afternoon, she found herself parked across the street from Tregear's apartment. Whatever the cost to her personally, she had to hear the answer from his own lips.

Still, it took her ten minutes to summon the will to get out of her car.

The instant she was on the street, Tregear's front door opened. He stood in the entrance, waiting for her.

Somehow, that made it easier. She would seem such a fool, to him and to herself, if she got back in the car and drove away; it took far less courage just to walk across the street to where he was standing.

"I'm glad to see you," he said. "Please, come in."

Ellen found she wasn't in a mood for the social amenities. She merely brushed by him as if he were the wallpaper. Inside, with the door closed, she discovered that she was angry, primarily at herself. But she wasn't scared, and that was something.

"Can I offer you anything?"

She ignored his question. She never took her eyes from his face. When he smiled she discovered she was furious.

"What is going on?" she shouted. "Why are you jerking us around?"

"Pardon me?"

"Did you know about the semen samples from Sally Wilkes?"

"Not until this morning. Your lab is a little behind in its postings."

"Okay, you didn't. But I did. Yesterday I took some hair samples out of your shower drain . . ."

"I know."

"You know? Well, if you want, you can have my badge for it," she went on sulkily. Somehow, his knowing took the edge off her anger. "They weren't a match anyway. But you know who the murderer is, don't you."

"Yes. I do."

"Then why didn't you *say so*?"

"Think about it." He smiled again, as if she were suggesting the impossible. "If I walked into your office and said I knew who killed Sally Wilkes, but I couldn't tell you his name or where he was, what would you think? 'Here's another crank. Next he'll confess that he's the Zodiac.' I've been laughed at before."

She could see the logic of it, but she was past logic. She wanted him to stop smiling at her.

And then she remembered it was a homicide they were talking about, and this man was waiting to reveal to her the murderer's identity.

You could see it in his eyes. He might smile, but his eyes were full of anguish. This was a man who labored under a burden.

And they held her. For Ellen it was one of those rare moments in life when she lost all sense of her own private existence. She could only experience it, helplessly, the way one experiences any mystery. The only thing that was real was the expression in Tregear's eyes.

Then Ellen remembered herself and took a tentative step back.

"We have to talk," she said, suddenly unable to look at the man.

Tregear nodded. "We have to talk."

They were still just inside the door. He made a gesture toward his front room, but he didn't follow her immediately. It occurred to Ellen that he was probably giving her some time to compose herself.

And she needed it. When she sat down on the sofa, she discovered that her hands were shaking.

When Tregear came in he was carrying two glasses of white wine. He set one down on the table in front of the sofa and then retired to his chair. He was keeping a safe distance.

"Your partner doesn't like me," he said quietly. "Why is that?"

"Because he thinks you cut up women as a pastime."

"And who put that idea into his head?"

"I did."

Tregear actually seemed pleased. He took a sip of his wine and then made a tiny gesture with his head, as if to say, *Try it.*

Ellen tasted the wine and discovered it was Pinot Grigio, her absolute preference. Only, this was a label that cost about twenty-five dollars a bottle, and the last time she had splurged on it was the day her transfer to Homicide had been approved.

Was there *anything* about her this guy didn't know?

"He thinks you're teasing us," she went on. "He thinks you want us to know it's you, even if we can never prove it."

"That would put an effective end to my career as a serial killer. But then undoubtedly he also thinks that I'm insane and that therefore my judgment might be a little impaired."

"I suppose so."

"But he's right about being teased—your killer is a game player." Tregear set his wineglass down on a small table on the left side of his chair. "So tell me about the semen sample. It's completely out of character."

"You don't think he fucks his victims?" Ellen asked, in her best ingénue voice. Her use of so crude a word was a small act of revenge that apparently went unnoticed.

"Beyond murder and torture, I have very little idea what he does with them. But leaving behind that kind of evidence is a mistake he's never made before."

"I don't think he made a mistake. I think he did it on purpose."

And then she told him about the red panties on Sally Wilkes' corpse and the glass in her kitchen.

"It probably won't be on the computer before late today, but I think it'll turn out to be a match with the semen. I think he wants us to know."

For a long moment, Tregear seemed lost inside himself. Then, finally, he looked up at the ceiling and said, just above a whisper, " 'Oh Daddy, Daddy, you're still number one . . .' "

And then, abruptly, he stood up.

"I'll only be a few minutes," he told her, and vanished up the stairs.

Those "few minutes" were among the hardest of Ellen's life, as she realized how utterly she had put herself in this man's power. Tregear could crack open her banking records like a walnut shell. He would find out about the ATM charge for five hundred dollars she had made that morning. One phone call to Internal Affairs and her career in the SFPD would come to an abrupt end.

And what would prevent him? The fact that they had had a little moment when she had found herself staring into his eyes like a teenager in front of a rock star?

When he came back, Tregear was holding a sheet of paper in his hand. He laid it faceup on the coffee table—it was about half covered with a double-spaced typeface—then knelt down, took a pen out of his shirt pocket, and wrote his signature.

"This will cover you," he said. "It's a release for DNA testing of a blood sample. Have you got an evidence bag in your pocket?"

"Yes." She took it out and showed it to him.

"Good. Now here comes the hard part."

He took a neatly folded white handkerchief out of his trousers pocket and set it on the arm of his chair. Then he sat down and reached back into his shirt pocket to extract a small silver folding knife, the kind gentlemen used to carry to cut the ends off their cigars.

Before Ellen could say anything, he opened the knife and slit the tip of his right index finger. For almost a full minute he let his finger bleed into the handkerchief. It was a deep cut and there was a lot of blood.

"That should do it." He smiled and closed his right hand into a fist. "Now, if you don't mind, I'll just go get a Band-Aid."

While he was gone, Ellen put the handkerchief into her evidence bag. She picked it up by one corner. It was really a mess.

When Tregear returned his finger was wrapped in gauze. He sat down again and dropped his right hand over the arm of his chair, as if trying to keep it out of sight.

He took a sip of his wine.

"I hope this will bring about an attitude adjustment in your partner," he said. "You can tell him I called you on your cell phone and asked you to come alone. You might leave a message on his voicemail, just to cover yourself."

He lifted his right hand and looked at it. The gauze had already bled through.

"I'm afraid I didn't do a very good job."

"Come upstairs to the bathroom and I'll fix it for you."

Tregear smiled. It was the smile of someone who was in on a secret.

"You mean the bathroom where you feloniously stole my hair samples."

"The very place."

. . .

He sat on the toilet seat like a good boy, making no protest while she cleaned out the cut and then coated it with Neosporin. Like every cop, she had had first aid training, so she did a pretty good job.

"Could you come back and change the dressings for me tomorrow?" he asked, making it sound like a joke.

"I might."

Suddenly Ellen realized that she was happy. It was a relief that this man was not a mass murderer. Actually, he seemed to be a rather nice person about whom it was therefore possible to entertain tender sentiments that had been lurking in the shadows, just out of sight. She found herself wondering if, like Ken the photographer, Stephen Tregear might like to take her to dinner.

"How did you know about the Pinot Grigio?" she asked, not quite sure why all at once it seemed such an important question.

"I didn't. It's the only wine I keep in the house."

What a delightful coincidence. She was so pleased she couldn't help smiling.

But apparently it didn't strike him the same way. The expression on his face was almost grim.

"Come downstairs," he said, "and you can hear the story of my life."

10

After her three years in Juvenile Offenders, Ellen thought that nothing about the little tragedies of domestic life would ever surprise her again. She had seen it all, she thought. Every kind of neglect or abuse. Children clinging to parents who were half-crazed with drugs or alcohol, begging for love—or absolution for their imagined sins.

For Ellen, the breaking point had been a fourteen-year-old girl arrested in the Tenderloin district at two o'clock in the morning. The charge was prostitution. She was grabbed in a street sweep and taken by paddy wagon with half a dozen other hookers to the closest station house. Because she was obviously underage she was sent to juvie, where Ellen interviewed her the next morning.

Her name was Julie Pailey, and she was a long way from being a pro. Ellen had searched her purse, in which she found forty-five dollars, a comb, a lipstick and no condoms.

Forty-five dollars. It must have been a slow night.

"Do you have any idea the sorts of things that can happen to you out there?" Ellen had asked her. "You could get robbed, which usually involves a black eye or a broken nose, unless the guy gets overzealous and kills you. And the way you're going you're almost certain to catch a venereal disease. What in God's name were you thinking about?"

This produced no response. She seemed apathetic, her gaze fixed on the top of the interview table, but there weren't any needle tracks on her arms and she didn't appear to be on anything. Ellen thought probably she was just frightened.

"Talk to me, girl." Ellen reached out and patted the back of the girl's hand. "Tell me where you live."

After a long while, Julie gave an address in the Mission District.

"How long has it been since you've had anything to eat?"

When she didn't receive any answer beyond a shake of the head, Ellen sent out for a cheeseburger and fries. Julie devoured them. She just about inhaled them. It was a revelation of sorts—with forty-five dollars in her purse she was almost starving. What could make her so afraid of spending her money?

After nearly an hour of indirect questions, really just invitations to talk, Julie began to open up. She lived with her pa. She had no idea where Mom was. She hadn't been to school in a while. This had been only her third night on the streets.

Fill in the blanks. How could her father not know what she was doing? He knew. How could he countenance such a thing? He wanted the money. For what? It was a safe bet it wasn't to pay the rent.

"Tell me about your pa."

"He sleeps a lot."

"Was it his idea you peddle your tail?"

"I don't know."

"Then it *was* his idea."

"No."

Abused children became intensely loyal to their parents. What choice did they have? Whether out of fear or a victim's abject love for her tormenter, Julie wasn't going to roll over on her old man.

She was a sweet little thing, and her loyalty to a no doubt undeserving father did her no harm in Ellen's eyes. Ellen liked her. She wanted to protect her, to give her the life to which every child was entitled—and this one perhaps more than most.

But it was clear that she was a little girl who would be better off in juvenile hall, where at least nobody could get at her, so Ellen wrote out her recommendations and scheduled a medical exam for later that morning. For the time being, the girl would be safe, and maybe, once Domestic Services had investigated Pa and revealed him as the unsavory bastard he no doubt was, some sort of placement could be found for her and she could get back into what passed for normal life among fourteen-year-old girls.

Except that, her medical exam complete, some idiot had decided she should be allowed to go home to her family.

It was after four in the afternoon when Ellen found out. Her shift was nearly over, but she didn't let that stop her. She clawed through her notes until she found the Mission District address and headed for the underground parking garage, taking the stairway three steps at a time because the elevator was too slow.

She was at the front door of the apartment building in ten minutes. A check of the mailboxes listed a Pailey in 203, which was up a flight of stairs and at the end of the dingiest corridor Ellen had ever seen.

She knocked on the door and waited. No answer. The second time she knocked louder, using her fist as a hammer. No answer. "Police," she shouted. No answer.

At this point she took out her badge and looped it over the breast pocket of her jacket, stepped back and, in the best tradition of the department, slammed into the door with the full length of her shoe sole.

The door popped right open.

There were two bedrooms, in the larger of which she found Pa, stretched out on the bed, alive but unresponsive.

Good, Ellen thought to herself. Maybe he'll die of an overdose. Maybe I just won't be in too much of a hurry to call for an ambulance.

But in the second, smaller bedroom she found Julie in the closet, hanging from a noose made with clothesline.

Ellen cut her down, but it was too late. Julie had been dead for probably an hour. Her hands were free and there was a beauty case lying overturned on the other side of the closet, suggesting she had kicked it away. There was even a note sticking out from the right side pocket of her jeans, with the words "I'm sorry" written with red Magic Marker.

Her face was covered with red patches, which, had she lived a little longer, would have colored into dramatic bruises.

When Ellen called 911 she was nearly incoherent. She was sitting on the floor with Julie's head cradled in her lap, sobbing.

It took the emergency team five minutes and an injection to get any kind of coherent response from Pa.

After the bodies, both living and dead, had been taken out on stretchers, Ellen was left alone with her futile attempts to imagine what must have happened. There must have been some sort of violent confrontation before Dad retreated into his favored recreational drug and his daughter into death. What he had done to her was obvious, but what had he said to her? What had he threatened her with? Perhaps only the withdrawal of his love.

And what difference did it make? Whatever he did or said, he as good as killed her. The coroner's report would list Julie Pailey's death as a suicide, but in truth she had been murdered.

At seven that evening, when the evidence people were busy and there was nothing left for her to do, Ellen went home to feed Gwendolyn, drink half a bottle of Pinot Grigio and cry herself to sleep.

The next morning she put in for a transfer. Enough was enough. It was either transfer or quit. She knew she could never face another case like this one.

And in its way, Homicide had been a relief. The victims were all dead, and you didn't have to watch their suffering. It was bad enough, but at least it didn't break your heart.

The little tragedies of domestic life did. But none of them could have prepared her for the story Stephen Tregear had to tell.

11

His earliest memory, he said, was not of a place but of the journey between places. Riding in a pickup truck between his father and mother, on the move.

His father was a restless soul, always ready to pack up and leave, always in search of a new town and a fresh start. He was a clever man who could do almost any work. In one place he would be an air-conditioning service man, in another a plumber or an electrician or a carpenter or telephone systems technician. He never had a license for any of these things but never wanted for employment. There were always people ready to hire him and let him work off the books, because he didn't ask for much money and his knowledge and skill beggared those of men with all the right certifications.

So the family traveled around, living like gypsies. Young Stephen could remember Lawton, Oklahoma; Crockett, Texas; Jefferson City, Missouri; Mound City, Arkansas; Peoria, Illinois; Scottsdale, Arizona, and a dozen other places, big and small.

His mother was only a vague smear of recollection, disconnected from specific events or time. A story about a fox and a rabbit, the details of which were as indistinct as a Monet haystack. The pressure of her hand against his cheek. A thin scar on her thumb—whether right or left he could no longer recall.

He remembered the sound of her voice. "Come on, Stevie Boy. Time for bed. Did you remember to brush your teeth?" Even after twenty-five years he heard it in his dreams. He remembered her face, and the way her eyes crinkled when she smiled.

The memory of her smile was vivid. She seemed hardly able to look at him without smiling.

When Stephen was seven, she simply disappeared. His father told him she had left, didn't love them anymore, had gone away. Her son had cried and cried but, finally, inevitably, had accepted it all as true. He and his father had continued their travels.

Schools were places you wandered in and out of. Some of them were like concentration camps but, never mind, you would soon be gone and this or that town would fade into memory. Only the road was real.

They lived in rented houses, usually a mile or so outside of town, sometimes near a wood or surrounded by cornfields. They were lonely places, with no one else nearby.

And the life father and son lived in those houses was strange and silent—strange perhaps only in memory, but the silence he remembered as something almost tangible. There were no visitors. There were only the two of them, and his father was a difficult man to approach.

The silence made him miss his mother all the more. It was as if her departure had dropped him into a dark place where he was utterly alone.

And the houses were always cold, always sunless, even in summer. Was this also just a trick of recollection? Was the cold something to be read on a thermometer, or was it merely a projection of his state of mind? He could no longer be sure.

What sustained him? His memories of his mother, who had loved him. That love was not a myth he had created for himself. It had been a fact of daily life.

And because he knew his mother had loved him, he began to suspect his father's scanty version of her disappearance from their lives.

"She just took off," he said. "She packed up her clothes and went. Maybe she got in with some fella she liked better'n us.

"Now don't ever ask me any more questions, because I don't like to think about it."

By the time he was nine years old, or perhaps ten, Stephen had worked out for himself that his father was lying. His mother would never have left him behind. Therefore, she had been driven away, or had herself been left behind or she was dead.

And there had been no scene, no tears or shouting. Only silence.

It was not that Stephen didn't love his father. He could no more stop loving his father than he could stop breathing. So his conclusions were drawn reluctantly. They were forced upon him by his attempts to find some order in his life, some coherent explanation of events.

And they did not obsess him, at least not until he began to push against adolescence. He had plenty of other things to think about.

Occasionally his father would take him along to jobs, and he taught his son the elements of many different crafts. His father was a good teacher: orderly, precise and patient. Those were good times.

At other times Stephen would be alone in the empty house. His father wouldn't come home for dinner, wouldn't come home until the next day, once in a while wouldn't come home for two or three days together. There was never any explanation.

Stephen could take care of himself. He could cook, in an elementary way, and he cleaned up after himself because his father hated a mess.

What he feared, above all else, was abandonment. Would his father finally not come back at all? Was that what had happened to his mother? Had he simply left her somewhere?

And the world in which he would be alone was such a fearful place. He knew this from the newspapers.

Wherever they happened to be, his father always brought home the local papers. It was his evening entertainment, to spread them out on the kitchen table and read them. Stephen never saw his father read a book, but the newspapers were a kind of passion with him.

And their pages were full of death.

Much of the time Stephen was alone in the house, and what school-work he brought home was ridiculously easy. So he picked up his father's habit of reading the news. There were always murders.

It would start with the discovery of a body. A woman's corpse would be found in some out-of-the-way place. The police didn't like to comment, but generally someone would provide the shocking details. Then the county medical examiner would release his report—wrongful death. The investigation would drag on and on and, eventually, there would be another, suspiciously similar crime. The papers would be full of it.

And sometimes versions of the story would find their way into school yard gossip. The little girls would talk about how their mothers had started taking them to and from school.

At first, Stephen assumed that murders just happened, that they were a normal occurrence, like thunderstorms. Women just got cut up every now and then. It was like being killed in a traffic accident.

It was only gradually that he began to understand that, wherever he and his father went, the newspapers would start carrying murder stories.

It was just bad luck, he thought. Only toward the very end did he begin to consider the possibility that luck had nothing to do with it.

In the meantime he had another mystery to solve—the fate of his mother.

They were migrants. They traveled light. The houses his father rented were always furnished. They didn't really own anything they couldn't put in the back of the pickup truck.

But there was always one suitcase that Stephen never saw open. Dad would take it up to his room and put it in the closet. They just carried it around with them.

Finally, one day when Stephen was alone in the house, he decided he would have a look. He went upstairs to his father's room, opened the closet door and took the suitcase out. It was a white, hard-shell Samsonite. He discovered that it was locked.

This presented a problem.

But a lock implied a key, and Stephen knew that his father kept all his keys on a ring he carried around in his pants pocket.

When his father returned, Stephen said, "Dad, it looks like rain. You want to get the truck into the garage?"

His father was sitting at the kitchen table, reading a newspaper. At first he seemed not even to have heard, but then, without even looking up, he took the keys out of his pocket and dropped them on the table.

"You do it," he said.

"Okay."

Stephen was eleven and tall for his age, and he had been able to reach the gas pedal for over a year. So driving was just another of the skills his father had taught him. On back roads where there weren't any cops, his father would let him have the wheel. He wasn't bad at it.

The garage was just a shack, detached from the house, and it was kept padlocked. Most of the time Dad couldn't be bothered and would just park his truck in front of the house. But these days he was working as a painter and he had a couple of canvas tarps in the cargo bed. It wouldn't do to let them get wet.

It was summer, and even at seven in the evening there was plenty of light. Stephen went through his father's keys as he walked out to unlock the garage. There was the key to the truck, the house key, one for the padlock on the garage, another for his toolbox and a smaller key with a short blade that might do well enough for a suitcase.

Stephen was tempted to take this one off the key ring and put it in his pocket, but he gave up the idea almost at once because his father would probably notice there was a key missing.

But at least now he knew where it was.

Over a workbench that nobody ever used was a single lightbulb dangling from the garage ceiling. Stephen pulled the string to turn it on and scanned around for something that might allow him to take an impression of the key.

There was a small can of wood dough, which he managed to pry open with the house key. He found a piece of cardboard about the length of his finger and smeared some of the wood dough over it, rolling it smooth with the side of the can.

By then he was beginning to feel horribly exposed and decided he had been inside the garage long enough. He went back to get the truck.

Once he had the truck bedded down, he pressed the suitcase key blade into the wood dough, first one side and then the other. Then he closed the can, putting it back where he had found it, and wiped the key clean on his shirttail. The entire operation took no more than about thirty seconds.

He switched off the garage light.

Of course, now there was the problem of what to do with his key print. It needed time for the wood dough to harden, so he couldn't very well leave it out in the rain. And he dreaded taking it inside the house with him because Dad would expect his keys back first thing. He considered just chucking it away and forgetting the whole business, but then what if his father found it in the yard the next morning?

How long had he been outside? Four, maybe five minutes. Dad probably hadn't finished the paper. The stairs were less than six feet from the front door. The kitchen was in the back of the house. He set the piece of cardboard on the third step and then went into the kitchen.

Dad was still sitting there. He didn't even raise his eyes when his son walked in and set the keys down on the kitchen table.

Stephen went to the refrigerator and took out a can of Coke.

"I got some reading," he said, his voice as flat as he could make it.

His father looked up, seemed to consider the matter for about three seconds and then nodded.

"Okay."

From the stairs he picked up the piece of cardboard and carefully carried it up to his room. He put it in his desk drawer. He would think of a better hiding place tomorrow.

Then, for perhaps twenty minutes, sitting at his desk, holding a math book he had checked out of the public library, only the fear of being heard kept him from sobbing. He wanted to go back downstairs and confess everything to Dad. He was a bad boy. His father was certainly right and his mother had deserted them. He hated her, but even more he hated himself.

Gradually the fit began to wear off, yielding to a sullen misery. His mother had loved him. It was impossible to believe anything else. And she was gone.

What else mattered?

About an hour later, his father came up the stairs, pushed the door open a few inches and looked in. "Go to bed, Steve."

"Okay, Dad."

His father went back downstairs.

Stephen slept in his underwear and, as he was taking off his trousers, he happened to glance at the desk drawer that held his key impression. Suddenly he was afraid his father would come in while he was asleep and search his room. He had never done anything like that—at least not that Stephen knew about—but Stephen had never before given him a motive.

The wood dough had hardened nicely. He had a winter jacket with pockets deep enough to keep his hands warm. He slipped the impression into the right-hand pocket, closed the closet and went to bed.

As he waited to fall asleep, he began to experience a certain feeling of triumph.

· · ·

Over the next few days, Stephen considered the possibility of casting a key from the impressions in the wood dough. He thought of melting down a tin can, but he had no idea how to do that, or how to handle the metal once it liquefied. Besides, it would probably just burn up the wood dough. Finally he gave up on the idea.

But could he file down an existing key to fit the impression? The luggage key was small and there were only two teeth on the blade, about an eighth of an inch apart. It seemed a realistic possibility. All he needed was a key and a small file.

The key was not a problem. Rented houses were full of long-forgotten keys. Stephen found one in the basement, in the top drawer of a beat-up old dresser some previous tenant had left behind.

The tools were almost as easy.

Stephen enjoyed considerable liberty. He and his father lived about two miles outside a place called Lewisburg and he could hike into town any time he felt like it. He didn't have to ask permission. Dad didn't care what he did.

There was a movie theater in Lewisburg, and Stephen went to the first matinee every Sunday afternoon, when the price was two dollars. He earned the money from odd jobs around town. After a residence of four months, he knew all the storekeepers, and he would drop in and ask, "You got anything needs doing?"

Sometimes he pushed a broom, sometimes he washed the windows, sometimes he helped with the stock. He was a good worker, careful and clean, and he was cheap.

It took him exactly a week to earn enough to pay for a Six Piece Needle File Set (price, $4.49) and a pair of locking pliers (price $2.39) he could use as a vise, but he would have to skip the movies that Sunday.

Another week went into making the key.

Dad was a pretty good locksmith, although he was rarely employed at it, saying the pay wasn't that great and he didn't like being shut up in a shop all day. But he changed all the locks on every new house they moved into, cutting his own keys. In about ten minutes he could cut a key by hand, which was almost a lost art. Stephen had had plenty of opportunities to observe the work.

But making this key involved special difficulties.

First he had to find a place to do it, since it wouldn't do to leave any brass filings around the house. He found a spot outside, across the road, beside a creek where there was plenty of concealment and the sound of the fast-rushing water would partially cover the scraping of the file. He even found a tree hollow where he could hide his tools.

He could do this. All he needed was to take his time and be very, very careful.

Then, when he had the key so that it matched the impression perfectly, and took it home to try it out, he discovered that it was too thick to fit the lock. This meant another trip to the hardware store— and another movie missed—to purchase a flat file (price $2.49). He then had to hunt up a discarded brick so he would have a flat surface on which to plane the key down.

Still, in the end he had his key.

He carried it around in his pocket most of the next day, waiting for school to end, but when he got home Dad was already there, reading his newspapers at the kitchen table. The next day was a Saturday, so Stephen had to wait through the weekend with the key hidden under his mattress.

Finally Monday came. He waited through school, then took the bus home. His father was nowhere around.

The key fit and the suitcase lock snapped open. Inside were women's clothes, two pairs of flat women's shoes and a red wallet. He recognized the wallet at once. It was his mother's.

Inside the wallet he found a driver's license, issued by the State of Ohio some fourteen years previous and bearing his mother's picture and signature. The name on the license was Elizabeth Dabney, which must have been her maiden name. The address given was 1380 Route 9, Circleville, Ohio 43113.

It was the first time he had seen his mother's face in four years. He held the license in his two hands and wept bitterly.

In the change purse he found his mother's wedding ring.

That was enough. He put the ring back in the change purse, dropped the wallet into the suitcase and closed the suitcase, reminding himself to relock it.

He got out of the closet, out of his father's room and out of the house as quickly as he could. He went across the road and down to the creek, where he sat with his knees under his chin, his arms wrapped around his legs, for a long time.

At least, he assumed it was a long time. He was perfectly unaware of the passage of time. He was completely absorbed in his private misery.

He wished to God he had forgotten all about his mother. He wished he had never looked inside that suitcase.

When the shadows of the trees became long and dark over the water, he knew he would have to go home. He would have to face his father and keep all of this inside himself. There wasn't any choice.

• • •

Two weeks later, Dad traded in his pickup truck and bought a van, a dark blue Chevy Astro.

"She was ready to die on us," he said about the truck. "A hundred and seventy thousand hard miles. We'll be able to carry more stuff in the van."

"Are we leaving here?"

"Yeah." Dad nodded slowly, as if the idea had just occurred to him. "Time to shake the dust again. We'll leave Saturday, after I've been paid. That'll give us Friday evening to load up."

And Saturday morning they were on Interstate 64, heading for Arkansas. Stephen, who hadn't had much sleep the night before, was dozing when his father reached over and shook him awake.

"Did you return that library book?" he asked.

"Yeah. Sure. Day before yesterday."

"What was it called?"

Stephen tried to remember, wondering what difference it made. "*Advanced Mathematics*. It was a sort of introduction to calculus."

"Is that what you were studying in school?"

"Oh Lord, no." Stephen found the question amusing. "They're still doing long division."

"Then what good's that stuff gonna do you?"

"I just like it."

"Why?"

"I like solving problems."

His father considered this answer for perhaps three seconds and then threw back his head and laughed.

"I'll just bet you do, sport. I'll just bet."

12

Mound City, Arkansas (population, approximately 300) was their last home. A developer was putting up some condos in Marion, and Dad got a job doing electrical work. He rented a house about a half-hour walk from the Mississippi River.

It was the middle of summer and the temperature outside would be close to eighty degrees by daybreak. The countryside was flat and uninteresting. With school out, there was nothing to do. Dad seemed to come home only to sleep. Sometimes he would be gone the whole weekend.

Mound City was just a village full of bedrooms. There was no library and hardly any businesses. On foot, which was the only way Stephen was going to get anywhere, West Memphis was a good hour and a half away. For about two weeks he walked it nearly every day, looking for odd jobs. It was something to do. But the local kids, turned loose from school, were also looking and didn't relish the competition. After he got beat up a second time, Stephen decided to stay home.

And at home he was left with plenty of time to think.

He kept coming back to the fact of his mother's suitcase, trying to find some way to exonerate his father. Why did he have her wedding ring? Had she given it to him, a parting gesture? That was at least imaginable. But why would she leave her clothes and wallet? Had she run away with nothing?

By the time she disappeared, the driver's license would have been some years past its expiration date. If she had renewed it, or gotten another in some other state, why would she have kept the old one in her wallet? In all his memories of their travels, his father had driven. It was always Dad who went to the store. Stephen had no memory of his mother ever having driven the truck. Given Dad's choice of houses—solitary places, a mile or more outside of town—she would have been almost a prisoner.

No, not *almost* a prisoner. A prisoner.

Then how had she escaped, except into death?

The third Saturday after they arrived in Mound City was Stephen's twelfth birthday. His father hadn't come home Friday night and didn't show up again until late Sunday afternoon. He just came home, sat down to eat his dinner, which he had brought with him in a McDonald's bag, then went to bed. The birthday was never mentioned.

Always before there had been something. Not a present, usually. Rarely a present, or even a card. But usually a smile and a "Happy Birthday, Steve."

This year, silence.

And that silence underlined a change in the relationship between father and son that had begun . . . when? When they arrived in Arkansas? Before? Stephen couldn't be sure.

But recent. Dad had started getting careless about some things, like groceries. He didn't always make sure, before he disappeared for a few days, that there was enough in the refrigerator. Stephen's recent birthday dinner had consisted of a few handfuls of Sugar Corn Pops and a beer. That was all there was.

It was almost like Dad thought he was living alone.

Maybe that was it. Maybe, in his head, he had already parted from his son. And, if so, what was going to happen to Stephen? Would he disappear like his mother?

Who would notice? Did anyone in this place even know he existed? Probably not. He wasn't registered in school, and there was no trace of his presence on earth that wouldn't fill a suitcase. A suitcase like his mother's.

A man and his son live four months in one town, off by themselves, and then take to the road for God alone knew where. In the new town the son is almost invisible. Who would inquire if he vanished?

In the week that followed, Stephen began to grow really frightened. He felt as if he could see his grave being dug, as if he could hear the hiss of the shovel as it sliced into the dirt.

Dad hadn't started bringing home the local newspapers yet, and there were no books in the house. There was, however, a television set. All the stations seemed to be broadcasting from across the river in Memphis. There were the networks, a couple of movie channels, traffic, some cooking shows and a station that ran the local news on a constantly repeating basis.

On the Monday after Stephen's birthday, there was a story about the nude body of an unidentified woman found in a refuse bin behind the Walmart on Elvis Presley Boulevard. The police were offering no details but were treating it as a homicide. On Wednesday morning a captain of inspectors read a statement that the woman had been identified but that her identity would not be released pending notification of her family. By four o'clock that afternoon the local news was running the photograph, obviously somebody's snapshot, of a reasonably attractive blonde named Tiffany Klaff, age thirty-one.

Tuesday evening, when he came home from the condo site, Dad brought a couple of the Memphis papers with him. He was still reading them at the kitchen table when Stephen went to bed.

Two days later the story made it to the networks when the coroner released his preliminary report. Tiffany Klaff had been systematically beaten to death. She was discovered with duct tape over her mouth, and her arms, knees and lower back had all been broken, apparently before she died of a blunt instrument trauma to the head. The coroner described her injuries as "particularly savage."

For several days, Stephen found it difficult to sleep. He found he had to take a nap in the middle of the day, when he was alone in the house. For the first time that he could remember, he was afraid of the dark.

And then, over the next three or four weeks, things began returning to their normal pattern. Dad started keeping food in the house. One night he even took Stephen into West Memphis for a pizza. Once he read aloud from a newspaper review of a book about the history of mathematics.

"That sounds like it would be right up your street," he said, as if he had just arrived at an important conclusion. "You ought to get that one out of the library."

"The library is six or seven miles from here."

"Is that a fact? Well, maybe I can drive you in before I go to work tomorrow."

The next morning he left early, having apparently forgotten all about the library. But that wasn't surprising. He usually forgot things like that. What was surprising was that he had thought of it in the first place.

Gradually, Stephen began to relax.

As fear subsided, so did suspicion. After all, he told himself, he was barely twelve years old. How could he really understand what had happened between his parents? The adult world was a foreign country to him. Maybe his father had simply put his mother on a bus back to Ohio. Maybe she had just left stuff behind.

A part of him even began to believe it.

The Tiffany Klaff investigation disappeared from television and was mentioned only briefly in the newspapers Dad brought home.

His mind had been playing tricks on him, he decided. He was bored and needed a distraction.

Then he remembered the book review Dad had read him. *A History of Mathematics*. The library in West Memphis might have a copy. Anyway, it would be something to do.

The next morning, as soon as his father had left for work, Stephen set out on his expedition. He arrived slightly after ten and inquired at the front desk. Klem's *History of Mathematics* was not in the catalog, but they might be able to get it through interlibrary loan. For that, he was told, he would need a library card. Did he have a library card? No. The nice lady told him to come back with a parent. The cards were free to all residents of Crittenden County and his would be mailed to his home address.

"Okay. Thank you. But today can I just look around?"

"Of course you can. You just won't be able to check anything out."

In the stacks there was a small mathematics section, consisting mainly of high school and college textbooks. No Klem. Stephen took down a thick volume titled *Calculus I*. Sitting in a chair in the main reading room, he worked his way quickly through the first ten or so pages.

I can do this, he thought to himself. He was reasonably sure he could have the whole book completed by the end of the summer.

The problem was, there was no chance of getting a library card. If he asked Dad to take him in to get one, Dad would say "sure" and then forget all about it. If then Stephen tried to remind him, he would just get angry, then agree, then forget about it all over again. Stephen wasn't going to get him inside the library. That wasn't the way it worked.

So he would do it here, in the library, which was air-conditioned and comfortable and full of people.

For the next several days, Stephen's mind was happily occupied with slope theory, integrals and chain rules. The librarian, when she figured out what he was doing, didn't ask any awkward questions but kept him supplied with paper and pencils and found him a small table to use as a writing desk.

"You understand this stuff?" she asked him once.

"Yes. It's not difficult."

"How old are you?"

"Twelve."

She went away, shaking her head.

At three in the afternoon, he would give the calculus book and his scribbled-over pages to the librarian, who put them on a shelf in the back room, then he would walk back to Mound City. He had studied a map and figured out a short route, so the walk both ways only took him about two and a half hours. Usually he got home before his father returned from work.

One time he didn't. Dad was in the kitchen, drinking a beer and reading the newspaper.

"Where you been?" he asked, without looking up. "I got home an hour ago."

"I was at the library in West Memphis. I'm learning calculus."

Dad raised his head. "They got teachers there?"

"No. I'm learning it out of a book."

"Okay."

The subject, apparently, was closed, and for a quarter of an hour neither of them spoke. Stephen went to the refrigerator and got out a Coke.

"You feel like some fried chicken for dinner? They got a KFC up in Marion."

"Okay."

His father seemed pleased, so he threw in a bonus.

"On the way I'll show you the job site," he said. "It's comin' along pretty good."

It was one of the happiest times Stephen could remember. The future Crittenden Gables was still little more than a series of wooden skeletons, but the floors were laid and in several places the wiring already wound up from floor to floor like exposed nerve fibers. They walked around together, and Dad explained all the stages of construction while his son listened proudly. His father, he was quite sure, could have built the whole place by himself.

Then they went to the KFC and had fried chicken and biscuits. It was dark before they got home.

● ● ●

About ten days later, Dad didn't come home Friday evening. It was late Saturday when the van pulled up and parked in the garage by the side of the house. Stephen watched through his bedroom window. His father came back outside. He staggered slightly and there was what looked like a bottle clutched in his left hand. He walked toward the front of the house. He had forgotten to close the garage door.

Stephen went downstairs.

"Hi."

Dad hardly seemed to have heard him, or to have noticed his presence. He went into the kitchen and collapsed into a chair, setting a pint bottle of Southern Comfort down on the table in front of him. The whiskey in the bottle was about a third of the way down.

He looked up and saw his son. It seemed to take a few seconds before he recognized him.

"Go to bed, Steve," he said, in a toneless voice. He was pretty well boiled.

"Okay. 'Night, Dad."

"Get me a glass first."

"Sure."

Stephen opened the cupboard and took down a water glass, setting it on the table next to the bottle. Then he turned and left the room.

In his bedroom he switched off the light, being careful to leave the door open about an inch. When his father came up, Stephen wanted him to think he had gone to bed.

Something was going on. Aside from a few beers, Dad wasn't much of a drinker. Once in a great while he would come home under the influence, but Stephen had never seen him like this.

He had to wait almost an hour before he heard heavy footsteps on the stairs. His father's room was directly across from his, at the top of the landing. He heard muffled sounds and then the loud, protesting squeak of bedsprings. His father's light was still on. After a few minutes Stephen thought he heard a gentle snoring.

In his stocking feet, he went across the landing. Dad was belly-down on the bed, in his underwear.

Stephen switched off the light and went back to his own room to fetch his shoes.

On his way down the stairs, he told himself that he was just going out to close the garage door, but he knew that wasn't quite the truth. Something was wrong and nothing in his previous experience of his father could tell him what. Right now, the only place he could go to look for an answer was the van.

Standing in front of the open garage, he looked up at the house. His father's room was on the other side. Even if Dad was broad awake, he wouldn't be able to see a light from the garage.

Still, without turning on the overhead, Stephen put his hand on the driver-side door handle. He pressed the button and the door opened. Not surprisingly, Dad had forgotten to lock it.

Almost the instant he opened the door, he was assailed by a faint odor, like raw hamburger gone bad—but really like nothing he could have described.

The interior light had popped on and he could see that there was nothing in the front compartment to account for the smell.

That left the cargo space.

Stephen closed the door, and he was left once again in darkness. He turned on the overhead light in the garage. Somehow he didn't want to open the back of the van in the dark.

He pulled on the rear door handle and the interior light came on again.

At first he didn't realize what he was looking at. Just an object wrapped in the clear plastic drop cloths that painters use. And then he realized that it was a face.

A woman's face, staring out at him through the clouded plastic. Her eyes were open, and her mouth. She seemed to be screaming.

Of course there was no sound, because she was dead.

Stephen stared at her in fascinated horror. It wasn't real. It couldn't be.

But the smell was much stronger, the smell of a corpse beginning to putrefy.

Suddenly his stomach clenched and he experienced a wave of nausea. He couldn't help himself. He bent over and vomited.

When he stopped gagging he understood at once the significance of what had happened. His vomit, yellow and thick, was on the garage floor and all over the back of the van. It was on his shoes and the bottoms of his trousers. There was no point in trying to clean it up—the smell would linger for days.

And Dad would know, couldn't help knowing, that his son had come down here at night and found a dead body in the back of the van.

And Dad would surely kill him. Just as he had killed Stephen's mother. The fact that he would be murdering his son, his own blood, would not restrain him.

Stephen closed the rear door of the van and turned off the overhead garage light. He stepped out onto the driveway and looked at the house, which was dark.

And he realized that he could never enter that house again, not if he wanted to live. His one chance was to run.

And so he ran.

13

And by running, he entered into a life of desperate fear. Somehow it never occurred to him to turn his father in to the police. His only hope was flight.

All of the crucial decisions were made that first night. His father was a restless sleeper, almost an insomniac. He would wake up in a few hours and go downstairs to make himself a cup of tea. It would probably occur to him that he had forgotten to close the garage and, given what was in the back of the van, he would almost certainly go outside to correct that error. Then he would know everything.

The next step would be to get rid of the body. Then he would start hunting.

Stephen tried to think like his father. What would Dad expect him to do? To head into town probably. Or to try to hitch a ride. He would know that his son had no money, had nothing but the clothes he was wearing.

So Stephen made up his mind to stay off the roads and to head north, away from West Memphis. But if he just wandered around he would quickly become lost. Then someone would find him and call the police. And the police, eventually, would call his father.

He could imagine how that would go. By then the body in the van would have been left for the animals on some stretch of waste ground. Dad knew how to cover his tracks.

"The kid's crazy," he would say. "He's been a problem ever since his mother died."

And the police would nod and grin and turn Stephen over to his father's vengeance.

So, instead, he would follow the railroad tracks. He picked them up about two miles from the house and walked the tracks all night.

By dawn he was hungry and exhausted. He stopped by a shack, windowless, deserted and locked, about twenty feet from the rail line. He sat down, leaned back against a wall where he could not be seen from the tracks and instantly fell asleep.

He was awakened by a train whistle. What seemed like an endless line of freight cars began moving slowly past the shack. Stephen lay on the ground, concealed in the high grass, and watched. Just ahead there was a sharp curve in the tracks and the train slowed to walking pace in order to make the turn. He noticed that there were iron ladders on the sides of the freight cars, almost at the end.

Could he reach one of those ladders, without being seen, and climb up on the roof of the car? He might be able to hitch a ride for thirty or forty miles before one of the crew even noticed he was there.

He decided to try it.

It was easy. He just ran alongside, grabbed a rung of the ladder and swung himself up. He was on top of the car in maybe fifteen seconds.

On the roof he lay flat, expecting any moment someone would come and throw him off. No one came.

He rode all the way to Blytheville, a distance of some sixty miles, where the train stopped to unload a couple of cars. It was just past noon. Stephen climbed down and headed into town. He had to get some food somehow.

Blytheville was his baptism in crime. He walked into a convenience store, took a package of beef jerky, a box of cookies and a bottle of ginger ale, started toward the counter as if he had every intention in the world of buying them, and then bolted for the door. He was around the corner and lost from sight before the clerk behind the counter even realized what was happening.

Interestingly, there was no pursuit. There were several customers in the store and perhaps the clerk was afraid to leave.

Stephen found an alley doorway and sat down to feed. He ate until he was almost ready to burst. Then he stood up, took a huge pee behind a trash bin and headed back to the railroad yard.

For the next three months he lived a vagrant life, dodging the police and the welfare authorities. He bathed and washed his threadbare clothes in any stretch of deserted river he could find. He took odd jobs when he could and stole when he couldn't. He was running for his life, so he put shame and conscience aside.

By October he had gotten as far north as Ohio. Ohio was as good a goal as any. He remembered the address on his mother's driver's license.

Hitching the rail lines took him to Circleville. It was a walk of slightly more than half a mile to Route 9.

The house at 1380 was no palace. The lot was enclosed by a picket fence and the house itself probably hadn't been painted any time in the last five or six years. But the grass in the yard was freshly cut and there were clay planters full of ferns on either side of the front door. The place had a general air of struggling respectability.

Stephen knocked on the door, which after about a minute was opened by a woman who could have been anywhere between fifty and sixty. She was small and thin, and her face looked oddly familiar.

"Are you Mrs. Dabney?" he asked, his heart beating so loud he could hear it in his ears.

"Yes, I'm Mrs. Dabney," the woman answered. "Do I know you?"

"No." Stephen shook his head, as if the admission grieved him.

"Then what can I do for you?"

"Did you have a daughter named Elizabeth?"

Mrs. Dabney looked stricken. Her eyes suddenly filled with tears. "Yes, I did."

"How long since you've heard from her?"

Taking a handkerchief out of a pocket in her apron, Mrs. Dabney wiped her eyes.

"A long time," she said. "Almost thirteen years—thirteen years next month."

"Then she must be dead. I'm her son."

There was a long silence, after which Mrs. Dabney said, "I think you better come inside, young man."

• • •

The first thing she did was phone her husband. Stephen could hear snippets of the conversation from where he sat in the kitchen.

"Yes, I believe him, Phil. . . . You should see him."

Then she came back and asked him if he'd like anything to eat.

While he ate his sandwich and drank his milk, she sat across the table from him, holding her hands against her meager bosom. She didn't speak until he was finished.

"What do you know about my daughter?" she asked finally.

Stephen might have seemed to be considering his answer, but he wasn't. He wasn't even thinking about that. Instead, he felt a great wave of pity for this woman. It was almost as if he could feel her distress as well as see it. Then he shrugged.

"Very little, really. She disappeared when I was seven. One day she just wasn't there."

"Then tell me about your father."

"His name was—is—Walter Rayne. He travels around a lot. He can do just about any kind of work. He's tall and he has light brown hair. Like mine. He has a purplish birthmark on the back of his right hand."

"That's him. That's the man Betty ran off with."

"Is that what you called her? Betty?"

"Yes."

She never took her eyes from his face. Sometimes she would squint slightly, the way some people do when they are trying to bring an object into focus.

"How did you know where to find us?"

"There was a suitcase. I found an old driver's license in her wallet. It had this address on it."

"Was there anything else?"

"Some clothes and a wedding ring."

"Then he did marry her?"

"I guess."

A few minutes later Stephen heard a car drive up and stop, then a man came in through the outside door to the kitchen. He was wearing a canvas hat and a heavy Windbreaker with a plaid pattern. He wore rimless glasses and was just at the threshold of being old.

Stephen got to his feet.

The man stood beside Mrs. Dabney and put his hand on her shoulder, which took away any doubt about his identity. Then he held out his hand to Stephen, and Stephen took it.

"I'm Phil Dabney," he said, giving Stephen's hand a vigorous shake. He didn't really seem that friendly. "My wife tells me you claim to be our daughter Betty's boy."

"He *is* Betty's boy," Mrs. Dabney broke in. "He knows too much to be anybody else. Besides, Phil, look at his eyes. Those are Betty's eyes."

Phil Dabney stared into Stephen's face, and then, suddenly, he seemed to be afraid of what he saw there.

"By God," he said, with a kind of awe, "so they are."

The three of them sat around the kitchen table talking until it began to grow dark outside. Then Mrs. Dabney, whose first name Stephen still didn't know, got up and started her preparations for supper. When she was away from the table, Phil Dabney leaned forward and, in a low voice, asked the question that must have been preying on his mind ever since he came through the door.

"What happened to your mother?"

"She's dead," Stephen answered. "My father killed her."

"How do you know that?"

"Because that's what he does. He kills women."

. . .

Dinner was largely ignored. No one wanted to eat while Stephen told the story of the dead woman he had found in his father's van. No one was hungry after that, since something of the sort must have been Betty's fate.

But for Mr. and Mrs. Dabney there was a consolation prize for learning what had happened to their long-missing daughter. Finally Mrs. Dabney reached out and took Stephen's hand.

"I'm your grandmother," she said. "My name is Wilma Dabney."

Stephen looked from her to her husband and back again, his eyes filling with tears.

"Do you believe me?"

"It's impossible to believe anything else," Phil Dabney said, taking his grandson's other hand in his own. "I guess you'll live with us now."

He looked at his wife as if asking her permission.

"He can have Betty's old room," Mrs. Dabney said.

And from that night, for the next four years, Stephen lived with his grandparents, whom he called Gramps and Gram and, collectively "the folks," which seemed to suit them. For four years he got to know normal life.

. . .

It is not always true that familiarity breeds contempt. The more Stephen came to know his grandparents, the more they became his exemplars.

And he quickly came to understand that he needed exemplars. It didn't take him long to figure out how strange had been life as he knew it with his father.

I've been living on Mars, he thought to himself one day, about a month after he arrived in Circleville. I don't know the customs here on Earth.

So he set about learning, in a way analogous to how he was eventually to learn foreign languages. He acquired the grammar and vocabulary by studying his grandparents, and then he went out and tried to put it together into sentences. Perhaps he would never acquire quite the right accent, but he would achieve a certain fluency and that might be enough.

Phil Dabney, his grandson quickly discovered, was an intelligent man whose moral world had little room for ambiguities. He lived according to his own notion of what constituted a gentleman, an idea defined entirely by conduct. A gentleman did not lie, cheat, steal or resort to violence. A gentleman treated other people with sympathy and respect. A gentleman did not use bad language.

Stephen had grown up in a household where other standards applied. The first time he used a curse word, his grandfather took him aside and explained to him, calmly and with great kindness, that that sort of language simply would not do. "I'm glad your grandmother wasn't here," he said. "She's a lady and it would have distressed her. The best thing would be if you dropped such expressions altogether."

Stephen tried. He never again swore in his grandparents' house. Later, after he had joined the Navy, it was more of a struggle, but he persevered.

His grandmother taught him to be human. He watched her deal with his grandfather, with her friends and neighbors, with tradesmen and strangers, and gradually he began picking up the skills of ordinary life.

She taught him table manners, with which he was little familiar, and, quite unconsciously, she taught him how to recognize the humanity of other people. She taught him how to open himself to life.

And she talked to him about his mother—enough to fill in the gaps in his memories and make her real.

"She was a smart girl, good in school, but too innocent," his grandmother told him. "She believed everyone was good. She saw everyone just the way they wanted to be seen. I never liked your father—I just didn't think he fit together right. But your mother thought he was an angel from heaven. And one day she was just gone. She didn't even leave a note."

Stephen had watched his grandmother struggling with her grief. She got up from the kitchen table, where they had been sitting, and went over to open a cabinet above the stove. There was nothing inside she wanted. It was just something to do, to give herself a tiny respite from her memories.

"And now she's in heaven."

· · ·

And then there was education of a more formal kind.

At first he went to the middle school, but after six months, when his teachers decided he had exhausted their resources, he was promoted to the high school. There he was a prize student, except that his mathematics teachers didn't know what to do with him. So it was arranged that, twice a week, on Tuesdays and Fridays, his grandmother would drive him into Columbus, to Ohio State University, to receive instruction in the mathematics department there. She would drop him off at the corner of North High and East Seventeenth and then go shopping for three hours. On the drive home, for fear of boring her, he talked about everything but math.

Not, probably, that he would have bored her, for his grandparents seemed interested in everything he did or said or thought. At dinner they would have real, actual conversations. For the first time since his mother's disappearance, Stephen knew what it was to be cared about.

By the time he was fourteen Stephen was doing independent work in mathematics, and at fifteen he wrote a paper on probability theory that his advisor at Ohio State encouraged him to submit for publication. A month later the paper appeared on the Internet.

Two months after that his advisor, Professor Aland, called Stephen in for a talk.

"Your paper has caused quite a stir," he said. "You should start thinking about the next step."

Professor Aland was about thirty, a tall, bony man with a black beard and eyes that suggested some permanent dissatisfaction with life.

"Well, I'm writing another paper . . ."

But with a languid wave of his hand, Aland indicated that he meant something else.

"I mean, what should be the next step in your education. You're wasting your time here."

Stephen's first thought was that he must have done something wrong. He probably looked stricken, because Aland smiled.

"Steve, you should be in graduate school."

"*Grad*uate school—I haven't even finished high school."

Stephen's chair was against a bookcase, at an angle that permitted a glimpse out of the room's only window. It was winter term and snow was falling in gray drifts. The world suddenly appeared very bleak.

"I remember high school as somewhere between a gulag and a revival meeting," Aland told him. "I should think you'd be glad to escape."

He let his gaze wander up to the ceiling, happily oblivious to Stephen's reaction.

"In any case, high school is a trivial obstacle. Universities have all the same courses—except, perhaps, home ec and auto shop."

He smiled again, to indicate he had made a little joke.

"Where would I go? Here?"

His advisor shot him a glance suggesting his question was in the worst possible taste.

"Oh God, no. Stanford, perhaps, although MIT would be better."

"I was just thinking a state school would be cheaper."

"Steve, *I* went to MIT, and my father was a bookkeeper. Two days ago the chairman of the math department, who just happens to be my old dissertation advisor, phoned me about you. I don't think there'll be any problem about money. And you'll have Harvard just up the street if you want to dabble in the arts. In my day, we used to refer to Harvard as 'the Charm School.' "

Another joke—another little smile.

"I'll have to talk to my folks about this."

"Fair enough."

That evening, after dinner, the Dabneys held a council of war. Stephen explained the offer, as far as he understood it. A combined BS/MS program, full tuition, access to Harvard courses in the humanities.

"So what's the problem?" his grandfather asked. He shook his head as if mystified.

"The problem is, I don't want it. I'm fifteen—nobody's going to have anything to do with me. My friends are all here, taking American history in high school. At MIT I'd be a freak."

"Then say no."

"How do I do that?" Stephen laughed in pure exasperation. "How do I say no to something like this? How do I shut that door?"

"We could say no for you." His grandmother said, as if the idea had struck her with the force of revelation. "Your grandfather could phone this professor . . . whatever his name is . . ."

"Aland."

"Aland, then. He can phone this Professor Aland and tell him we think you're too young. You're not yet mature enough. We're afraid those college boys might lead you astray."

"Gram, you're a genius."

• • •

There was school, there was his family and there was the public library. He brought books home all the time, starting with Klem's *History of Mathematics*. He read ancient history and nineteenth-century novels, books about philosophy and archaeology and, perhaps not surprisingly, criminology. His grandparents never tired of reminding him of the first question he asked when he understood that he would be staying with them: "Can I have a library card?"

For the rest, he was happy. Circleville wasn't a bad place to grow up. He lived under the name of Steve Dabney and he had friends whom he was allowed to invite home. He was even popular with the girls. What more was there to ask for?

But all of this ended abruptly on a June evening when Stephen was sixteen.

He was not present for the beginning of that particular tragedy. He could only piece together what must have happened. All he knew for certain was that his father came back into his life, with catastrophic results.

How did Dad find him? He didn't know—he might never know. Had he been looking for his son all this time, or had he just stumbled back into central Ohio and decided to see how things were going with his late wife's family? Stephen was never in a position to ask.

What he knew for certain was that, around seven-fifteen that night in June, his grandfather went to answer the doorbell and was stabbed to death the instant he opened the door. He might never even have recognized his murderer. Stephen could only hope he had not.

What his grandmother must have suffered he was glad not to know.

The school year had just ended and Stephen and a group of his friends were celebrating their release. They had somehow obtained a case of beer, which they drank in somebody's backyard with more bravado than pleasure. One of the girls threatened to do a striptease, but, to everyone's intense disappointment, by the time she was down to her underwear she lost her nerve. She spent most of what remained of the evening sitting next to Stephen, describing the frightful immoralities she planned to commit when finally she escaped to college.

About nine-thirty, their host's parents came home and told everyone to leave.

It was a half-hour walk back to his grandparents' house and Stephen wasn't in a hurry. It was a lovely night and tomorrow he could sleep late and Gram would make him French toast for breakfast.

As they always were when he came back at night, the lights were on over the front door. The unusual thing was the light streaming out through the living room window. Gram was a great believer that respectable people kept their blinds drawn, but they were open tonight.

Stephen's hand was in his pocket, fishing for the door key, before he looked down and noticed a dark patch on the welcome mat. Whatever it was, there was more of it spattered on the side of one of the planters and even on the leaves of the ferns.

He knelt down to see what it was, rubbing his fingers against the spot on the welcome mat. They came up red.

It was blood, not completely dried.

He experienced a moment of panic during which he wanted to break down the front door, but then he remembered the light from the living room window. All he had to do was to step back and walk across ten feet of lawn to look straight in.

It was like a stage set. Every lamp in the room was turned on. And, sitting on the sofa, blood staining the front of her dress, was Stephen's grandmother. She was leaning a little to one side, and she was obviously dead.

On the floor at her feet, lying on his back, was Gramps. His eyes were open, but he wasn't seeing anything.

It was like an invitation, Stephen thought to himself. Somebody was inviting him to come rushing into that house.

He didn't have to wonder who that someone might be.

So, instead of going through the front door, or any door, he went across the street to a neighbor and used his phone to call the police, telling them to send an ambulance.

A patrol car was there within three minutes. An officer opened the car door and came out onto the sidewalk. Stephen pointed to the illuminated front window and told him what he would see through it. A minute later the ambulance arrived.

"I think somebody better go in there," the officer said. "You got a key, kid?"

Stephen handed him the key.

"If the man who did this is still inside," he said, his voice shaking, "he'll be waiting."

"Stay out of it, kid. Go sit in the car."

The medics were taking things out of the back of the ambulance when the police officer turned the key in the front door lock. He pushed open the door and instantly there was an explosion. A flash of light and a sudden roar, followed by black smoke. Even inside the patrol car, Stephen could feel the concussion.

The police officer must have been killed instantly.

14

Stephen Tregear, sitting in his rented apartment in San Francisco, held out a second glass of wine he had poured for Inspector Ellen Ridley. He was quite calm, and that night of horror was many years in the past.

"It was a booby trap, of course," he said. "There wasn't much of a fire. The explosion blew most of it out, and the front room wasn't touched at all. They got my grandparents out, but of course they had both been dead for some hours.

"At first the police thought that I'd probably done it, but I had an alibi going back to the early afternoon. Even then, I don't think they took very seriously the story I told them about my father.

"I've often wondered if the police might have believed me back in Arkansas, when I could have taken them to my father's garage and shown them that woman's body. In a sense, perhaps my grandparents' blood—and all the blood since—is on my head because all I could think to do was run away and save my own life."

"You were twelve years old," Ellen told him. It seemed excuse enough.

"There is that."

Tregear made a little dismissive gesture with his right hand. He wasn't looking for any excuses.

Ellen would have liked to touch him, perhaps just to have patted him on the knee and given him the comfort of a little ordinary sympathy, but it seemed impossible. She was a cop, after all, listening to evidence about a series of murders, but that wasn't the real reason she couldn't bring herself to do it. At that moment he seemed so remote, as if in his own eyes he stood already condemned, beyond the reach of any human gesture.

And then he smiled and shook his head.

"Anyway, I knew I had to disappear again or I would die too. My father is a tenacious man. So as soon as my grandparents were buried I got on a bus to Columbus. From there I went to Chicago, where I burned my social security card and driver's license and enlisted in the Navy as Stephen Tregear. I was underage but tall. So when I told them I was eighteen they didn't question it."

"How did you hit on Tregear?" Ellen asked. "It's an unusual name."

"I got it out of a Trollope novel."

Tregear smiled, as if he had just made a lame joke.

"What's your real name?"

"I don't have any idea." He shrugged and set his wineglass down on the table beside his chair. "Stephen is real, but my father has used so many aliases that I suspect there could have been a few last names before Rayne. I haven't a clue where I was born, so I'll never find a birth certificate. Tregear, I suspect, is going to have to do."

"And you've been hunting your father ever since you left the Navy?"

"Even before," Tregear answered, in a tone that suggested it was a self-evident proposition. "I'll never be safe until he's dead or in jail. I'll have to go on living like a hermit for the rest of my short life because no one close to me is safe. I have to find him before he finds me."

"Is he looking?"

"Always."

•   •   •

For years, he told her, from as soon as he had figured out the reach the Internet gave him, he had been casually fishing in its waters, searching for some trace of his father. He couldn't just walk away. Walter—he had already become "Walter" in his imagination, a stranger—Walter was out there, killing people, and Tregear was the only person left alive who knew. At first, he told himself, it was little more than a hobby.

In those days he was stationed in New London, Connecticut. He was only a seaman first class, but the Navy allowed him private quarters on the base and considerable latitude. He had a "discretionary fund," officially for buying equipment but in fact for any use he cared to make of it. He was not required to keep records.

So he had himself quite a setup. He had a T-1 connection and the fastest desktop money could buy in those days, running Unix and a whole slew of tracking software he had written himself.

Then one morning a news story popped up on his screen.

In Norman, Oklahoma, a woman had been found dead along a jogging trail. She had sustained what the police spokesman called "savage injuries." It was the second such discovery in as many months.

"Savage injuries." The phrase struck a chord. It was two or three days before he remembered Tiffany Klaff, dead in a Memphis trash bin—her injuries had been described as "particularly savage."

Tregear already had the police reports from Memphis. He tapped into the Norman police database and downloaded everything they had. It was eerily familiar. Was it Walter? Who could say?

There were two more murders in Norman and then, as suddenly as they had begun, they stopped.

He started backtracking, finding other, similar strings of homicides. Gradually patterns began to emerge. An analysis of method, using Memphis as a baseline, led to the conclusion that at least a percentage of them were the work of a single individual.

Would the parallels hold up? He tried to remember every town he and his father had lived in during their years of wandering. But the files in some locations had never been computerized. He would have to go in person and check the paper records.

The Navy was generous with furloughs. They were always prepared to grant him four or five days off, no questions asked. But he had to be a good boy and not try to leave the country or shake off his watchers. He covered a lot of ground and the results were interesting.

But then, toward the end of his second tour, when he had only a few days to go and hadn't put in for reenlistment, the Navy started to get a little nervous.

There wasn't much they could do about it because legally he was about to become a civilian.

His boss, the only officer to whom he reported directly, was a Commander Renfield, who held some sort of murky position in the area where the Signal Corps and Naval Intelligence overlapped. Renfield was a nice enough fellow but a worrier. He was round-faced and bald, and whenever he became nervous the top of his head would break out in sweat. The approaching end of Tregear's tour was almost more than he could bear.

He called Tregear into his office for what he referred to as "a little chin-wag."

"We gather you're working on something big," he said, with one buttock resting on the corner of his desk. "And *we* think the Navy is the best place for you to pursue it. We have resources the private sector just can't match. We'll give you anything you need—anything you want."

So that was it. They thought he was working on some software project. They couldn't crack his machines, so they imagined he was about to go rogue and sell out to Microsoft or somebody.

"I am working on something," Tregear answered. "But it has no military or commercial application. It's private. You don't want to know."

"Then why haven't you reenlisted?"

"I plan to. I just need time to do some field research."

"How long?"

Tregear shrugged. "Thirty days. Maybe a few months. I don't know."

"You have thirty days after separation to reenlist without loss of pay and rank—"

This made Tregear laugh.

"What will you do?" he asked, "send me back to boot camp? I'm a seaman first class, not an admiral."

"You could be—just about. You could write your own ticket in the Navy. You know that."

"I'm a high school dropout."

"Oh, come off it, Steve!"

"Yes, sir."

Tregear offered a ratty grin.

"If you sign now," Renfield announced, suddenly very official, "I'll grant you an extended furlough. We'll call it 'compassionate leave.' And you'll have your reenlistment bonus for expenses. The usual conditions will of course apply."

"Don't push it, *Sir*. In three days I can walk out of here a private citizen and a taxpayer. Keep your bonus."

Renfield could only shake his head.

"Steve, you're Navy property and will be for this lifetime. We've got our claws into you and we're never, ever going to let you go. We can't risk it."

"Are you worried I'll defect?"

"It's a thought. But we also can't have some Third World thug snatching you off the street. Face it. You'll be under guard, of one kind or another, until you're old and gray and too senile to represent a threat to national security."

There was nothing about any of this that Tregear hadn't figured out already. He saw the logic, even the necessity of the thing. He didn't even resent it.

Besides, the Navy had been good to him.

"Okay. Where do I sign?"

Before the ink was dry, Renfield had a question.

"Where are you going?"

"Frederick, Maryland."

· · ·

And what did Frederick, Maryland, have going for it? Two unsolved homicides.

In late May of that year an Army corporal named Jo Anne Rudd, age thirty-two, had been found naked and dead, stretched out on a picnic table in Baker Park. There were burn marks over the whole front of her body, and the autopsy revealed that she had been systematically tortured for at least three days before she died from having her throat cut. She had been stationed at Fort Detrick, just north of the city, and had been listed as AWOL for five days.

The usual. No fingerprints, no fiber evidence, no witnesses, no signs of sexual assault. No nothing. Just a corpse that might as well have been put on that picnic table by the hand of God.

Then, in mid-July, just five days before Seaman Tregear had his conversation with Commander Renfield, a forty-three-year-old widow named Grace Newcomb, an apartment dweller from the west side of town, known to her neighbors as somewhat undiscriminating in her choice of gentleman friends, turned up in the Carroll Creek Canal, slightly more than half a mile from where Corporal Rudd had been discovered. The body was fully clothed. At first it was believed she might have fallen in and drowned, but then at autopsy it turned out that her spine had been neatly severed in two places. Cause of death: suffocation brought on by paralysis. The pathologist speculated that she might have remained alive and conscious for a few hours after the injuries had been inflicted. Again, no trace of her murderer.

Stephen Tregear arrived on the second of August. He traveled by train, from New London to New York, from New York to Washington, DC, and from DC on the commuter line to Frederick. He was wearing brand-new civilian clothes and, in addition to his suitcase, also new, he carried a briefcase full of carefully organized computer printouts and his own twenty-eight-page summary and analysis. In his innocence he imagined that the police might find all this information both interesting and useful.

It was evening when he arrived, so he walked from the train station to the Mt. City Lodge, where he had a reservation. He had dinner and went up to his room, where he let the television lull him to sleep.

The next morning he phoned the police department and asked to speak to a Sergeant Hill, whose name he had seen in several newspaper articles dealing with the two murders. Sergeant Hill was not available. Would he care to leave a message?

"Sergeant Hill, my name is Stephen Rayne"—the Navy had insisted that he travel under an alias, so why not the one he was born with?—"and I am in possession of information that bears on the recent homicides of Jo Anne Rudd and Grace Newcomb. I am staying at the Mt City Lodge, Room two-five-six. I will wait for your call."

And he did wait. That day and the next, he hardly left his room. At two o'clock on the third day, he walked over to the police station on West Patrick Street, where they were so suspicious of his briefcase that they made him open it.

Tregear gave his alias and made an elliptical reference to his business.

"Sergeant Hill is unavailable."

"Is he in the building?"

The receptionist, who was a uniformed policewoman, offered him a hard stare and finally, with apparent reluctance, nodded.

"He's here."

"Then I'll just take a seat."

He waited until a quarter to five, when a large, bluff-looking man of about forty, wearing a plaid sport coat that was just a shade too small for him, came out into the lobby through a door around the corner from where Tregear had been sitting.

"You Rayne?" the man asked coldly.

"Yes." Tregear stood up. "I'm Stephen Rayne."

"I'm Hill. Come with me. I can give you about ten minutes."

Tregear was shown into an office small enough that, with its desk and three chairs, it was hardly navigable. Hill sat down behind the desk.

"Now," he began, placing his hands flat on the desk, "you say you have information. Did you witness either of these crimes?"

"No."

"And I gather you're not from around here?"

"No."

Hill shook his head. He was bored in advance.

"Okay. Let's hear it."

Tregear spent his ten minutes outlining six homicides from various parts of the country, drawing parallels to the two Frederick cases. Then he produced his summary.

"If you read this, you'll see that all of these murders are the work of a single individual. At the end I draw attention to what can be known about this person. He's in his early forties, light brown hair, left-handed, a small purplish birthmark on his right hand. He works in the building trades."

Sergeant Hill picked up the summary and seemed to weigh it in his hand. Then he let it drop back to the table.

"You know this guy?" he asked. "For instance, you know his *name*?"

"I do know him, yes. But I don't know his current name. I haven't seen him in twelve years, and he's used a lot of different names."

"But what was his name when you knew him?"

"Walter Rayne."

"I see. A relative of yours?"

"Yes."

"I see." Hill stood up. "Well, I'll look into this, Mr. Rayne. And if I need to talk to you again I'll call."

He didn't bother to ask for an address or a telephone number, so Tregear wrote them out for him on the first page of his summary.

"I'll be in town for at least a few more weeks," he said.

"Thank you, Mr. Rayne."

They shook hands, and Sergeant Hill smiled perfunctorily. The interview was over.

Tregear stood on the steps of the police building, holding his empty briefcase, feeling disappointed. He had the distinct impression the sergeant thought he was some sort of mental case. All the things he should have said flashed through his mind: "I saw a dead body in his car." "He murdered my grandparents—phone the Circleville police." "If you know enough math to count to ten, the statistical case is overwhelming."

Probably every day Hill talked to somebody who thought he had the answer. "Jo Anne Rudd died for the sins of the world." "Grace Newcomb was killed by Bigfoot."

Instead of going back to his hotel, Tregear headed into the center of town, where he hoped to find a decent dinner and drink way more beer than was good for him and forget the whole thing.

• • •

The next morning Tregear came within a gesture of getting back on the train to DC and spending the rest of his furlough curled up with the first woman who showed any interest. He actually went down to the station and checked the schedule, but it was a Saturday so the trains weren't running. He decided he would go sightseeing instead.

The hotel had thoughtfully provided a magazine that contained a map of Historic Frederick. Tregear, who tended to be obsessive about maps, had torn it out and stuffed it into his wallet.

And, just to add a little something to the whole endeavor, he thought he might try to spot his babysitters.

The etiquette was that you didn't make life any harder than necessary for the watchers. You didn't suddenly duck out of buildings by a side door, or cross and then immediately cross back on a busy street so that they made themselves obvious. The watchers, after all, were Navy, just like you, and rendering their lives miserable demonstrated a lack of team spirit.

However, it was hard to follow a person on foot, wandering more or less randomly through an urban landscape, without giving yourself away.

But these guys were very good. It was two days before Tregear was sure about even one of them, and that was almost by accident.

Tregear found Frederick interesting. From the quantity of building that had gone on in what was now called the downtown, he concluded that the city must have enjoyed considerable prosperity in the three or four decades preceding the Civil War, and it was easy to imagine what the place must have been like when Lee's army came marching through.

One could still see the building where Maryland delegates would have assembled to vote for secession if Lincoln hadn't first had most of them arrested. There was even a Museum of Civil War Medicine on Patrick Street, and its bookstore was where Tregear identified his first babysitter.

The giveaway was his sunglasses.

He was the sort no one noticed. Probably in his early twenties, about five ten and a hundred and fifty pounds, wearing tan shorts and a gray T-shirt, he was indistinguishable from the vast army of college kids with not much to do over their summer. He was standing well away from the front window, holding a book titled *Death is in the Breeze* about eight inches from his face. And he was wearing sunglasses.

They were the wraparound kind and very dark. It was, after all, August and probably a majority of the people one saw on the street were wearing sunglasses. But this pilgrim still had them on in a dimly lit room, and he was pretending to read. It didn't ring true.

Tregear went outside and headed west, away from the center of town. The guy in the sunglasses didn't follow him. In fact, Tregear didn't see him again for another three hours, until he was standing beside the canal on the Carroll Parkway, just where the water went underground for about two blocks. There was a dog park just across the street and Mr. Sunglasses was standing beside the chain link fence, talking to a man with an Irish setter.

Over the next three days, Tregear concluded that they must have been running about a six-man team on him. He identified two more—a tall man with particularly hairy arms, wearing a straw hat, and a Near Eastern type, short with a bad haircut.

He tried to be considerate. He stayed in his hotel room at night and he took enough time with his meals to save everyone's digestion. He tried to go to interesting places, preferably where everyone would have a chance to sit down once in a while.

By the end of the fifth day, a Wednesday, he still hadn't spotted any watchers beyond the first three. They were very good.

And he still hadn't heard anything from Detective Sergeant Hill and had more or less decided he wasn't going to.

Afterward, he often wondered whether, if he hadn't been so intent on his watchers, he might have cast his net a little wider and noticed someone else on his tail.

Because there was, as he found out Thursday night.

He was having dinner in front of Brewer's Alley, a restaurant on North Market Street that, as the name implied, served beer brewed on the premises. It was seven-thirty in the evening and voluptuously hot. People were passing by on the sidewalk. The barbecue chicken salad was delicious and the beer was better. Life was good.

Tregear was sitting alone at his table, and then suddenly he wasn't. A man came into the little trellised patio and sat down in the chair opposite. He was in his late twenties, in such perfect physical condition that he seemed to glow from the inside, and his dark blond hair was cut just long enough to take a part. He might as well have had "Annapolis" stamped on his forehead.

"Seaman Tregear," he said, as if the name and rank were some sort of secret between them, "there is a car parked up the street. We'll drive you straight back to New London tonight."

"I'm on leave. Go away."

The man reached into his shirt pocket and pulled out a plastic card. He set it on the table, just in front of Tregear's left hand.

Tregear picked it up and looked at it, then set it back down again.

"Go away, *sir*."

Lieutenant Seward, USN, didn't like that answer. His face visibly hardened.

"The car is waiting, Seaman. You're coming. That's an order."

"I only follow orders when I'm on duty," Tregear answered. "I'm not on duty. By the way, would you like a beer?"

"I can arrest you, if that's what you want." The lieutenant smiled tightly, just to show he wasn't a bad guy. "I can take you back to New London in chains."

"If you do, I'll probably get so depressed I won't be able to re-member my own name, let alone how the Navy's code sequences work. We'll see how the brass likes that, *sir*."

The lieutenant let out a little gasp, as if exasperated and amused at the same time.

"I'll have that beer now, if you wouldn't mind," he said.

Tregear flagged down a waiter.

"You sure you wouldn't like a little something with it?" Tregear asked. He had halfway decided to forgive the man. After all, Seward was an officer and a gentleman, which meant he probably couldn't help himself.

The beer came in a glass that was already sweating in the warm August evening.

"They warned me you might be tough to handle," Lieutenant Seward announced. Then he took a sip and seemed elaborately pleased. "But I have to get you out of here. There isn't a choice. Your watchers have discovered that someone else is watching too."

"Who?"

The lieutenant shrugged. "We assume the competition."

"How many?"

"Just one that we know of. But there could be others."

"Just one? Describe him."

For a few seconds the lieutenant merely stared into space, giving the impression he couldn't understand why what some nameless thug looked like could make any difference. Then, apparently, he decided to relent.

"Forties, maybe six one, maybe a hundred and seventy pounds, light brown hair, wearing jeans and a work shirt—down here, he probably thinks that looking like a redneck is a great disguise."

He laughed, until he saw that Tregear wasn't.

"Anything else?"

"Else?" The lieutenant shook his head, then suddenly seemed to remember. "They think he's left-handed, but they're not sure."

"Anybody get a really close look at him?"

"We've got some long-distance photos—if you insist."

"Where are they?"

"In the car." The lieutenant smiled, a warning that he was about to spring his cleverly concealed trap. "Which is where you should be, right now."

There wasn't any point in arguing. Tregear didn't even want to argue. He was too scared. He paid his tab and they were out of there.

"I need to stop by the hotel to get my stuff."

"It's being attended to."

The lieutenant raised his arm and, about thirty feet up the street, the two back doors of a peanut butter–brown station wagon sprang open. The man who got out on the sidewalk side was tall, with very hairy arms. Tonight he had left his straw hat behind.

They put Tregear in the backseat, in the middle, as if afraid that he might try to bolt.

"Show me the pictures."

The lieutenant, who was in front, on the passenger side, handed back a manila envelope. There were perhaps a dozen photographs, but Tregear only needed one.

"He's not the competition," he said. "He's much scarier than that."

• • •

Nobody was interested.

Tregear discovered that his mouth had gone completely dry. He didn't begin to relax until they were in New Jersey, when he discovered he was very, very tired. He missed New York altogether and didn't wake up until they reached New Haven.

Around noon of the next day a chambermaid at the Mt City Lodge in Frederick opened the door to Room 256 and almost stumbled over a corpse in civilian clothes but subsequently identified as Petty Officer Third Class Frank Piersal, age twenty-three. He had died of a single knife thrust to the throat, probably from behind, probably by someone who was left-handed.

The listed occupant of the room, a Mr. Stephen Rayne, who was described by the bell clerk as having used his left hand to sign his registration card, had disappeared and was wanted for questioning by the Frederick Police Department.

Back in New London, when Tregear's commanding officer showed him Piersal's photograph, he recognized him as Mr. Sunglasses.

"Of course nobody thinks you did it. We'll have a word with the Frederick police," Commander Renfield explained. "Piersal was sent to pick up your stuff while you were still having dinner. Whoever killed him was probably waiting for you."

"He's just as dead, whether I killed him or not."

And then he tried to explain.

"Piersal was killed by my father. The last I heard his name was Walter Rayne, but he's probably changed it sixteen times since then. He's already killed two women in Frederick, plus God alone knows how many besides. Send one of these photos to the Frederick police and tell them this is their killer. Or I'll go tell them—maybe now they'll believe me."

"This is really true?" Renfield asked him.

"You bet. If you want corroborating evidence, I've got gobs of it."

"I'll let Security know. It's their decision."

But Security did nothing. They didn't want Tregear anywhere near a criminal case, even if they could prove beyond a doubt he was as innocent as a lamb. They didn't want the publicity. They didn't want Tregear's name and/or photo in any reports—let alone the newspapers. They didn't want any part of any of it. Tregear, to the world outside the Navy, wasn't admitted to exist.

The photos, they claimed, were useless for purposes of identification.

"You tried," Renfield told him.

"Not hard enough."

• • •

"So eventually I put in for separation, and here I am," Tregear said, and smiled wearily. "But I learned a few valuable lessons out of the experience."

"Like what?"

Ellen had long since finished her wine and was a little surprised to discover she was still holding the glass. She set it down on the table in front of the sofa.

"What did you learn?" she asked, as if she thought a clarification was in order.

Tregear made a despairing little gesture with his right hand, suggesting that the cost of such knowledge must always be paid in guilt.

"I learned that I couldn't approach the police directly," he said, "both because they wouldn't believe me and because Walter might be listening at the keyhole. And I've learned that I have to keep my distance. I accomplished nothing in Frederick and Piersal died in my place. If I'd stayed away, he'd still be alive.

"So from time to time I've made the police anonymous presents of information, which have usually been ignored, and I've been waiting for a situation like this, where the police would come to me."

15

As she walked back to where her car was parked, Ellen discovered that she was what her father, the shrink, would have described as "conflicted." The cop was feeling triumphant. She was on the cutting edge of the sort of homicide investigation they wrote books about, and the adrenaline was pounding through her veins. But Ellen Ridley, the woman who was not always a cop, discovered she was a shade disappointed.

Well, what had she expected? Stephen Tregear had just unburdened himself of the most horrific story she had ever heard.

"I think I have to talk to my partner," was all she had said.

"That strikes me as a very good idea. Tell him he's welcome any time."

But was she welcome? Welcome in a way Sam wouldn't have appreciated? That was perhaps a little unclear.

When she was behind the wheel of her car, with the door firmly closed, she phoned Dispatch. She found herself wondering if Tregear had some way of listening in.

"Where is Sam?" she asked.

"Oh hi, Ellie! I love you too," a woman's voice answered. "He's in the office, breaking in a new chair. You want to talk to him?"

"It can wait."

Frankly, she wasn't sure what she was going to say to him.

. . .

Sam was at his desk, drinking coffee out of a paper cup. He didn't look happy.

"The lieutenant wants us off Tregear by tomorrow," he said, after he had glanced up at Ellen and then briefly scowled. "If Captain Marvel lodges another complaint, we're going to have a problem.

"And, by the way, what in blazes are you doing here? It's your day off."

"Tregear won't complain anymore," Ellen said. She reached into her jacket pocket and pulled out the evidence bag with Tregear's blood-soaked handkerchief inside. She dropped it on the desk.

Sam stared at it as if it were a dead cat.

"What is this?"

"A very large sample of Stephen Tregear's DNA. I also have his signed release."

"And with your very own eyes you saw this stuff coming out of his veins?"

"Yes, sir."

And how did you manage that?"

"Didn't you know, Sam? Men are like putty in my hands."

Sam looked back down at the evidence bag and actually sighed, a sound filled with the most terrible resignation.

"I think you better tell me about this."

•   •   •

"He phoned me, Sam."

They were driving back toward Fisherman's Wharf. Sam had had some very unkind things to say about his partner's police techniques, and Ellen hoped this would be the last lie she would have to tell him.

"He's willing to cooperate. He's innocent. The killer is his father and he's been tracking the bastard for years. He's prepared to give us everything he knows."

"He's not innocent until the DNA report says he's innocent."

"Oh, come on! Then why would he have given us all that nice blood, except to prove he's not Our Boy. Do you think he's going to just hand us something that can put him on death row?"

Sam didn't answer. In truth, there was no answer.

"Okay, so he's innocent." Sam glowered at the traffic. "But he still sounds like a crazy. That story of his is like something out of the funny papers."

Ellen experienced a quick flash of anger. Stephen Tregear wasn't crazy—it was cruel and bitterly unfair to dismiss him like that.

But the anger passed as quickly as it had come. What did she expect? What would have been her reaction if someone had told her the same story? *It's like something out of the funny papers.* Sam hadn't seen the look in the man's eyes.

"You've got to talk to the guy, Sam."

"That's just exactly what I'm gonna do."

After he had finished listening to Ellen's story, he had picked up the phone and called Stephen Tregear. He realized it was late in the day, he said, but would Mr. Tregear consent to see them? The extremity of his politeness was itself a bad sign.

"And after we finish with this nut job," he said to Ellen, setting the receiver carefully back in its cradle, "I'm going home to Daly City and my wife's pot roast."

Tregear met them at his front door. They all took their previous positions in his living room. It was like a class reunion.

"My partner has told me quite a story," Sam began. He smiled pleasantly, which meant that he was really seething. "I'm just not sure how much of it I can believe."

Tregear reached into his trousers pocket and pulled out a small black object, which he set on the coffee table in front of Sam.

"That's a thumb drive," he said. "It holds thirty-two gigabytes and it's just about full. Almost everything I know about the man who at one time called himself Walter Rayne is on there."

"*Almost* everything?"

Tregear smiled, perhaps a little wistfully. "He's my father. Not everything is reducible to words and pictures."

"How do you feel about him?"

To Ellen, who knew him, it seemed that Sam took a certain cruel pleasure in the question, but Tregear appeared not to notice.

"How do I feel? Is that important?"

"Maybe."

"He murdered my mother and my grandparents. He'll murder me if he gets the chance. How would you imagine I feel about him?"

But how could anyone imagine? Even Sam, who had seen everything, could not have imagined. And Tregear knew that. Ellen could see it in his eyes.

"Do you hate him?" Sam asked—implying that so complicated a relationship could be boiled down to a single emotion.

"No. But I'm afraid of him, so it comes to much the same thing."

Tregear stared off into empty space for a moment and then glanced at Ellen and smiled, as if at some missed opportunity.

"But I'm forgetting my manners," he continued. "Can I offer either of you anything?"

The answer was a curt "No, thanks."

They talked for perhaps half an hour, during which Sam never asked why Tregear was so sure Sally Wilkes' murderer was the man who, for the sake of convenience, they referred to as Walter Rayne. He seemed little interested in the evidence. What seemed to engross his attention were the psychology and motives of Stephen Tregear.

At one point he picked up the thumb drive and held it in his open hand, staring at it as if by itself it might be the answer to some riddle.

"You've given this a good share of your life," he said, not even looking at Tregear. He made it sound like an accusation.

"For the last ten or so years, it almost has been my life."

"Why?"

"That seems an odd question from a homicide detective." Tregear smiled and moved his shoulders in a vague shrug, perhaps implying an apology or perhaps not. "For years women have been dying lonely, unspeakable deaths—my mother was almost certainly one of them. By now my father's victims must number in the hundreds. It's difficult to ignore."

Sam appeared to consider the answer, giving no hint about his conclusions. The thumb drive disappeared into his jacket pocket.

After a while Sam climbed to his feet. The interview seemed to be over.

When they got to their car, Sam dropped the thumb drive in Ellen's lap.

"I'll leave you at the department," he said. He was inflicting a punishment. "You can start printing out whatever's on this thing. Like I said, I'm going home."

"Okay, boss."

•   •   •

When Tregear closed the door on his two guests it felt almost as if the apartment had been hermetically sealed. He could not remember a time when he had felt so cut off from the human race, not since boyhood.

Would they come back? Or, more important, would *she* come back? Or would they simply write him off as another nut case? By now, perhaps, the very weight of the evidence he had collected might tell against him.

This time she had said hardly a word—she had let her partner do all the talking, and it was clear that her partner didn't much like him. But all he had to do was close his eyes and remember what she had been like only a few hours ago.

Could you come back and change the dressings for me tomorrow? I might.

It was wonderful to see the way she smiled when she said it. It was wonderful to have a woman flirt with you like that.

Tregear had been so long alone that it was difficult to imagine being with someone. Aside from the briefest encounters, he had stayed away from women. He had no right to put them in the line of fire.

But Ellen Ridley was already there. She was a cop working a homicide case, and Tregear's father was Suspect Number One. She was in it, with both feet, and it had nothing to do with him.

It was almost a relief.

Of course, their little moment of connection had occurred before he told her about Life with Walter. Maybe now she shared her partner's distaste. Maybe that was why she had stayed so quiet. Maybe now she saw him as some sort of freak, almost an accomplice in his father's crimes.

Maybe he even was.

The sins of the fathers shall be visited upon the sons.

In a sense, perhaps my grandparents' blood—and all the blood since—is on my head because all I could think to do was run away and save my own life.

You were twelve years old.

Was that exoneration enough?

Tregear had read enough about the tendency of abused children to assume the guilt for their parents' failures, but it had never seemed to him to apply to his own case. That night, when he had found the dead woman in his father's van, he had run away. It had never even occurred to him to do anything else. He had been twelve years old and afraid for his own life. And his father was his father. All of his excuses seemed a little beside the point.

The sins of the fathers shall be visited upon the sons. There seemed a certain justice in that.

And maybe, upon reflection, Ellen Ridley had come to agree.

Or maybe not.

Tregear regarded himself as having few enough claims on the world's forgiveness, but perhaps, just this once . . .

He knew he would never be able to forgive himself if he didn't at least ask.

. . .

When she was at her desk, Ellen stuck the thumb drive into a USB port, waited for the ancient computer to recognize it and then started calling files up on screen for a look.

It quickly became apparent that Tregear's data was vast. It would take days to print it out and boxes and boxes of paper. Budget would have a fit.

Within five minutes she was reading Walter Rayne's dossier. It was pretty thin.

Tregear knew more about Walter Rayne than anyone on earth, and even he didn't know much. The one exception was his list of known aliases, and that was impressive. Walter Bauer, Walter Brown, Walter Carter, Walter Ellis—there was even a Walter Scott.

And under any and all of these names, the man had no IRS history, no social security account, no banking history, no credit history. He had lived his whole life under the radar. Officially, he didn't exist. They didn't exist.

Which led inevitably to the conclusion that he was not Walter Rayne, that Walter Rayne was just another invention and that whoever he really was had disappeared a long time ago. His life before his son's memories of him was therefore probably unrecoverable.

Unless, of course, they caught him. It would be interesting in that case to run his fingerprints and find out if anyone, anywhere, had a match.

And if not, he would remain forever an enigma, a man who had conjured himself out of thin air.

The file on his work habits was much more rewarding. His son was right—the man seemed to know how to do everything.

Tregear's personal recollections attested to the father's knowledge of the building trades. Walter Rayne had worked as a carpenter, electrician, roofer, plumber, tile layer, plasterer and painter. He knew heating and air-conditioning, security systems, sprinkler systems, telephone systems and insulation. He knew explosives.

His patterns of employment were a matter of inference and conjecture. There was a ten-year blank following the twelve-year-old Stephen's flight from Mound City, Arkansas, but from the age of twenty-two, from his vantage in the Navy, Tregear had been tracking his father.

The material on the thumb drive was extensively cross-referenced. The work history file contained pointers to a list of homicides committed over the last twelve years. There were hundreds of them, from all over the country. All of the victims were women. Each entry included the victim's name, her date of death and the location. Many of them contained pointers to case histories and all of them were color coded: black for "confirmed not," yellow for "possible," blue for "probable" and red for "highly probable."

The case histories contained detailed summaries, in which Tregear began to emerge as a critic and connoisseur of the homicidal arts. He discussed motive and psychology—interestingly, as separate categories—method, patterns of victim selection and refinement of cruelty. He even tried to articulate an impression of victim response, discussing them as the first audience of their murderer's performance.

With each succeeding year, the black and yellow cases became fewer and fewer and the blue and red cases increased. This resulted, no doubt, from Tregear's accumulated understanding of his father's patterns.

A close study of the "probable" killings revealed that both father and son were rapidly sharpening their skills.

• • •

At six-thirty Ellen remembered that she had a ferret and a college roommate to feed and reluctantly shut down her computer. It was time to go home and be something else besides a cop.

From the beginning, from the discovery of Rita Blandish in a hotel bathtub, this case had ceased to engage her merely as a homicide detective. And now it had acquired yet another dimension. It was no longer about just another sociopath who went around murdering women who were no more real to him than the bad guys in a video game. It was that, but it was also about his son's obsessive quest to find and stop him. Now, for Ellen, once she had heard his story and had sifted through even a small fraction of the data he had so painstakingly accumulated, it was as much about Stephen Tregear as it was about Walter.

Ellen, a homicide detective and the daughter of a psychiatrist, knew that violent criminals were frequently the abused children of violent parents, and that the degree of inheritability was higher in men than in women. She kept reminding herself that, beyond the obvious, she knew very little about Stephen Tregear. He was intellectually brilliant and personally charming, but so had been Gilles de Rais and Ted Bundy.

Do you hate him? Sam had asked.

No. But I'm afraid of him, so it comes to much the same thing.

But did it? Ellen suspected the truth couldn't be captured in so neat an equation.

Did some part of him still love his father? Or was he enough like his father that he was incapable of love?

Ellen didn't believe that, but she also recognized that she didn't want to believe it.

I've often wondered if the police might have believed me back in Arkansas. . . . In a sense, perhaps my grandparents' blood—and all the blood since—is on my head because all I could think to do was run away and save my own life.

You were twelve years old.

There is that.

But Tregear wasn't making any excuses for himself. In his crushing sense of responsibility, and his acceptance of it, there was something tragic—in the sense Aeschylus had understood such things.

Monsters knew nothing of remorse.

Gwendolyn was still asleep in her hammock and Mindy was either still at work or in the arms of her new boyfriend when Ellen opened her apartment door and let herself in. She put a Lean Cuisine in the microwave and poured herself a glass of wine, sitting down at the kitchen table to drink it. After Tregear's Santa Margherita it tasted like nail polish remover.

The microwave, which emitted four beeps when the cooking time was over and then one a minute thereafter until the door was opened, was a long time rousing Ellen from her fit of abstraction. At first she couldn't remember what the sound meant, then she smiled and shook her head as if coming out of a trance.

She had been thinking about Tregear, or perhaps less thinking about him than simply conjuring him up in her imagination. She was remembering the expression of his eyes while he talked about his frightful childhood. If she tried, she could screen out the sound of his voice and concentrate on his face alone.

In the years since achieving the rank of inspector, Ellen had interviewed hundreds of criminal suspects, and one of the things she had learned was to watch people's faces. The con artists, the narcissistic wheeler-dealers who looked down on the rest of the human race with amused contempt and thought they had refined lying into an art form, were all ham actors who could be counted on to overplay their parts. Their faces betrayed them, and especially their eyes.

Tregear hadn't been playing a part. If there had been anything of a performance it had consisted of an attempt to distance himself from the things he was describing.

He was on the level—either that or he was the Laurence Olivier of psychopaths. He was probably intelligent enough for that. It might just be that all the blunted career criminals and child rapists and drug-crazed, abusive parents of her experience hadn't prepared her for an instrument as sharply honed as Stephen Tregear's mind. There was always that possibility.

But again, it was not something she could take seriously. Tregear was not a suspect in this case. There was no evidence he had ever harmed anyone.

So she decided there was no harm in allowing herself the pleasure of recalling his face.

· · ·

All the next day, from 7:30 A.M. on, apart from occasional trips to the ladies' room and the departmental coffeepot, Ellen hardly left her desk. And gradually her intensity of focus had its effect on the other

occupants of the duty room. Everyone knew that their Ellie was working the Wilkes case and, from her level of concentration and the quantities of paper she was running through the printer, they began to form
the impression that she was on to something. The noise level fell away
almost to a whisper, and people kept glancing in her direction, as if
expecting a miracle.

Finally, around two in the afternoon, Barney Phelps, a ten-year
homicide man, approached her from behind and leaned cautiously
over her shoulder. He picked up her paper coffee cup, checked to confirm that it was empty, then set it back down.

"Ellie, come on—you can't live on that sludge. You're gonna get
yourself really wired. Take half an hour and find yourself some real
food."

"No time" was the answer. Ellen never took her eyes from the computer screen.

"Well then, if I went around the corner to the diner and got you a
nice bottle of iced tea and some chicken salad on a bagel, would you
eat it?'

"Sure."

The bagel sandwich and the iced tea sat on her desk for twenty
minutes before she even noticed that they were there.

At a quarter to six, Ellen turned off her computer. She raised her
arms and stretched like a cat.

"Well?"

Barney spoke for the whole room. Ellen turned to him and smiled,
like a bride on her father's arm.

"I know how we're going to catch him," she said sweetly.

16

The next morning, at eight o'clock when Sam returned from his day off, there was a stack of reports on his desk approximately the length of *War and Peace*.

Ellen was working. She only noticed his presence when he sat down, noisily, on his chair. Then she looked up and greeted him with a cheery "Howdy."

Sam scowled at her and placed his right hand on the stack of papers, as if he were about to take his oath on them.

"What in God's name is all this?"

"It's what'll put our killer on death row," she answered brightly. "And I figured it out all by myself. Well, with a little help from Steve."

"Steve?" Sam peered into her face. He seemed to be trying to remember who she was. "*Steve?*"

"Tregear."

"I see. We're on a first-name basis now?"

"Sort of."

With a shrug that suggested it might not be the oddest thing he had heard in his long career, Sam turned his attention back to the pile on his desk.

"I'm supposed to read all this?" he asked. "You couldn't give me the *Reader's Digest* version?"

For the next three hours, Ellen took him on a guided tour. After the first fifteen minutes Sam reached into his breast pocket and took out his reading glasses, which was a good sign.

She concentrated on the red murders, leading him through the summaries and explaining the analyses. She drew his attention to the system of cross-references and tried to do justice to Tregear's intricate patterns of inference.

"And you buy this horseshit?" he asked at one point—his use of the term did not necessarily imply dismissal.

At that precise moment, 9:47 A.M., the phone on Sam's desk rang. He picked up the receiver, made a few grunting sounds as he listened, then said, to whoever was on the other end, "Well, that's interesting." Thereupon, he hung up.

"Tregear isn't our killer," he said blandly. "But our killer is a close male relative. Don't look so smug."

"Now, to get back to my original question: And you buy this horseshit?"

Ellen decided that the tactful thing to do was to avoid gloating and just answer the question.

"Sam, I looked up a paper Tregear wrote when he was fifteen. It was published under his grandparents' last name, Stephen Dabney, which is why we missed it. I could only understand about every fifth word, but from the frequency with which it's cited in the math journals it must be pretty good. It's on probability theory. This guy knows how to weigh the odds."

Sam merely nodded, and they went back to the case histories.

When the performance was over, Sam threw himself back in his chair, which emitted a shuddering groan.

"Tregear's a smart son of a bitch, I'll give him that."

He closed his eyes for a moment and looked almost as if he were about to fall asleep. But then he opened them again, and their expression suggested nothing so much as suspicion.

"The question is, how does all this get us any closer to finding the guy?"

Ellen raised her hands, palms up, and smiled.

"By using Tregear's criteria of selection," she announced triumphantly. "Aside from method, how does he establish that a group of murders are all being committed by a single perpetrator? What clinches it for him? He looks at the work orders."

Sam shook his head. "I don't follow you."

Ellen spread three red case histories out on the desk. These women had all died in St. Louis, Missouri, over a four-month period six years ago. On the last page of each report there was a heading labeled "Work History," which listed the service calls made to the victim's residence in the final three months of their lives. In each list, one item was highlighted in red: "Al's Roofing."

"We follow in Tregear's footsteps," Ellen explained, almost fiercely, "We go to the victims' records and we find out who paid a visit to all three."

Sam put his left hand behind his neck and began scratching in the meditative way that meant he was thinking.

"We're on the verge, Ellie," he said at last. "You've done really good work. But before we jump I think we should talk to Tregear again, just to see what he thinks."

"I agree."

. . .

When Ellen phoned, Tregear invited them to lunch.

"You can have a choice between sliced brisket of beef and lasagna. Plus, of course, salad and Pinot Grigio."

"Do you have any beer? Sam only drinks beer."

"There's a liquor store with a huge refrigerator just two blocks from me. What does he favor?"

"He likes India pale ale."

"I'll see what I can do." And then, after a short pause, "How about dinner tonight? I mean, just the two of us."

Sam was at his desk, staring at her quizzically, and Tregear was asking for a date. It was a moment of more than usual awkwardness.

It was also time for a make-or-break decision. Tregear, she sensed, was basically a shy man and too well mannered ever to keep inflicting his attentions on a woman who had already turned him down once. And she could think of a dozen reasons why encouraging a personal relationship with Tregear would probably be unprofessional and a mistake. She didn't care if it was unprofessional, and she was prepared to risk a mistake.

"That sounds good," she answered.

"We're having lunch there," she said, as soon as she set the phone down.

"I see." Sam's face didn't register any reaction, and then he smiled. It could have meant anything. "Okay."

They drove to Fisherman's Wharf in silence, but when the car was parked in front of Tregear's apartment, Ellen turned to her partner and touched his arm, almost pleadingly.

"Sam, be a little nice. Please? Try to forget you ever thought he killed anybody."

Sam merely grunted.

As they were walking across the street, Tregear's door opened and there he was. He had a smile on his face appropriate to a visit from a favorite aunt. The first person he actually spoke to was Sam.

"I have Harpoon IPA on ice," he said. "Is that acceptable?"

"More than acceptable, Mr. Tregear."

"Call me Steve. Please."

"Okay. Steve." Then he actually offered his hand. "Ellie here thinks I owe you an apology. What do you think?"

"For suspecting me of murder? An understandable mistake. Don't mention it."

Tregear laughed, then they all laughed. After that they were fine together.

"Lunch will be ready in five minutes," Tregear announced. "It's all from Trader Joe's, so it's heat and serve, but it's not bad."

It was more than not bad. Nobody could decide between the brisket and the lasagna, so everybody had some of each. The salad was not terrible, in spite of the anchovy dressing, and nobody complained about what they were drinking.

Conversation was at first general, and Ellen was pleased to see Sam making an effort to get to know this highly unusual man with his brilliant mind and his dreadful childhood.

But eventually, inevitably, the talk turned to Walter. That was what Tregear called him, so for Ellen and Sam too this murderer, their "Boy," as they had sometimes called him, became simply Walter.

They outlined to Tregear how they proposed to catch him, and Tregear listened respectfully and in silence. Then Sam asked him what he thought.

"I think you'll have exactly one chance," Tregear answered. "If you muff it, and he gets wind you're sniffing around after him, he'll vanish like mist and you'll never hear from him again. And after a while women will start dying somewhere else."

He shook his head slowly and closed his eyes, as if at some painful memory.

"Don't make the mistake so many have made, myself included. Don't underestimate him. He's very smart, and he's gotten very good at this."

Then he seemed to snap back from his trance.

"Let's say you identify the company. What then?"

"Then we check their records until we find out who made the calls," Sam answered. He looked at Ellen as if the question made no sense to him.

"If you send a badge around, you'll never catch him. Believe me, he'll go to ground."

"How do you figure?"

Tregear smiled, not very pleasantly.

"You have to understand something about Walter," he began. "To women he's like catnip. He has to be in his fifties now, but there's no evidence he's lost his touch. The company you find will probably be small, the sort that's willing to cut a few corners—that's his pattern. The office staff is likely to be one woman, probably single, probably in her late thirties to early forties, and Walter will have her licking his hand. She'll tip him off. She'll be on the phone to him as soon as you walk out the door.

"I have a suggestion."

It was obvious that Sam wanted to say something, to offer some defense of department procedure, but he was wise enough to wait. He merely nodded. He was listening.

"Give me the company name. I'll get inside their system. I'll give you the work orders. I'll give you the employee files, with names, addresses and car license plates. I'll print them out and hand them to you. Then you can just pick him up."

"That's illegal." Sam raised his hand up to about eye level, letting it wander in aimless little circles. It was an eloquent gesture of futility. "We need either a search warrant, for which we have to have probable cause, or we need their willing cooperation. In either case we can't just hack into their computers—and we can't let you do it either. We're cops, remember?"

"Once you have his address and current alias, you can put a case together."

Sam leaned forward and emitted a single, muffled syllable of laughter.

"Mr. Tregear—Steve. You're a very smart guy, but you're not a criminal lawyer or a cop. I don't think you appreciate how hard it is to get a conviction for capital murder. If we break the rules, he'll walk."

"Okay. It was only a suggestion."

It occurred to Ellen, who had kept quiet during this exchange, that it was almost as if she were watching a Greek tragedy. Tregear was right, but Sam was bound by the rules of procedure. She had the terrible feeling that it would end badly.

"Could we use someone from one of the licensing boards?" she asked suddenly. Both men turned to her as if they had forgotten she was in the room. "A contractor operates under a state license. Somebody from the state board goes in to make sure they're up to code, or something like that."

"It's a thought." Sam nodded meditatively. "I don't know if we can get away with it, but we can run it by Legal.

"Time to go back to work."

He stood up, which instantly got Tregear to his feet, and the two men shook hands. It was like watching a couple of prizefighters touch gloves.

"Well, thank you for coming," Tregear said.

In the general movement toward the front door, Ellen glanced at Tregear.

"How's the finger?" she asked.

He smiled and said, "It's mending."

"I suppose he might suit you," Sam said, once they were back in the car. "God knows, he's screwy enough."

Ellen could only laugh. "You don't miss much, do you, boss?"

• • •

When they got back to the squad room, Ellen phoned her friend in the DA's office. Mindy was not impressed with the idea.

"Sorry, Toots, but it'll have to be a police show from end to end. It's either probable cause or you get their permission. You use a subterfuge, it's an invasion of privacy."

When Ellen told Sam, he merely shrugged.

"Okay, we'll worry about lovesick secretaries another day," he announced. "For now, it's time to knock on doors. You take Wilkes and Hudson, since they were both in apartments here in town, and

I'll take Blandish. I think she lived in a house over in Oakland. God, I hate Oakland. I always get lost."

Kathy Hudson had lived in a regular apartment building, with a super. He was perfectly willing to go through his records and, yes, they had had the air-conditioning guy in when the main vent in that unit had frozen up. He gave Ellen a copy of the invoice, which read, "Allied Heating and Cooling." The date was just a few days shy of a month before Kathy had been found in a neighbor's car trunk.

As soon as she was back on the street, Ellen's cell phone rang.

"Are we still on for dinner?" Tregear asked.

"Yes. Sure. I said so."

"You said, 'That sounds good,' which isn't quite the same as 'yes.' I just wanted to hear you say it when Sam wasn't around."

"How do you know he isn't around now?"

"Sam is in Oakland."

In one of those barely conscious acts that seem to have nothing to do with the will, Ellen found her eyes wandering over the sidewalk on the other side of the street. And then suddenly she realized she was looking for Tregear.

But, then, he wouldn't be there. He seemed like God gazing down from heaven.

"And am I ever going to find out how you know that?" she asked.

"You will if you have dinner with me."

"Then make it a good story."

"Would you like me to pick you up?"

"No. I'll come over there." She figured she would need an hour in her apartment, to get changed, feed Gwendolyn and explain to Mindy that she was having dinner with a material witness. "Figure seven-thirty?"

"Okay. Where would you rather eat, my place or out?"

"I'll leave that to you."

She clicked off her cell phone, thinking how odd it was that this man, who seemed to know everything, had needed to hear again that they had a date. Somehow it pleased her, although she couldn't have said why.

I suppose he might suit you. God knows, he's screwy enough.

Apparently Sam knew a thing or two.

• • •

Mrs. Patterson, Sally Wilkes' landlady, remembered Ellen and didn't seem very glad to see her again. The apartment, of course, was still sealed, and that was a grievance. But she recalled that there had been a problem with the heat and a man had come to replace the thermostats.

"You don't think *he* killed her, do you? He was such a *nice* man."

"Probably not," Ellen said, smiling her best professional smile. "We're just checking anyone who might have had access. Do you remember what he looked like?"

"Young. Fifties, I'd say."

Mrs. Patterson's eyes took on a dreamy cast as, apparently, she enjoyed the recollection. Ellen remembered what Tregear had said: *To women he's like catnip.*

Well, like father like son. Suddenly she was really looking forward to her evening.

With vast reluctance, Mrs. Patterson consulted her checkbook. There was an entry just a month back, $212.17 to Allied Heating and Cooling.

Bingo. This was it. It just felt right.

When Ellen got back to her car, she phoned Sam and told him she had struck pay dirt.

"Any luck with Rita?"

"Not a thing. She lived with a couple of girlfriends, and I have the impression they paid their bills with nookie. Anyway, they claim there haven't been any servicemen in the house over the past year."

Of course not. And, anyway, why would anyone living in Oakland call a San Francisco company? They would want someone local.

"She was killed at the Marriott," Ellen told him. "You want me to run over there and ask if they've had anyone in?"

"If you would be so kind."

But the Marriott was a blank. With 329 rooms, they had their own maintenance staff, thank you very much. So maybe Rita had been just a target of opportunity.

But now she had a match on two cases. It was enough.

· · ·

As it turned out, they went to a restaurant on the Wharf. It was only a few blocks from Tregear's apartment and he said it would give them more time to talk.

On the way their shoulders kept brushing against each other in a way that seemed perfectly natural, as if from long-standing habit.

In the restaurant there was a little interval for regaining one's self-possession as they were seated and could busy themselves with the contents of the menu.

"Would you like some wine?" he asked while the waiter, who seemed to regard Tregear as his personal possession, hovered behind his chair.

"Yes. Thank you."

"Pinot Grigio?"

She merely nodded, and the matter was settled.

When they were alone again, she had thought he would want to hear about her reaction to his material, but he never brought the subject up. Instead, he wanted to hear about her.

"I hardly know anything about you," he said. "Aside from your taste in wine and the fact that you drive a four-year-old Toyota, you're a mystery to me."

He smiled, a trifle uncertainly, and it occurred to Ellen that this was not a man who simply assumed you found him irresistible. That kind of unself-conscious modesty was in itself almost irresistible. He could even order a bottle of wine without seeming to suggest that he was one of the world's great connoisseurs.

"What would you like to know?"

"Whatever there is to know—whatever you care to tell me. I'll settle for why you decided to become a cop."

"You shouldn't ask me questions I'm not sure I have the answer to," she said, allowing a little hint of laughter creep into her voice. "I don't know, except that it's about real life."

"Is homicide real life?"

She almost said, *You of all people should know,* but she restrained herself. Instead she said, "It beats Atherton."

"You don't like Atherton?

He smiled again, and Ellen began to think she might be developing a taste for Tregear's smiles.

"It's not real life. It's like a ritzy department store where everyone spends their time shopping for things they don't really need. After a while you wonder what you're doing there."

For a moment his eyes drifted away as he seemed to consider the matter. He didn't give the impression he was reaching any conclusions.

"Given the life you've led, that probably strikes you as self-indulgent nonsense."

Instantly it occurred to her that she might have made some ghastly mistake, but he only shook his head.

"No, I know exactly what you mean," he said. "Nobody wants to live in a cage, even if it's gilded." And then he laughed. "Actually, that isn't even halfway true. Probably most people would be perfectly happy in a gilded cage."

"Most people in Atherton seem happy with it."

"That's because they can't see the bars."

Yes, she thought. That was precisely the truth of it—at least, it was her truth. The two of them had started out from such different places and somehow managed to arrive at the same point.

There was a basket of sourdough French bread on the table. She took a piece and buttered it thickly—it was a way to distract herself a little, and she needed distracting. She felt almost as if she were falling under a spell.

Besides, sourdough French bread was one of the chief reasons why Ellen knew she could never live anywhere except the San Francisco Bay Area, and butter was a vice she indulged only in restaurants.

The wine came, and the waiter, with the air of someone who knew how these things were done, poured a little into Tregear's glass and waited expectantly for him to taste it.

"It's fine. It's wonderful," Tregear said, and the waiter seemed satisfied.

It was just a little ceremony, something by which restaurants above a certain price point defined themselves. And for Tregear, it seemed, that was all it was, a little ceremony, like shaking hands. Something he was willing to put up with to avoid injuring anyone's self-esteem.

So the waiter filled their glasses and went away, content.

And it occurred to Ellen, almost as a happy recollection, what a nice man Tregear was, how considerate he was. And not by design but by character.

"So tell me something else about yourself." Tregear was still holding his wineglasss. Then he appeared to remember its existence and set it down. "How you liked Berkeley, for instance. Or your six all-time favorite movies. Anything."

By the time dinner came, they had settled that neither of them liked Ingmar Bergman films, that Earl Hines was the greatest jazz pianist who ever lived and that unhealthy desserts were the best kind.

When dinner arrived, Ellen was telling him all about her problems with her mother.

"It's terrible. I'm thirty years old and every time I'm around her she acts like I'm getting ready for my first prom."

"And so I take it being a homicide detective isn't her idea of a suitable career?"

"You guessed it. Marriage to a board member at Wells Fargo would have been her idea of a suitable career."

Tregear smiled the faintest of smiles. Probably he was thinking of the mother he could hardly remember and the father who just wanted to kill him.

"I'm sorry," Ellen said, suddenly penitent. "I must sound to you like a perfect brat."

"No, you don't." The smile broadened just a trace. "I'm glad you told me."

And then he smiled suddenly the way one does upon seeing the joke.

"Everyone, it seems, has trouble with the folks."

While they ate they talked about San Francisco, and Ellen described to him how cold the Pacific was and the quantities of jellyfish that got washed up on Ocean Beach.

"It isn't really much of a beach, but you can walk up toward the Cliff House and watch the sea lions on Seal Rock. I like sea lions."

"Breathes there a man with soul so dead that he doesn't like sea lions?"

They both laughed. They both liked sea lions, and wasn't that wonderful.

They talked about other things as well. Tregear, it seemed, was interested in music, particularly jazz, and was extremely disappointed to learn that Turk Murphy had been dead for decades.

"I heard one of his records once, when I was in the Navy. Oh well. Another of life's missed opportunities."

"They named a street after him." Ellen shrugged. "Actually, it's only a block long. It's up in North Beach."

The idea that the city fathers would name a street after a trombone player—even if it was only one block—seemed to please Tregear.

"I think I'd like to go visit it," he said.

Dessert—crème brûlée—was eaten in near silence. It was as if they shared a secret that they couldn't mention, even to each other.

Once she looked up and caught a look in his eyes of almost wistful longing, as if he believed she would be forever beyond his reach, and she felt in the core of her being that he had to be the most beautiful man she had ever seen.

And in half an hour or so, it occurred to her, less as a decision than as a discovery, they would go to bed together. The idea made her smile, and she hoped he could see that smile, and read it correctly.

• • •

It was about that simple. On the walk back to his apartment they held hands, and once inside his door she turned to him, put her arms around his neck and gave him a kiss that told him there wasn't anything to negotiate. After that it just happened, as if it had never crossed either of their minds that it wouldn't.

And it was perfect. There was no other way Ellen could have described it. It didn't have anything to do with technique or staying power. Nobody had anything to prove. It wasn't an athletic event, just a man and a woman coming together because on some level too fundamental for analysis they needed each other.

After the first time, the thought crossed Ellen's mind that it had been a long, long drought and she probably really needed this drink of water. But the first time was only the first time, and there was a second and third, and each time was just as good, or perhaps even better. They would make love and sleep and wake and make love again. And it was making love. It wasn't just sex.

She didn't know how he felt, and she wasn't sure it would make any difference. He might be using her, and if that were true she wanted to be used. But she didn't think he was using her. This man was everything that Brad and her other lovers had never dreamed of being.

17

In the town of Half Moon Bay, some twenty-five miles down the coast road from San Francisco, stood a house set in the midst of fields that smelled of brussels sprouts. It had been left abandoned for nearly eight years, so the owner was happy to have it occupied even at a cheap rent, with only a one month deposit, particularly since the new tenant had offered to fix it up for just the cost of materials. He was a single man in his fifties, a pleasant sort and apparently very capable. After two days he had the well running again and after five the old wiring had been stripped out and replaced and it was safe to turn the electricity back on.

In that first week the landlord had come out nearly every day to see for himself how things were progressing. But after a while his tenant made it clear, without actually putting the thing into words, that he regarded these little visits as an intrusion and that he preferred his privacy, after which the landlord left him alone.

The tenant's name was Walter Stride.

And, aside from the landlord, hardly anyone in Half Moon Bay even knew of Mr. Stride's existence. He worked in San Francisco and did his shopping either there or in Pacifica, which was on his way home. He must have rented a post office box somewhere because he never got any mail, and no one ever saw him in the local restaurants and bars. The only signs of his existence were the rent payments, in cash, that were regularly delivered to his landlord's office and the house lights that could be seen from Highway 1.

. . .

Walter had quickly recovered from his pique at the landlord. After all, the guy was just trying to be friendly. Walter could appreciate that, although cultivating friendships was not very high among his priorities.

The way he saw it, one friend was one too many. Friends were a nuisance and a danger.

But the landlord struck him as a good sort and had taken the hint. Walter would reward him in a way he could appreciate, by taking good care of the property. He himself preferred a tidy house. He had been careful to put a big plastic tarp down on the basement floor to keep Sally Wilkes' blood from ruining the linoleum.

Sally had been his guest for a pleasant evening at home. That was the sort of relationship he preferred to cultivate. She suffered so eloquently that it had been really a pity when he had to tape her mouth closed. The next one would be better because by then he would have the basement properly soundproofed.

He had the next one all picked out. He was looking forward to her because she would come of her own free will. It was more amusing when they chose their fate. Sally, for all her youth, had known better than to trust strange men. He had had to grab her as she walked to her car, which was both dangerous and unsatisfying.

It was a blessing that age made women foolish. Harriet Murdoch was a forty-something realtor who lived and worked across the hills in San Carlos. She was divorced and her son was safely distant in some college in Los Angeles. Walter had met her in a bar two weeks ago.

By comparison with a lot of places he had lived, the Peninsula seemed rich. In all of the towns following one another along that finger of land, with San Francisco at its tip, the general impression was of prosperity. You had to look to discover a real slum.

Under the circumstances, finding the right kind of bar had been a challenge. Women with comfortable incomes tended to be suspicious to begin with, and snobs. They wouldn't look at a man who didn't wear a suit, and Walter didn't even own a suit. He wanted someplace where he would fit in, where no one would notice him and where he would have a chance to work his charm.

The right kind of bar had been a place on El Camino Real, which was the main artery up and down the Peninsula. Pete's Tavern was on a corner, next to a discount furniture store. The neon signs in the window advertised Budweiser and Miller Lite.

Walter was on his second beer and on the verge of calling it a night, when this fake blonde came in and sat down on the next bar stool but one from him. She was clutching her purse in both hands as she

ordered something called a Pink Lady that came in a martini glass
and really was pink.

She glanced at him, just once, and then seemed absorbed in the
bottle collection on the wall behind the bar. But she was interested.

Of course, she would be. That was why she was there.

Everything about her suggested she was on the prowl. She was just
a little too well turned out to be anything else. The dress, the hair,
the makeup—it was all too perfect. She might have just stopped in on
her way to someone's wedding.

Taking his time, Walter watched the bartender make her drink,
which seemed a major project, and waited until it had been served to
her on a little scalloped coaster and she had had her first sip.

"What's in that thing?" he asked finally.

Very slowly, she turned her head to look at him. Then, without
smiling, she answered, "Plymouth gin, grenadine, a teaspoon of cream
and an egg white."

"And then they shake it up?"

"Yes."

Walter smiled at her in a way that suggested nothing except the
sweetness of his nature.

"Well, it looks pretty."

Then she smiled, and said, "Yes, it does." And by then Walter knew
he had her.

With the second Pink Lady, which Walter bought, they adjourned
to a booth. It wasn't until they were sitting in the booth that he asked
her name.

This was a license for the conversation to turn personal. On these
occasions he always wore a wedding ring, which seemed to make
women feel safer. This one he had bought in a pawnshop in Fort
Worth.

He told Harriet he was a widower. Strictly speaking, this was the
truth.

Then she told him about her divorce, and about her son away in
college and about how much she missed him.

"I have a son," he confessed. "I haven't seen him in years."

She was very sympathetic, particularly since he didn't go into details. Doubtless she sensed the subject was painful for him, which was
precisely the impression he wished to create.

It was eleven-fifteen, and Harriet had just finished her third drink, when he decided it was time to quit.

"I'd like to see you again," Walter told her, and his eyes had that pleading expression women found so hard to resist. "If you give me your phone number, I'll call you tomorrow."

It was amusing to watch the play of expression on her face. On the one hand she was disappointed, since she clearly had thought she was going to get laid this very night, but on the other hand she now saw before her the prospect of acquiring a gentleman friend, perhaps even a relationship that might last into the indefinite future.

It was a measure of her desperation when a woman started prowling the bars. Harriet was desperate. She took the bait. She fished a ballpoint pen out of her purse and wrote out two numbers on a cocktail napkin—one her home phone and the other her cell.

Now it was her turn to make her eyes plead. *Please, just phone me,* she seemed to be begging. *I'll make you happy. I'll give you my body and my love, and everything else you ever dreamed of.*

Of course, if she had known what Walter's dreams were like, she might have thought better of it.

They had had dinner together a few times, in restaurants where neither of them was known. He didn't stint. He took her to nice places, places where he had to wear a sport coat. And she was drawing all the desired conclusions.

"My wife's been dead for a few years now, and I loved her dear. But a man has to move on or he dies inside himself." All of which, of course, implied, *I'm tired of being alone.*

Still, he avoided any definite proposals beyond another dinner. He didn't even presume to a little necking at her front door, and after the second date it was all he could do to avoid being dragged inside and ravaged. This woman was so hungry to feel a man's weight on her that all the way back to the van she kept brushing against him.

But Walter was playing coy, and it was working. When, with beguilingly embarrassed hesitation, he finally asked her to come along to his place for a nightcap, she would dance all the way.

But that was a little down the road, and in the meantime he had to stay focused. Police in the San Francisco Bay Area had had a lot of experience with serial killers and he needed to keep his wits about him.

This new stuff the doctor in San Mateo had given him wasn't helping. It eased the misery in his gut, but the tradeoff was an odd, detached feeling, an indifference that was scary.

He had had abdominal pains for about five months and had gone
to some quack in Seattle who wanted to run all kinds of tests and
wrote him a prescription, something just to take the edge off. It wasn't
much better than aspirin—Walter had to take three times the dose to
get any relief. He never went back. He didn't need any tests because
he knew what it was.

Working on the house in Half Moon Bay, he would forget his pain,
sometimes for hours at a time. Work took you out of yourself. You
forgot to suffer the way you might forget to have lunch. Pain was
just a habit. If you didn't think about it, it wasn't there.

And for the times when it was there, he had a new prescription
that seemed to do the job. He could sleep—better, in fact, than before he got sick, because the new stuff seemed to keep his dreams
within acceptable limits of horror. But it also left him feeling blunted.

His father's preferred narcotics had been corn whiskey and the
Bible, and in the end neither had worked. The old man had howled
all the way to the grave. "The devil is come down onto you, having
great wrath, because he knoweth that he hath but a short time," he
used to say, when he was sober enough to know that he was dying.
He would shout the words at his fifteen-year-old son, never quite clar-
ifying whether young Walter was the subject or the object of the verse.

Because, of course, he had long since acquired an understanding
of his only child's dark ways.

Yet any son born to that wicked old man would have been stamped
in his cradle as the devil's own. Walter's father had seen evil in everyone except himself, and he had taken great and obvious pleasure in
contemplating the torments of the damned.

He styled himself a man of God, a preacher, an apostle of the Word.
And from time to time, when he needed money, he would set up a
storefront church and scratch together a congregation. Then, after a
while, when nobody came anymore, the reverend would take to the
road again.

"Many are called, few are chosen," he would say.

And when his flocks disappointed him, which was often, in com-
pensation the shepherd would beat his son.

At last, in the extremity of his final illness, God's holy apostle ended up in the charity ward of the county hospital, just another emaciated old man lying under a thin blanket, waiting for death.

The year before, Walter had quit school and was working as an apprentice, helping to build yet one more strip mall. He lived in a boardinghouse and took a city bus to the construction site, and every evening he stopped off to see his father. His reasons had nothing to do with love or respect. Walter just wanted to see the old man die.

One night he arrived, just at sunset, and the nurse, who felt compassion for his youth and what she interpreted as his filial affection, took him aside and told him, "If you have anything you need to tell him before he goes, this is the time. He's stopped speaking. When he's conscious he seems to understand what you say to him, but he goes in and out. I don't give it more than another day before he slips into a coma."

So Walter sat down beside his father's bed, in that long room with its rows and rows of the dying, and he smiled when the apostle at last opened his eyes. He waited patiently until he was sure his dad recognized him.

"They tell me it won't be long before you go under for good and all," he said quietly. "Personally, I'll be sorry. I've enjoyed watching you die."

Yes, Daddy heard him. You could see it in his eyes.

"For years I've thought about killing you myself, but now I'm glad I didn't. I couldn't have made you suffer the way God has. It's what He does best."

His father's mouth opened, but nothing came out except a faint wheezing sound.

"You know, I never agreed with you about hell," Walter went on, his voice low and soothing, as if he were talking to a sick child. "I don't think it waits for us after death. I think it's here and now. So I guess you're safe. You'll just die, and crumble into unfeeling dust. God has punished you in this world.

"And you'd be wise to hope I'm right, because if anyone ever deserved the everlasting fire, it's you. God hates you, you old bastard. God hates us all, and He's right."

Hatred, Walter always believed, was the most durable of the emotions, the one dearest to God. And in that instant, at the very threshold of death, his father was consumed with hatred for his son. There was no room for anything else.

And that was just the way Walter wanted it.

"Your Bible is full of fairy tales," he said, smiling, stroking his father's hair with the tips of his fingers. "There is no redemption. There is only the horror He has created for us as our just punishment. I'm glad your death has been hard."

The nurse was wrong, and the apostle hung on a little longer. A second evening, and then a third, he was alert enough to understand everything his son had to tell him.

"You remember the girl who said I tried to rape her? You thought she was lying—or maybe just hoped it. She was telling the truth. And I've done worse since, much worse. I've taken life, just like God. And I'll go on doing God's work for Him. Maybe that way I'll become like God Himself and inherit from Him the curse of immortality. What do you think?

"'And in those days men shall seek death, and shall not find it; and shall desire to die, and death shall flee from them.' What do you think, Daddy? Was the prophet talking about me?"

Finally, on the fourth evening, he came and was told that his father was in a coma. His heartbeat was erratic, and they didn't expect him to last more than a few more hours.

Walter sat beside his bed, watching and waiting. And at two-seventeen in the morning the apostle breathed his last. Walter waited until he was sure his father's heart had stopped, then he got up and left, without a word to anyone.

Now, whenever he thought of God, he imagined Him with his father's face.

". . .because he knoweth that he hath but a short time."

18

At four in the morning Ellen found herself broad awake. She was in Tregear's bed and he was asleep beside her. The light from the street lamps filtered vaguely in through the bedroom blinds. She could just make out the curve of his back and she was filled with longing.

Yet what had awakened her was not lust but guilt. She felt she had betrayed him.

Either him or the department—she couldn't be true to both. So she had been a good cop. She had eaten dinner with Tregear, made love to him, and never told him that she knew where Walter was working.

It hadn't been a question of knowledge but of faith. Tregear knew more about this murderer than anyone living. He was probably the one human being on earth who would know Walter on sight. He understood his habits and his methods. If he said Walter would know if they sent a cop to his office, he was probably right.

He had been right about the secretary. Before leaving the Marriott, Ellen had looked up Allied Heating and Cooling in the yellow pages and given them a call. She had pretended to be a housewife with a furnace that wouldn't light and had had a brief conversation with the woman who answered the phone. Her voice sounded middle-aged, but there was a kind of brassiness to it that somehow managed to suggest that when her workday was over she would be going home to an empty space.

Maybe that was part of Walter's pattern, to pick a business where he knew he could win over the secretary. *To women he's like catnip.*

But she was loyal to procedure. Sam was right. A cop lives and dies by the rules because a cop serves the law.

Still, if they played by the rules Walter might disappear. And, eventually, Tregear would follow him. She wasn't sure she could bear that.

All at once Tregear began to stir. He rolled over and opened his eyes. He was smiling at her.

"Can't you sleep?" he asked. Under the covers, he touched her belly with the tips of his fingers. "Are you all right?"

"I'm all right. Let's get up and take a shower together."

It was an interesting experience to have a man put his arms behind your knees and just slide you up the tile wall like you weighed nothing. And to be all covered with soap and have that man enter you while he held you helpless was deeply stirring.

The shower lasted about forty-five minutes, and when they came out they were both really clean.

If it wasn't love, it would do. And she sensed it was love—at least for her.

Last night in bed, while her conscience was troubling her about her little secret, she had asked if it bothered him that she was a cop. He thought this was very funny.

"You're the only kind of lady friend I can have," he had said. "One who carries a nine-millimeter and knows how to use it."

After their shower together, they toweled each other off and went downstairs naked to have breakfast. Breakfast, it seemed, was the only meal Tregear knew how to make from scratch. For the rest, he ate out or lived on prepared food.

"I should make you dinner sometime," she said, as she sat at the kitchen table and watched him scramble eggs. "I'm not a bad cook. It's the only one of the feminine arts I've ever mastered."

"The *only* one? Making love doesn't count?"

He laughed at his own joke, but Ellen was already thinking of something else.

"I've been holding out on you." She shook her head. She hadn't meant to tell him, but now she couldn't help herself.

"What? You've got a husband and six kids?"

"No. I know where Walter is working."

He had his back to her as he was facing the stove. There was an almost imperceptible change in the slant of his shoulders, but no other sign that he had heard her. He went right on stirring the eggs.

For perhaps a minute he said nothing.

"Do you hate me for it?" she asked finally, desperate to hear his voice, even if he cursed her.

"No, I don't hate you," he answered, still keeping his back to her. "I'm not angry or even disappointed. You were doing your job."

He turned around, holding his egg pan in one hand and a spatula in the other, and smiled at her. Then he began to shovel eggs onto the two plates he had set out on the table.

"I'll tell you if you ask me to. Do you want me to tell you?"

When he was finished serving breakfast, he put the egg pan and spatula in the sink. Then he came to the table, kissed her and sat down.

"I'm not sure," he said. "If you tell me, and I use it, I'll have destroyed your career."

"And if you don't, Walter will get away and the body count will keep going up."

"Yes, it will." He hadn't touched his eggs yet. He seemed to have forgotten they were there. "I'm wondering if we can't work out a compromise."

Then he turned his attention to breakfast.

"Eat your eggs," he commanded, pointing to her plate with his fork. "They'll get cold."

They both ate in silence and when they were both finished, Tregear picked up the plates and carried them over to his sink.

"What kind of a compromise?" Ellen asked.

"I don't know."

He brought over their tea. Tregear used two bags of Irish Breakfast in each mug and he thought tea should be allowed to steep until it was the approximate color of molasses. It was dreadful stuff, almost as bad as police station coffee.

"You checked with the apartment managers?" he asked, sitting down. "You found out from them?"

"Yes."

"But you haven't filed your report yet?"

"No."

"When would you normally do that?"

"This morning, first thing."

"Then I'd have found out anyway. This morning, second thing. But I'm glad you at least told me you knew."

"What will you do?"

"You mean, how will I get inside their system?"

"Yes."

"I'll send them an e-mail with a little something attached. It's a code of my own devising that none of the commercial antivirus companies know anything about. They'll open the e-mail because it'll look like a service request, and the code will install itself. I'll know in about two minutes if I've scored, when it starts downloading their database files."

"And they'll never know?"

"They'll never know."

"And what will you do when *you* know?"

"I'll send you an e-mail with his name and address."

"That's it? No vigilante stuff?"

Tregear smiled and reached across the table to touch her naked breast with his index finger.

"I swear, by your right nipple, I won't get involved."

Suddenly both of them were laughing.

• • •

"Mercy me, you certainly look chipper this morning."

It was eight-fifteen and Sam had just come into the duty room with two cups of coffee, one of which he set on Ellen's desk. He sat down on the chair he was currently torturing and shook his head.

"And how was your date with Mr. Tregear last night?"

Ellen hit the "enter" key on her computer, which sent the report on her inquiries yesterday into the department database. Tregear would be reading it in five minutes.

"Sam, you're a dirty old man. By the way, I have the name of the company our very own Walter has been working for. Their office is on Gaven Street. What do you say we go roust them."

• • •

One hundred sixty-four Gaven Street was just a block south of the Embarcadero. It was in a warehouse district, utterly without charm. Allied Heating and Cooling was on the second floor, above a tile store.

The door was locked, but after Sam rapped on the glass a few times a woman came to answer. She was about forty, with short brown hair and too much makeup, and her voice belonged to the woman Ellen had talked to on the phone.

Sam showed his badge, and the temperature in the room dropped about twenty degrees.

"What do you want?" she asked.

"We want to look at your employment records," Sam told her, in his coldest interrogation voice. "It's in connection with a police inquiry." He pushed the door closed behind them.

"Well, the boss isn't in, and I can't authorize you to go pawing through our files."

She was stalling and she was nervous. Standing there, in the middle of that cluttered, ugly little room, she kept rubbing the heel of her left hand against her hip.

"Are you going to make me get a search warrant?" he asked her. "Because, if you do, we'll all have to sit here for a couple of hours until it arrives, and I bore easily. I'll probably start looking around. I won't be able to help myself. And I'll probably end up calling in the fire marshal and he'll probably find a dozen violations of code, which will probably force him to shut you down. Will that fill your boss's soul with joy? What do you think?"

"Go ahead. Do what you want—you will anyway."

She wasn't happy. She glared at Sam as if she hated him, and she probably did.

"I appreciate your reasonable and civic-minded attitude," Sam told her, sounding like he was addressing a Girl Scout troop. Then he nodded at Ellen. "Inspector Ridley will now spend a little time on your computer."

At that precise moment, Ellen's cell phone emitted a few musical notes and the screen lit up. She had a text message.

There are only four employees: the owner, someone else with the same last name, so probably a relative, the secretary, and a Walter Stride, hired five months ago. His address is 212 Quarry Road, Half Moon Bay. His cell phone number is 415-555-0123. I am putting a trace on it now. Can you come back tonight?

Nevertheless, she went through the motions. She spent twenty minutes pretending to find Walter Stride's personnel file. Then she announced, "He's not here. There's nothing about a Juan Carrasco."

Sam, bless him, never missed a beat.

"Then I can only apologize to you, ma'am, for wasting your time." He actually made a little bow to the secretary. "Have a good day."

On the way down the stairs, he put his hand on Ellen's shoulder, as if to arrest her flight.

"Who the hell is Juan Carrasco, you clever girl?"

"A character in a movie. I didn't want her to—"

"I know damn well what you didn't want her to do. You know, it occurred to me in there that Tregear was probably right about her." They had already reached their car before he asked the really important question. "Did you find Walter?"

"Yes. But here's the part you won't like. He's outside our jurisdiction."

"Where?"

"Half Moon Bay."

"Oh shit!"

. . .

Mary Plant had worked for Allied Heating and Cooling for six years, ever since her divorce, when she discovered she couldn't live on her alimony checks. It was not a wonderful job. The pay was only slightly better than a waitress's, and Herb, the owner, was unhappily married and liked to grope her. She had pretty much concluded that this was all life would ever hold for her—a job that just allowed her to pay the rent on a walkup studio apartment, purchased at the price of her self-respect. Then Walter had come into the office.

Walter was so sweet, so tender. For a woman whose sex life had been restricted to Herb fondling her tits and her husband, an alcoholic with no imagination who had quickly made their marriage into a dirty joke, Walter was little short of a revelation. They had hit it off at once. Then he started taking her to lunch. Soon he was a regular visitor to her walkup, where he treated her body with a kind of reverence. With him, and for the first time in her life, she felt no shame. Oh, the things they got up to!

And Walter was like her, one of the world's victims.

"I did five years for a robbery. I was nineteen and stupid. When they let me out the only job I could get was in a car wash. Everybody's got a right to a second chance, and I had to have a fresh start. So I jumped parole and created a new identity for myself. Stride was my mother's maiden name. But they never give up. They've hounded me for twenty-five years. And if they ever catch me they'll put me inside until I'm old and gray and good for nothing. I'm telling you this because I trust you."

"And if they ever come to the office, I'll warn you. Walter, I love you. I'd die if I thought I'd never feel your hands on me again. If you have to run, we'll run together."

Maybe this thing today was nothing. Probably it was nothing. The cops were looking for someone else. Mary tried hard to convince herself they were telling the truth, because if Walter had to disappear he might go all noble and it was possible she would never see him again. She wouldn't know how to bear that.

It was the slack season. Summer was coming, but in San Francisco nobody worried very much about air-conditioning. Mary had lots of time to think.

It wasn't nothing. The cops had lied. Well, maybe they had lied. She couldn't take the chance. She couldn't live with herself if she let Walter die in prison.

She ate lunch at her desk, and over her tuna sandwich she decided she had better phone.

. . .

"You have no idea what a protocol mess this is," Sam had told her as they drove back to the department. "Half Moon Bay is just a wide spot in the road, but they'll feel insulted if the request is made by anybody below the rank of captain. And their idea of police work is traffic and the drunks on Saturday night.

"If Walter lived in the Mission District, I'd send a SWAT team. My sense is he's not the type to come quietly. Does Half Moon Bay even have SWAT? They'll have to borrow, and that means more delay."

"But we have to get rolling on this," Ellen said. She knew she was stating the obvious and it bothered her that she sounded like she was pleading. But she was pleading. She kept remembering what Tregear had said: *If you muff it, he'll vanish like a ghost.* Had they already muffed it? *To women he's like catnip.* Was that secretary already on the phone to Walter?

Sam nodded, as if he could read her mind.

"Never fear. Captain Jacobs was my shift commander when I was a rookie. I'll talk to him the minute we get back.

"What about the lieutenant?"

"To hell with Hempel."

19

Captain Roman de Lores of the Half Moon Bay Police Department received the call a few minutes after eleven in the morning. An arrest warrant would be faxed in two minutes. The suspect was wanted in connection with two, possibly three homicides in San Francisco. He was to be considered extremely dangerous. Captain de Lores scribbled down the address and waited for the fax. Then he had to decide what to do.

This was precisely the sort of mess he had come to Half Moon Bay to escape. De Lores had been seven years on the San Francisco force and had worked his way up to inspector. By then his marriage was in deep trouble and, when he and his wife went into counseling, the therapist had told him that the stress of his job was the problem. He knew instantly that the diagnosis was correct, so he quit. He had tried running a security service for a while, but that had gone nowhere, and then he accepted the job in Half Moon Bay, where he had grown up. It was a quiet little town, a fishing village with a fair amount of tourist trade, and the work was restful. A big case was some kid's stolen iPod. In his ten years there had been exactly two murders, both of which were cleared up within twenty-four hours.

He didn't need this. He didn't want any part of it. But the arrest had to be made.

His own force was hopelessly inadequate. He knew that. None of them had ever gone up against somebody like this. Captain Jacobs had put him on the phone with the sergeant who was working the case, and he had recommended SWAT. The closest SWAT team was in San Mateo. Captain de Lores made the call.

. . .

"I think we should be there."

Ellen was having a lot of trouble paying attention to her reports. The computer screen kept blurring in front of her eyes.

"We can't. We'd be visiting firemen. Our presence would be resented."

Then Sam suddenly raised his head. Pythagoras had probably looked like that when he discovered his theorem.

"On the other hand, we could just go out to Half Moon Bay and play tourist. We could have crab salad for lunch."

"Now you're talking."

It was twenty-three minutes past noon, and they had barely reached Daly City, when Ellen's cell sounded its plaintive little tune to tell her she had a text message.

She tipped him. That was all it said.

Ellen stared at the screen for about fifteen seconds, feeling as if a sliver of ice were being forced through her heart. Then she closed the phone and put it in her pocket.

"Walter knows," she said finally. "That secretary phoned him."

Sam never glanced at her. Instead, he focused all his rage on the traffic.

"Tregear." He shook his head. "Goddamn him."

"You're mad at him because he was right? We should have listened to him."

"Maybe so."

It was probably a full minute before he spoke again.

"De Lores made inspector in four years, so he isn't stupid. He'll have a man watching the house. If Walter runs, they'll be all over him."

"If he's even home."

"That's right. If he's even home."

·   ·   ·

And he wasn't home. He was in a parking lot at a public beach a few miles down the coast, where he busily switched license plates with the car next to his van. That would do for a few days, but pretty soon he would have to get rid of the van. The police were way too close this time.

Walter knew how they had made him, of course. They were tracking the services calls. It was just surprising they had thought of that so quickly.

To be inconsistent was a point of pride with him. All of his little escapades were individual works of art, with no apparent connections among them. The whore in the hotel was just something that happened—on his day off Walter had gone into the Marriott to use the restroom, and one thing led to another. It had been an improvisation. The other two women had been carefully planned, but perhaps he was getting sloppy.

Still, the police shouldn't have made the connection with Allied this early.

Obviously he couldn't go back to the house, which was unfortunate. With a little more warning he would have burned the place to the ground, but now they would have his things. There would be fingerprints. Unless they were idiots, they would find a few traces of Sally Wilkes in the basement.

He wondered what they were doing. Had they gone inside yet, or did they just have the house staked out and were waiting for him to come back?

Well, there wasn't any good reason why he couldn't go have a look.

About a mile from his house there was a low hill, and behind it a dirt road that led from nowhere to nothing. It was an unwanted place, forgotten by everyone.

Walter parked his van at the side of the road and climbed up the hill. In his left hand he carried a very good pair of field glasses. As he approached the crest of the hill, he got down on his hands and knees. He found a spot where he would be concealed by some brush and lay flat to watch the show.

· · ·

Except there was no show. At least, not yet.

An unmarked police car waited on Highway 92, about a quarter of a mile from the entrance to Quarry Road, which was a dead end. Regular patrol cars were in town, looking for Walter Stride's van. As soon as anybody saw him, SWAT would move in.

In the meantime there was nothing to do except wait, which meant that Sam got his crab salad for lunch.

They sat outdoors at a round table. Ellen was playing with her iced tea, stirring it relentlessly with her straw. She couldn't think about food.

"Steve should be out here," she said finally.

Sam put his fork down and stared at his salad as if bidding it farewell.

"He's really gotten to you, hasn't he."

"Yes, he's really gotten to me. But he should be out here anyway."

"He's a civilian."

This seemed to strike Ellen as funny, or preposterous, or both.

"Walter is gone. He's probably fifty miles from here, driving a car that won't be reported stolen until tomorrow, when he'll be in New Mexico, or Oklahoma or God knows where."

"We don't know that."

"Oh yes, we do. Steve did a triangulation on his cell phone. It hasn't moved in an hour, which means that Walter dumped it. It's within a hundred yards of where we're sitting. Day after tomorrow somebody will probably find it in a litter basket. He's gone."

"We have to be sure. In three hours, if he hasn't turned up, SWAT will move on the house."

"Then promise me that when the house is clear, we fetch Steve. He should walk the grid with us when we do the place. He'll see things we'll miss."

"Okay. But babysit him. He gets to look, but that's all."

"Agreed."

Sam studied her face for a moment and then shrugged and went back to his salad.

"I wouldn't have thought he was your type," he said, without looking up. "I thought your tastes ran to college boys with three degrees and all the right friends."

"That's my mother," Ellen answered, amused in spite of herself.

"Are you going to take him home to the folks? I'd love to see that."

"We haven't gotten that far yet."

Ellen took a sip of her tea and looked around at the other patrons. She was embarrassed, although she wasn't sure why. If she had a friend in this world, it was Sam.

And then it occurred to her that she was embarrassed by the idea of bringing Steve for a cozy family dinner in Atherton.

Why was that? Probably because he hadn't graduated from the

right sort of school—or any school, for that matter. Because her mother would make snide little asides and check to see if he had axle grease under his fingernails.

Her father's perspective would be a little broader, since there had already been one plebian in his family.

"My grandfather's baby sister married beneath her," he had told her once. "My great-uncle Johnny never got past the fifth grade. He grew up during the Depression, and his father died when he was ten, so he had to go to work.

"I got to know him while I was in high school. He had been plant manager for a peanut butter company, of all things, but he was retired by then. He was a clever man, a machinist. If something broke down, Johnny could fix it. He and my great-aunt lived in Alameda, in a house he had built himself—and I mean all by himself. He had bought the lot cheap and within a year he had the house up, well built and beautifully designed.

"He and Mid—my great-aunt's name was Mildred, but everyone called her Mid—took a cruise when they were both in their seventies. To Panama. Johnny was crazy to see the canal. He wanted to see how they managed the locks.

"That was what interested him, how things worked. He was not a philosopher, but he liked to read history and he had a point of view: 'What did the Renaissance achieve, except to give some aristocrats a pretty place to go to church? But the Industrial Revolution, which was about machines, changed everything for everybody. The common man now lives in a state of physical comfort medieval kings would have envied.'

"And he wasn't boasting. He simply understood that men like him had remade the world.

"And Mid was a happy woman. She knew she had hit the jackpot. Johnny was a lovely man, one of nature's aristocrats."

So was Steve. He was a working-class waif and a high school dropout. He was also brilliant. He could solve any puzzle. The Navy thought he was a national treasure. There were books on his shelves in three foreign languages.

To hell with her mother, she decided. When she got the chance, she would take him home. It would be fun.

"Would you like to know just how far we *have* gotten?" she asked suddenly, without knowing quite why. Perhaps she just wanted to confess.

"Oh, that's apparent." Sam laughed.

When Sam had finished his salad, they went to an art gallery and admired the seascapes. After two hours of this, they were rescued by Sam's cell phone.

He listened for a moment and then answered, "No. We're here. We've been enjoying the local cuisine. We can be there in five minutes."

He folded up his phone and announced, "SWAT is ready to clear the house."

All through the drive, Ellen kept thinking about Tregear's story of his grandparents' murder, of how the house had been booby-trapped. When she mentioned it to Sam, he just shook his head.

"They know Walter has used explosives. They've probably brought their dogs with them." He grinned. "Nevertheless, we'll wait outside until they're finished."

"Can I phone Steve?"

"Sure."

By the time they arrived at 212 Quarry Road, which was about as isolated a spot as one could imagine, SWAT was already inside the house. And, yes, they had brought dogs.

Sam and Ellen went over to wait with Captain de Lores.

After about ten minutes the SWAT team started coming back out through the front door, their helmets peeled off and their gun barrels down. The house was clear.

"Nobody home," the SWAT commander announced, smiling wearily. "I'm always a little disappointed when we don't get the bad guy."

"So am I," Sam agreed, with a perfectly straight face. "Think of the money you might have saved the taxpayers."

Everyone laughed appreciatively.

"Well," he said to Ellen, "shall we go in for a look?"

The house had two stories. There was a kitchen and living room downstairs and two bedrooms upstairs. One of the bedrooms was just an empty space. The rest of the place was furnished sparsely, but everything was very tidy. Walter seemed to be the sort who made his bed every morning. He might have been anyone, living his ordinary life.

The basement was something else again.

It wasn't very large, maybe twenty by twenty. There was a small furnace in one corner. The center of the room was occupied by a rough wooden table, with large iron hooks at either end and pieces of rope dangling from them. There were bloodstains on the ropes and on the table itself, which rested on a green plastic drop cloth.

"One supposes this is where Sally Wilkes got dissected," Sam said, collectedly as his eyes roamed over the table. "Forensics is going to be very busy down here."

"God, it's like a medieval dungeon."

Sam was already squatting down, examining the table from underneath.

"It's well built," he said. "If you sanded it a little, you could put it in your living room. I don't suppose he'd let this thing just sit here for the next tenant to discover. He probably planned to take it apart and burn it. The drop cloth suggests he wasn't interested in leaving any traces."

"Do you think he might have built a new one every place he went?"

"Probably."

"Jesus."

They went back outside, where Captain de Lores was waiting.

"With your permission," Sam told him, "I'd like to bring our people down here to do the evidence. Our suspect isn't going to show his face again in your jurisdiction—or mine either, for that matter. It would just be administratively easier if everything was in one place."

"And your people have more experience with this sort of thing." The captain nodded. He wasn't feeling slighted. He was merely stating a fact. "Okay then, call them in."

The two men shook hands and Captain de Lores got in his squad car and drove away, leaving Sam and Ellen alone with their crime scene.

Twenty minutes later, Tregear showed up. He got out of his car, a gray Subaru with a scratch on the right front fender, and shook hands with Sam. He smiled at Ellen.

"He's gone." That was all he said.

"We fucked up. You were right." Sam wasn't enjoying the taste of defeat.

"You couldn't help it," Tregear told him. "You had to do this a certain way. You didn't have a choice. But you got closer to him than anybody I know about." He pointed to the house with his chin. "What's inside?"

"A bachelor's pad, standing on top of a chamber of horrors."

"Let's go look."

. . .

Walter enjoyed watching the SWAT team and wished there had been time to arrange a more suitable welcome for them. He particularly liked the dogs—as if they would have made any difference. Then he watched SWAT leave, and then the Half Moon Bay Police.

Then a gray car drove up and a man got out. He was wearing a pair of tan trousers and a light blue T-shirt, so he wasn't official.

Walter knew it was Steve, his son, almost the moment he first saw him. The man in the T-shirt had his father's hair, without the gray, and he wore his watch on the right wrist. But it was the way he walked that made Walter's heart stop. Steve had always been a graceful boy. He could make a stroll down a country road look like a dance number.

Walter knew it was Steve even before he turned his head and showed his face.

Of course. All the thick-skulled cops in the world would never have found him by themselves. Steve was hunting him. Still.

His son was the one person in the world he was afraid of. Walter had known, from the day the kid had run away from home, maybe even from before, that Steve wasn't going to leave it alone and get on with his life. One day, Steve was going to settle accounts.

He knew that Steve had opened his mother's suitcase. In hindsight, Walter couldn't understand why he had kept the thing all those years, but he had. Probably he was just sentimental by nature. And the kid had got the suitcase open.

Clever little bastard. Walter couldn't help a feeling of pride in his son's ingenuity. Twelve years old. And he hadn't picked the lock—a kid that age would have left scratch marks all over the thing—which meant that somehow he had gotten hold of a key. How the hell had he ever managed it?

But the fact was, he had been inside the suitcase. He had seen his mother's stuff and had drawn the obvious conclusion.

Then he had found that bitch's corpse in the van, and away he went.

In a way, Walter blamed himself. If he hadn't come home stewed he would have remembered to lock the garage and Steve never would have known the difference. But that filthy whore had upset him. She had died hard, shouting and cursing, and she wouldn't shut up no matter how hard he hit her. They were in the parking lot behind a bar and he got scared someone might come out and find them, so he wrapped her up in a tarp and sailed on out of there. His nerves had needed a little soothing.

But the business with Steve had been a lesson to him. After that he kept off the hard stuff.

When the boy ran off, Walter hadn't bothered with much of a search. How long could a twelve-year-old survive on his own? The cops would pick him up, or some pederast would leave him dead somewhere.

But he had survived, and he had found his grandparents. It was almost an accident that Walter had discovered him. He was in the neighborhood, and on the off chance. . .

But Steve seemed to have a talent for survival.

And then eight or nine years passed and Walter was working in Maryland. He had gotten off work early one afternoon and was enjoying a beer in some cozy little dive, minding his own business. He was seated near the window, observing the rich spectacle of life, when out of nowhere appeared his baby boy.

It was the purest chance. He happened to be facing west and a figure moving in that same direction, walking on the other side of the street, almost seemed to sneak right past him. In an instant he was no more than an outline, striding into the sun. But there was something about the way he moved that drew the eye . . .

And then it dawned on him. Steve. It simply couldn't be anybody else. So Walter had followed him until his son disappeared into a hotel.

An hour later, Walter called. "'Scuse me," he said, in his best downhome accent. "This is the lost and found at the railway station. Somebody left an envelope full of stuff in the men's room—paper'n like. Looks like the kinda stuff he'd prob'ly want back. They's a reservation slip for y'r place in the name o' Stephen . . . I can't quite make it out. You had any Stephens in the last hour 'r so?"

"Yes, one. A Stephen Rayne. You want me to put you through to his room?"

"Oh, wait a minute. Somebody just passed me a note. Yes. He called just a minute ago. Problem solved, darlin'. Thank you."

Stephen Rayne. Walter had dropped Rayne as soon as he got out of Arkansas, which was the evening of the day after Steve ran away.

By the grace of God, Walter had caught up with him again in Maryland, but some other guy had come through that hotel room door and died in his place.

Afterward, he hung around just long enough to find out what had been going on. At first, the police had thought Steve killed that sailor boy—the local newspaper had been full of it. But, reading between the lines of that idiot cop Hill's statements, it was clear Steve had come to him with information and been dismissed as a nut job.

And then, suddenly, Stephen Rayne just vanished from the news. The police didn't like him anymore as a suspect. It was as if someone had told them to forget all about it.

It had happened a couple of other times that Walter had had to pack up and move out a little earlier than planned. Today was the closest the law had ever been, but there had been a few other near misses. They were getting help. Someone was telling them about all his little ways, someone who really understood how he worked, even how he thought.

It couldn't be anyone but Steve. The police just weren't that clever, and they were local. Someone was tracking him from state to state. Who else but his own sweet son?

And in all that time Walter had never been able to find his pursuer. Not since Maryland. Steve was like a mirage. You saw him, but he wasn't there. You ran to catch him and he disappeared. Steve was the ghost of his sins, a black shape haunting his dreams.

And now Walter had found him again, had seen him in the flesh. And, once more, he was just a man after all.

Sometimes, with His perverse sense of humor, God answers our prayers.

20

Inside the house, Tregear displayed no emotion. It occurred to Ellen that they might as well have been strolling through a museum.

Upstairs he pointed to the made bed. "He always did that, every morning. He must have had a strict upbringing. Even I'll leave a bed unmade."

In the bathroom he used his pen to open the medicine chest. He pointed to a squat orange container, the kind in which pharmacies dispense their pills.

"Percocet, sixty hundred fifty milligrams. He must be hurting because that's the highest dose. When you get the doctor's name off the bottle, he should have an interesting story to tell.

"There'll be fingerprints all over the place, and you'll be able to get hair samples out of the shower drain." He glanced at Ellen and smiled. "You'll know a lot about him before you're done."

The kitchen had a pantry. Tregear opened it and read the labels.

"Same stuff," he announced. "Wheat Chex for breakfast, cream of tomato soup, Ritz crackers, English Breakfast tea. If you look in the refrigerator you'll find a carton of jumbo eggs and a six-pack of Coors beer. I'll bet there's a half gallon of chocolate ripple ice cream in the freezer."

Ellen used a dish towel to open the refrigerator.

"A perfect score," she said.

Tregear nodded, suggesting there had never been any doubt, then turned his attention to the sink. "You'll notice there aren't any dirty dishes," he said, almost as if the observation gave him some sort of pleasure. "They're all washed and put away. Walter hates dirty dishes."

The kitchen was just large enough for a table and one chair. There was a stack of newspapers beside the chair, and one on the table, open to page four. There was a two-column story on the Sally Wilkes murder.

"Walter has been reading his reviews."

"Do you want to see the basement?" Ellen asked.

"No." Tregear shook his head. "I think I'll spare myself that—I'll wait for the photos. I think I'm done here."

They went outside, where the Evidence people were unpacking their truck. Tregear looked at his watch.

"It's four-fifteen, and it's been a long day," he said. "Why don't you come home with me."

"Better yet, come to my place and I'll make you dinner."

. . .

On the drive back to San Francisco, Tregear apparently didn't feel like talking. He switched on the car radio and hit the CD button, and the interior space was suddenly flooded with Bach organ music. It was a little like attending a funeral.

As directed, Tregear parked in front of the hardware store and they climbed the stairs to her apartment. Once inside, Ellen disappeared into the kitchen, where she uncorked a bottle of domestic Pinot Grigio ($8.99 a bottle).

When she came back out, she found Tregear standing in front of Gwendolyn's cage. She handed him a glass and he took a sip.

"Your friend and I have been sizing each other up," he said matter-of-factly. "I gather he's not accustomed to strangers."

"*He* is a *she*." Ellen opened the cage door. "Gwendolyn, come and meet the nice man."

Gwendolyn used Ellen's right arm as a walkway and then settled on her left shoulder, which was farther from Tregear, whom she regarded with evident suspicion.

"She's interested," Ellen said quietly. "She's curious. Let's try something."

Ellen let her right hand rest on Tregear's shoulder. Gwendolyn seemed to consider this new situation and then changed her own position over to Ellen's right shoulder. Then, after about a minute, she started making her way stealthily along Ellen's arm. When she reached Tregear's shoulder, she looked back at Ellen, who then took her hand away.

"It appears you've made a new friend," she said.

Gwendolyn began investigating Tregear's hair, as if testing it for footholds.

They sat down on the sofa and drank their wine. Gwendolyn was still on Tregear's shoulder, although he seemed not to notice her.

"So how long have you had him—*her?*" he asked, setting his glass down on the table in front of them. "How long have you had her?"

"About seven years." Ellen reached over and gathered Gwendolyn up. "I was vacationing at Lake Tahoe and saw her in a pet store window in Carson City. I went in, put my hand inside the cage to pet her and she climbed right up my arm. Sometimes I think she picked me rather than the other way around. She was just a baby then."

Tregear smiled and began to say something, but the words seemed to catch in his throat. His expression was suddenly odd, as if he couldn't understand what was happening to him, and then he buried his face in his hands and began to sob.

It was the most pathetic sound Ellen could remember hearing, a mingling of grief and fear for which there was no comfort. She knelt on the sofa beside him and put her arms around his shoulders. There was nothing more she could do. No words were adequate. Words would have to wait until the spasm passed.

And it did. After three or four minutes he took a handkerchief out of his trousers pocket and wiped his face. His hands were still trembling.

"Sorry about that," he said. "Where's the bathroom?"

Ellen made a vague gesture down the hall, and after a few seconds she could hear water running.

When he came back again, it was as if the whole episode had never happened.

"What would you like for dinner?" she asked him, simply to be able to say something.

"Anything. Whatever."

"How about leftover lasagna? Gwendolyn doesn't like lasagna, so she won't make a pest of herself."

"Perfect."

By the time the lasagna was ready, their wineglasses needed refilling. Ellen kept moving back and forth between the kitchen and the

living room because she sensed that Tregear wasn't ready to talk. They
ate in silence, balancing the plates on their laps.

"Would you like something for dessert?" she asked. "I have ice
cream."

But Tregear seemed not to have heard her.

"We lost him, Ellie," he said. "We'll never have another chance like
this one."

Ellen shook her head and sat down beside him.

"We'll have his fingerprints, and his DNA. We'll be able to tie him
to the Wilkes murder. If he sticks his head up again, we'll have enough
to put him on death row."

"That's the problem. He'll learn caution from this episode. He'll
think it through and figure out how you found him. Then he'll change
his patterns."

"Maybe not." Ellen managed a cautious smile. "Serial killers are
usually pretty compulsive about method. Maybe he won't be able to
change."

Tregear took a deep, almost convulsive breath and then let it out
very slowly.

"You have to understand something, Ellie." He shook his head and
his eyes were full of pity, as if he were about to strip her of her last
illusion. "Most serial killers are in the grip of some sexual obsession.
The hunt is like foreplay. If they change the method they lose the thrill.
But with Walter this isn't about sex. It's about power, the power of
life and death. It's about being like God. And as God is capricious
and sudden, so is he. As God is cruel, so is he."

"Do you believe in God, Steve?"

She hadn't meant to ask the question. She couldn't imagine why she
had. But there it was. Tregear only smiled and shook his head again.

"No. But Walter does."

. . .

They didn't make love that night. Tregear seemed completely un-
manned. And they hardly slept. They just lay in bed, holding each
other, each the other's refuge against the world. And it occurred to
Ellen that she had never felt so close to any other human being.

"I'll have to be on my travels again," he said at one point. "When
he starts up in some other place, I'll have to follow."

"Do you think he knows you followed him here?"

"Yes. He doesn't know where to find me, and if we bumped into each other on the street I doubt if he would recognize me. But he knows I'm after him. I've got the Internet, but I'm no smarter than he is. He knows."

"I think you're the smartest man I've ever known."

"That's because you've never met Walter." Tregear laughed, but the laugh was cut short. "I hope you never do."

• • •

About a quarter to six the next morning, Tregear left Ellen asleep to get himself a glass of water in the kitchen. The apartment was laid out so that the only entrance to the kitchen was through the living room, where he found a strange woman asleep on the sofa.

As he wasn't wearing anything except his boxer shorts, Tregear decided to forget about the water and retreated back into the bedroom. By then Ellen was awake.

"There's somebody sleeping in your living room," he said, as if he couldn't imagine why anyone would be interested to know that.

"Oh, yes. That's Mindy. She was my college roommate and hasn't found an apartment yet. She works in the DA's office and she's between husbands—it's a long story."

Tregear nodded. "Perhaps I should get dressed."

"That's not a bad idea."

By six-thirty everyone was ready for breakfast. Mindy was sitting at the kitchen table, nursing a cup of coffee while Ellen made oatmeal with blueberries.

"So when did that happen?" Mindy asked, tilting her head toward the living room, where Tregear was renewing his acquaintance with Gwendolyn.

"The day before yesterday."

"A whirlwind romance?"

"You could say that."

Ellen kept her back to the table as she stirred the oatmeal with perhaps more intensity than was strictly required and experienced the absolute impossibility of explaining someone like Tregear.

"I thought you didn't much care for casual sex."

"There's nothing casual about it."

Ellen brought out a bowl of oatmeal for Tregear and placed it on the coffee table, since Tregear seemed to be deeply involved in playing with Gwendolyn. He made feinting movements with his hand, as if to grab her, and she was dancing back and forth on the sofa cushions in excitement.

"I haven't seen her do anything like that in a year," Ellen said. "I thought she was getting old, but maybe she was just bored. You seem to be good for her."

Tregear picked up the bowl of oatmeal, and Gwendolyn, sensing that the game was over, climbed onto his right shoulder and stared at Mindy accusingly.

Breakfast conversation stumbled along, with occasional compliments on the quality of the oatmeal and the odd, faintly probing question for Ellen's new beau.

"Have you lived in San Francisco long?"

"No. Only a few months."

"Do you work here in town?"

"I work for the Navy."

"Oh." Mindy took a moment to absorb the fact that Tregear said he worked *for* the Navy, which implied he was not *in* the Navy. "What do you do?"

"I create mysteries."

Tregear smiled in a way that suggested there wouldn't be any further explanations.

Finally Mindy decided it was time she adjourned to the bathroom.

"Will you come to my place tonight?" Tregear asked, as soon as he and Ellen were alone. "I promise I won't come unstuck again."

"Sure." She looked around her for a moment, as if measuring the room. "You know, if this is going to become a regular deal, maybe I should bring a change of clothes."

"That's a good idea, but maybe a better idea would be if you just moved in."

"It's a little early," she answered—and then immediately recognized that it was the wrong answer. "Would you like that?"

"Oh yes. I'd like it fine." And then his face darkened. "But it's probably a bad idea. We won't have a lot of time."

"Before you go on the hunt again?"

She smiled, just to let him know she understood. Events were not in their control.

"Well, if we don't have a lot of time maybe we should make the most of what we do have. If you like, I'll pack a suitcase tonight. Can I bring Gwendolyn?"

"By all means, bring Gwendolyn."

"Then can you give me a ride to work? I left my car in the police garage."

• • •

When she got to the department, she was greeted by a rare sight. Sam was in front of the computer.

"I can't use this goddamn thing," he said, without looking up from the screen. "They've been at it all night down in Half Moon Bay, and the data is coming in faster than I can get this fucking machine to show it to me. You take over."

"Only if you get me some coffee. I didn't sleep much last night."

There was the ghost of a smile on Sam's face, instantly suppressed.

"Steve was having a very bad time," she said. All at once it seemed desperately important to make Sam understand. "I think being inside that house wasn't easy for him."

"That doesn't come as much of a surprise."

"No. No, it doesn't."

They seemed to have exhausted the subject, so Ellen smiled and said, "Get out of my chair."

"Okay." Sam stood up. "I'll go around the corner for the coffee. Nobody's made any fresh here since yesterday."

"Good. Good plan."

By the time Sam came back and set a cup of Ralph's Finest Columbian on her desk, there was a blizzard of paper coming out of the printer.

"It's a bonanza," Ellen announced cheerfully. "They've got prints galore. Walter seems to be losing his hair, so the bathroom was full of it. They're bringing in blood samples from the basement. They think, but they're not sure, that it's from two individuals."

"Maybe Kathy Hudson died down there too."

"Maybe so." She smiled. It was such a pleasant subject. "And there's more. They found what they think is vomit in the bathroom. Walter is a clean freak, but he seems to have missed a spot around the back of the toilet bowl. I wonder what they can tell from that?"

"Maybe only that somebody threw up."

But Ellen seemed to have missed the joke entirely—possibly because she hadn't been listening.

"Steve showed me a bottle of pills in the medicine chest. Painkillers. I wonder what's wrong with him."

"Usually the prescribing physician's name is on the bottle. Or we can get it from the pharmacy."

"That's what Steve said."

For a moment Ellen was silent, staring at nothing. Then she looked up at Sam with the rigid intensity of a bird dog.

"I think we should work that angle," she said. "I think we should do that right now."

Sam nodded. "I'll phone and get somebody to hunt up the bottle."

In five minutes they had the name. Mark Fairburn, MD. In another two minutes they found him in the online edition of the California Medical Directory. There was a telephone number and an address in San Mateo.

When Sam phoned, he got the doctor's exchange. The lady who answered seemed annoyed.

"The office isn't open on Sunday," she announced, with considerable asperity.

"Then what's his home phone number? This is the San Francisco police."

"Sure."

"Lady, I'll bet you have a San Francisco phone book. Look up the number and ask for Sergeant Tyler in Homicide. I want to hear from you within the next two minutes. And when you call, give me the emergency number for the building."

They got their answer in a minute and a half. But no one was answering at the Fairburn residence.

"Jesus. Who isn't home at eight-thirty on a Sunday morning?"

"Some people go to church, Sam."

"Oh. Yeah."

At nine-thirty, Sam called again. The phone rang and rang, but nobody picked up.

Sam swept his hat from his desk.

"You want to take a drive?"

On the way Ellen phoned the building number. "Can you have someone there to open up Dr. Fairburn's office?"

"You'll find it open, lady. You're not the first to call."

Three-quarters of an hour later they were in the parking lot of a medical building on El Camino Real. When they went inside, of course Dr. Fairburn's door was locked.

The upper half of the door was frosted glass, but one could see shadows moving around inside. Sam rapped at the glass.

"Come on, open up," he muttered. "Come on."

He kept at it until someone came to the door.

It was one of those moments of species recognition. Nobody had to tell Ellen that the guy who opened the door was a cop.

"What are you doing here, Sam?"

The man was in his middle forties, heavily built and bored-looking. He held out his hand and Sam took it.

"We want to talk to the doc," he answered.

"Well, you're a little late. He went jogging last night and ran into a bullet."

"No kidding." And then Sam remembered his manners. "This is my partner, Ellen Ridley. Ellen, Pete Castaldi. We go back. Can we come inside, Pete?"

Rather than answer, Detective Castaldi simply moved out of the way.

"So what did you want to talk to him about?" Detective Castaldi seemed only mildly interested.

"We wanted to know why he's prescribing painkillers to our prime suspect in three homicides."

"So who's the suspect?"

Sam appeared to find the question amusing.

"Well, he's been a lot of different people. Yesterday his name was Walter Stride, but I imagine he's somebody else by now."

"Walter Stride." Castaldi wrote the name down in his notebook. "Well, we're going to have to go through all of the good doctor's records, on the off chance he was killed by a dissatisfied customer. I suppose we can start with Walter Stride. I'll let you know if we find anything."

"He'd probably stick with Walter, but he could have been using one of his other aliases. Look for somebody who became a patient within the last six months."

"You think your Walter may have killed Fairburn?"

"I think it would be an enormous coincidence if he didn't." Then he shook Castaldi's hand again. "We'll get out of your way, Pete. Nice to see you."

When they were back in the parking lot, Sam took off his hat and looked into it, his fingers moving along the inside of the band.

"You know, I think I'm getting senile," he said, putting his hat back on. "They put the patient's name on prescriptions and I forgot to have them check it when I phoned. Probably it doesn't matter anyway."

"Why wouldn't it matter? We can save those guys some work."

Sam just shook his head.

"They're not going to find Walter's records, under any name. He already had them when he killed the doctor. It's the only thing that makes any sense."

Ellen was mystified, and she must have looked it.

"Didn't Tregear say his father had worked as a locksmith? He came here last night, picked the lock and stole his file. Then he shot Fairburn. Why kill the doc when everything anybody would want to know is in his files? Do you see?"

Yes, Ellen saw.

"Then the question becomes . . ." She paused as the idea jelled in her mind. "The question is, what doesn't he want us to know?"

"That's my girl."

21

The lab was very busy. The blood samples from the basement were established to have come from two different individuals. A match with Sally Wilkes was made late that afternoon, but the second sample would take longer because it was more degraded. Hair samples from the suspect's bathroom were a DNA match with the semen found in Sally Wilkes.

The police had their case. They just didn't have Walter.

The secretary at Allied Heating and Cooling was their one tenuous link, so Sam phoned the owner, who gave him a Burrows Street address. They drove down and invited her to come back to the station for a conversation. Walter's cell phone had been found in Half Moon Bay, and the last call received had been from Allied. Thus it was made clear to Mary Plant that her refusal to cooperate would guarantee a charge of obstructing justice.

She was left in a holding room while Sam and the lieutenant debated the wisdom of letting Ellen conduct the interview.

"The current theory is that the secretary's got a letch for our suspect," Sam explained. "I think she'll be more likely to open up about it if she's talking to another woman."

"Ellen doesn't have the experience. I want you in there."

Hempel, who had never demonstrated any particular flair for interrogation, sat behind his desk with his arms crossed, apparently convinced that he had made his point.

"Come off it, Dave." Sam lit a Camel, suddenly filling the room with blue smoke. "She's never going to get any experience if we don't let her try. Besides, she's clever. She's the best choice."

Hemple, two beats behind as usual, suddenly looked suspicious.

"What makes you think the Plant woman was having it on

with . . ." He took a moment to consult the case file. ". . . Walter Stride, if that's his real name."

"It almost certainly isn't. Besides, I said it was a theory, not a proven fact. It appears to be the way Walter works."

"You seem to know an awful lot about this guy."

Sam managed a tight smile. He felt not the slightest temptation to let Dave Hempel in on the secret of Stephen Tregear's involvement.

"Intuition, Dave. A lifetime of police work. Now. Does Ellen conduct the interview? Otherwise I'll charge Mary Plant, and we'll end up with a lawyer in the room."

When Sam came out of the lieutenant's office, he smiled.

"She's all yours," he told Ellen. "Go get her. The tapes are running."

. . .

Ellen went into the holding room with a manila folder under her arm. She sat down across from Mary Plant and laid the folder on the table, and then seemed to forget its existence.

She smiled at Mary, as if to say, *No hard feelings because I understand.*

Then she was all business.

"Let me tell you how Walter Stride spends his spare time," she began. And then she laid out the case—the two homicides, the blood samples recovered from Walter's basement, the DNA evidence, the semen sample taken from Sally Wilkes' body.

By this time Mary was in tears. She seemed to find the semen evidence particularly hard to bear.

"Would you like to see the pictures of his victims?" Ellen asked, sounding like she was granting a favor. "Would you like to see what Walter does to women?"

Mary shook her head. By then she was sobbing convulsively.

But Ellen opened the manila folder and lined up the photographs so that they faced Mary Plant.

"Look at them," she said softly. "You need to look at them."

Ellen waited in sympathetic patience while Walter's girlfriend stared in horror at his handiwork.

After about one minute, Ellen put the photographs back in their folder. Then she offered Mary a box of tissues. She even offered to bring her some tea.

"No, thank you." Mary shook her head. Gradually she began to calm down.

"Look, Mrs. Plant—Mary—you have to understand your legal position. Walter got away because you warned him. He's still out there, walking around, sharpening his knives, getting ready for his next victim. We have you for obstruction of justice and as an accomplice after and, if he kills again, before the fact. We're talking about prison time here.

"But we really don't want you. We want Walter. He played you. From all accounts, he's an attractive man, and you're just human like the rest of us. He made you feel good, didn't he."

Mary nodded, as if the joints in her neck were stiff. She dabbed at her eyes, and it wasn't just for effect.

"Tell me about him," Ellen said. It was an invitation, from one woman to another, to confess her pain.

And that was what Mary did. At first she hardly mentioned Walter. She talked about her ex-husband and about the boss's hands. She talked about loneliness and the desperation that assails a woman by herself in the years after she turns forty.

And Ellen listened, making little agreeing noises the tape recorder never caught. Her job had never made her hard, and probably never would. She really did understand. She was not free from pity and the wish to comfort.

Finally Mary began to describe the first time she met Walter, what a handsome man he was and how sweet. At that moment, knowing the evil he had done, and that she had been betrayed yet again, she was still in love with him.

She told Ellen things she thought she would never tell anyone. She described what it felt like to have his hands on her, to know that someone could still want her and care about her.

In a world of sad stories, this was the one Ellen knew she would always remember.

And in the act of confession, Mary had accepted this policewoman as her friend. It was not the fear of prison that would move her, but the fact that at last one other person understood.

"There's something you can do for us," Ellen said at last. "We need a description. There are no photographs of Walter. He could walk into this building right now, and we wouldn't know him. He's faceless,

and that's his protection. We need to know what he looks like. Will
you help us?"

"Yes." That was all she said, just "Yes."

"We'll have someone in here in a few minutes," Ellen said, retreat-
ing into her identity as a cop. "He's called a sketch artist, although
they use a computer these days. He'll help you put together a likeness. Then you can go home."

"I hate doing this," Mary said.

"I know, but it has to be done."

           •   •   •

"That was masterful," Sam told her. He was almost obscenely pleased.
"That was goddamn good work."

Ellen really didn't want to be congratulated. She felt too much kin-
ship with Mary Plant to know any sense of triumph. After all, she
was in love with Walter's son.

"Promise me, Sam. Promise me that if the sketch artist gives us
something useful, Mary Plant walks."

"What does anybody care about Mary Plant? The prisons are over-
crowded as it is."

"Thanks, Sam."

It was four-fifteen. The sketch artist was already at work. There
was nothing to do except hook into his feed and watch Walter's face
come together on Ellen's computer screen.

Ellen wished she could go home. As of this morning, home was
now a high-end apartment near Fisherman's Wharf, where Walter's
son would pour her a glass of Pinot Grigio and listen to her troubles.

Probably Steve was watching the same feed, seeing his father's face
take shape. What must he feel?

           •   •   •

Almost as soon as she was out of police headquarters, Ellen's cell
phone rang. It was her father.

"Your mother and I are in town for a matinee. We wondered if
you might be free for dinner," he said.

Her first impulse was to beg off, but then she thought better of it.
It would be an interesting experiment.

In fact, she decided, it was a golden opportunity. The thing had to be done sometime or other, and perhaps it was better that the first shock took place in a restaurant rather than at home in Atherton.

"Can I bring someone?"

There was a slight hesitation, and then her father said, "Sure. A friend of yours?"

"You could call him that."

The only remaining question was, how did she present this to Steve?

They had been officially living together for only a few hours , but Tregear had given her a key to the front door. As soon as she was inside, she called his name and was greeted with a faint "I'm up here." She found him in his work room. Gwendolyn was standing on his shoulder, her front paws in his hair as she peered over his head. They were both staring at the image of Tregear's father on the computer screen.

"That's Walter," he said, without looking at her. "Older and heavier, but it's him. It's him to the life."

"Steve, I want to ask you a favor."

Tregear tapped a key and the image collapsed.

"Name it," he said. He seemed almost to be defying her to think of something he wouldn't do for her.

"Will you have dinner with my parents tonight?"

"Sure. Where?"

Father and daughter had settled on Tarantino's, a fish place on the Wharf. It was about a four-minute walk from Tregear's apartment and Daddy liked crab. It was also socially neutral, so Ellen wouldn't have to find out whether Steve knew which fork to use.

It was only on occasions such as these that she realized how inescapably she was still her mommy's girl.

"I just need to go back to my apartment for a few minutes to get some clothes," Ellen said.

• • •

Getting dressed was a revelation for both of them. Ellen had stopped by her apartment and picked up a black sleeveless dress and heels. It would be the first time Tregear had ever seen her in a dress, and this one fitted over her trim figure like a second skin. When she turned around she found him studying the change with obvious appreciation.

Then he cocked his head a little to one side and his eyes narrowed speculatively.

"You should wear that outfit with a pale gray shawl," he said. "Besides, it gets cold up here at night. There's a knit shop in the Cannery. Let's stop there on the way and see what we can find."

"Okay."

He himself wore a white turtleneck shirt and a silk sport coat of indefinable color. The effect was decidedly but effortlessly patrician. He had a couple of expensive items in his wardrobe, probably because there was little enough else for him to spend his money on, but there was no display about him. He seemed indifferent to effect, as if it never crossed his mind that anyone would notice his clothes.

You are a beautiful man, she said, nowhere but in her mind.

The shop in the Cannery had exactly the right shawl, a silk fishnet, almost iridescent. Tregear took it off a peg and draped it over Ellen's shoulders, his hands lingering briefly on her arms.

"You were right," she said, smiling at him in the full-length mirror. "It's perfect."

"You're perfect," he answered. "Now let's go eat."

Her parents had already arrived and were sitting at a table next to a window that opened out onto the Bay. Daddy was working on his customary predinner cocktail, and he stood up when he saw his daughter and her date approaching. Ellen made the introductions and the two men shook hands, Steve addressing her father as "Dr. Ridley."

Now how the hell did he know that? she wondered, but then she stopped wondering because she knew. By now he probably knew her great-grandmother's maiden name.

"And this is my mother."

Mrs. Ridley offered her hand and submitted to the briefest possible pressure from Steve's. For the moment at least, she seemed prepared to suspend judgment.

They sat down and the waiter came. Ellen decided to be extravagant and ordered a Pimm's Cup, complete with cucumber, and Steve waved the man away, saying he was fine.

Conversation got off to an awkward start. Daddy wanted to know about his little girl's new guy. "So what is it you do?"

"I work for the Navy," Tregear said, smiling as if the admission embarrassed him. "At least, they sign my paychecks. I don't know what I do to earn them."

"It's classified, Daddy. Steve is a security specialist."

Daddy seemed prepared to hear more, but his wife raised her eyebrows, which meant she had chalked up at least one black mark against the new beau, who was something technical—like the man who fixed your sprinkler system. Ellen decided to steer the conversation in some safer direction.

They talked about movies, and this drifted into a discussion of movies based on novels, and then somebody mentioned *Pride and Prejudice*, and the two men took up the question of which of the several movie versions would have been least offensive to Jane Austen. Ellen was content merely to listen because she sensed her father was having such a marvelous time.

Mrs. Ridley remained silent, apparently not even listening. It was one of her unconscious biases that intellectual conversation at dinner was vulgar.

"Laurence Olivier was the best Darcy," Dr. Ridley announced, "but the 1940 film was hopelessly sentimental. Jane Austen was never sentimental."

Steve pursed his lips slightly, suggesting that he was unconvinced.

"You wouldn't call *Persuasion* sentimental?" he asked, as if merely soliciting an opinion.

"No." Dr. Ridley shook his head, perhaps a little too vehemently. "*Persuasion* is romantic, which is not the same thing."

"I remember once hearing a definition of Romanticism as 'the struggle to maintain an illusioned view of life.' On that basis, aren't 'romantic' and 'sentimental' virtually synonymous?"

"That's an interesting definition. Where did you read it?"

Tregear merely shrugged. "I didn't say I read it. I said I heard it. I don't even remember where."

Dr. Ridley seemed disappointed, but he recovered quickly.

By the time dinner was served, they had achieved a wary truce about Jane Austen. The waiter brought Dr. Ridley his crab, along with a nutcracker to use on the claws. Mrs. Ridley had ordered sole, her habitual choice, and studiously avoided noticing her husband's careful dissection of the crab.

Ellen and Steve, refusing to take sides, had both ordered abalone steaks.

While they ate, Dr. Ridley described a seminar he had recently attended at UC Medical, which had been titled "The Neurology of Decision Making." A small discussion had arisen over the concept of free will, which the panel members had seemed to regard as tasteless and beside the point.

"What do you think, Steve? Is there such a thing as free will?"

It was less a question than a challenge, another move in the intellectual game, and Tregear smiled to show that he understood it as such.

"For me, and for most people, free will is doing what I want to do. By that reckoning the will is more or less free depending on the circumstances. But we don't choose what to want. We just want it, and then we build a belief structure to justify wanting it. Desire is a cause, and action is an effect. We aren't free of that. As Kant pointed out, experience isn't intelligible without the idea of cause and effect. So it becomes a question of definition."

"Like the definition of 'Romanticism'?"

"Something like that."

No one was interested in dessert, but Dr. Ridley wanted a cup of tea. When it came, Tregear pushed his chair back a little.

"I'll leave you three now," he said, standing up. "Ellie, I'm sure you'd like a little time alone with your parents, and I'm sure they would with you. I'll see you later."

The two men shook hands and mumbled the usual assurances about what a pleasure it had been. And then Tregear was gone.

"Well, that was abrupt," Mrs. Ridley said, virtually the first words she had uttered through the whole meal.

"But well meant." Ellen smiled. "Don't tell me you're not glad, or you'll hurt my feelings."

"I am glad." Dr. Ridley reached across and patted the back of his daughter's hand. "But only to have time with you."

"Then you liked him?"

"Yes. Far better than most of your boyfriends I've met. What was the name of that one you brought home from Berkeley? Marvin?"

"Melvin." She laughed at the recollection. "Melvin the Student Revolutionary. Steve isn't anything like that."

"Well, he's certainly better educated. Where did he go to school?"

"Circleville High." She paused, enjoying her mother's reaction— Mrs. Ridley was too shocked even to speak. "And he dropped out of that."

"I think you're pulling my leg, Ellie," her father said. "I don't believe you."

"Believe me. He's led a very strange life."

"Oh Ellie, who have you gotten yourself involved with now?" Mrs. Ridley, her face a mask of anguish, slowly shook her head. "Who doesn't go to college these days?"

Ellen reached across the table and took her mother's hand.

"I want you to understand, Mommy," she said. "I really do. But there are things I can't tell you. Suffice it to say that, for reasons outside of his control, the usual opportunities were closed to him. And now it doesn't make any difference."

"How can't it make any difference?"

Mrs. Ridley was exasperated, as if her daughter were talking gibberish.

"Mommy, why do most people go to college?" Ellen smiled, still holding her mother's hand. This once, she thought, it was important to make herself understood. "They do it to prove something—how smart they are or how much they know. But Steve doesn't have to prove anything. He doesn't need any mentors. He's taught himself everything from ancient Greek to string theory. He probably thinks that universities are for the lame and the halt.

"He doesn't fit into the familiar categories, Mommy. He's beyond any category. He's a very unusual man."

"But then is he . . . ?" Mrs. Ridley gasped.

"Normal? No." Ellen shook her head. "Brilliant, considerate, sweet-natured, yes. Interesting? Oh yes. But never normal."

Mrs. Ridley said nothing, merely shook her head and looked worried. She understood what Ellen was saying, but it frightened her. How could a man who was beyond any category be good for her daughter?

"What does he really do for the Navy?" her father asked.

Ellen allowed herself a syllable of laughter. "All I know is that it has to do with codes, Daddy. And if I knew more than that, they'd probably lock me up as a security risk. The Navy seems to regard him as some sort of secret weapon."

"Well, I rather like him," Dr. Ridley announced. "If fact, I like him very much. I'd like to know him better. Do you think I'll get the chance?"

"I don't know, Daddy. It isn't up to him and me."

22

When he broke into Dr. Fairburn's office, Walter had had the presence of mind to look around for some Percocet. By then he hadn't taken a pill in about eight hours and he was in a lot of pain. He found a locked cabinet, which seemed a likely possibility, and had it open in about ten seconds. It was a junkie's wet dream. There were blister packs containing samples of probably thirty or forty different medications, including Percocet.

By the time he shot the doctor, Walter was feeling much better.

For years he had always kept a packed suitcase in his van. It was his escape kit, containing clothes, money, his considerable collection of false driver's licenses and social security cards, and a small, .32-caliber automatic in a plastic sandwich bag. It seemed a reasonable precaution, although this was the first time he had needed it.

This had been a close call.

It was already dark, and the doctor had been dead about an hour, when Walter checked into a motel in San Carlos. After an exciting day, he was asleep within minutes.

He dreamed about his son—about the boy, age nine or ten, who had loved him as abjectly as any woman. In his imagination, and therefore in his dreams, the boy and the man he had become were two separate people. The boy had become the man the day he ran away.

In his dream he was just waking up. Steve was at the foot of his bed.

"There's a dead lady in the back of the van, Dad. She's beginning to stink."

"After a while they get that way, son."

"What's she doing in the van?"

"I met her over in Memphis. I bought her a drink and she said she'd give me a blow job for fifty bucks, so I took her outside and beat her to death. Then I put her in the van."

"Can I come next time?"

Then he really was awake and it was just shy of eight o'clock. He spent the rest of the morning watching TV. He didn't want to think about anything, and TV was good for that.

Around noon he took a shower and got dressed. Then he drove around until he found a diner, where he ordered pancakes and coffee.

He had bought a newspaper, which he read with his meal. There was nothing about Dr. Fairburn's murder, although there had been a mention on the TV news.

There was nothing, not one word, about yesterday's events in Half Moon Bay. The police apparently were keeping a lid on it. Walter felt vaguely cheated.

He decided it was time for a public performance, something the newspaper readers of San Francisco would really enjoy. Something to let Steve know that he hadn't heard the last of his old dad.

But not yet. Not for a few days. Walter decided he would give everybody time to get nice and comfortable.

. . .

Late that afternoon, Harriet Murdock was sitting at her desk in the realty offices of Wade & Bradley, wishing she had something to do. Business was slow. She had been to two open houses that morning, and she couldn't imagine why anyone would want to live in either one of them. She hated her job, she decided. But she was trapped in it, the way she was trapped in her life.

Thus she had no great expectations when her cell phone started ringing, not until she heard Walter's voice.

"You want to meet me after five for drinks? Then maybe dinner? Please say yes."

There wasn't any doubt she was going to say yes.

"Where would you like to meet?" she asked, trying to keep the excitement out of her voice.

"Somewhere they serve Pink Ladies."

She left work at three, which would give her two hours to pull herself together. She took a shower and shaved her legs, just in case, and then went to work on her makeup.

She finally chose a dress, white with diagonal zebra stripes and a flouncy collar, and then she had misgivings. Wasn't it perhaps just a little much? A little too come-hither? No. To hell with it. She put it on and looked at herself in the full-length mirror. If Walter got the idea she was available, so much the better.

She also wore perfume, which she hardly ever did. Shalimar. Like the dress, it was obvious. She put it on behind her ears and between her breasts—again, just in case.

Now. What did she have in the house to eat?

• • •

They met where they had first met, in the bar on El Camino Real. The instant he saw the dress, Walter knew that everything was going to work out as planned.

He was sitting in their booth, and he rose to meet her. He took her hand and, for the first time, kissed her on the cheek.

"You look lovely," he told her. "You look just lovely."

When she was seated, he went to the bar and ordered a Coors and a Pink Lady. The bartender had been forewarned, so the Pink Lady was already put together and just needed another turn with the electric drink mixer. He brought them back to the table.

"I can't get over how nice you look," he said. "You look a treat."

It didn't take very much of this before Harriet was blushing down to the roots of her dyed hair.

They talked for a while, about the weather and the lousy real estate market, and how glad they were to see each other. And somewhere Walter slipped in that he was living in a motel for the next few days. His rented house, it seemed, had turned out to be alive with vermin and was being fumigated.

It was almost immediately after receiving this bit of news that Harriet suggested, "Why don't we have dinner at my place?"

Why not, indeed.

"And maybe you could leave your van at the motel. I'll follow you there in my car and then drive you back to my place. I have nosy neighbors."

Walter, he thought to himself, you've just been invited to spend the night.

Harriet owned a house, which was convenient. She had lived there with her husband until the divorce and now she lived there alone, without enjoying it much.

Dinner was steak and a baked potato and salad, and Harriet was the dessert. She practically crawled to him on her hands and knees. He pulled down the zipper of her dress while she was unbuttoning his fly.

And she wasn't bad at it. She knew that, after a certain age, gentlemen needed some encouragement. By the time she was done he was nice and hard, and then she straddled his lap and guided him in. She enjoyed herself so much that, by the time they were finished, she was pink as a lobster all the way down to her nipples.

They slept that night in her double bed. She went to sleep holding his member, which was about half-erect. She was a very happy girl.

He was awake a little longer, trying to decide when and how he should kill her.

It would have to be here in the house. That was sure. The basement in Half Moon Bay would have allowed for a proper send-off, but right now it was probably crawling with police technicians, scraping up blood samples. So the house would have to do.

And the house was a little tract cracker box, where the neighbors were twenty feet away. So it wouldn't suit if Harriet started screaming. That was a pity. Walter always enjoyed the screaming. But she would have to suffer, so he would tape her mouth shut and do her in the bathtub.

But not tonight. And probably not tomorrow. Harriet would have a few days of unblemished bliss before she paid the debt she owed to God.

About two in the morning, she woke up and wanted him to make love to her again. He was happy to oblige. He gave the preliminaries lots of attention, and by the time he pushed into her she was shuddering with pleasure. Ten minutes later she was damp with sweat and couldn't do anything except cling to him and whisper, "I love you," over and over again. She fell asleep like that.

The next morning she got up, took a shower and announced that she had to go to work. She asked if he needed a ride back to the motel, but her eyes were pleading, *Please stay, please be here when I come home.*

"I'll take the day off," he told her.

"I'll come home for lunch," was her answer.

Walter went back to sleep. He was tired.

Usually his dreams were terrible, but this morning he dreamed about his wife, whom he remembered from the days of their court-ship as easy and sweet, surrendering her virginity to him without so much as a pretense of resistance. He had taken intense pleasure in her, which in the innocence of his youth he confused with love. He had thought she might lead him away from his wicked ways, but then, after about two months, she became pregnant and things changed. Even before it was born, she loved the baby more than him. So he killed a woman in Kansas, stabbing her in the throat with a pair of scissors, to celebrate the birth of his son.

The boy became his consolation prize. Stephen, whom Walter had named after his own hated father, was a nice baby who, the day after he was born, had wrapped his hand around Walter's little finger and looked into his face with the most amazed expression.

Stephen kept his mother alive for seven years. Walter spared her until his son was old enough to get by without her, and then Betty had filled a shallow grave in North Carolina, to be dug up a year later by somebody's hunting dog.

Walter, sitting in a coffee shop in Norfolk, Virginia, had read about it in the newspaper and had laughed.

And for a while the boy was only his.

He woke up thinking about his son. He remembered standing in a classroom with some math teacher who thought Steve had been cheating on an exam because he didn't write down all the steps of his solution.

"Nobody can solve a problem like that in his head," the man had said.

"Just because you can't doesn't mean that he can't. That boy is smarter than either one of us. Why don't you set him a test? Give him a problem, cold, and see if he can solve it."

The outcome had been a foregone conclusion. The poor bastard had had to apologize to a ten-year-old boy and had quit teaching at the end of the year.

Steve was a smart son of a bitch. It was a pleasure to teach him things. You only had to show something to him once and it was his forever. Walter had taught him many skills.

And then, finally, he had learned too much.

Walter shook his head, smiling to himself. Nobody else could have tracked him this far, nobody but his baby boy. He was a stranger now, working with the police, hunting his father the way a Labrador retriever hunts a pheasant, but you had to admire him.

Walter was intensely proud of his son, even as he tried to figure a way to kill him.

. . .

When Harriet came back at noon, she was eager again. She wanted to be bent over the living-room sofa. But Walter explained to her that, after a certain age, the desire is there but the capacity is not, and that she should have patience and wait until this evening.

She accepted this, because what she really wanted was not so much penetration as attention. This Walter gave her, feeding her lunch and caressing her hair. She went back to the real estate agency happy and full of hope.

But Walter had no sympathy for her because he had never known that longing for love. Harriet's need for affection struck him as merely a silly and shameful weakness. He prided himself on loving no one. What were other people except shadows? They hardly existed. Their pain and their suffering meant nothing.

Even his son he would brush away like a shadow.

But he was a gifted actor and could play any part. When Harriet came home at fifteen minutes after five, he listened to her history of the day and appeared to enter into all her griefs. He consoled her and caressed her, and made her feel that no one had ever understood her the way he did.

And then he made her a cocktail, his own approximation of a Pink Lady, but with a little something added that would be sure to put her out for about an hour. He wouldn't need any more time than that.

. . .

It was about six-thirty when Harriet began to stir. By then Walter had stripped off her clothes and covered her mouth with about three layers of duct tape—first one straight across and then another that came down at an angle from the side of her nose, looped under her chin and then came back up to the other side. More duct tape secured her hands behind her back, and yet more bound her legs at the ankle so that her left foot was over her right and her knees were apart.

She was lying faceup in the tub, in the bathroom her son probably used when he was home, her head away from the tap end. Walter would have preferred to have had the toilet seat under him rather than having to kneel, but this was the most convenient position. Besides, for the close work he had in mind it would have been a bit of a reach from the toilet.

Finally she became what probably would pass for conscious, except that she seemed to have no idea where she was or that there was anything odd about being in a bathtub with her mouth taped shut.

But in a few minutes, fear would come of its own. Walter was prepared to be patient.

When she seemed to recognize him, he smiled at her and began to stroke her hair. Even then she didn't seem to be at all alarmed.

"Possibly you're beginning to wonder what you're doing here," he said, his voice silky and intimate. "Can you imagine why you woke up in the bathtub, with your hands and feet tied and a gag over your mouth? No? Then let me show you something."

Harriet, to her credit, seemed to be genuinely interested in cooking, and her cutlery was all first rate. Walter held up for her inspection a small knife he had taken out of the block on her kitchen counter. It was all one piece of sterling steel with a needle-sharp point and of a German brand that wouldn't have been available at Walmart. Harriet recognized it and her eyes went wide with terror.

That was more like it.

"It's time for you to die, Harriet, and it's God's will that you suffer first. You won't have an easy death, but then hardly anybody does."

He rested the point of the blade on a spot just to the outside of her left eye, and then he pressed the heel of his right hand against her chin so she couldn't move her head. After a few seconds to let the suspense build, he pressed down until the knife had cut all the way to the bone and then started dragging the point across to the angle of her jaw.

Harriet tried to scream, but it came out as more of a grunt. And by the time he was finished she was trembling uncontrollably. Among other injuries he had severed her trigeminal nerve, probably in two places, and there was no pain like that.

There was a lot of blood, so Walter, who was a fastidious man, stood up to rinse off his hands in the bathroom sink. He left the knife resting on the rim of the tub.

While he was drying off with a face towel, he looked at Harriet and smiled. She was still trembling and her eyes were wet with tears.

"That's just a taste," he said kindly, as if he were explaining something to a child. "I'm afraid your cleaning woman is going to have her work cut out for her. And then, later on, when we've finished here, perhaps we'll take a drive in your car."

23

In the days following the discovery of Walter's house, Tregear had watched the evidence accumulate. He read the reports and assessments, examined the photographs and listened to the recordings of interviews. Ellen told him the chatter that never found its way into the police computers. He knew everything, and nothing.

His working assumption was that Walter would now vanish and then, after a month or two, resurface in some other place. But two facts kept nagging at him. There was the semen sample, the first DNA evidence Walter had ever left, which seemed to reflect a deliberate choice. And there was the murder of the doctor in San Mateo and the presumed theft of the medical records.

Why had he wanted his DNA found and why had he killed the doctor? Neither made any apparent sense. If Walter ever came to trial the DNA would guarantee conviction, so why was he signing his work? And what could possibly have been in Dr. Fairburn's memory or records that he wanted so badly to hide?

The two acts seemed to contradict each other. One was virtually an admission of guilt and the other was a completely unnecessary concealment.

Walter had almost come to grief from falling into a habit. Two of his victims were women he encountered in his work, and he had thus left a thread that could be followed back to him. Most murderers were caught because they were careless, and Walter had grown careless. And now the police had his fingerprints and his likeness and sufficient physical evidence to convince any jury. Walter had made a mistake, but anyone could make a mistake. Mistakes didn't really demand explanation.

But the semen and the doctor's murder demanded explanations, and Tregear didn't have any.

"Maybe he wants to get caught," Ellen had suggested. "Lots of murderers want to get caught. You should listen to their confessions. They can't stop telling you how guilty they are. They just want it to be over."

They were eating dinner, Chinese takeout, at the kitchen table. Ellen kept sliding her foot up Tregear's trouser leg, but she wasn't getting much of a reaction. Tregear was somewhere else.

"The semen sample wouldn't get him caught," he answered, glumly. "Semen doesn't come with a return address."

"Well, I'm grateful to Walter because his semen got you off the suspect list."

It was an attempt at humor, just a little banter to get poor old Steve to stop obsessing. But it didn't work. She could tell that from the way his head slid over a little to one side. He was thinking. He was back in that dark place he shared with his father.

"Maybe that was the idea—not to exonerate me but to get you to pay attention to me."

The Chinese dinner lay on the table between them, forgotten. All Ellen could see was the expression on her lover's face, and for the first time it occurred to her that his mind might be spinning out of control.

"Why would he want to do that? He didn't even know you were here. He probably still doesn't."

"He knows. He's known since Maryland that I was tracking him. The few times I've been able to get someone to listen, he probably had enough of a scare to remind him. I'm sure he can almost feel my breath on his neck.

"Maybe he spotted me at one of the crime scenes."

Suddenly he became very still.

"Yes. Now it makes perfect sense. Kathy Hudson in the trunk of somebody else's car—you remembered me from there. He must have been around somewhere. You'd never catch him at it, but he's probably got a shortwave radio and it's the kind of circus he'd enjoy.

"And since I'm not an established member of the. . . What does Sam call it?"

"The Fan Club."

"Right." Tregear nodded, as if the term itself held some sort of importance. "Since I'm not a member, Walter would assume you would regard me at least potentially as a suspect."

"And he guessed right about that."

But Tregear might not even have heard.

"So he'd want you to know that I wasn't your killer but at the same time that I had special knowledge. He'd want you to know I wasn't just another nut."

"But why?"

Ellen reached across the table to touch his hand. It all made a screwy kind of sense, the way so many neurotic fantasies seemed to make sense. But she just couldn't bring herself to believe it.

"Why would he want us to take you seriously when you know so much about him?"

"Perhaps to flush me out. To get you to involve me in the investigation. The way you did when you called me in to walk the house with you. I wonder if he was watching."

"That's paranoid." She shook her head. "I think you need a vacation. Let's go up to Yosemite for a week and admire the wildflowers."

All at once he looked up and smiled.

"That sounds lovely," he said. "When this is over—if I'm still alive—let's do that."

·   ·   ·

Suddenly, for no reason he could identify, Tregear found himself broad awake. He raised his head a little, enough to see the LCD display on the clock on his dresser, and determined that it was two-fifteen in the morning. For perhaps five minutes he lay quite still, listening. He heard nothing but the occasional sound of a car on North Point Street— that and Ellen's slow, steady breathing as she lay asleep beside him.

Dear God, how he loved her. It was all he could do to keep himself from touching her. Let her sleep, he thought. He hoped her sleep was dreamless.

It was the wrong time to fall in love. But would there ever be any right time? Love just made everything harder because now he had so much more to lose than just his life.

In all the time since he had found that woman's corpse in his father's van, how many years had he had in which to feel something

like normal? Four years with his grandparents, and then Walter had
come back and killed them. Then maybe six years in the Navy. But
even then he had felt as if he needed eyes in the back of his head. Did
he even know what "normal" felt like?

How many years since he had been on the hunt? Maybe twelve.
And it had led him to San Francisco, with Walter going berserk.

And here he had met Ellen, who now slept beside him—who had
shown him, by her mere presence in it, how inhumanly strange his
life had become.

He was so tired. So very, very tired.

What had she said? Something about admiring the wildflowers.
What a wonderful idea.

He stared up at the ceiling, which was just a black space that might
as well have been open to the vast emptiness of oblivion. Sometimes
Tregear felt that, with just a little effort, he could step off the edge
and disappear forever.

But not now, not yet. Walter was still out there.

Gradually, Tregear drifted back to sleep.

• • •

Around 3:00 A.M. that same morning, Officer Jim Lawell was coming out the front door of a diner on Sloat Boulevard. There was a
brown paper bag in his right hand. He was holding it by the bottom
because one of the paper coffee cups inside seemed to be leaking and
he didn't want the bag to tear.

His partner, Herb Balmis, was behind the wheel of the patrol car.
Herb always got hungry about this hour, so there was a chocolate-
covered doughnut, wrapped in wax paper, resting on the lids of the
coffee cups.

Jim got in on the passenger side and handed Herb one of the cof-
fees and the doughnut. Herb opened the wax paper, being careful to
peel it from the doughnut's chocolate coating, then shook his head in
apparent disbelief.

"This thing looks like it was made yesterday morning," he said.
"It looks embalmed, and probably tastes like it."

"That won't stop you from eating it."

"No." Herb had to laugh. "No, it won't."

In about two minutes the doughnut was gone, along with about half of Herb's coffee, which was still scalding hot. He put the rest in the left cup holder on the dash and said, "Let's roll," as he eased the car into reverse. He always said that.

They traveled west on Sloat and then south down Skyline Boulevard. They usually followed Skyline down to John Muir Drive and then back north along Lake Merced, but not tonight. Tonight they found a car parked just at the mouth of Harding Park Road. It was a white compact and its flashers were going. They parked parallel to it, on the other side of the road.

"Go have a look," Herb said. "I'm still digesting."

Officer Lawell got out of the patrol car and clicked on his flashlight, passing the beam slowly back and forth over a Chevy Camaro, about three years old. There appeared to be no one inside.

He approached the front of the vehicle and touched the hood with his fingertips to discover that it was still warm. Probably just engine trouble, he thought

Then he raised his light to the windshield and saw something that made him change his mind.

It was a handprint. It was on the driver's side, and Lawell could see the steering wheel beneath it. The strange thing was that it looked red.

He moved closer and could see why. The handprint was on the inside of the windshield and was in blood. Up close, he could see drip lines coming down from it.

He went back to the patrol car and told Herb about it.

"I'll phone it in," Herb said. "It's out of our league."

"Okay."

Lawell went back for another look. This time he walked all the way around the Chevy until he came to the trunk, where he found the words "OPEN ME" written in blood on the lid, in four-inch capitals.

The book said you should detain any witnesses, preserve the scene and not touch anything. Well, there weren't any witnesses, and Officer Lawell was happy to preserve the scene and not touch anything. Above all, he was happy not to open that trunk.

• • •

The inspector who got the call had just been posted to Homicide. His name was Donald Krodel. He had had his gold shield for four years and was considered a comer.

Hence the early assignment to the Land of the Blessed.

He was on his way back from a slam dunk domestic murder, where the guy had shot his wife three times while she was lying asleep in bed and then gone to the refrigerator to get himself a beer. When the police arrived he had surrendered quite meekly. Krodel wasn't the primary on the case. He had been called in only as backup, in case there was trouble. There hadn't been any trouble. He was going home.

And then there was this bloody handprint thing.

He didn't mind. His case had been in Ingleside, only two miles away, which in San Francisco translated into about five minutes. Besides, the handprint made it sound like a real mystery.

When he got to the scene, nobody was there except a couple of uniforms, their car and *the* car.

Krodel did his own tour of inspection, looked at the handprint and looked at the bloody lettering on the trunk: "OPEN ME."

Time to accept the invitation.

The door on the driver's side was unlocked, and the handle yielded to the leverage of a ballpoint pen. The trunk latch was just inside the door. Krodel crouched down, took a pair of latex gloves from his jacket pocket and put them on. Then he pulled the latch.

The two uniforms were over by their patrol car. They wanted no part of this. After he saw what was in the trunk, neither did Krodel.

A human female, naked and very dead, stared up at him from the well, which was a pool of congealing blood. She had been cut open on her face, on her breasts and across her belly. She was a mess.

Krodel took a handkerchief and pushed the trunk lid closed again.

"Get on the horn and call Evidence," he told the older of the two uniforms—whom he noticed had crumbs on his black shirt. "Tell them they'll be doing the whole car. And tell them we need the medical examiner."

The medical examiner and his ambulance were there within thirty minutes. By then two more patrol cars were on the scene to help with the inevitable crowd, some of whom were already arriving. Within forty-five minutes, the Evidence crew had both doors open and were going over the front and rear compartments. The trunk was also open as the ME did his preliminary examination.

"She's been dead between three and four hours," he said, presumably to Krodel, who was standing a discreet six feet behind and to the right of him. "Come and have a look at this."

With Krodel as an audience, he took the dead woman by the wrist and lifted her arm.

"You see? Only minimal resistance. Very little rigor. She was almost certainly alive when whoever did this put her in the trunk. Otherwise, it's difficult to account for the quantity of blood."

"Look at that." The ME pointed to a slash across her throat.

"Is that what killed her?"

"It's not likely. There isn't enough blood. I think it was torture. It's pretty sure she was alive and conscious while all of this was being done to her. We'll know for certain when we see her histamine levels.

"And notice the absence of defensive wounds on her hands. I think he tied her up and then went to work on her. Probably the big wound across her abdomen is what caused death. After that, she would have bled out in a few minutes."

"So you think he put her in the trunk and *then* cut her open?"

"It seems likely. That way she would die alone and in the dark."

While the ME's assistants were removing the body—something he really didn't want to watch—Krodel went to have a chat with the Evidence technicians.

"Finding anything?" he asked.

"Oh yeah. Prints all over the place. And all the paperwork for the car. It's all bagged and on the front seat, if you'd like a look."

The insurance card and registration were in the name of one Harriet Murdock, of 231 Brittan Avenue in San Carlos. Krodel climbed into one of the patrol cars and tapped into the DMV link. He fed the name and address into the search form and came up with a driver's license. The woman in the photograph looked a lot like their corpse.

Krodel phoned Homicide and reported what he had found. San Carlos was miles down the Peninsula, way out of their jurisdiction. The locals would have to deal with the house.

· · ·

At five-fifteen that morning, three patrol cars pulled up silently in front of 231 Brittan Avenue. The uniformed officers started fanning out around the house. They opened the latched wooden gate to the backyard, and within ten seconds had all the exits to the building secured.

Detective Michael Golding, who was in charge, gave the signal and a uniform with a jackhammer broke in the front door. Detective Golding, his pistol held in both hands and pointing up, was the first in.

There was no one in the living room. The kitchen and dining room were secure. They found a door to the basement and two of the uniforms went down to check it out. The bedrooms were upstairs. Golding and a uniform started doing the rooms. Every closet, every door was checked.

There was nobody home.

"Detective, I think you should have a look at this."

It was the bathroom off the master bedroom. It contained a bathtub with a showerhead, and the bathtub was smeared with blood. The tiled wall was bloody. Blood had leaked over the side of the tub onto the floor.

This is where he did her, Golding thought to himself.

In a second bathroom, which contained a shower stall, they found traces of blood on the stall floor. The washcloth was still damp.

"And this is where he cleaned up afterward."

There was also something a little peculiar in the master bedroom. A vanity table was against one wall, and there was a pile of stuff—a hairbrush and comb, a couple of perfume bottles, a couple of lace doilies and a plastic tissue box cover, white with roses painted on it— lying on the floor. It looked as if someone had simply swept them all off the table.

There was one object on the table, precisely in the center. It was an Ohio driver license, issued decades before. The woman in the picture looked very young.

Golding led the uniforms out of the house. They had done their job. Now it was time to bring in the Evidence teams.

• • •

It was Ellen's day off. At nine in the morning she and Tregear were enjoying a late breakfast of buttermilk pancakes and sausage. Gwendolyn was perched on Tregear's shoulder because she liked sausage and had figured out that Tregear was the softer touch. Later, they were going to the Steinhart Aquarium to look at the alligators.

"Did your mother teach you how to make this stuff?" he asked. The pancakes seemed to be a big hit.

"Of course not. I went to a special school. All the refined young ladies of Atherton attended the Pancake Academy."

"Okay."

Tregear, apparently, wasn't sure if she was joking or not.

Before she could explain, her cell phone rang. It was Sam.

"Walter's back," he told her. "This morning he left us a body in the trunk of a car. He also left his handprint, in blood, on the windshield. The lab made the match about fifteen minutes ago. I think you should come in."

"I'll leave here in five minutes."

"And bring Tregear with you. They found something in the victim's house we need him to look at."

·   ·   ·

They took Ellen's car and parked in the department garage. Then they took the elevator up to the third floor. Tregear could feel eyes on him when they walked into the duty room. *Who's the civilian?*

Sam was at his desk. He stood up to shake Tregear's hand.

"Let me show you what we've got," he said. Then all three of them sat down in front of the computer screen.

It was a slide show. First the car, parked halfway up on the shoulder, then the bloody handprint, then the body in the trunk.

"You see that wound on her throat?" Sam said, tapping the screen with his fingernail. "I got a call from the morgue a few minutes ago. They're still in the middle of the autopsy, but they thought we'd be interested to know that at some point he cut up her larynx. Maybe she was getting too noisy.

"The fingerprints of course confirm it—Walter's prints were all over the inside of that car—but otherwise I wouldn't have thought it was him. It's pretty sloppy work for him."

"He meant it to be sloppy," Tregear answered, struggling to keep the tension from his voice. "He wanted you to know it was him. He's rubbing your noses in it."

"Not just our noses, I think."

Sam hit a key and another image came up on the screen. It was a photograph of what looked like a driver license resting on some sort of table.

"This was found in Harriet Murdock's bedroom," he said. Using the mouse, he highlighted and enlarged the driver license.

"Is there anything you can tell us about this?"

Tregear studied the photograph for perhaps fifteen seconds, all the while feeling his bowels turn to ice water. Finally he couldn't bear it any longer—he simply had to be alone. He got up and walked over to a window, where he stood, looking down at the traffic.

Of all the lousy things his father had done over the years, this one small cruelty offended him the most. He could have left her out of it.

Then he went back and sat down again.

"The woman in the picture is my mother," he said, his voice as even as he could manage. "Walter kept the license in a locked suitcase in his closet, along with her clothes, wallet and wedding ring. I was eleven years old the last time I saw this."

"Why do you think he wanted this found?"

Tregear merely shrugged, as if little disposed to speculate, so Ellen answered for him.

"It's a challenge," she announced, her voice betraying perhaps a shade more resentment than she intended. "It's a little message from father to son. This is all a game to him, so he wants to be sporting about it and let Steve know he's on to him."

24

Things had reached such a pass that Sam felt he had no choice but to take it all to the lieutenant. Hempel was not pleased.

"You've got a major serial killer running around San Francisco, cutting up women like they were paper dolls, and you've got his son sitting out there in the duty room. When was I supposed to hear about this, Sam?"

"You're hearing about it now."

"So where does all this put us?"

At first Sam merely shrugged. Then he thought about it for a few seconds, looked Hempel straight in the face and smiled.

"Not too bad," he said. "Not too bad. Tregear's going to help us catch this jelly bean. We're going to use him for bait."

"I don't think so."

"He's not giving us a choice, Dave. He says he'll either work with us or against us. If he has to go it alone, he'll publish his name, address and telephone number in the *Chronicle* and see what happens."

"He can't do that."

"How are you going to stop him?"

Hempel thought about it for a minute and then his face brightened.

"We'll call the Navy," he announced. "They'll put him in the brig. They seem to think they can't keep their ships afloat without this guy. We'll let the Navy stop him."

So Hempel made the call, and forty-five minutes later Lieutenant Commander Hal Roland was sitting in the same chair so recently occupied by Inspector Sergeant Sam Tyler.

Hempel told him the whole story.

For a long moment Hal Roland said nothing. He merely stared at his sleeve, wondering if the narrow stripe would ever catch up with the other two. His hopes for promotion seemed to be dimming by the second.

"You've got to rein him in," Hempel said finally.

Roland looked up and tried to smile.

"The Navy doesn't have an impressive record for 'reining in' Tregear. I don't know what you expect me to do."

"Get him to see reason. He's a civilian. He doesn't understand the risks he's taking."

Roland shook his head. He seemed on the verge of laughter.

"I doubt there's very much about this situation Tregear doesn't understand. He understands most things better than most people."

"He could get himself killed."

"Well, we can't have that." He glanced down at his sleeve again. The narrow stripe had a terribly permanent look.

"I think I need to talk to Tregear," he said.

The two men met in an empty holding room, sitting across from each other at a small table. Roland had taken off his jacket, hoping to give the discussion a less official quality.

He knew he had no leverage. The lieutenant was right. Tregear was a civilian. He had a contract with the Department of Defense, but what could they do if he simply stopped working? They would beg and plead and promise him anything he wanted, so Roland would beg and plead for them.

"This man—your father," he began, hoping to strike the right note. "We can deal with this for you."

"How, Hal? Just exactly how are you going to deal with it?"

"We can put you somewhere he can't touch you, and we let the police catch him."

"He's been at this for thirty years and more, and the police haven't caught him yet."

"They know more about him now. Thanks to you. They'll catch him." Roland raised his hands a little way from the desk, as if to fend off any possible objections. "Or somebody will catch him. We'll turn it over to the Justice Department, and they'll make it a priority. Every FBI office in the country will have his prints and description. They'll be on the streets in every town in the USA, and they'll find him."

Tregear's immediate reaction was laughter—except that "laughter" wasn't quite the right word. It was more a slightly hysterical giggle. It was an unnerving sound, suggestive of the possibility that the man might just be coming unstuck.

"And how many women die in the meantime? After all these years, his score is probably in the hundreds. How many more? Twenty? Thirty?"

"And what happens if he kills you?" Roland leaned forward so that their faces weren't more than a few feet apart. "You know, all this time you've worked for the Navy, you haven't been sitting in front of your computer screen writing video games. You're protecting your country. You're protecting the men and women you served with. Their lives matter too."

His speech, Roland felt sure, would not be without effect. He was an Annapolis graduate and he was not cynical about patriotism, but he felt intuitively that the instinct for survival, once wrapped up in the flag, would be irresistible.

But apparently not. Tregear sagged visibly and with a vague movement of his hand waved the appeal away.

"I'm tired," he said, and the mere sound of his voice was evidence of it. "My father has been hounding me since I was twelve years old. I've been hunting him because I knew my life depended on finding him first. Now he wants it to be finished, and so do I."

Okay. The Navy taught the virtues of a flexible response. If one thing wouldn't work, Roland decided, he would try another.

"Then will you let us help you?"

"I'm listening."

.   .   .

Roland stayed until shortly after one o'clock and then drove back to Treasure Island to make his arrangements. Sam, Ellen and Tregear drove over to the county morgue, where the autopsy on Harriet Murdock was just finishing up.

Allen Shaw, MD, the chief medical examiner, was waiting for them in his office.

"And what is your role here?" he asked Tregear, as they were being introduced.

"He's on loan from the Navy," Sam answered blandly. "He's

constructing a computer model of homicides so we can cross-check the evidence."

Shaw did not appear to be entirely convinced, and his response was to ignore Tregear's presence.

"Well, I can tell you a few things for openers," he began, sitting down behind his desk, which was covered with manila folders, various loose pieces of paper and several photographs of unspeakable horror. "The Murdock woman didn't die quickly. The killer took his time. The abdominal wound was the ultimate cause of death. She had had sexual intercourse within the last few hours of her life—apparently, judging from the quantity of semen and the general condition of her labia, quite a bit of it. It was real sex, unlike the Wilkes case, and it was consensual. She was wearing a diaphragm.

"The serology and the DNA work will be done sometime tomorrow."

"Do you think this is the work of the Wilkes killer?" Sam asked, and then shrugged, as if dismissing his own question. "Just, what's your impression, Doc? I won't hold you to it."

"I would guess it's the same man." Dr. Shaw looked down at his desk and picked up a pencil. He apparently just wanted something to do with his hands because all he did was tap at his blotter with the eraser. "We won't know until the DNA is finished, but I'm betting it was. The method was different, but in both this and the Wilkes case the bodies were moved to carefully stage-managed discovery sites. Besides, Sally Wilkes suffered and this one suffered. Both of them were killed by a righteous monster, and how many of those can there be walking around?"

• • •

"I'm hungry," Sam announced when they were back out on the sidewalk. "Let's get something to eat."

They found a diner, the kind with Formica tabletops and napkin dispensers and no liquor license. They all ordered hamburgers, which was the safe choice.

"He must have seen me," Tregear said, while they were waiting. "He must have been watching while we searched his house."

Suddenly, to Ellen's ears, the idea no longer sounded so paranoid.

"How do you know that?" Sam asked.

Tregear raised his eyes to Sam's face, who offered a vague shrug to let him know that it was just a question, that he wasn't challenging him.

"Think about the timing. I walk into that house and four days later my mother's old driver's license is found on a dead woman's vanity table. Besides, you're his audience and he's yours. He wouldn't have been able to resist the show."

Probably unconsciously, Tregear shook his head. He clearly wasn't pleased with his conclusions.

"So now I'm the bait," he said.

"Yes, you're the bait." Ellen looked up at him with something like real anger. "We'll be dangling you in front of a psychopath."

"That's the idea."

"You could end up like those women."

"I don't think so."

They were interrupted by the waitress with their orders. The hamburgers, to Sam's obvious disgust, came with potato chips instead of fries. The waitress seemed unimpressed with his protest and brought him a bottle of ketchup.

"Why not?" Sam asked him finally, after he had tasted his lunch. "Are you counting on family affection?"

"No, I'm counting on the Navy." Tregear laughed. It wasn't a cheerful sound. "I've made a deal with them. They'll maintain a cordon around me wherever I go, loose enough that they won't spook Walter. At least, that's the plan."

"He doesn't have to be standing next to you to kill you," Ellen pointed out. She didn't like the plan very much, and the tone of resignation in Tregear's voice frightened her. "He could lure you someplace and be five blocks away with a high-powered rifle."

"I don't think he'll try anything like that." Tregear smiled at her. "He'll want to talk, and that will give me some time. We've got a lot of catching up to do."

25

Ellen spent a restless night in her own apartment and at 4:00 A.M., by which time she was convinced that sleep was an empty promise, she was in her living room with a cup of coffee and Gwendolyn asleep in her lap, watching a 1940s doctor movie featuring not a single actor whose face she recognized. She had missed the first half, so she had no idea what the story was about.

Steve probably would have been able to fill it in for her. Steve loved movies, particularly if they were old and low budget. But Steve wasn't around.

Steve had banished her.

"I don't want you anywhere near me," he had said. "Until this thing is over, I don't even want to talk to you on the phone."

She understood that he was trying to protect her, that he didn't want her caught in the cross fire between him and his father, but after all she was a cop with a nine-millimeter automatic strapped to her belt, and *he* was the one who needed protecting. Aside from the M-16 the Navy had taught him how to use in boot camp, Steve, as it turned out, had never fired a gun in his life.

"I've got the Shore Patrol to keep me safe," he had told her. "Walter doesn't know anything about you, and that's the way it has to stay."

So now she was back to sleeping alone. Except that she wasn't sleeping.

"Well, that didn't last very long," Mindy had announced, as if the discovery should be headlined in the *Chronicle*.

"We didn't break up," Ellen told her. "It's more complicated than that."

After which it became necessary, for more than one reason, to explain the whole situation to Mindy. Perhaps, it crossed Ellen's mind, having laid it all out for Mindy, she might even begin to understand it herself.

"You heard about the body they found in a car trunk down on Skyline? That seems to have done it. Our killer seems to have decided on some sort of blood feud, and Steve is being noble. The problem is, I don't particularly want him being noble."

"Maybe not, but under the circumstances what else could you expect him to do?"

Mindy's expression became oddly speculative.

"When you've got this beast in a cage," she said at last, "I want the case, and I don't care if I have to seduce the DA to get it. The book rights will finance my retirement."

Somehow this struck Ellen as immensely funny, and it wasn't very long before they were both laughing.

"But I don't think it'll go down that way," Ellen said finally, when she could keep a straight face. "I don't think this one will ever allow himself to be taken alive."

"Well, isn't that just a fucking shame."

And then they both started laughing all over again.

Fortunately, tonight Mindy was all tucked up with Whatever His Name Was, so Ellen could sit on the couch with Gwendolyn, watching a commercial for aluminum siding.

When the movie came back on, the Old Doctor, the Young Doctor's mentor and father figure, was talking into a Dictaphone. His voice sounded endlessly sincere and compassionate and it was all very quaint.

She was about to switch to another channel when suddenly she found herself staring at the image of an elderly actor holding a clumsy-looking microphone. How, exactly, would that process work? she asked herself. The doctor's voice was going onto a cylinder, and then a secretary would put the cylinder on another machine and listen to it through headphones as she typed the notes. Then the notes would go in a file folder.

What did they do these days?

Ellen's father was a doctor, so she knew the answer. Doctors usually didn't know how to type—certainly her father didn't—so they still used dictation machines of one kind or another, and the tape cassettes or memory chips were sent to a transcription service.

But what came back? Maybe a paper printout, maybe a computer file on a CD. Maybe by now they just e-mailed them back.

So if Walter had lifted the file folder, which would have contained a printout of a file on one of the front office computers, there was probably still a backup.

Had the San Mateo cops gone through the hard drives? Were Walter's records still there?

The clock on her cable box said four forty-five. Sam's dachshunds wouldn't get him up until five-thirty. She might as well go take a shower.

By five forty-five she was at her desk in the duty room, but she exercised restraint and didn't call Sam until six.

Millie answered. Sam was out emptying the dogs. No, he wasn't carrying his cell phone. It was still on his night table.

"Can you have him call me as soon as he gets back? I'm at work."

Millie promised.

Twenty minutes later, Sam called.

"Your friend the San Mateo cop—what was his name?"

"Pete Castaldi."

"Can you phone and find out if they've gone through Dr. Fairburn's computers? I think Walter's records might be there."

"Okay."

It was almost seven-thirty by the time Sam called back.

"They looked through the files, but they didn't find anything for Walter Stride," he said. "They think Fairburn was killed by a mugger. His wallet was missing."

"Can you get us into that office?"

"They won't like it, Ellie."

"Then you'll just have to be especially charming about it. Can you meet me there?"

"Oh, I suppose."

By a quarter after eight she was in the parking lot of the medical building in San Mateo. There was a patrol car waiting for her, and when she showed her badge the uniform took her in to Fairburn's office and used his key.

"I don't have to tell you to lock up after yourself, do I?"

"No. You don't."

Ellen started with the computer on the receptionist's desk. There were lots of patient records, raw transcriptions in Word format, but a search on "Stride" turned up nothing. A search on "Walter" yielded three records, all related to an eighteen-year-old being treated for the clap.

Had their Walter gotten here ahead of her? It didn't seem likely. Ellen had looked in the Recycle Bin and it still held files dated from before Fairburn's murder, so Walter hadn't emptied it.

At eight forty-five Sam showed up.

"Any luck?" he asked. He didn't make the question sound hopeful.

"Not yet, but the morning is young."

He sat down on the couch in the waiting room, took off his hat and set it on the seat beside him. He was obviously prepared to be very bored.

"If my expertise is required, just let me know," he said, then leaned back into the couch, folded his arms across his chest and closed his eyes.

In desperation, Ellen had begun searching the records by date when the door opened and a woman in her forties, dressed in a red T-shirt and gray cropped pants, stepped inside and froze, staring at Sam in amazement.

"Who are you?" she asked.

Sam opened one eye and fumbled for his badge.

"Cops. Go away."

"Wait a minute!" Ellen stood up and came out into the waiting room. "Do you work here?" she asked the woman.

"Yeah. I'm the receptionist." She had dark hair with streaks of blond in it. She looked like she would have been exactly Walter's type. She shrugged. "At least, I was. Now they're just keeping me on for a few weeks to tidy up."

Ellen gestured with her hand. "Come with me."

They sat down together on the two chairs in front of the late Dr. Fairburn's desk.

"What's your name?"

"Carol." The ex-receptionist shrugged again. It seemed to be her habitual response to life. "Carol Brush."

"Do you want some coffee, Carol?"

"Hell, no. The coffee here is foul. Doctors are all cheap sons of bitches."

"Do you remember a patient named Walter Stride?"

Yes, Carol remembered. You could read it in her eyes.

"He was nice," she said, then smiled at the recollection.

"What was wrong with him?"

"I don't know—pain. Just pain."

"Did you do the filing around here?"

"Yeah." She laughed. "I was it. I was the whole staff."

"And you didn't see his file?"

"No. The first and only time he had an appointment was just four days before . . ."

"I understand."

Within about five minutes Ellen really did understand. She understood that Dr. Fairburn had paid his overworked receptionist less per week than his wife might spend on an umbrella, that the doctor's widow only came in to sign the checks and begrudged every nickel, that there wasn't going to be a severance bonus, that Carol Brush was lonely and poor and resentful.

She also understood how the office was run, that the doctor, like Ellen's father, dictated his notes and employed a transcription service, and that the notes were mailed back on a CD.

"What have you been doing with the mail?"

"I sort out the checks and the bills and leave them for Mrs. Fairburn." Carol pointed to the small pile of envelopes on the doctor's desk. The rest I dump in an empty filing cabinet."

"What time does the mail usually come?"

"Just after lunch. The postman pushes it through the slot in the door."

Ellen smiled. "Why don't you take the day off," she said. "Right now there's nothing for you to do here, and we're going to need the place to ourselves."

"Don't tell Mrs. Fairburn if she comes." Carol shook her head vigorously. "Say I'm out running an errand, or she'll dock me for it."

"I won't tell."

Carol Brush left, tiptoeing over the linoleum floor of the waiting room and closing the office door as quietly as possible so as not to awaken Sam, who had fallen asleep on the couch.

Ellen instantly went to the filing cabinet Carol had pointed out to her and started going through the old mail. She found two padded mailing envelopes from Pacific Transcriptions. The second contained Dr. Fairburn's notes on Walter Stride.

"Moderate to severe lower abdominal pain, radiating up the back to necessitate sleeping in a chair. Condition worsening over previous 4 months. Rx Percocet 650mg. Scan. Blood work. Possible pancreatic involvement."

A quick search of the receptionist's phone directory indicated a radiology practice and a lab, both in the building. Since both offices would know Carol Brush's voice, it would be necessary to walk down the hall and flash a badge.

When she went out to the waiting room, Ellen discovered that Sam was awake.

"Did you find what you were looking for?" he asked, pushing back his hair with his left hand.

"Yes, I did. And now I want you to wander down to Suite two thirty-three and check if they have Walter's X-rays. Then I'll buy you lunch."

"You got a deal. Are we done here?"

"Yes."

"Then I'll meet you at the cars."

Ellen herself went to the lab in the basement, where she was told that, yes, Walter Stride had had an appointment to have blood drawn, but he never showed up. A minute or two after she got out to the parking lot, Sam joined her and reported that the radiologists didn't have any film on Walter because he had missed his appointment.

There was a diner two blocks away. Ellen, who hadn't had breakfast, ordered an omelet, and Sam decided to risk all on their crab cake.

"So what's the matter with Walter?" he asked while carefully inspecting his spoon. "I trust it's nothing serious."

Ellen showed him a printout of Dr. Fairburn's notes. Sam took out his reading glasses.

"'Pancreatic involvement'—sounds ominous." Sam raised his eyebrows speculatively. "You don't suppose he'll go and die on us, do you?"

Their orders came. Ellen tested her omelet with a fork. It had a consistency like India rubber.

"I think it's interesting that he didn't show up for his other appointments," she announced, giving the omelet another jab.

"And what do you conclude from that?"

Sam tasted his crab cake, made a face and then reached for the ketchup bottle.

"I conclude that he only wanted Fairburn to write him a prescription. He wasn't interested in a diagnosis."

Ellen took a bite of her eggs and then set down her fork, thinking she might not need it anymore.

"If you had so much back pain you had to sleep sitting up in a chair," she went on, folding her hands together, "wouldn't you want to know what's the matter with you?"

"Sure."

"Then maybe he already knows."

Sam, who had been completely absorbed in his lunch, stopped eating and looked up at her. Gradually, he began to smile.

"Wouldn't that explain a few things, Sam?"

"You mean like why he didn't just disappear after we tossed his house?"

"Yes. And this last murder—the bloody handprint, leaving his dead wife's driver's license for us to find in the victim's house."

Ellen shook her head, as if she were a little disappointed in their suspect.

"It's not his style. Walter has a history of committing nearly perfect murders. No fingerprints, no fibers, no evidence. But Harriet Murdock was pure theater, with Walter at center stage. Given how much we know about him, he has to realize that if he hangs around eventually we'll catch him. But what if he also realizes that he's going to be dead in a few months? Then all he has to do is beat the clock. He's taunting us."

Sam nodded and then resumed work on his crab cake.

"It's a good theory," he said, without looking up.

"But you don't buy it?"

"Oh, I buy it. With one reservation."

"And what's that?"

Sam took a sip of his coffee and then set the cup down with elaborate delicacy. He raised his eyes to Ellen's face and then shrugged.

"The one reservation is that Walter isn't playing to us." He smiled sadly, as if aware that he was demolishing some treasured illusion. "Most of the time you'd be right. These crazies, they get a little press and they start thinking it's a duel between them and the cops. They write letters, they phone us up. It becomes a game."

The smile collapsed.

"I think, however, we need to be a little humble about Walter," he said. "I suspect he doesn't give a damn about us. He probably imagines he can stay ahead of us forever. It's not us he's taunting. It's not us he's leaving messages for. It's Tregear."

26

While Ellen and Sam were finishing their lunch, Walter was just getting up. He had slept fitfully for fourteen hours and still felt exhausted. He badly needed a pain pill.

He had gotten up once during the night to vomit and the bathroom still smelled of it. After washing down the pill with half a glass of tepid water, he looked at himself in the mirror and was not encouraged by what he saw. His face was as yellow as saffron.

It occurred to him that his slide into oblivion was picking up speed. He found the thought of food nauseating and his clothes were beginning to hang on him.

As he waited for the Percocet to kick in, he stared out through the venetian blinds of his motel room window. There wasn't much to see, only a strip of road with a gas station and a liquor store on the other side.

Out of how many windows had he looked down at some variation of the same scene? Men created for themselves landscapes of dreary horror, places to drag out their pointless, wretched lives. And pristine nature was no different. Only people who had lived all their lives in cities could delude themselves that every forest and field wasn't crowded with brutal, ugly suffering.

It was a hateful world and he would not be sorry to leave it.

When he started to feel better, he lay down on the bed, on his side to keep the pressure off his back, and picked up the Gideon Bible on his night table. He amused himself by reading the Twenty-second Psalm. When he had finished it he closed his eyes and fell asleep again.

It was nightfall before he woke up. By then the pain was almost gone. He even felt hungry. He took a quick shower and dressed and then went down to the motel lobby to buy a couple of candy bars and a can of Coke out of the vending machines.

By the time he had finished the candy bars, Walter was in a much better mood. He was planning his evening entertainment.

He had finally gotten rid of the van, leaving it in the long-term parking lot at the airport. From there he had stolen an olive-gray Kia, the sort of car no one would pay any attention to. As was his practice when he did not feel rushed, he had switched the Kia's plates with a pair from another car in the next row and then left the van in a slot some distance away. He figured he might have close to a week before the Kia was even reported stolen.

He drove it across town to a section of North Beach that seemed to be all restaurants and bars. It was nine o'clock on a weeknight, so the crowds were thin. He parked on the street. He wouldn't be long.

Ten years ago Walter had bought an antique bayonet in a second-hand store. It might have dated back to the First World War, or even earlier. The blade was a foot long and took a good edge. Since a quick kill wasn't nearly as much fun, he had never used it.

But tonight, because he would have to work out in the open—and because, anyway, the victim was purely incidental—he carried the sheathed bayonet down the inside of his trouser leg, the grip sticking up over his belt and concealed under his jacket.

He saw a woman walking down the sidewalk alone and fell into step about thirty feet behind her. He had picked her because she was young, no more than thirty, wasn't wearing a coat and was talking on her cell phone. She had come out of a yuppie bar called La Questa and with any luck at all was heading back to her car. There was something urgent in her stride, which suggested that she had had a disappointing evening.

He followed her for a block and a half, then she turned into a parking lot not much bigger than a squash court, surrounded on three sides by tall buildings. The booth at the entrance was dark. There were no overhead lights. As soon as she turned into the lot she was in deep shadow. Walter followed soundlessly behind her, the distance between them closing fast. He took out the bayonet, holding it low.

She never saw him until she opened her car door and the inside light came on. Then it was too late. She started to take a step back and the bayonet slipped effortlessly in under her ribs, puncturing her left lung before it pierced her heart. For a few seconds she just stood there. She stared into his eyes without comprehension and then her mouth opened. All that came out was a thin dribble of blood. And then suddenly, as if she had at last realized that she was dead, she collapsed.

Her keys were still in the door lock. Walter took them and opened the car trunk. Then he lifted the body from the asphalt and put it inside. She had dropped her purse, so he picked it up and searched it, taking out the cell phone, then placed the purse in the trunk beside her. He didn't want them to have any trouble identifying her.

Then he took a ballpoint pen from his shirt pocket and wrote "815A" on the inside of her right forearm. He posed the body carefully so that the writing would be immediately visible.

He closed the trunk lid.

When he reached the sidewalk, where there was light from the streetlamps, he checked himself over carefully and was pleased that there was no blood.

He was feeling weak and tired and he needed another pain pill. He probably needed some sleep too. He would take a shower when he got back to the motel room.

He found a traffic ticket under the windshield wiper of the Kia. Somehow it annoyed him. He wadded it up into a ball and threw it against the plate glass window of a storefront. It bounced off and landed on the sidewalk.

Then he remembered he had to call the police. His watch read 9:25, but that was too early. He would call at eleven, using the woman's cell. He would have to stay awake until then. He would watch TV.

•   •   •

Ellen took the call at ten minutes to midnight. She had been asleep for perhaps half an hour, but she was starkly awake the instant the phone rang. She knew what it meant.

A body, female, had been found in the trunk of a car in North Beach. She scribbled down the address and climbed into her clothes.

"They're expecting you," the dispatcher had said. Well, they should be. Since Harriet Murdock, any suspected homicide in which the victim was female rated a call to either Tyler or Ridley, and at night it was Ellen because she lived in the city and was therefore closer.

North Beach wasn't far away. Within ten minutes she was standing in the parking lot, staring down into a car trunk containing a woman, probably in her late twenties, with the hilt of a knife sticking out just in front of her left arm. The angle indicated that the thrust was upward, probably tearing a good-size hole in her heart. From the look of her, she hadn't been dead for more than a few hours.

There was hardly any blood, just a stain on her blouse where she had been stabbed, and a little on her mouth and chin. Ellen felt reasonably sure that this one had died right here, probably while trying to get into her car. The keys were still in the trunk lock, put there no doubt by whoever killed her.

Had that been Walter? She wasn't sure. Walter liked them to suffer, and this woman had died from one instant to the next. It seemed possible she hadn't even had time to realize she was being murdered.

Ellen was using a standard department-issue flashlight she had taken from the patrol car that was presently blocking off the entrance to the parking lot. At two or three feet, the distance available to her as she examined the body, it cast a narrow beam. For a moment it came to rest on the handbag, which was open and lying next to the dead woman's knee. It was a nice bag, made of butter-smooth tan leather. It was open. The wallet was still inside and there was still money in it—Ellen could see the corners of a few bills sticking out.

So this hadn't been a robbery. The killer's motives were more personal.

Then Ellen moved the light again and saw the writing on the victim's arm:. "815A," in inch-high block letters.

Oh, Jesus.

She went back to the patrol car and pulled the radio microphone off its hook.

"This is Inspector Ridley," she almost shouted. "I want some foot soldiers out here. We've got a hot one. And send somebody with photographic equipment and a printer. We'll need to reproduce the photo on the victim's driver's license and start showing it around, right now. I want every bartender and waiter in the vicinity to see her picture tonight."

Then she phoned Sam.

"We're going to be here for a while," she told him. "I need you to make sure I don't make any mistakes."

"Is it Walter?"

"I can't be sure, but I think so."

Within twenty minutes the forensic people showed up. Within half
an hour there were probably eight more uniforms milling around,
waiting for someone to tell them what to do. For starters, Ellen had
half of them out patrolling the neighborhood, checking the sidewalks
and the streets, the trash cans and the license plates of parked cars,
looking for anything out of the ordinary.

By then Sam had arrived. Ellen filled him in on what she had so
far and he nodded his approval.

"You don't need me to babysit you, girl," he said, then grinned.
"Still, I wouldn't have missed this for the world."

"I want to show you something, Sam."

They went over to the car, where three evidence technicians
were dusting everything in sight. One of them was in front of the open
trunk, using an iron bar to lift the dead woman's purse out by its
straps.

"I want an inventory on what's in that bag," Ellen said. She was
more excited than she realized, and her tone of voice reflected it. "I
want everything, right down to the dates on the nickels in her change
purse, and I want it twenty minutes ago."

The technician was a woman, about Ellen's age, and she was unimpressed.

"Standard operating procedure, Inspector," she said blandly. "This
isn't our first homicide."

Ellen raised her hands and smiled apologetically. "Sorry."

"That's okay."

And then, just to show there were no hard feelings, the technician
shook her head.

"I'll tell you one thing right now that's funny," she said. "No cell
phone. You ever see a woman walking around with a bag like this
who didn't carry a cell phone?"

"Maybe she dropped it when she was killed."

"Not if she died here, and I'm betting she did. We've looked."

She turned away and trotted off to the forensics truck with her
trophy.

"You know, you've got to learn to be nicer to people," Sam told
her, only half-seriously. "Now, what did you want to show me?"

They went around to the trunk, and Ellen shined her flashlight on
the victim's forearm.

"You see that?" she asked, unnecessarily. "What do you make of that?"

"'Eight-fifteen A.'" Sam shook his head. "Damned if I know. You think it's Walter? You think he's playing games with us again?"

Ellen gave no evidence that she had even heard.

"You remember Sally Wilkes?" she said finally. It wasn't really a question. "And that one last night—also in a car trunk. You remember how staged it all was? This is like that.

"I'm thinking he killed her there," she went on, pointing to the door on the driver's side. "I'm thinking he picked her at random and she led him to the car. He stabs her, and she drops her purse. Then he puts her in the trunk and goes back to pick up the purse to put it in here with her, so we'll have it right away and we won't have to fool around finding out who she is."

"So far I'm with you."

"Then look at the way she's posed. If he'd simply dumped her in and closed the lid, her right arm would have fallen to her side with the elbow turning out. The elbows always go out—it's the way the bones are articulated—but that way we wouldn't have been able to read his little message. He posed her."

"You think he killed this woman just to send us a note?" Sam looked puzzled.

"And the note gives us a time," Ellen said, with something like awe in her voice. "Eight-fifteen A.M.."

"There's hope for you yet, girl."

This made then both laugh.

"Inspector."

They both turned to see a uniform standing by the front of the car. He was holding a slip of paper about the size of his hand. He offered it to Ellen.

"I found this a block and a half down the street," he said. "Who throws away a parking ticket?"

And that was just exactly what it was, a parking ticket. The time indicated was 9:10 P.M. Also noted were the make, model, color and license tag of the vehicle.

Ellen showed it to Sam, who looked at it for a few seconds then raised his eyes to the uniform.

"What's your name, Officer?"

The uniform, a gangly blond kid of about twenty, snapped to attention and said, "Ludlow, sir. Timothy J."

Sam nodded, as if making a mental note of it. "Well, Officer Ludlow, you've earned your keep tonight."

Ludlow, Timothy J., smiled broadly then was gone, probably to paw through every trash barrel within a mile radius.

"Is that how it's done?" Ellen asked, amused in spite of herself.

"Yes, girl, that's how it's done."

• • •

Forensics lifted the victim's driver's license out of her wallet with a pair of tweezers, and within five minutes surprisingly good five-by-six photos of her were coming out of their portable printer. Ellen passed them around to the remaining uniforms and told them to go find out how Eugenia Lockwood had spent the last few hours of her life.

It was two in the morning when they removed the dead woman from the trunk of her car and she began her journey to the morgue. The car itself would be towed downtown and a team would spend half a day going over it for hair, fibers and prints, but Ellen didn't think they would find anything.

By three-thirty the site was pretty well closed down. The parking lot was taped off and a patrol car and two men were left inside to keep people out. Tomorrow morning, in daylight, the evidence people would make another sweep and then it would be business as usual, as if nothing had ever happened.

Ellen didn't go home. She drove straight to headquarters and sat down at her desk to write her report. She wanted everything that was known about the death of Eugenia Lockwood to be in the database by the time the sun rose. She wanted it all to be right there for Steve when he sat down in front of his computer with a cup of his vile tea.

She couldn't see him or even talk to him on the phone, but she wanted him to know that she was there for him, keying in every detail of this latest sad story. And maybe he would appreciate that she had spent a sleepless night so that he could have it all before breakfast. It was the only way she had right now to make him understand that he was always in her thoughts.

The parking ticket Officer Ludlow had found crumpled up on the sidewalk was in an evidence bag and was working its way through Forensics. Probably by the end of the day someone would take a statement from the traffic officer who wrote it. Then someone else would have to do a search for the owner. Ellen guessed it was probably a blind lead.

The reports were beginning to come in from the uniforms who had checked the bars and restaurants. The bartender at a place called La Questa had looked at Eugenia Lockwood's photo and recognized her. She had sat at the bar and downed two glasses of white wine. She hadn't seemed to be expecting anyone and nobody had hit on her. She had left sometime between nine-fifteen and nine-thirty.

The autopsy hadn't started yet, but the murder weapon had been identified as a regulation Navy bayonet, Spanish-American War vintage. There wasn't another mark on the body, and the technician who called in the identification was quite sure Eugenia had died almost instantly from a single stab wound.

The report on the victim's purse was in. No prints except the victim's and nothing unusual among the contents. There was $84.26 in the wallet. There was no cell phone, and one hadn't been found at the scene.

Was that meaningful? Why would anybody, even Walter, steal Eugenia Lockwood's cell phone? People forget their cell phones all the time. Maybe it would turn up when they searched her home.

The address was on Larkin Street, which meant it was probably an apartment.

So, what were they left with? A random, motiveless murder and four digits written on the victim's arm. It didn't seem like much.

• • •

At six-thirty that morning, before he had even brewed his tea, Stephen Tregear turned on the computer in his workroom. Within two minutes he was reading the police reports on the homicide of Eugenia Lockwood. The news failed to surprise him.

Walter seemed in a hurry, and it never crossed Tregear's mind that this latest murder was not his father's work. If he had had any doubts, the four digits on the victim's forearm would have erased them. Like Ellen, he interpreted them as a time signature: 8:15 A.M.

The question then became, what happened at 8:15 A.M.? Perhaps without realizing it, Ellen provided the answer.

"No cell phone was recovered from the victim's purse or at the scene. Its absence has been noted as surprising."

Very surprising. Something like 93 percent of adults under thirty owned a cell phone, and the figures were higher for women than for men. Eugenia Lockwood, according to her driver's license, was twenty-eight.

Within three minutes Tregear had confirmed that, yes, Eugenia Lockwood had owned a cell phone. He also had the number.

He dialed it. After one ring it rolled to a recording of a rather breathy female voice: "This is Eugenia. I can't take your call right now . . ."

Of course. Dad didn't want his whereabouts traced, so he had switched the thing off. He would be available only at the time indicated.

Tregear looked at his watch. It was six fifty-five. He had an hour and twenty minutes to kill, so he went downstairs to his kitchen and scrambled himself a couple of eggs. He also brewed a mug of tea. He was going to need it.

It was finally beginning. After all these years, it was finally going to happen.

By the time he finished breakfast it was seven-twenty. He had fifty-five minutes to kill, so he took his half-full mug of tea upstairs and spent the time reading over the rest of the case files.

At eight-fifteen he pulled up his sound recording and tracking software and dialed the late Eugenia Lockwood's cell phone number. The phone rang exactly twice, then he heard the voice that had haunted his dreams for over twenty years.

"Yes?"

"Good morning, Dad."

27

What do you say to your father when he's a serial murderer, when he's killed your mother and your grandparents, when he's tried twice to kill you?

"How are you feeling, Dad?"

"Fine, son. Fine. Never better." This last punctuated with a faint chuckle.

"Why are you laughing, Dad? Because it's true or because it's not?"

"Just glad to hear your voice, son. It's been such a long time."

At first Tregear didn't know what to say. He felt overwhelmed by contradictory emotions. He felt like he was twelve years old again.

And then he remembered the corpse in his father's van, staring out at him through the plastic sheeting that was her shroud.

"Dad? Dad? Are you sick?"

"You mean sick in the head?" He laughed. "Probably."

"No. I just want to know why you're taking painkillers."

A slight pause, no longer than a few heartbeats. "Well, that's just a little stomach trouble, son. Nothing to worry about. You saw the bottle in my medicine cabinet?"

"Yes. And I think you're lying to me. I think you killed that doctor just so nobody would know how sick you really are."

"You always were a clever son of a bitch, Steve. You do me credit."

"Is there any chance I can get you to turn yourself in?" Tregear asked, almost pleadingly.

"I don't think so. I don't want to lie chained to a bed in some prison hospital. Besides, I still have unfinished business."

For a long moment there was silence. Tregear began to worry that his father would just hang up on him. He didn't want that. The tracking software was rapidly narrowing in on the signal source, and he wanted to keep Walter talking.

And, if he was honest with himself, he didn't want the conversation to end that way. He kept remembering the time his father had shown him the building site in Marion—all the times before his father had become a terrifying stranger. Walter.

"Is that why you're sticking around? They've got your fingerprints and your description. You can't hide anymore, Dad. They'll nail you."

"I'm not worried about them, Steve. You're the one who scares me."

"But it's the police who will kill you."

"They're welcome to try."

"Then why are we talking, Dad? What is this conversation about?"

"Maybe just for the pleasure of hearing your voice," he answered. "You are my son, after all."

"And you can hear my voice anytime you want. I'm calling you on my cell phone, and it's always with me. The phone you're talking on is a Blackberry Curve 8900. You can read my number off the display."

"Now how the hell did you know that?"

"How the hell did I know you were in San Francisco? It's an interesting question, isn't it."

"Do you know where I am right now?"

"Could be, Dad. The net is tightening."

"Well then, now that we've found each other again, let's stay in touch, son."

Before Tregear could say anything, the signal went dead. The tracking software had focused on an area of the Mission District, somewhere east of Van Ness Avenue and between Sixteenth and Twentieth streets. There were probably twenty-five thousand people currently occupying that space, so it wasn't very useful information.

Besides, Dad—Walter—was smart enough to turn off the phone and get out of there.

So. What did he have? Not much. A voice recording and a search area that would probably be out of date within the next ten minutes.

Tregear no longer even knew why he had made the call.

Yes, he did. He hadn't been able to help himself, and his father had guessed as much. And to achieve this brief conversation, a twenty-eight-year-old woman named Eugenia Lockwood had died in a shadowed parking lot.

· · ·

Sam appeared in the duty room at a few minutes after ten. He had been up half the night and today was his day off, but after six hours of sleep he knew he should be on the job, if only to keep Ellen from a state of collapse.

The instant he saw her, crouched in front of her computer, he knew his instinct had been correct. She had come straight in from the crime scene. She probably hadn't had more than two hours' sleep out of the past thirty-six. She looked like yesterday's hangover.

"You should go home," he told her.

She glanced up at him, giving no indication that she had even heard, then said, "Listen to this."

She hit a key and a voice recording started to play. It was the 911 call from last night, telling the police that they might find something interesting in the trunk of a car parked just south of Powell and Chestnut.

"Now listen to this." The second voice recording was Tregear and his father, and the father's voice was identical to last night's 911 caller.

Sam listened closely and, when the second recording was over, said, "Play it again."

The total impression, twice round, was even more bizarre.

"He shouldn't have done it," Ellen said, sounding more bitter than perhaps she intended. "Steve should have cleared it with us. Or just stayed the hell out."

"You think so?" Sam cocked his head a little to one side, as if he doubted she really believed what she was saying. "What would have happened if you or I had made that call? After the first word we've have been listening to a dial tone. You heard him. Walter isn't concerned with us—it's all between the two of them. This way we have good evidence that Walter is our perp in the Lockwood killing, we have the transcript and we have a line of communication to the Devil himself."

"So once again Tregear is way ahead of us."

She made it sound like a defeat, which meant that she was still angry. Sam put his hand on Ellen's shoulder and crouched down a little to look into her face.

"Tregear? You're just mad at him because he kicked you out. Well, what did you expect? The guy knows what Walter does to women. He's just trying to protect you."

There were tears in her eyes when she spoke again.

"But who's going to protect him?"

"Go home, Ellie." Sam shook his head. "You're worn out."

Ellen drew herself up and looked away. "My shift doesn't end until four-thirty."

"Your shift started at midnight and its ten-forty. Remember me? I'm your sergeant. Go home." He picked up the wad of printouts that was on Ellen's desk, looked at them with distaste, then set them back down. "I have to talk to Hempel."

"Okay. Then I'm going with you." The expression on her face was one of imperfectly suppressed defiance. "Remember me? I'm the case officer."

"Then you'll go home?"

"Then I'll go home."

So now both of them would get to tell Dave Hempel, who would have to tell the powers that be, that they had a situation on their hands.

Sam tapped his knuckle once against the glass and opened the door to the lieutenant's office.

Hempel glanced up and frowned. "What is it this time?"

After a leisurely inspection of the chairs, Sam sat down on the one that was out of the light from the window. He smiled.

"He's killed another one," he announced brightly. "Officer Ridley will give you the gruesome details."

Hempel looked at her, as if only then aware of her presence, and she sat down. Her recital took about five minutes. When it was over Hempel looked pained, as if he could already read the headlines.

"You're sure it's Walter?"

"We have solid evidence," Ellen announced cheerfully. "This makes four, if you don't count the doctor or the prostitute at the Marriott."

She could almost watch the dark thoughts chasing through the lieu-tenant's brain, and Ellen didn't blame him. Nobody liked an emer-gency. Emergencies always brought a flood of criticism, and the men upstairs, all captains and above, all lifers, policemen unto death, all worried about their next assignment and their next promotion, didn't like criticism. They wanted to ride their own momentum into some-thing sweet in the commissioner's office.

And all of those guys, who hadn't worked the street in years and years, would be looking to Dave Hempel to make this go away.

"We'll form a task force," the lieutenant proclaimed, as if he were preaching a crusade.

"Oh God!" Sam was so upset that he actually took his hat off.

"It's the only way."

Which meant it would look good in the newspapers. It would look like somebody was actually doing something, when in fact it would only tie up about twenty people with answering the phones. False tips, false confessions, nuts popping up like mushrooms sprouting on a rotten log.

"You can't make his identity public," Ellen said, as if to the wall. Her voice was all the more chilling for its lack of emphasis. "No picture, no names, no history. Walter wouldn't like it."

Hempel looked annoyed.

"And we're supposed to worry about whether the murderer of four, maybe five women likes his press notices?" He shook his head. "Of course we'll identify him. Maybe somebody will recognize him. Anyway, the citizens of San Francisco have a right to know that their police force has been doing its job."

"Is that what it's about? I thought we were just supposed to catch him."

Instantly Ellen realized that she had made a mistake. She had prodded Hempel in every desk cop's most vulnerable spot—his deep reverence for public relations.

But there was nothing to do except soldier on.

"Lieutenant, you have to understand something about our Walter. He's like a kid playing a video game. The screaming, the blood . . . it's all a fantasy. On a purely theoretical level he probably understands that there are laws against homicide, but he really doesn't think that his little amusements are any of our business. He already knows that we're on to him and he's not afraid of us, so a press conference isn't going to make him run away and stop bothering us. He'll resent it. He'll see it as a personal insult, a violation of his privacy. And he'll take his revenge."

She glanced at Sam, who was still clenching his hat.

"She's probably right," he said, staring at Hempel's office window as if it were a lost opportunity. "We don't want to stir this guy up."

"Well, from the rate he's going I'd say he's pretty stirred up already." Hempel smiled faintly, appearing to savor his little joke.

"Lieutenant, this is—"

"Inspector Ridley, I think we can excuse you now." Hempel's smile seemed frozen in place. "Sergeant Tyler and I have things to discuss."

"Go home, Ellie," Sam murmured. "Get some sleep."

The message was clear. She wasn't changing anybody's mind. She should get out of there before she did her career any more harm.

On the drive home, her anger was probably the only thing that kept her awake.

• • •

"And you'll lead it," Hempel announced, as soon as he and Sam were alone. He smiled, the way a man does when he's exacting revenge.

"The hell I will."

"You'll lead it. You're the senior inspector in charge." The lieutenant was very happy. He had solved his problem. "I'll schedule a press conference for four o'clock, in time for the evening news. Go prepare your statement. And put together a press kit on our suspect."

Upon his return to the duty room, Sam observed that Ellen's chair was empty. Apparently she had followed orders and gone home.

Damn. Sam hated the idea of stepping up in front of the television cameras and being the public face of the San Francisco Police Department. His wife would doubtless tape his ninety seconds of fame and insist that he watch it, and his neighbors in Daly City would rib him for a month.

Ellie would have done it much better. For one thing, she wasn't a frowzy middle-aged street cop wearing the wrong tie. Ellie had gone to college. For her it would be like standing up in lit class and reading a paper on the erotic symbolism in "Mother Goose." She would give a polished performance.

And now she was on her way home to a Lean Cuisine and bed. Lucky girl, she would probably miss the whole sorry show.

And she wouldn't even be around to correct his grammar.

• • •

But by four o'clock, despite vast misgivings, Sam was standing behind a lectern in the press room, blinking into the television lights. He had a prepared statement in his sweating hand and there were stacks of the press kit on a table behind him.

The press kit was mercifully brief, consisting of the few confirmed facts about Walter and the artist's sketch based on Mary Plant's description. Hempel had wanted something encyclopedic, just to prove the police were on their toes, but Sam knew better. He would give the public only what might help the investigation and no more. Otherwise the inevitable avalanche of false leads would be geometrically more vast and intractable.

"Last night," he began, "sometime between nine and nine-fifteen, there was a homicide in North Beach. The victim was a young woman—her name is not being released pending notification of her family—and she died of a single stab wound. Her body was found in the trunk of her car following an anonymous call to 9-1-1.

"Last night's tragedy was the latest in a series of homicides occurring in and around San Francisco which, on the basis of forensic and other evidence, the police are convinced are the work of a single individual."

Sam took off his glasses and wiped them with a handkerchief as he waited for the furor to subside. It was inevitable. Serial killers were reasonably rare, even in California, and they sold more newspapers than a celebrity divorce.

"The suspect appears to be a white male in his middle fifties, working in the building trades or as a handyman. Our office is in possession of DNA evidence and fingerprints. We have a physical description and an artist's rendering, which will be made available to the press. The suspect is armed and must be considered extremely dangerous. If any member of the public recognizes this man, they should call the police immediately. They should under no circumstances approach the suspect themselves.

"We have reason to believe the suspect may be involved in a series of homicides, in various parts of the country and stretching over a period of several years . . ."

Sam's announcement took less than two minutes, but the questions ran on for an hour and a half. The press room walls seemed to vibrate with the noise. It was like the shouting of a lynch mob.

• • •

Ellen was awake and eating a chicken pot pie in her pajamas when the six o'clock news came on. Sam's press conference was the lead segment and the background stories went on for another ten minutes.

At first she could hardly believe it. Sam? Why not some captain from Administration, some faceless bureaucrat in a blue uniform, safely distanced from the investigation? Now Walter would know who was hunting him. Hempel might as well have painted a bull's-eye on Sam's forehead.

During the commercial break her cell phone rang.

"Did I wake you up?" Sam asked timidly. Of course, that wasn't the reason he had called.

"No. I watched you on TV. You were pretty good."

"Was I okay?"

"You were more than okay. You were dignified and precise, and you didn't give too much away. You were great."

"He fucking forced me to do it."

"Hempel?"

"Yeah. I'm going to need you tomorrow to organize this stupid task force. It'll take all morning just to find enough chairs. It's going to be a pig's dinner."

"I know. It'll be all right."

"I'm worried that it might scare Walter off. If he bolts, and then nothing happens for the next month, the newspapers will eat us whole."

"He won't bolt, Sam. He's got unfinished business here. Besides, he's probably enjoying the publicity."

"Well, I'm not."

For just a second or two Ellen hesitated. She knew what she wanted to say and that she would never forgive herself if something bad happened and she hadn't said it, but she also knew Sam would think she was getting hysterical.

Still, it had to be said.

"Sam, will you do me a favor?"

"Sure. Name it."

"Stay on your toes. Walter probably watches the news. He saw your face and he knows your name. Hempel should never have let you get up in front of those microphones."

"Ellie, do you know how many death threats I've had in my career?"

"Lots, I'll bet. And most of them were just noise."

"All of them were just noise."

"Well, this is different. This is Walter. He won't threaten. He'll just do it."

"Sure. Okay."

Ellen could only shake her head. *Sure. Okay.* It was the best she was going to get.

"I'll see you tomorrow morning, Sam. Early."

"That's right, little girl. Early."

After she had clicked off the phone, Ellen could not overcome a sense of uneasiness. A terrible blunder had just been committed, of that she felt sure. This task force was nothing more than a political stunt, a completely unnecessary leap into the unknown.

Now perhaps the hunters would become the hunted.

• • •

Walter, as he watched the television news, was not happy. He did not like this turn of events. It was one thing to read about one's exploits in the newspaper, but television was another matter. It was way too personal.

And he didn't like the drawing. The resemblance struck him as less than perfect—they had made him look like a shoplifter—and he didn't like the fact of the thing. Its mere existence was offensive. How the hell had they come by it?

Then he remembered Mary Plant. It was either Mary or the receptionist at the doctor's office, and he put his money on Mary. The receptionist had seen him only once, but Mary really, really knew what he looked like.

Steve, of course, was out. Steve hadn't set eyes on him in over twenty years, and the face in the drawing was middle-aged.

Middle-aged and weary. It was not the way he wanted people to see him—he didn't want people to see him at all. Vastly more important, it was not the way he saw himself.

That cop who had conducted the press briefing—what was his name? They had flashed it on the screen, but Walter couldn't remember. He would watch the late news, and this time he would write it down.

That cop was getting into things that were none of his business.

28

Tregear had also watched the press conference and also felt it was a mistake.

He had an impression of his father, shaped by his early memories and years of meticulous research, as a careful, deliberate man. Even his apparently random migrations were always plotted out in advance. He knew where he was going and what he would find there. Everything was planned.

Yet since he had been driven from the house in Half Moon Bay, Walter seemed to be improvising. Last night he had murdered a woman, a stranger. He had picked her at random, then stabbed her to death in a parking lot, then walked away. It was almost as out of character as the prostitute at the Marriott.

In all likelihood, the prostitute had been another target of opportunity, but at least the act of killing her would have accorded with Walter's ideas of fun.

He lures her into an empty hotel room and gets her to take off her clothes. So far, from her point of view, it's all business as usual. Then he points a pistol at her.

It was possible to imagine what the last five minutes of her life were like. "If you make a sound, I'll gut shoot you. You'll die in agony. You might live to suffer a few hours, but they won't be able to save you. Now come with me."

And then takes her into the bathroom and makes her get down on her hands and knees in the bathtub. He pushes her face down against the drain and then slides the pistol barrel into her anus. He might talk to her for a few minutes, listening to her plead, savoring her fear, then he squeezes the trigger, twice. Had Walter then pulled her head up by the hair so he could watch her face as she died?

Doubtless it wasn't as satisfying as taking Sally Wilkes down to his basement, strapping her to a table and then pulling her guts out while she was still alive, but Walter would have enjoyed himself in that hotel room.

Eugenia Lockwood, however, was something else entirely. An hour before the press conference, Tregear had read the autopsy report, and she had died almost instantly, probably without ever realizing what was happening to her, without even time to be afraid.

Where was the fun in that?

The answer seemed to be that Walter had lost interest in tormenting individual women and was now tormenting the police.

And now they had taken the bait.

There was emerging in Walter a terrifying heedlessness. The police could have his fingerprints and his DNA—he had made them a present of his DNA. They could have all the clues and evidence they wanted. He didn't seem to care.

Tregear turned off the television in his workroom and went down to the kitchen to make himself a cup of tea. He would drink it alone. Ellen wouldn't be there to tell him how dreadful it was. He missed her horribly.

As he waited for the water to boil, his cell phone rang. For an instant of wild hope he thought it might be Ellen. In spite of everything he had said and believed about the dangers, he wanted it to be Ellen.

But it wasn't. The screen displayed Eugenia Lockwood's phone number.

"Did you watch the news? How does it feel to have a celebrity in the family?"

"Hi, Dad."

"Did you see it?"

"I saw it." Tregear searched for something else to say. "They only credited you with four. They're not sure about the one at the Marriott."

"I noticed that. You can tell them from me that the score so far is five, plus the doctor. I killed the whore too."

"I'll pass it along. I'm sure they'll be grateful for the correction."

"You should have been there, son. She complained that the front sight hurt her asshole."

"I can't say I'm sorry I missed it, Dad."

"That's because you have an underdeveloped sense of humor."

Tregear could feel his heart pounding. He noticed that the tea kettle was boiling furiously and he pulled the plug out of the wall socket. He was grateful for that little distraction. It helped him find his voice again.

"Could be."

Apparently Walter didn't like that answer, because there was a silence that probably lasted ten or twelve seconds. Tregear could hear traffic sounds in the background, just loud enough to suggest that his father was out of doors somewhere.

"You can tell them something else from me," Walter said finally. "You can tell them that I've decided to raise the stakes."

Then Tregear found himself listening to a dial tone.

.   .   .

At seven-thirty that evening, Tregear phoned Homicide. He expected merely to leave a message but apparently Sam was still in the building and he was put through directly.

"Hello, Steve—what have you got for me?"

"I had a call from Walter. You can move the Marriott hooker into the 'confirmed' column. He told me all about it."

"Give credit where credit is due?"

"That's about right."

"Anything else?"

"He says he's decided to 'raise the stakes.' Those were his words."

"Any idea what he means?"

"Yes. It's not anything you'll have trouble guessing."

"More dead bodies?"

"That's the prevailing currency."

There was a brief interruption, during which Tregear could hear Sam complaining to someone who had not renewed the coffee urn. Then he came back with another question.

"Can you come in tomorrow morning?"

"What for?"

"To make Ellie happy, and to talk to me."

"What time?"

"Early."

.   .   .

Ellen was at her desk by 7:00 A.M. Within forty-five minutes she had the technical people hooking up communications equipment in a couple of unused waiting rooms, and she had a squad of recent police academy graduates, rescued from traffic duty, to man the phones.

When Sam came in, at a quarter to eight, he rewarded her with a chocolate-covered doughnut and a gigantic paper cup of Starbucks Caffè Misto.

"I've sworn off the house brew," he said. "When we catch him, I'll use it to poison Walter. He'll die by lethal ingestion."

He paused, clearly waiting for some appreciative response to his joke, but Ellen's attention was elsewhere.

"What am I supposed to do with that?" She made a disparaging little gesture toward the doughnut. "Doughnuts are bad for you. Have you ever seen me eat a doughnut?"

"Doughnuts are part of the police subculture, but if you don't want it you can always give it to Tregear. He could use the calories."

The phone rang. Sam picked up the receiver, listened for a few seconds and said, "Yeah. Send him up." His smile was catlike.

"Guess who."

For a moment Ellen didn't say anything. She seemed to be trying to make up her mind about whether or not she should be angry.

"What's he doing here, Sam?"

"He's here by invitation. Mine."

The elevator at the opposite end of the hallway made a loud pinging noise.

"That's him," Sam announced. "I'm going to have a talk with him—you know, get his perspective on how things are developing—and then you might want to find a nice, quiet interrogation room where you can take his statement. If you feel like it, you can arrest him as a material witness. I don't suppose he'll mind."

They saw him first through one of the plate glass windows that ran along the whole inside wall of the duty room. He was wearing the same tan Windbreaker he'd worn in the film taken the morning Sally Wilkes had been found. When he saw Ellen, he smiled.

"Mr. Tregear. Such a pleasure."

Sam stood up and offered his hand, which Tregear accepted without taking his eyes from Ellen's face.

"Let's find somewhere we can talk."

That turned out to be the lieutenant's office. Hempel was attending a conference at city hall, agreeing with everything the mayor said, and wouldn't be showing his face until after lunch. Sam sat down behind the desk.

"Why don't you begin by filling Inspector Ridley in about last night's conversation with Walter?"

Tregear and Ellen were sitting in the two visitors' chairs, and Ellen flashed him a look of instantly suppressed astonishment.

"He surprised me," Tregear said, clearly offering an apology. "I wasn't able to record the call, so I phoned Sam. Pardon me—Inspector Sergeant Tyler. I wrote out a transcript, as near as I can remember."

He fished a sheet of paper, folded in thirds, from an inside pocket and put it on the desk.

"I've set up my equipment so that all future calls to my cell will copy to a sound file."

"So what did he say?" Ellen asked, not even glancing at the folded transcript.

"It's all there." Tregear nodded toward the desk. "You can read it."

Sam picked up the paper, opened it and handed it to Ellen. She read it through without apparent reaction, then handed it back to Sam.

"What did I tell you?" she asked, as if the two of them were alone in the room. "We've hurt his feelings, so he's going to punish us. He's going to 'raise the stakes,' which means he's going to go from killing people we don't know to killing people we do."

"Maybe he'll shoot the mayor," Sam answered, smiling faintly.

"He isn't mad at the mayor, Sam. The mayor didn't put his picture up on TV. He's mad at us."

Sam glanced at Tregear, who merely shrugged—he wasn't disagreeing.

"Which means he's mad at you, Sam," Ellen went on, still ignoring Tregear's presence. "And probably Mary Plant, since he'll have figured out that she gave us his face, but mainly you."

The perfect host, Sam turned his attention to Tregear.

"What do you think?" he asked, giving the impression that he found all this just a touch absurd. "Should I start coming to work in a Kevlar vest?"

"I think she's probably right," Tregear answered. Then he looked at Ellen and smiled.

"This is all about him," he went on. "Your motives and feelings don't mean anything to him. He's like a child who isn't getting his way. He'll hit back."

"And he'll probably try for you at home," Ellen put in. The idea had just formed in her mind. "He can't get at you here, but he won't have any trouble finding out where you live. You should get Millie out of the house."

Still amused, Sam turned to Tregear.

"Millie is Mrs. Tyler," he announced, as if he thought the question might have been preying on Tregear's mind.

Tregear nodded. "It's good advice," he said.

"Why did he phone you?" Ellen asked, relenting a little. "Did he think you wouldn't tell us?"

"No, he knows I'll convey the message." Tregear made a despairing little gesture with his left hand. "It's part of the act—his little pantomime. He's playing Dear Old Dad. He'll kill me first chance he gets and he's knows I know it, but he likes to play the role."

"But . . ." Sam seemed at a loss. "He is your father."

"So what?"

"So he'd really kill you?"

"Yes. I think that's what this is all about. For some reason of his own, he needs my death."

"Why would that be?" It was Ellen who asked the question. "Because you've been hunting him?"

"I don't think so. Five years ago, even five months ago, I might have said yes. I might have flattered myself that he was afraid of me."

"Why shouldn't he be afraid of you?" Ellen leaned toward him. "He said as much himself yesterday morning. 'You're the one I'm afraid of.' And he's right. If we'd done it your way in Half Moon Bay, he'd be dead or in jail right now."

"You'll never put him in a cell. He won't ever just surrender. And I don't think he's afraid of death. He's leaving a trail of evidence the Brownies could follow. He wants a showdown, but it isn't out of fear."

"Then why?"

"Maybe to get even." Tregear could only shrug, perhaps to suggest his own doubts about the theory. "I got away from him. Twice. Three times, if you count running away when I was twelve. Maybe he just wants to prove that I'm not smarter than he is."

• • •

When he was alone, after Ellie had dragged Tregear off somewhere, Sam kept thinking about retirement. He had been a cop for twenty-four years, an inspector for nineteen, on Homicide for fourteen. If he wanted to, he could start cashing his pension checks next month.

But did he want to? He wasn't sure. Aside from a stint in the Marines, being a cop was almost the only job he had ever had. What else was there for him to do? He didn't want to spend the rest of his life surf fishing.

But was Homicide any better? About once a month it occurred to him that he was bored with murders. The average murderer was some dunce who just about caught himself. Then there were the drug killings, which were rarely solved, but which didn't matter because that particular crime almost counted as a public service. And finally there were cases like this one, real mysteries. But what kind of a job was it in which finding a corpse in the trunk of someone's car constituted a refreshing break from the routine?

And now Ellen was telling him that his life might be in danger.

But it did occur to him that he might as well follow her advice and send Millie down to her sister's in Palo Alto, just until Walter was off the streets.

• • •

But strictly speaking Walter wasn't on the streets. He was at the public library, trying to figure out how the computer worked.

Eventually he stumbled on the Search function and then things got easier. When he typed in "Samuel Tyler" he was rewarded with a long list of references, most of them newspaper articles about criminal cases. He learned that twenty years previous then Patrolman Tyler had received a departmental commendation for saving a three-year-old girl from a fire. Upon promotion to inspector, he had worked in Vice and then Robbery for five years before reaching Homicide. His list of arrests was impressive. He had a wife named Mildred and a married daughter who lived in Bakersfield. The daughter's wedding had been held at St. Andrew's Catholic Church in Daly City.

A search of the Daly City phone book revealed a "Tyler, Mildred" living at 441 Belhaven Avenue.

That was easy.

29

Tregear left Homicide a few minutes before eleven. They couldn't even have lunch in the diner around the corner because he didn't want to risk being seen with Ellen. But at least they had had a few hours together, a little interval in which to feel human.

And then it was back to work.

Ellen sat at her desk with the evidence reports from the Lockwood crime scene. They made an eight-inch-high stack of manila folders. She was a third of the way through it before she found the parking ticket discovered by Officer Ludlow, Timothy J. She brought the DMV link up on her screen and typed in the plate number.

Wait a minute. The ticket described a gray Kia, but the plates belonged on a white Ford. The Ford was registered to a Stanley Eco of 221 Winding Road in Belmont. It would be interesting to know where Mr. Eco thought his car was. Ellen dialed the phone number.

A woman answered. "Hello?"

"Is this the Eco residence?"

"Yes."

"This is Inspector Ridley from the San Francisco Police Department. Could I speak to Mr. Eco, please?"

"He's at work. This is Mrs. Eco." By then a thread of anxiety had found its way into her voice. "Can I help you?"

"I hope so, ma'am. We're looking into a possible grand theft auto of a gray Kia, license plate number 6AOB291. Have you or your husband reported such a car lost or stolen recently?"

"That's the number on my husband's car—but it's white, it isn't gray."

"Where is the car now, ma'am?"

"It's in the garage, where it's supposed to be," Mrs. Eco almost shouted. "What is this all about?"

"There's nothing to be worried about, ma'am. But I will need to verify that the car is in your possession. Could you arrange to be home for the next few hours?"

"Well . . . I suppose so."

"And, please, don't touch the car."

As soon as she was finished with Mrs. Eco, Ellen phoned Evidence and gave them the address.

"I've got a lead on Walter's car," she told Sam. "He switched the plates."

Two minutes later she was in her Toyota, leaving the police garage.

Traffic was light and Ellen was in Belmont in a little over forty-five minutes. She drove up Ralston Avenue and found the Eco house in a tangle of streets west of the Alameda de las Pulgas. It was a beige two-bedroom tract house, probably built right after the Second World War. It was clinging to the down slope of a hill, so the driveway was quite steep.

The door was answered by a fiftyish woman with unconvincingly black hair. She looked up at the street, where Ellen had parked, and seemed relieved not to see a squad car.

Ellen held up her badge for Mrs. Eco's inspection.

"I suppose you'd better come in," was all the invitation she received.

The front door opened directly into a living room that was no more than about twelve by twenty. On the far side there was a wooden table and chairs and a china cabinet to demarcate it as the dining area. The inside of the house was oppressively hot, as if no one ever opened a window.

Mrs. Eco had not asked her to sit down.

"Ma'am, as I told you over the phone, I'm with the San Francisco Police Department." Ellen smiled thinly. She was taking her revenge. "I have no jurisdiction in Belmont, so if you would rather deal with the local police I can have them here in ten minutes."

"Oh, no! I . . . Please." Mrs. Eco turned her face slightly away and seemed to draw some spiritual comfort from contemplating her fireplace. "I'm sure . . ."

"Then I wonder if I might look at the car."

Ellen phrased it as the most distant surmise, which was her way of relenting.

The garage was accessible through the kitchen and had space for two cars. The white one was on the left. There were three wooden steps down to the cement floor, and Mrs. Eco stood on the landing and pushed a button just to her right that lifted up the door to the outside.

"Those aren't Stan's plates," she said, standing with Ellen behind the car. "How could that have happened?"

"Mrs. Eco, how does your husband normally get to work?"

"By train. I drive him down to the station in the morning. He works in the city."

"So the car is usually in your garage?"

"Yes." Mrs. Eco nodded sharply—but only once, as if a doubt had begun to creep into her mind. "Except when he travels. He's a compliance officer for Bank of America, and they send him all over the place, even up to Seattle. Most of the time he flies, but sometimes he drives."

"Has the car been away from home over the past week?"

"Yes. Stan flew to San Diego. He drove to the airport and left the car in long-term parking. He just got back Wednesday."

"How long was he gone?"

"Four days."

"Then that's probably when the plates were switched."

Ellen looked up the driveway to the street, where an unmarked panel truck had pulled up behind her car. The doors popped open and two men in coveralls came out, each carrying a dark brown canvas satchel.

The boys of Evidence had arrived.

"I want prints, front and back of the car," she told them. "And print Mrs. Eco here. Her husband works for a bank, so his will be on file. And I want the plates."

She turned to Mrs. Eco, who looked aghast, and smiled.

"One of these gentlemen will take your fingerprints." While she was talking, she brought out her notepad and jotted down the license number. "Don't worry. The ink rubs right off and it's only for purposes of elimination. Your husband's prints and yours are going to be all over this car, and we just need to know what we're looking at."

"But the plates . . ." Mrs. Eco's voice was pitched somewhere between outrage and pleading. "We can't drive the car if it doesn't have any plates."

"They're evidence in a felony investigation. I'll have the DMV send you a new set. I'll tell them to put a rush on it."

Using the laptop in the Evidence truck, Ellen fed the license number into the department database. The car was not listed as stolen, so the odds were the owner had put it in the long-term parking lot at the airport, the same place the Eco car had been parked, and hadn't yet come back to discover his loss. A check of the DMV site listed a 2009 Kia, color gray, plate number 2FLN211, as registered to a Chester Mowry, 2504 Middlefield Road in Berkeley.

She phoned Sam.

"Have you got any friends in the Berkeley PD?"

"Sure. What's up, girl?"

Ellen gave him everything that she had. "Unless he's ditched it already, that's what Walter's driving around in. We need to know chapter and verse about that car, including the contents."

"I'll make the call."

Driving back to San Francisco, Ellen couldn't help but feel reasonably pleased with herself. The parking ticket had yielded the description and, unless Walter had switched plates again, she now had the license number of his car. If he had left his prints on the Eco car, it would place him at the scene of Eugenia Lockwood's murder. The noose was growing tighter.

Patrol cars could be out looking for a gray Kia already this evening—no, tomorrow. The alert would have to be part of the morning's oral briefing. They couldn't broadcast it today because Walter might be listening to the police band.

By the time she got back to the city it would be four and her shift would be over. She would stop in at the department anyway, just to see if anything interesting had come in and to say good night to Sam, if he was still there.

He wasn't, but there was a note on her desk stating that the Berkeley PD reported that no one was answering the phone at 2504 Middlefield Road but that they would send someone around that evening. Sam had given them her cell phone number.

Out of boredom as much as anything else, Ellen went back to the

DMV website for a second look. She found the name of the Oakland dealership that had sold the car to Mr. Mowry.

Finally, she wrote up her report and posted it to the department database.

Having at last run out of excuses, she went down to the garage to reclaim her car for the drive back to her apartment, where Gwendolyn, who seemed to miss Steve, would eat her dinner and then sulk for the rest of the evening.

· · ·

As it happened, Sam had signed out early and driven through town to a diner on the Great Highway, where he could sit in a booth by the window and watch the waves breaking along Ocean Beach. As always, being a reminder of the pointlessness of all human struggle, the sight brought him to a state of pleasant melancholy. The waves had been running up this stretch of sand for a million years before the first murderer was born and would still be at it after the human race had given up and turned it all back over to the sea lions. The waves were without intention or wrath. They just went on and on.

Sometimes it was necessary to stop measuring time hour by hour and just sit back and eat your meat loaf special. Sometimes it was the only way to stay sane.

There was no one waiting for him at home, not even the dogs. As instructed, Millie had cleared out and gone to her sister's, taking the tribe with her. Millie's sister owned an elderly German shepherd who seemed to enjoy the company.

Tonight his only company would be a six-pack of Sierra Nevada IPA—and, of course, Walter's dark shadow.

He could imagine how the evening would run. Halfway through his second bottle he would turn on the television, hoping the noise would drown out his thoughts. When that didn't work he would go outside to occupy a lounge chair on the back porch. Eventually, when he could no longer see his neighbor's house, he would turn on the porch light and watch the bugs as they searched for a way through the screen. By this time he would be into his fourth ale.

And Walter, silent and listening, would be right there with him, sometimes taking fitful shape in the darkness beyond the porch light. Walter the monster, who had raised murder into an art form.

In his fourteen years with Homicide, Sam had hunted two serial killers and actually caught one of them. The other had fled to Los Angeles, where he committed three more murders and was arrested, entirely accidently, by a rookie traffic cop who had pulled him over for not using his turn signal. Afterward, Sam had flown down to interview him. They had spent most of an afternoon together.

Both men were currently on San Quentin's death row, where they regularly gave interviews and sorted through their fan mail, objects of intense interest to people who would remain forever strangers.

Somewhere Sam had read that life was most successfully viewed through a single window, but he was inclined to regard this as no more than a clever turn of phrase. Both Keith Jarvis and Eddie Massie were so obsessed with their various grievances that neither had been very successful at much of anything except murder. Probably both were far happier on death row, where the current logjam in capital case appeals meant they were much more likely to die of old age than lethal injection. They would have decades in which to enjoy the smug sense of having at last beat the system.

Up close and personal, both had proved to be disappointments, pathetically deficient in every human quality except malice and cunning.

But Walter, according to his son, was a different animal. He was intelligent and charming, and not so much blind to human feeling as merely indifferent. He understood people, but without any complicating sympathy. There was no sense in which he was compensating for anything or getting even. He just enjoyed torturing women the way teenagers enjoyed slasher movies.

It might even be true. After all, Tregear was the resident expert on Walter.

Sam pulled into his driveway and pressed the remote that opened his garage door. He put his headlights on high beam and sat in his car for a moment, studying the interior of the garage. Millie's car was gone, already down in Palo Alto, and there was nothing inside except the lawn mower and, against the back wall, a long shelf supporting the usual collection of dried-up paint cans.

"You're getting spooked, Sam," he whispered to himself. "Cut it out."

From force of habit, he parked his car on the driveway and actually had the door open before he remembered to close the garage.

He followed the flagstones around to the backyard. The porch enclosed the entire rear of the house, and its door was never locked. As he crossed the deck he decided it probably needed restaining. The kitchen door had a double bolt and as he turned the key in the lock he caught himself listening for the dogs. But they were with Millie, in Palo Alto.

The house was dark, so he turned on the overhead light in the kitchen and went to the refrigerator for a beer. He poured it into a tall glass, tasted it, then left both the bottle and the glass on the kitchen counter when he went into the bedroom.

He took off his sport coat and hung it in the closet, then he unclipped the handcuff case and the holster from his belt and opened the top drawer of the highboy dresser and dropped the handcuff case inside. Usually the holster followed it, but tonight Sam could not seem to let it go. He just stood there, holding it in his hand as if trying to remember what it was.

The holster held a standard police-issue .38 revolver with a four-inch barrel. It was the weapon he had carried since he was a rookie and had never fired except at the pistol range. He hated the damn thing for the way the grip gouged at his kidney every time he sat down. The gun was merely one of the inconveniences of being a cop.

But maybe not tonight.

This is different. This is Walter, Ellen had said.

Sam took the revolver out of its holster. Maybe just this once he'd keep it with him.

He went back out to the kitchen and tasted his beer again. Having lost just a little of its chill, it was perfect.

The television in the living room would stay off tonight. To hell with it.

He went out to the porch, the glass of beer in one hand, the gun in the other. The lounge chair welcomed him. He set the revolver down on the wooden floor, where he could reach it easily with his right hand, and put the beer on the table.

The porch light was on, but the yard was full of murky shadows. Sam could just make out the top of the fence and the vague outline of a neighbor's tree. Anybody could be out there. He got up, switched on the backyard floods and killed the porch light. Then he sat down again. He felt much better.

It was a warm night, and windless. He could hear a cricket some-where, and the usual traffic sounds, but nothing else. He drank his beer and felt himself beginning to relax. When it was finished he went into the kitchen and got another.

. . .

Sergeant Sam's house was a squat, one-story building with rather small windows, set back about thirty feet from the sidewalk on slightly rising ground. Walter had been involved in the construction of so many houses just like it that he had no trouble imagining the interior layout—a master bedroom in front, to the left of the living room with a hallway in between. There would be a second bedroom behind the master, a dining room behind the living room and the kitchen all the way in the rear.

The front windows were dark, but there was a car parked in the driveway. Walter put his hand on the hood and discovered it was warm. Somebody was home.

The garage was separated from the house by a flagstone walkway that seemed to lead to the backyard. Standing there in his rubber-soled shoes, Walter could see that the outdoor lights were on in the back-yard. There were no lights in the front yard. Did that mean there was a porch in the back where the sergeant was perhaps even now taking his ease?

The question of Sergeant Sam's location in the house was critical. After all, the man was a cop and cops carried guns. It wouldn't do to give him any warning—one couldn't simply break in through the front door and start going room to room.

Besides, there was no hurry. Better to take one's time and do the thing right. Nobody would start paying any attention until the first shot was fired.

There was a Mrs. Sam. Mildred. Where was she?

The garage had one window and there was enough light to look inside and see space for a second car. So where was it?

Why was the other car parked on the driveway instead of in the garage?

Walter did not particularly want to kill the sergeant's wife. It wasn't enough. It was even possible that Sam might be very happy to get rid of Mildred. He didn't care to do the guy any favors.

He wanted to kill Sam. Only Sam would do.

So what did the car parked outside tell him?

Sam would leave in the morning and not come back until late afternoon. Mrs. Sam would be in and out all day, running the mysterious errands that constitute a housewife's life. She would want to be at home when her husband returned. Therefore, she would park her car in the garage and Sam would park in the driveway. QED, as Steve used to say.

Unless, of course, she worked.

Walter went back to the car and looked in the driver's side window. It was a man's car. The front seat was set all the way back and there was trash in the console. Women were tidier than that.

It was Sam's car. Sam was home and his missus was most likely off somewhere. Perfect.

Which still left the problem of where exactly Sam was in the house.

There was nothing going on in Sam's living room. Walter had already had a good look and the front of the house was dark, without even the bluish glow of a television set.

That left the back, where a light was on.

The path between the house and the garage led to a wooden gate, about four feet high, and a section of picket fence that filled the remaining space to the garage.

Standing close to the gate, Walter could see that the back of the house was indeed enclosed by a screened porch. About six feet this side of where the porch started there was a door and a set of cement stairs leading up to it. The odds were short that it was a kitchen door and that the kitchen was also directly accessible from the porch.

A man sitting at his ease on his own back porch has no reason to keep quiet, so Walter stood still and listened. After a few minutes he was rewarded with a dull click, the sound of a glass or mug being set down on a wooden table.

It was Sergeant Sam's cocktail hour.

This greatly simplified the task at hand. All Walter had to do was walk back to the side of the porch, take aim through the wire mesh and start shooting.

The only problem was the gate because the gate was closed. It would be hard to open noiselessly and the attempt, should it fail, would give Sam about a five-second heads-up. If he had his gun with him, that could be awkward.

Then Sam made everything easy by getting up. There was the scrape of furniture against the porch floor, followed almost immediately by the sound of a door being opened. Sam was going back into the house.

Walter did not move until light came through the glass panes of the side door, which meant that Sam was in the kitchen getting himself a refill. Then Walter opened the gate latch with only the faintest possible sound and the gate swung open silently on its hinges.

He stood out of sight, just at the edge of the screen, holding his .32 in both hands and waiting for Sam to come back out. Finally there was the sound of a door opening and then footsteps on the porch's wooden floor.

Now.

He stepped out and was at first surprised by how dark the porch was. Sam was still on his feet, only a vague shape in the darkness. Walter fired once and the shape instantly went down.

He could only wait. The shadow on the floor did not move. After perhaps thirty seconds Walter thought he heard a soft moan.

The son of a bitch was still alive.

Walter considered if he should go in there and finish the job, but there were too many risks. Sam might have his piece on him and even a dying man can kill you. Besides, people might ignore the sound of one shot—one shot could be a car backfiring. But two shots rated a call to the police.

Better just to let Sergeant Sam bleed out. Time to leave.

30

E llen had just finished dinner when her cell phone rang. She thought it would be the Berkeley police, reporting in about Mr. Mowry, but the area code was San Francisco.

With a slight shock she realized it was Steve.

"Hello," she said, as seductively as she could manage. "How are you?"

There was a silence that lasted perhaps a second. Was he embarrassed?

"Ellie," he responded finally, "Walter's car is parked about half a block from Sam's house."

"When?"

"Right now. Get everything you can over there. Send an ambulance."

"How do you know this?" The question instantly seemed irrelevant and stupid. "You're sure?"

"I'm sure. I'll meet you there."

And then the line went dead.

For perhaps five seconds Ellen stared at her cell phone, unable to move beyond her own astonishment. Gradually an image began to form in her mind—it was Sam, lying facedown in a pool of blood.

She made the call.

It was seven forty-five and the evening rush hour was just beginning to tail off. Ellen was not prepared to put up with traffic. She took the flasher from her backseat and stuck it on the roof of her car. She had never used it before, so she spent a second or two figuring out that the power cable plugged into her cigarette lighter.

When the roads were clear she could make it to Sam's in a little more than half an hour. Today, her horn blaring, she did it in twenty-three minutes.

Almost as soon as she made the turn onto Belhaven Avenue she spotted what looked like Walter's car, parked about two doors down from Sam's house. Ellen pulled in behind it, got out and stopped just long enough to check the license plate.

6AOB291, big as life.

The next thing she noticed was the quiet. Belhaven Avenue was just another suburban street on a Friday evening. There were no police cars, no ambulance, no cops milling around.

This was not what she had expected.

Then she looked across the street and saw an elderly couple standing on their front lawn, and she knew at once what had happened.

Ellen had phoned in the call to the SFPD exchange and they had called the Daly City cops, who didn't know a thing in the world about Walter and were slow to react. Maybe they would send around a patrol car in another ten minutes, maybe not.

So she was alone here, and Walter was probably inside Sam's house. Had the couple across the street heard a shot? Was that what had brought them out? It didn't seem like the right time to ask.

It didn't matter. If Sam was down he was down, but down wasn't the same as dead. Sam was her partner and you didn't let your partner die just because there was no backup. You had to do something.

Ellen drew her nine-millimeter and started across Sam's front lawn.

She was perhaps five feet from the sidewalk when a man appeared, coming down the walkway between the house and the garage. For an instant she thought it might be Sam, but then she knew it wasn't.

It was Walter, and there was a gun in his hand.

"Drop it!" she shouted. "Drop it now."

He just laughed.

Ellen didn't hesitate. She raised her weapon and fired.

Walter appeared to stagger a bit, then he raised his weapon. She could almost feel herself in his sights when she fired again.

And then everything stopped.

. . .

Ellen never heard the shot that hit her. Suddenly she was just flat on her back. She could feel the grass beneath her hand and it felt cool.

She was conscious, but very little more. She seemed to have no will, but there was also no fear. She could listen and watch. That was it.

Walter was standing over her. He was holding a small automatic in his right hand. His *right* hand? Now why was that? He was pointing it at her.

And then she heard the sound of a police siren. It seemed to be coming from all directions at once. It hurt her head.

Or maybe her head just hurt for some other reason. She didn't know.

Walter seemed ready to finish her, and she found herself wondering abstractedly if it would hurt. And then Walter brought his hand up. He seemed to be listening.

"Your lucky night, little girl," he said—Ellen recognized his voice from the sound files. "Maybe you'll be more useful alive than dead. Get on your feet."

She would have liked to explain to him that that didn't seem possible. She tried, but talking was suddenly a very complicated business that was just going to have to wait.

Walter kicked her in the hip, not very hard, and then apparently gave up. Suddenly his hand was on the collar of her jacket and he was dragging her over the lawn like a sack of fertilizer.

By the time they reached the flagstone walkway she had had enough and she managed to say, "Let go."

Walter stopped and released her, and Ellen discovered that she could just roll over so that she was on her hands and knees.

Then Walter grabbed her collar again and pulled her up to a standing position. When she didn't fall down right away he pushed her along toward the back of the house.

"You're all right," he said, as if he suspected she had been faking. "Come on, walk."

By the time they reached the screen door to the porch, Ellen had snapped out of her trance. She touched her forehead where it seemed to hurt the most and when she brought her hand away her fingertips were coated with blood. The concussion must have knocked her silly for a bit. She had the mother of all headaches, but otherwise she seemed to be in working order.

Although getting up the wooden stairs to the porch was something of an ordeal.

When she saw Sam lying there she forgot everything else. She pulled herself free of Walter's grip and dropped down on her knees beside her partner.

"Sam," she murmured, almost sobbing the word. "Sam, can you hear me?"

Slowly Sam opened his eyes. His breathing was labored, suggesting that he was in great pain. Blood was welling out from a bullet hole on his right side, just below his rib cage.

He seemed to be trying to speak. Ellen gathered up his right hand in both of hers and crouched down to hear him.

"My gun," he whispered. "It's on the floor."

He dragged his eyes down and to the right, as if pointing.

The sirens were much louder now and one of them ground to a halt.

Simply because she did not dare to look for the gun, Ellen turned around to look at Walter, who by now had slumped into a chair. There was blood in two places on his shirt, one on the right side and the other on the left, between the armpit and collarbone. His left arm was hanging limp.

The right-side wound probably amounted to nothing more than a few broken ribs, but the one on the left side was bad. It was bleeding heavily, so that his shirt was soaked down to his belt, and the nerve centers that controlled the left arm were likely in shreds.

And Walter was left-handed.

"They're *com*ing," she said to him, giving her voice a little lilt and flashing a ratty grin. "From the sound of it one just pulled up in front of the house, and I can hear others. In the time it takes to count to ten, they'll have you in a box. Think about it, Walter. There's nothing between us and the great wide world except some screening. If you stay in that chair it won't be more than sixty seconds before a SWAT sniper takes your head off."

But Walter only smiled.

"So you know my name?" he asked finally. "Then I'll bet you know my son."

· · ·

Tregear arrived almost simultaneously with the first police units. He drove up Belhaven Avenue and saw Ellen's car and then the olive-gray

Kia in front of it and drew all the obvious conclusions. He parked across the street from Sam's house.

As he started to open his car door, a man in a light blue sweatshirt with cutoff sleeves came by and pushed the door closed again. He put his hand on the roof and leaned down, smiling, not very nicely, as he pushed his sunglasses up into his curly black hair. There was a detective's badge dangling from a chain around his neck.

"Take off, buddy," he said. "We've got a situation here."

"I'm part of the situation." The cop had to get out of the way fast as Tregear opened his door and stepped out. "Who's in charge?"

"Jesus, mister!"

"I'll ask again. Who's in charge?"

"Nobody's in charge—we just got here. Who the fuck are you?"

Tregear dismissed the question with an impatient shrug.

"Have there been shots fired?" he asked.

"Yeah. Shots have been fired." The cop, who was probably in his middle twenties and certainly fancied himself, nodded vigorously. "Now, you're gonna find yourself under arrest if you don't get outa here. And I mean right now!"

Tregear didn't trouble himself to answer. Instead, as if dismissing the cop from existence, he turned, crossed the street and walked up on Sam's front lawn. As soon as he got to the flagstones he found traces of blood.

"Oh, God!"

"I'm sorry, sir, but I'm going to have to insist you leave now."

Tregear turned to face a different policeman, this one probably forty, in slacks and a Windbreaker, also with a badge hanging from a chain around his neck. His badge said, "Sergeant."

"Are you in charge here?" Tregear asked him.

The sergeant nodded.

"For the moment, yes. I'm Sergeant Brinkley, Daly City Police. And, like I said, you'll have to leave now, sir."

"This is Sam Tyler's house. That's right, isn't it?"

The sergeant nodded again. "Yes, sir. Everyone knows Sam."

Implying, of course, that such information was common knowledge and bought nobody any special favors.

"The call was phoned in by an Inspector Ridley of the SFPD," Tregear announced, almost as if offering a dare. "Sam is her partner and that's her car down there, parked behind the gray Kia, which, incidentally, is the subject of a fugitive warrant. Sam is in there, either wounded or dead—it's anybody's guess—and Inspector Ridley is with him."

For an instant he glared at the sergeant with something almost amounting to hatred. By now he was really angry and the emotion frightened him a little.

"They are being held hostage by a monster. Did you see Sam's press conference? Doesn't anybody watch the news anymore? What else would you like to know?"

The sergeant's eyes narrowed. "Who the hell are you, mister?"

It was a good question. Aside from Sam and Ellen, who were presently unavailable, hardly a soul in San Francisco Homicide had ever even heard of him. And this was Daly City.

Tregear took out his wallet and extracted Hal Roland's card. He handed it to the sergeant.

"My name is Stephen Tregear," he said. "Ask him."

. . .

"Do you know my baby boy?"

Walter smiled, then his head tilted a little to one side as his eyes narrowed.

"I remember you," he went on, in the tone of someone recalling a pleasant experience. "You were at the house. You showed up after the boys in the black jackets struck out. And Sam here was with you. And then, after a while, Steve arrived."

He shook his head and laughed.

"Isn't that funny? I'd forgotten about it until just now. I remember thinking, 'For a cop, she's damn cute.'"

Suddenly his face contracted with pain. When the spasm was over he looked down at his left shoulder.

"And you're a damn good shot too. But I don't hold that against you."

With his right hand he made a gesture toward the wall of the house.

"Why don't you be a good girl and snick off these floodlights?"

Ellen stood up and went over to the switch panel beside the door. In an instant the light in the backyard seemed to shudder and then disappear. She waited for her eyes to adjust to the darkness.

It wasn't any later than eight-thirty and still twilight. The porch was darker than the yard. It might be another half hour before anyone outside would find the darkness inconvenient.

Sam's gun was still lying on the floor just under the lounge chair, now covered by its impenetrable shadow. Apparently Walter hadn't noticed it.

"You need to be in a hospital," she said, without looking at Walter. "Otherwise you're not going to finish the evening alive—either the cops will kill you or you'll bleed to death."

Walter might as well have not heard. He was studying Ellen's face.

"I remember something else," he said. "You and Steve went into my house together. Did he give you a guided tour of all his daddy's little ways? And then you drove off with him in his car. Are you two sweet on each other?"

The idea seemed to amuse him.

"It wouldn't surprise me. You know, you remind me a little of Steve's mother."

As she listened, Ellen let her face turn to stone. She didn't want Walter to see her fear.

She remembered thinking how paranoid Steve had sounded when he wondered if his father had been watching that day. But he had been right. This most evil of men had seen them together, and had guessed the rest.

"What about it?" she asked him—anything to get him thinking about something else. "How do you want to leave here, on a stretcher or in a body bag? I don't suppose you've got very long to make up your mind."

"Death doesn't hold any terrors for me, Miss . . ."

"Ridley." She offered him a fast, unpleasant little smile. "Inspector Ridley to my friends."

"I'll leave here when it suits me," he answered calmly, all the while regarding her with the eyes of a predatory animal. "I have only one thing left to do in this world and God, in one of His rare displays of mercy, has put into my hands the means to do it. I'm very happy to meet you, Inspector Ridley."

•   •   •

The sounds of movement around them had finally forced Walter to accept the logic of his position.

"Come on," he said, standing up. "They're getting too close. Let's go inside."

"Let me do something for Sam," Ellen pleaded. "I've got to try to stop the bleeding."

She and Walter faced off across a distance of perhaps twenty feet. They were little more than shadows to each other, but Ellen could still see the gun in his right hand.

Suddenly he pointed it at where Sam was lying on the floor.

"If you like I can put him out of his misery right now," he said calmly.

"No."

"Then it's time to get moving." With the gun he motioned toward the kitchen door. "After you."

At one point Sam's gun was no more than a yard from Ellen's foot. She thought of making a dive for it but gave up on the idea. The odds were too long and then Walter would only shoot Sam. She hated to leave it behind, but there wasn't a choice.

In the kitchen he made Ellen sit on the floor, on the far side of the room, while he examined the contents of the refrigerator.

"Ah, beer!" He took out a carton with four bottles remaining and placed it on the counter next to the sink. "Maybe our Sam isn't all bad after all."

He found a bottle opener in a drawer and dropped it into one of the empty slots in the beer carton. Then he stepped away from the counter and motioned to Ellen to get up.

"Here, you get to carry it into the dining room."

The dining room, predictably, had only one window and it was curtained. Walter pulled down the shade and then drew the curtains closed. Then he flipped the light switch and the chandelier came on.

He studied it for a moment with evident disapproval.

"Vulgar crap. Belongs in a whorehouse."

There was a sideboard, the upper section of which was a glassed-in display case filled with antique cups and saucers. The lower section was a cabinet with double doors concealing its contents, but its top was a flat surface at present occupied by nothing except a silver tray.

Walter looked at Ellen and motioned for her to put the beer on the tray.

"Now lie down on the floor, facedown," he said. "Go on. Over there."

She did as she was told. She was about as far away from him as the size of the room allowed, and she watched as he stuck the pistol in his belt and then used his one good arm to upend the dining room table and lean it against the window.

"You can get up now."

His face was sweaty and was beginning to acquire a waxy pallor. By then the whole left side of his shirt was soaked in blood. He was hurting.

"Let's go see if Sam's got any aspirin," he said.

A search of the bathroom turned up a bottle of Excedrin and, under the sink, a reasonably well equipped first aid kit. There was also a bottle of rubbing alcohol. Ellen got to carry it all back to the dining room.

Walter took one of the large end chairs and pulled it over to a corner near the outside wall. He opened a beer and used it to wash down a handful of Excedrin.

It occurred to Ellen that aspirin in that quantity might thin Walter's blood and make him bleed to death faster. She didn't know, but it was something to hope for.

"Sit down," he told her and then, after raising his eyes to look at her, "how's your head?"

Without thinking, Ellen reached up to touch the wound on the right side of her forehead. It was still wet.

"What do you care?" she answered, wiping her bloody fingers on her jacket.

Walter merely shrugged and began unbuttoning his shirt.

It was a painful spectacle to watch. Walter's lower right side was a mess, the bullet having bounced around on the ribs and then exited messily just above the kidney. In places the shirt fabric stuck to the wound and had to be ripped free. Walter calmly set his pistol down on the sideboard, which was just within reach, opened the first aid kit, soaked a large square of gauze in the alcohol and began to clean up the ragged tears in his flesh.

"It's not the worst," he said quietly. "One time on a construction job in Arizona some idiot working two floors above me slipped and knocked over his toolbox. The building was just an open skeleton, so it all rained down on me. I got a claw hammer stuck in my arm and a crosscut saw damn near took my head off."

He cut strips of adhesive tape and pressed them down at the edges of a couple of gauze pads. He covered the wound in front easily enough, but the exit wound was beyond his reach.

"You want me to do that?" Ellen asked.

"Would you mind?"

He set the gauze pad down on the sideboard and picked up his automatic. Ellen got up from her chair and taped the pad over an oblong wound that was still oozing blood—apparently the bullet had exited sideways.

"Thank you," Walter said, when she had sat down again.

"You're welcome. I apologize for the discomfort. I'd intended to kill you."

Walter's first reaction was surprise and then he started to laugh. He was still laughing when he set the pistol back down and started to work on his left shoulder.

"You almost did," he said, still chuckling. "My arm isn't worth much. I can still move the thumb and first finger a little, but that's about it.

"You must be pretty good at your job," he went on. "How did you get here so fast?"

"Steve phoned. He was tracking your car."

"No shit!" Walter shook his head, as if such a thing defied belief. "How do you suppose he could do a thing like that?"

"I don't know. He didn't tell me. He's a very clever man."

For a moment Walter seemed lost in amazement, then his expression darkened.

"I suppose that's how it works," he said sullenly. "My son the magician sniffs after me at a safe distance and then, when he's got the scent in his nose, he sends in somebody like you for the kill."

"He isn't after your life."

"No? Recent experience would suggest otherwise."

"He doesn't want to kill you." Ellen studied Walter's face, searching for some resemblance to the man she loved. In that moment it was hard to believe they were even the same species. "He just wants to put a stop to you."

"He wants to put me in a cage?" The idea seemed to constitute a grievance.

"Or a hospital, or on the dark side of the moon—anywhere you can't go on killing people."

"But you just said you tried to kill me." Walter smiled, as if the irony of the situation appealed to him. "Then what's the difference?"

Ellen shrugged, a gesture hinting at the pointlessness of the discussion.

"It's my job. I don't do it for fun."

She watched Walter smiling at her and felt the fear grow cold inside her. She could not remember another time she had been this afraid. But instinct told her she had to hide it. Fear would only excite him. Fear was what he lived on.

"That's not to say I wouldn't like another chance," she said. "Maybe next time my aim will be better."

But Walter wasn't paying attention. He seemed absorbed in the difficulties of getting something out of the left pocket of his trousers. At last his efforts were successful and what he held in his hand was a cell phone.

"I think I'll just call up Sonny Boy," he announced. "Invite him to the party."

31

I talked to your Commander Roland," Sergeant Brinkley announced, when he came back to where Tregear was sitting on the bumper of a police car, under the watchful eye of the cop in the cut-off sweatshirt. "He says you're some kind of computer spook but that we can believe anything you have to tell us about this case. He also says we shouldn't let you do anything rash and he'll be here in half an hour."

"In half an hour Sam Tyler and Ellen Ridley will probably both be dead."

The sergeant made a gesture with his hand, as if somehow discounting the risk.

"We're going to have a little talk with our suspect in there, give him a chance to surrender. Most of the time in hostage situations, they end up coming out meek as lambs."

"Not this one." Tregear stood up. "Roland said you could believe me, so believe this. Your 'suspect,' who happens to be my father, is never going to just give up. He'll make you kill him or he'll kill himself, and he'll take as many people with him as he can."

"We have to give it a try." Brinkley did not look happy. "He's your father? What else can you tell us about him?"

"Nothing that's going to make everything all better."

"Do you know what he's doing here?"

"Sure." Tregear looked away and shrugged, as if embarrassed. "Walter didn't like the press conference . . ."

"Walter?"

"That's his name—the only one we can be sure of. Anyway, he took offense and came over here to teach Sam better manners by killing him. I found out about it, so I phoned Ellen. She got here first."

"You found out? How did that work? Did he tell you?"

"No. It was his car."

They both looked at the gray Kia on the other side of the street.

"He stole it. Ellen tracked it down, including the original dealership. I cracked their computer records and found out it had a GPS with an antitheft feature that begins transmitting if the car is started without the key. They even listed the MAC address, so I began sniffing around for it. When I found it I also found that it was parked over there."

"Jesus."

In the next instant Tregear's cell phone started ringing.

• • •

The number displayed on the cell phone's readout was Eugenia Lockwood's, dead not even forty-eight hours. After four rings, Tregear hit the answer button.

"Hello, Dad. How's your evening working out?"

He could hear Walter's laughter. It was the sort of joke that would appeal to him.

"Fine, son. Just fine. Are you having this call traced?"

"Why would I do that? Your car is parked on Belhaven Avenue in Daly City, so I assume you're not far away. How is Sam? Is he dead yet?"

"I *think* he's still alive—he was last time I saw him. But he wasn't looking too good. By the way, your girlfriend's here."

For just an instant Tregear couldn't find anything to say. He knew the pause was a giveaway, but he couldn't help himself. It was as if some part of his mind had refused to believe what he knew perfectly well to be the case, that Dad had Ellie . . .

"Which girlfriend is that?" he asked, perhaps just a shade too brightly. "You know, I lead such an active love life."

God, he could hardly believe how stupid that sounded. Walter could probably hear the desperation in his voice.

"Inspector Ridley, son—but you knew that."

"Well, be nice to her until I get there."

"I will, I promise. She's already tried to kill me once, but we're old friends now. By the way, when do you think you can make it?"

"I'm on my way, Dad. The traffic is bad, so give it about twenty minutes."

"That's about all the time she has, son."

And then the line went dead.

While Tregear had been on the phone with his father, a new man had arrived. He was presumably a cop, since no one tried to shoo him away, and from the fact that he wore a coat and tie he was presumably higher up the chain of command. This was confirmed by the body language of the conversation he was having with Sergeant Brinkley.

And, even worse, one of those boxy sedans all federal agencies bought by the fleet drove up and parked across the street. The door opened and Lieutenant Commander Hal Roland climbed out. As things happened, it was the first time Tregear had ever seen him in civilian clothes.

The two men nodded to one another from opposite sides of Belhaven Avenue and then Roland, with the intuitive sense of a born politician, turned his attention to the two senior policemen. He walked across the street to join them.

Not without me you don't, Tregear said to himself.

By the time he reached them, Roland was already explaining to the two cops how "national security issues" required the Navy to "assume responsibility." He was really enjoying himself. He was bringing in his own team, he told them. The Daly City police could withdraw.

"They're staying," Tregear said flatly. "There's no time for heroics. We've got . . ." He checked his watch. ". . . about seventeen minutes before I have to go over there and have a little reunion with my father. Otherwise he's going to blow Ellen Ridley's head off."

"I have the authority of the Assistant Secretary of the Navy—" Roland started to tell him.

"But you don't have mine."

It was an interesting moment. The cops, who had not been happy about Roland's taking command, were waiting to see who would win.

"It's very simple, Hal. My father has murdered probably hundreds of women, and all of them died alone, in some secret place, without a hope of rescue. That's not going to happen to Ellen Ridley."

"She's a cop," Roland answered, as if the fact were grounds for resentment. "She knew the risks."

Tregear smiled.

"Then let me put it in terms you'll find easier to comprehend. You get in my way on this, you interfere and Ellen dies, and I go to work for Norton Antivirus. The Navy can whistle for its codes and its security procedures. Have you got that?"

From the way his throat muscles were working, it appeared that there was something the lieutenant commander very badly wanted to swallow but that just wasn't going down.

To hell with him.

"Does anybody have a floor plan of the house?" Tregear asked, addressing his question to Sergeant Brinkley.

Brinkley glanced at Roland, who couldn't seem to meet anyone's eye, and the decision was made.

"In my car," he said.

. . .

Walter was not looking at all well. The gauze patches over his wounds were saturated with blood, which was leaking out of him as if nothing could stop it. He was sweating heavily and he was clearly in serious pain.

He was panting. Ellen had seen enough shooting victims to know the signs—Walter was bleeding internally and his shortness of breath meant that he was reaching a point where his diminishing blood supply wouldn't be able to carry enough oxygen to keep him alive.

"I give you less than an hour," she told him, breaking a long silence. "You're hemorrhaging. Pretty soon you'll begin to feel light-headed and after that you won't be anybody's problem anymore. You need to be in a hospital."

There was an antique clock on a little wooden wall shelf about three feet above and to the right of Ellen's head. It didn't keep very good time, being off by a little more than two hours, but it was running.

It was the object of Walter's rapt attention.

"I don't need an hour," he said. "He'll be here in another ten or twelve minutes, and after that my work in this world will be done."

From the look on his face he was Saint Sebastian, waiting for the angels to receive him.

"Why do you hate him so much?"

It was not a question Ellen had expected to hear herself asking.

"I don't hate him. He's my son."

"Then why are you so afraid of him?"

"I'm not afraid of him."

It was the first time she had heard Walter lie. The tell was how his eyes drifted down and to the left, as if he couldn't quite bring himself to look at her.

"You are afraid of him," she said. "I've heard you admit it. Even now, on the doorstep of eternity, you're afraid of him. Is it because he's smarter than you are?"

"When have I ever admitted it?"

"On the recordings." She smiled at him, almost pityingly. "He's recorded all your conversations, did you know that? He knows more about you than you do about yourself."

"You talk too much, sweetheart."

He picked up the gun and pointed it at her head. At that distance, with his right hand and in his condition, maybe he'd hit her and maybe he wouldn't. It seemed a chance worth taking.

"You just can't bear the thought of leaving him behind, can you."

The gun wavered slightly, which could mean a failure of resolve or merely bodily weakness. There was no way of knowing.

"Why don't I just kill you right now?" Walter said. "I'm sick of listening to you."

"Because you can't. I'm the bait, remember?"

He seemed to consider this for a moment, then slowly his gun hand came down until it curled up in his lap.

"Yeah. You're right."

He shook his head, not to signal any objection but merely, she sensed, to bring things back into focus. Then he raised his right hand and looked down at the pistol cradled in his palm. His eyes, when he raised them to Ellen's face, were empty of mercy. He smiled.

"Still, why don't you shut the fuck up or I'll just put one in your knee. Trust me, you won't feel so chatty then."

Except that they both knew what would happen at the first sound of gunfire. Ellen was almost ready to call his bluff but then thought better of it. Walter wasn't paying attention.

He appeared almost to have forgotten her existence. He took

another handful of Excedrin and was into his second beer, but none of it appeared to afford him any relief. The pain of his wounds seemed to make him restless. He could not keep still.

"How long have you known him?" he asked finally.

"Who?"

"My son—Steve. Who did you think? Willie Nelson?"

He allowed himself one short syllable of laughter and then his face collapsed into an expression of anguish and hatred.

"My son," he repeated. "Have you known him long?"

"Not long." She smiled at him mockingly. "Since a few days after we found Sally Wilkes. You remember her?"

He ignored the taunt. His mind seemed to be elsewhere.

"He was always a sweet boy," he said wistfully. "And smart. I'd show him a thing one time and he'd have it forever. If I ever loved anybody in my whole life I loved that boy."

"And now you want to kill him."

"It's none of your business."

Ellen could only shake her head. Sitting across from him like this, Walter seemed such an ordinary man. But the workings of his mind were unfathomable. He was a paradox concealed in a riddle—a riddle, probably, even to himself.

"Everything about you is my business," she said quietly. "I'm a homicide detective and you're a murderer. You made yourself my business."

But Walter wasn't listening. His eyes were on the wall clock above Ellen's head.

32

The screen on Sergeant Brinkley's laptop, which he had set up on the hood of his car, showed a schematic of Sam's house. The feed was from the Daly City Department of Records. Tregear had only to raise his eyes to see the real thing.

"Sam is probably here," he said, pointing to the broken line that indicated the back porch. "The blood trail suggests that Walter retreated in that direction, and Sam is no fool. I don't see where else Walter could have got the drop on him—certainly not inside the house."

Brinkley nodded.

"We've got guys behind the backyard fence, but the lights are off and they can't see much. If Sam is in there, and down, he'd be just about invisible."

There were two ambulances parked at the end of the street and police crews were busy putting up floodlights all around the house.

Brinkley tapped with his finger at the space labeled "Dining Room."

"My bet is your Walter is holed up here. There's only one window and he'll have lines of sight to both the front and the back doors."

"I think you're right," Tregear answered. "And he'll barricade the window."

The lieutenant, whose name was Klegg, made a low, whistling sound.

"He has to know there's no way out," he said.

"He's not looking for a way out." Tregear's expression, as his eyes rested on the lieutenant's face, suggested no emotion. He might have been explaining something to a child, without any hope of being understood. "He wants a little chat with his son, just to get everything straightened out, and then it's Armageddon."

"And you're the son." Brinkley shook his head. "Are you counting on that?"

"I'm not counting on anything."

"Then he'd actually do it? He'd really kill you?"

"He'll want to talk first, and then we'll see."

"Jesus."

"Just because somebody has to say it," the lieutenant began, "I'll tell you here and now, there's not a reason in the world why you have to do this."

"Yes, there is."

"You have to stop him." Roland, who had tagged along simply because he couldn't think what else to do, was almost clawing at the lieutenant's arm. "You can't let Tregear go in there. He's a national security asset. He belongs to the Navy."

"I think that's his choice," Klegg said.

"In a situation like this a relative is the best negotiator." Brinkley was speaking to his lieutenant, not to Roland. "It's a big risk, but my guess is Tregear has the best chance of ending this without bloodshed."

"I agree."

"It's ready, Lieutenant."

Who had spoken? A technician in blue coveralls, a kid who hardly looked twenty and who stood at the bottom of Sam's lawn, waiting for a signal.

Klegg nodded, and the next instant the floods went on and Sam's house was bathed in hard, white light, making it seem huge, imparting to it a sinister grandeur.

"Are your shooters in place?" Tregear asked.

"Yes."

"Then if Sam is on the porch I'll call you to come pick him up."

He checked his watch. He had about three minutes left.

It was a trick of the imagination, he knew, but suddenly Sam's one-story bungalow became the last home Tregear had shared with his father. He was twelve years old again, and Dad was asleep in a second-floor bedroom. He had just discovered the corpse in the van, but running away was no longer an option. He had to go into that house and face his worst nightmare, the man who had raised him, whom he had loved all his life.

"Tregear."

He turned his head and saw Sergeant Brinkley, who had something in his hand. It was a gun, a standard service revolver.

"Take it," Brinkley murmured, as if the offer had to remain their secret. "Give yourself a chance."

Tregear put his hand on the gun and, very gently, pushed it away.

"I can't," he said, in a voice so quiet he might have been talking to himself. "He's my father. I'd never be able to bring myself to use it."

"Okay." Brinkley reached back and put the revolver in its holster. "But the first shot fired, we're coming in."

Tregear flashed him a quick, frightened grin. "I'm counting on that."

He stepped down from the curb and started his slow walk across Belhaven Avenue. Each step seemed to require a separate act of will.

Tregear looked up into the night sky, nearly obliterated by the floodlights, searching for a star. It seemed the most important object of his life to see one point of light in the heavens, but there was none.

He had lied to the police—he had no real doubt Walter intended to kill him. But his first object was to get Ellie out of there, and that seemed possible. That was worth dying for.

Then he would just see, along the road to Come What May.

The gentle slope of Sam's front lawn was like a mountain under his feet. He wanted to get down on his hands and knees to climb it.

Finally he touched the corner of the house and somehow he felt better. Now he had something to do.

His cell phone rang.

"Where the hell are you?" It was his father's voice.

"I'm on the walkway, coming around to the back of the house."

"Well, move it."

"In my own sweet time, Dad."

He clicked the phone off.

In was three steps up from the flagstones to the porch, and before he took the first step Tregear could see Sam lying there, his feet toward him.

Tregear let the porch door slam shut behind him. Best to let Dad know he had arrived.

He knelt down and checked the pulse in Sam's throat. Sam never stirred. Then Tregear clicked a button on his cell phone.

"Sam's unconscious, but his heart is beating," he said. "Get your people in here."

He stood up and opened the kitchen door.

"Dad?" he shouted. "Where are you?"

He didn't really need to ask. The only light in the house was coming from a room to the left, down a short hall that led to the front.

"I'm here," the answer came, sounding thinner than over the phone. "You'll find me."

Tregear went down the hall and stopped just short of where the light poured out from an open doorway.

"Let me hear your voice, Dad."

"What would you like, a few choruses of 'Old Man River'?"

This was followed by laughter, which was in turn followed by a coughing fit that seemed to go on and on. But the sound let Tregear know that his father was on the other side of the room.

He stepped just inside the doorway while Walter was still trying to catch his breath.

"Ellie, are you all right?"

He asked without taking his eyes from his father, but he knew where she was—close enough that he could have touched her.

"I'm all right."

Tregear nodded, still without looking at her. He did not dare look at her. If he was to get her out of there alive he had to keep focused on Walter.

He had to create the impression that there was only him and Walter, that no one else mattered.

"Dad, in a few minutes you're going to hear noises coming from the porch. The medics will he picking up Sam, who you'll be happy to hear is still alive."

A flicker of wrath crossed Walter's face but was quickly suppressed. Walter was smart enough to grasp there was nothing he could do. If he went out there with the idea of stopping it a sniper would get him. If he shot Ellen Ridley—his only means of retaliation—Steve would disappear.

It was the first time that father and son had seen each other in over twenty years. Tregear had the sense that Walter was searching his face for some trace of the boy who had run away so long ago. Perhaps it was easier for Tregear to see the father he had fled.

Beyond this, he found it difficult to look at the clear signs of approaching death—the waxen, sweating face and the wounds in the naked flesh. Walter's left arm even had a faintly bluish cast to it, as if it had already begun to turn putrid.

He was holding an automatic in his right hand, but without pointing it at anyone.

"You've grown up," he said. "You still looked like a kid in Maryland. Twelve years has really made a difference."

"You look terrible," his son answered.

Walter shrugged, which seemed to require considerable effort.

"I've been better."

Tregear, watching, felt a surge of pity that surprised him.

"Give it up, Dad," he said quietly. "You need to be in a hospital."

"The cops would kill me before I ever left this room."

"Not if you walk out of here with me. What about it, Dad? Will you go to a hospital? Forget about Custer's Last Stand. Life is worth something."

"Not mine." Walter waved his right hand dismissively, and his face contracted with what looked like nausea. His skin actually seemed gray. "I'm dead either way. I've got cancer."

Even though Tregear had told himself something of the sort was likely, he discovered he was shocked. That this man, of all men, should die of anything so prosaic was astonishing.

"Are you sure?"

"Hell yes, I'm sure." Walter glared at his son with genuine hatred. "My father died of it at about my age. I remember the signs. I don't want to go out like that."

And then he grinned.

"Take a look at me and see yourself in another twenty years."

The threat didn't register. Tregear's attention was elsewhere. He could not remember another time when Walter had related any family history.

"How old were you when your father died?"

Walter lifted his head. The question appeared to surprise him.

"Fifteen." He shook his head and emitted a syllable of laughter. Then he made a face, is if there was a bad taste in his mouth. "He was as mean an old bastard as God ever suffered to breathe. The only things I ever learned from him were the Bible and how to take a whipping. I did better by you."

All at once Walter sagged in his chair, overcome by a kind of fainting spell, it seemed. Then he straightened up and brought the back of his right hand, still holding the gun, to his forehead.

"Any more questions?" he asked, grinning like a devil.

"Just one. What am I doing here?"

Dad appeared to find this extraordinarily funny. "Don't you think families should stay together?" he asked, between bouts of laughter.

Then he began to cough, but this time he raised his gun and pointed it directly at Tregear's chest. The coughing went on for at least a minute, and when it was done there were flecks of blood on Walter's lips and chin.

And through it all Tregear felt the likelihood that he was about to die and, oddly, he discovered that he was not afraid. The discovery depressed him. This was what it was to be the son of a man like his father, to carry the burden of his hereditary guilt.

"Where is my mother?" he asked. With the gun still aimed at his heart, the question he knew was a deliberate provocation. It could have ended everything. Perhaps it was even meant to.

"In heaven, maybe."

Walter was still gasping for breath, but he lowered the gun.

"I mean, where did you dump her body after you murdered her?"

"Who remembers? It was a long time ago."

"Did you at least bury her?"

"Will you shut the fuck up about your mother?" Walter shouted—or tried. His voice was thick, as if he were strangling. "How old were you then? Seven? It's ancient history. You probably don't even remember her."

"I remember her. I remember her and I loved her. You probably can't comprehend such a thing, and that's a dangerous failure of imagination because it blinds you to other people's motives."

Walter stood up. It was a ponderous, slow, painful thing to watch. The chair might have been his coffin at the moment of the Last Judgment. On his feet, he swayed slightly.

"I tried," he said, his eyes cast down. "I tried to live the television dream. I was fond of your mother, I really was. But it just got too hard."

It was pure theater. He was a man trapped in his own nature. It was beautifully played. He might even have believed it himself.

"And so of course you killed her. Had she found out what you were up to, or had you just gotten bored? Don't forget, I've seen how casually you can take life. I saw what you did to my grandparents."

"Oh, you mean Betty's folks?" He smiled his sly smile, as if to say, *Okay, so you don't buy it. No hard feelings.*

He sank backward into the chair, and instantly his face was a grimace of pain.

"Oh God! This is getting old real fast."

There were beads of sweat on his face, and a shudder passed through him, as if he felt a sudden chill. He looked fragile enough to crack like an egg.

"Go to the hospital, Dad. Don't put yourself through this."

"Death is hard, Steve. That's just a fact. God never meant us to leave life on a feather bed."

"It's not your time unless you want it to be."

"It's my time—close enough."

"You really want to die?"

Walter only shrugged. The subject seemed to bore him.

"Okay, Dad. That's your business. But you're not taking the whole world with you."

For the first time Tregear stepped fully inside the room. He walked over and stood in front of the chair on which Ellen was sitting, blocking her from his father's sight.

"Stand up," he murmured, glancing quickly over his shoulder. "Do exactly what I tell you."

Ellen rose behind him, and when she was on her feet she rested the palm of her hand between his shoulder blades. It was a brief gesture, lasting only seconds, but it told him what he needed to know. She would follow his lead.

Walter stared out at them through sullen, hate-filled eyes.

"I know what you've got in mind," he said, and a wicked smile twitched at his mouth. "But I'll probably get off two or three shots before she reaches the doorway. I'll aim low. I'll hit her in the legs and I'm bound to stop her. And then I'll kill her at my perfect convenience."

"I don't think so, Dad." Tregear shook his head. "Just let me tell you how it works from this point on. At the first sound of a shot the police will storm the house. They'll break down the doors, they'll come through the windows if they have to, but they'll come. At the outside you'll have maybe ten seconds. And then you'll die sitting there in that chair."

"But I'll take you with me."

Tregear managed a brief laugh. "You'll probably do that anyway. But the point is, our little conversation will be over."

"My guess is she's not worth that to you."

Over his shoulder, and in a voice that, were it not so breathless, would have been a shout, he said, "Run! Now!"

Ellen didn't hesitate. She ran for the doorway.

Walter raised his gun, but he didn't fire. And in an instant she was gone. He slumped back in his chair.

"That's twice you've scored on me," he said. "The question is, why is she worth it to you?" His eyes narrowed with suspicion. "Don't tell me you've gone and found love."

"There's that. But more than anything there's the fact that I should have turned you in back in Arkansas. By failing in that, by not taking that risk, I made myself an accomplice to all the monstrous things you've done since. You've killed all the women you're going to. I don't want Ellen to be your last victim."

"You're reserving that honor for yourself?" Walter laughed at his own joke.

"I'm not eligible. I've been your victim most of my life."

33

The ambulance crew who were lifting their patient onto a stretcher knew there was only twenty or so feet separating them from an armed psychopath, so when the kitchen door flew open they almost dropped poor Sam.

Ellen fell to her knees beside the stretcher and reached out her hand to touch Sam's face, but in the last instant she hesitated.

"Is he . . .?"

"Yeah, he's alive," the medic said, almost in a whisper as he was prepping him for an IV. "But just barely. We've got to get him out of here."

Within thirty seconds they were maneuvering the stretcher through the outside door, and Ellen hovered near Sam's head, touching his face with her fingertips, until, outside on the flagstone walkway, they lowered the wheels and she remembered that she wasn't going with him.

She found Sam's service pistol easily. It was lying in the shadow of the lounge chair, where apparently no one had noticed it. Then, as she sat on the floor, she opened the cylinder. There were five live rounds inside so she closed it, being careful to align the empty chamber with the firing pin.

Then, as she held the thing in the palm of her hand, all the fear she had been pushing aside flooded in on her and she began to weep.

She couldn't help it. She hated herself for it, hated the weakness she was exposing, but she simply could not hold it back.

At least she wasn't sobbing. Her tears flowed without a sound.

Finally she was able to force herself to stop. Then for several seconds she stared down at Sam's revolver.

She had no idea where her nine-millimeter automatic might be. It had been years since she had even held a revolver, but at the police academy she had trained with one no different from Sam's. She knew how to use it.

And now was the time.

. . .

"I never made you a victim," Walter said finally. He sounded hurt. "You just took off."

Tregear nodded, then sat down on the chair lately vacated by Ellen. "That's right. I just took off. After I found out that you'd lied about what happened to my mother. After I found a dead woman in the back of your van. I figured I was probably next. Does that strike you as an unreasonable conclusion?"

He folded his arms over his chest, apparently perfectly relaxed. His eyes seemed fixed on the toes of his shoes.

"Then you killed my grandparents," he went on, "setting the stage so all I had to do was look in the front window to see them dead. Don't say you didn't expect me to go rushing through the door which you had so cunningly booby-trapped.

"Then I had to run away again. I joined the Navy on the mistaken theory they would ship me out to sea and I'd be safe. I live under a name I took out of a novel. Until Ellie I've never allowed myself to get too close to anyone against that inevitable day when we'd cross paths again. And now here we are."

Finally, he looked at his father. He smiled, not very nicely. He was done.

"You've been chasing me." Walter stared at him sullenly. "You've hunted me for years. *I* was the quarry, not you. I've known that since you tried to sell me to the cops in Maryland. How many years ago was that? I would have left you alone."

"You could have left me alone in Ohio, but you didn't. Don't kid me, Dad. You've always been a great one for tying up loose ends.

"And now we're both done hunting. Within the next half hour or so, you'll probably be dead. I expect I'll be making the trip with you. And the circus will go on, probably for years. You'll be famous, Dad. They'll write books about you. But at least there won't be any more Eugenia Lockwoods, or Harriet Murdochs or Sally Wilkes."

"I did them all a favor."

"How do you figure that?"

"Isn't it obvious? Where have *you* been living?" Walter was so near death that the contemptuous little wave of his hand collapsed almost immediately. "Tell me, Steve, do you believe there is such a place as hell?"

"No."

"Well, there is. But it doesn't wait for us after death—my old man got that wrong. We're in it this minute. And it isn't sin that makes this world hell. That was another of my old man's mistakes. It just is. It is because God made it so, and He made it so because He hates us. Who was the guy who said that 'Hell is other people'?"

"Sartre."

"Well, he got that wrong. He got it wrong and my dad got it wrong. Hell is us. We're each our own hell. And God is right to hate us. So we suffer through every second of living, and suffering is the only way out. Those women are free. And soon I'll be free."

He closed his eyes. For about fifteen seconds Tregear wasn't sure he hadn't already crossed over. Then Walter drew a shallow, ragged breath and let it out.

Slowly, his attention refocused on his son. He smiled.

"You know, the way I feel and using my right hand, I'm not even sure I'd hit you."

"But you'll try, right?"

It was virtually a dare. Walter was not going to have the pleasure of seeing him afraid. Live or die, Tregear would deny him that satisfaction.

Walter looked down at the gun in his hand. He seemed to be measuring its weight.

"You're not afraid to die?" he asked.

"My fear is all used up, Dad."

And it was even true. Despair brought with it a kind of serenity. After all these years it was finally ending. The bill had at last come due. Death would almost be a relief.

The hand came up, and the gun with it. One squeeze of the trigger and the bullet would have gone through Tregear's throat.

For about ten seconds his life was measured out to him one breath at a time. He expected to die.

The shot that killed him would bring the SWAT team that had no doubt arrived by now and Walter would die sitting in that chair. Then, at last the nightmare would be over. Death was a price that seemed worth paying.

"Still not afraid?"

"Try me, Dad."

In an instant, the point of the gun twitched away. It was aimed at nothing.

He's toying with me, Tregear thought to himself. He'll wait until I really believe I might live, and then he'll kill me.

He stood up, taking his time so as not to spook his father into anything. He just preferred to be on his feet. It seemed a more dignified way to die.

. . .

The door to the kitchen was still open. With Sam's pistol held in both hands, Ellen stepped across the threshold.

There were no more tears, and her heart felt like ice. The only emotion she was conscious of was hatred.

She had hated very few people in her life—if asked, she probably would have said that she regarded such emotional extravagances as unprofessional—but in the last half hour or so she had learned to hate Walter. He had badly frightened her; he had killed little Rita Blandish. But neither of those was the real reason.

He was threatening to kill the man she loved. He wanted to rob her of more than her life. She hated him for that.

For working she preferred rubber-soled Mary Janes with a suede/poly-mesh upper and a Velcro strap. They weren't very stylish, but they were light and as comfortable as running shoes. They were also as silent as if you were barefoot. They never squeaked as she crossed the linoleum kitchen floor.

At the entrance to the hallway she heard the muffled drone of conversation. At first she could distinguish only Walter's voice, but a moment more and she heard Steve. She couldn't make out the words, but the cadence was as familiar to her as a favorite tune.

A memory came into her mind, vivid as any immediate event. Once, during the brief few days they had lived together, she had come back to Steve's apartment, gone up to his office and found him seated in his chair with Gwendolyn perched on his shoulder. Her front paws were in his hair as she looked over his head at the computer screen.

From almost the first moment Gwendolyn had trusted him, and in such matters animals were wiser than people.

Steve had come into this house, where he knew a man waited to kill him. He had brought no weapon, no defense except a vast courage, and he had put his own body between Ellen and death. It was the only way he knew. He was simply not meant to be a destroyer.

In that sense at least, he was not his father's son.

As she approached the doorway to Sam's dining room she could hear their conversation quite distinctly. Walter was gasping for air, as if every word was a hard-won victory over death.

"You're afraid to die," he said. "Maybe not this very moment, but in another hour you'd be glad to be still breathing. Some things you just have to learn the hard way."

That was it. There was no more time.

Her gun held in both hands, she stepped into the doorway. Walter was seated across the room from her, his little automatic pointed at Steve.

He turned his head in her direction and for an instant his eyes narrowed in surprise.

She had him cold. She pulled the trigger and his right arm went slack as a bullet hole appeared just below his left eye. He was already dead, but she couldn't stop herself. Without realizing what she did, she fired twice more and Walter slumped sideways in his chair.

She waited through the longest five seconds of her life, not letting her gaze wander from his now lifeless face, ready to kill him all over again.

There was no need.

She turned her head and for the first time, with something like surprise, saw Steve, not more than six feet away. He just stood there, staring at her as if at an apparition.

"I had to come back," she said.

34

Sam had been out of the hospital a month, but he hadn't yet recovered his strength. When he walked his dachshunds he used a cane. Ellen came to visit him every Sunday morning and they took the dogs out together.

Hard as they tried to avoid it, eventually the conversation always came around to The Case.

The media frenzy had died down at last. For three weeks it seemed there was no other story on the six o'clock news, but at last the public, and even the reporters, had grown bored with it. Walter's body was still in a refrigerated vault at the city morgue, but he was already relegated to the uninteresting past. Sometime or other it would all come back, when the books started to come out and if the much-talked-about TV movie ever got made, but for the present it was all just another case file in the computer.

For Sam and Ellen the story was never over.

Today's little tidbit was that the FBI had finally scored a hit on the fingerprints. Forty-two years ago an Indiana teenager named Walter Brewer had been arraigned in juvenile court on the charge of assault with intent to commit rape. Pending a hearing, the boy had been remanded to the custody of his father, Stephen Brewer, a local clergyman of unsavory reputation. Father and son had then promptly disappeared.

"The mills of the gods grind slowly," Sam announced as they walked up a difficult bit of hill on their way to a public park much beloved by his dachshunds. "Juvenile records from that long ago wouldn't even have made it into the computer. Somebody must have searched them by eye. Don't the cops in Indiana have anything better to do with their time?"

"Maybe some eighty-year-old juvie officer remembered the case," Ellen suggested. "It would be the sort of thing to stick in your mind."

"You mean a teenage rapist with Elmer Gantry for a father? In the Midwest they're probably as common as mushrooms."

They were silent until they reached the park, and then Sam sat down on a bench to rest and let Ellen walk the pack around to water the shrubbery.

When she came back, Sam took the dogs off their leads to let them wander about. Strictly speaking, this was illegal, but they were well behaved and never strayed very far from Daddy.

"I'll bet we'll hear a lot more about Walter Brewer." Sam was watching contemplatively as Daisy, the baby of the pack, dug in a flower bed. "Assault with intent doesn't sound like a first offense. Probably he was a bad boy before he reached puberty. The case files should make interesting reading."

He leaned forward, his hands laced together over the handle of his cane, and frowned.

"But I won't be reading them. When my convalescent leave is over, I'm putting in my papers and retiring. Millie is adamant."

For a moment Ellen was sufficiently distressed to be at a loss for words.

"What'll I do for a partner?" she asked finally.

"What are you doing for one now?"

"Nothing. I'm still cleaning up the bits and pieces from Walter."

"Well, when Walter is put to bed they'll give you a new partner, probably one as green as you were when I got you."

"Then who's going to be my Father Confessor and Guide?"

"You don't need one anymore. That's just another reason I'm retiring."

He glanced at Ellen, who seemed close to tears, then looked away.

"I'm not moving to Oregon or anything like that," he said. "You can still come and walk the dogs with me. You just don't need a mentor anymore. Your handling of the Walter case was masterful."

"I had help."

"Some—we always get *some* help—but not very much from me. If I'd retired last year you still would have broken the case."

"Not without Steve."

"Maybe not, but you made all the right moves, all on your own. You don't need me anymore, Ellie. You've earned your stripes. You're a big girl now."

He shrugged, as if owning to an absurd weakness.

"And I'm sick of it. I never want to see another dead body in a car trunk. I think I would have quit a long time ago if not for you. You've earned this. My retirement is your coming-of-age. You're a veteran homicide inspector now. *You'll* be the teacher."

It was time to change the subject.

"By the way, how is Steve these days?"

"I don't really know." Ellen shrugged. Today seemed a day for unpleasant revelations. "He's still in the hospital."

"And he still doesn't want to see you?"

"He's relented. Friday I got a call from his shrink. I'm going down there this afternoon."

"Well, give me a call afterwards and let me know how he is." Sam laughed suddenly. "He's a clever bugger. I'm glad he didn't take after his old man because we'd never have caught him."

"And now he's in the nut ward."

"Oh well, aren't we all?" Sam stood up and whistled for the dogs. "Time we were heading back. We have to celebrate my retirement. I think the lunch menu is beer and lasagna."

"In the kitchen?"

"Until Millie can pick out new wallpaper for the dining room."

*   *   *

Ellen left Daly City at one-fifteen. She had to make a two o'clock shuttle flight to the John Wayne Airport in Santa Ana, and then it was an hour's drive to Camp Pendleton. She had a four-thirty appointment with a Dr. Stockton at the Naval hospital there and she didn't want to be late. That interview was the last hurdle before seeing Steve, who had disappeared from view the night Walter died.

They had walked out of Sam's house together, holding on to each other as if each was afraid the other would fall over. Then because of her head wound the Daly City police had insisted on putting Ellen into an ambulance and taking her to the hospital.

She had not unreasonably assumed that the Navy would scoop up Steve and send him to the hospital, a medical examination being standard procedure after a hostage situation that ends in bloodshed. She had even thought they might meet again in the emergency room, but it didn't happen.

X-rays revealed that her skull was intact, so she was given some painkillers and told to go home. But she didn't go home. She found out where Sam was being treated and kept her vigil in the general surgery waiting room. After about ten o'clock she and Millie kept each other company until, about two, Sam was wheeled into Recovery and declared out of immediate danger.

Since she had been involved in a shooting, Ellen was put on paid leave and, pending the review, ordered to have no contact with anyone even remotely involved in the "incident," which by extension included everyone on the San Francisco and Daly City police forces and the district attorney's office.

Nevertheless, the evening of her first day in quarantine someone knocked on her apartment door. It turned out to be Mindy Epstein.

"I am not here," she said, slipping through the door. "I am home, getting hammered by my boyfriend. You haven't seen me anytime in the last ten days."

She sat down on the couch and asked for a glass of wine.

"So what's up?" Ellen asked. It seemed a reasonable question.

"I just wanted you to know that the DA's office is not prepared to involve itself in any way in this shooting. Nobody is even remotely interested in filing criminal charges. You're in the clear, kid. All you did was save the taxpayers a *lot* of money.

"Now, tell me what happened. Spare me nothing."

So Ellen gave her the whole story—about Tregear, about the anti-theft signal on the stolen car, about everything that happened at Sam's house that night.

"He went in there to get you out?" Mindy was frankly incredulous. "I don't believe you. They don't make men like that anymore."

"Nevertheless, that's what he did."

"Then what are you doing sitting alone in your apartment? Where the hell *is* he?"

"I don't know. I haven't seen him since that night."

By then they had exhausted the first bottle of wine and Ellen had to go into the kitchen for reinforcements. She couldn't find another bottle right away, so she sat down on one of the breakfast table chairs.

She didn't want to get up again. She felt numb—or, perhaps more accurately, detached. She wondered if it was the wine, but she didn't really think so.

After a while, Mindy came looking for her. Mindy found the other bottle of wine.

"Post-traumatic stress?" she asked.

Ellen looked up at her and smiled wanly. "No." She shook her head. "I'm just thinking about Steve. The Navy must have him stowed away somewhere, and I'm not sure, after all this, they're ever going to let him go. I don't know if I'll ever see him again. And if I don't, I'm just wondering what I'm going to do with the rest of my life."

"Do you love the guy?"

"Oh yeah."

"Then find him." Mindy sat down on the chair opposite and took Ellen's hand in hers, squeezing it hard. "You're a detective, so find him. And when you've got him back, don't ever let him loose again."

. . .

The next morning she drove down to Atherton to spend a few days with her parents. This might have been a mistake because when her mother saw the bloody gouge just above her left eyebrow she came close to hysterics.

"This is what comes of joining the police," she almost shrieked. "You'll carry that scar for the rest of your life."

"Probably," her daughter answered, smiling inwardly. Actually, she discovered, she was rather proud of her wound.

During that visit she had told her father the truth about Tregear. There was no point anymore in keeping it a secret—it wouldn't be possible to keep it a secret—and she wanted her father to know everything.

"You realize of course that there are certain risks involved in this relationship," he said. They were in his private sanctum and he was sitting behind his desk, which allowed him, she supposed, to maintain a certain professional detachment. "He's the son of a serial murderer, and sociopathic tendencies are to some degree hereditary."

"He's not a sociopath, Daddy."

"You know that?" He smiled, which was his way of announcing

skepticism. "Some of these guys are very skillful at mimicking normal emotions."

"Daddy, he walked into Sam's house, knowing his father would probably kill him. He risked his life to get me out of there. Would a sociopath do that?"

"No. No, he wouldn't."

He got up from behind his desk and leaned over to kiss his daughter on the forehead.

"I'm glad you told me," he said. "Maybe he even deserves you."

But it would have been nice to know that Steve agreed.

.   .   .

The Navy reported that Mr. Tregear, the only witness to Walter's death, was "unavailable" for a statement, but Walter had conveniently tried to murder two police officers, so the hearing was something of a formality. After five days she was cleared of any wrongdoing, and there was even talk of a commendation.

She didn't want the commendation. What she wanted was to hear from Steve.

But where was he? Before she left work on her first day back, she phoned Lieutenant Commander Hal Roland, who might reasonably be expected to know.

"He's perfectly safe, Ms. Ridley. The Navy has him."

"I figured that, *Mr.* Roland. But where? I need to get in touch with him."

"I'm afraid that won't be possible."

"Hal, as the case officer on Walter I'm going to have to write a report, which will doubtless find its way into the hands of your superiors—in fact, I'll make very sure that it does. Personally, I think you're a bumbling careerist. Is that how you would like my report to read, or would you rather be an able and conscientious defender of our nation's security?"

"I'll see what I can do."

By the time she had gotten home to feed Gwendolyn, she had an e-mail giving the address and telephone number of a Naval hospital at Camp Pendleton.

But this turned out, at least at first, to be just another stone wall.

"I'm sorry," someone in administration told her. "I don't have a complete list of our patients and, in any case, I'm not authorized to give out information on any of our patients or personnel. However, if you'll leave me your name and number I'll see that a message that you called reaches the appropriate department."

She kept phoning, and after almost two weeks someone from the psychiatric department called back.

"Mr. Tregear does not wish to receive any visitors."

• • •

On the flight down, Ellen sat nursing a glass of club soda, finally acknowledging to herself how scared she was. Steve was in a mental hospital, and she had spent her youth listening to her father's sad stories about people who went to such places. She had no idea what to expect. She had no idea if the man she was to encounter there would be the same man she had loved—and still loved, even to this anxious moment.

She had known Steve for less than two weeks before he disappeared down the rabbit hole. In that time it had crossed her mind once or twice that the strain was telling on him, that he was too self-contained, even too strong, that he held himself too straight. Perhaps he was brittle. Perhaps that was what happened—he had broken into pieces.

She kept remembering something Steve had said to her father, about free will and how we couldn't choose what we wanted. *We just want it,* he had said, *and then we build a belief structure to justify wanting it.* Walter had created a kind of inverted religion for himself that explained his inner turmoil and excused his savagery.

But what of Steve? His whole life he had been driven in one single direction, without real choice. And now perhaps he was free—provided he still had the capacity to choose.

She kept remembering the expression on his face the instant after Walter died. He had looked so stunned and appalled. After all, she had just killed his father. Would that moment haunt their relationship forever?

The one idea that brought her any comfort was that he had sent for her. Although it was just as possible that he wanted her to understand that, for him, there was no coming back.

She supposed she would find out.

· · ·

The hospital was like a resort hotel and Dr. Stockton was a very nice gray-haired man with green eyes and tangled black eyebrows, his one revolt against military correctness. He was dressed in Navy whites and the insignia on his collar put his rank at captain.

He met Ellen in his office and they sat across from each other in two chairs fronting his desk. It was all decidedly informal.

"Steve is a very easy patient to treat," he began. "Men of such extraordinary intelligence usually are. He talks, I listen and make notes. He's very analytical and figures most things out for himself. As soon as he came out of his catatonia, I knew he was going to mend."

"Catatonia?"

"Yes. You didn't know about that?"

"No."

"It started when he was being taken to the hospital. He got into the ambulance on his own and seemed perfectly fine, but by the time they arrived he had become silent and unresponsive. He didn't talk and he didn't listen. If someone led him he would submit to the pressure and follow, but if they stopped leading he stopped too. He had retreated into some back closet of his mind. It's not an uncommon reaction to severe emotional trauma.

"So they shipped him down here. I started seeing him on a daily basis. I'd ask him questions, which he wouldn't answer. He seemed not even to know I was there.

"Then, after two weeks, I came into his room and said, 'Good morning, Mr. Tregear,' and he answered, 'Good morning, Doctor.' He had decided to come back to life. It was that simple."

"Well, is he all right now?"

"He will be, but he isn't there yet. He has a lot to sort out. He's carrying an immense burden of irrational guilt over all those murdered women. Beyond that, this problem with his father has occupied most of his attention most of his life, and now it's gone. It's left behind something of an emotional vacuum."

Dr. Stockton smiled, just enough to suggest he recognized the irony of the situation.

"I know. His father was a monster. Why would anybody, particularly his abused and hunted son, miss him? But usually it's the fact of a relationship rather than its quality that makes it important. You can hate someone and, if you invest enough emotional energy into hating him, you will feel an emptiness, a kind of grief, when that person drops out of your life. The death of Steve's father means that he has to restructure his whole existence. He has to learn to live without fear, and right now he even misses the fear. He needs someone to fill the void. That's why I called you."

"He didn't ask you to?"

"No." The doctor shook his head. "He doesn't have any idea you're coming—if he did it would only give him something else to worry about. But, trust me, he'll be glad to see you. He talks about you a lot."

Ellen shrugged hopelessly.

"I'll bet he does. I killed his father right in front of his eyes."

"I know that from the police reports, but not from him."

"He's a gentleman."

"I doubt if that's the reason."

But Ellen was unconvinced.

"A month ago, when I finally tracked him down, they told me he'd given instructions: no visitors."

"He didn't want you to see him, not the way he was then. Now I think he needs you."

There followed a silence lasting perhaps fifteen seconds, during which Dr. Stockton seemed to be measuring something.

"He told me you lived together briefly."

"Just a few days." Ellen found she was embarrassed, although she couldn't have said why. "He made me move out because he was afraid for my safety."

"How do you feel about him now?"

"I'm in love with him." She shook her head. It didn't seem enough. Maybe no words were enough. "I'm absolutely mad about him, on top of which he saved my life. I can't tell you how much I love him."

"'Love'—it's a word that means so many different things." The doctor smiled again. "I'm sorry. I don't mean to trivialize. The question is, do you love him enough to look after him, to give him what he needs right now?"

"And what's that?"

"Love, time and patience."

"I have a full-time job, but I'll do my best."

"I'm sure you'll do fine. And the fact that you have a job shouldn't be a problem, because he needs time alone. But he also needs someone to lead him back to life. Move back in with him. Sleep with him, but don't expect miracles. Male sexuality is a very fragile business, and it may take him a while. But most of all protect him from the Boogie Man."

"The Boogie Man is dead."

"For Steve, the Boogie Man will never be dead."

"Won't he ever get over that?"

The doctor raised his impressive eyebrows, as if at the naïveté of the question.

"Ms. Ridley, you don't ever 'get over' the sort of thing he's been through. If you're lucky, you adjust to it."

"I'll bear that in mind."

"Good!" Dr. Stockton stood up. "Then I'll take you to where you can find him. Can you come back next weekend?"

"Sure. Absolutely."

"Fine. He doesn't really need this place anymore. It's been good for him. He's gotten the VIP treatment, as if he were an admiral with a little drinking problem. But in two weeks we're going to kick him out. Can you come down again then and collect him?"

"With bells on." Her hands flew up to her head as if she weren't sure it would stay on by itself. "With bells on," she repeated, laughing from sheer relief.

"That's the spirit. Now, come along with me . . ."

• • •

There was a state park just south of the hospital, and through it ran a sizable creek. The area was wooded and very pretty, just the place for an injured soul.

She found Steve sitting on a wooden bench, watching the water. He was so intent on the sight that she came within fifteen feet of him before he heard her tread on the dry leaves and turned around.

"Hi," she said. It was an awkward enough beginning.

At first he was merely startled, but then he smiled. Yes, he was glad to see her. He stood up and took a few steps toward her, and then, as if suddenly yielding to an impulse, reached out to her. He seemed not quite to have the courage to touch her.

"Thank you. Thank you for coming. I can't say—I . . ."

That was better. Ellen closed the distance between them and Steve put his arms around her. There was a desperate quality in his embrace. He seemed to be afraid she would run away.

Finally they made it to the bench and sat down together. Steve kept touching her—her hands, her face—as if trying to reassure himself that she was real. After a while she leaned her back up against him, took both his hands and put them over her breasts.

"It's me, and I still love you," she said.

"I'm a mess," was his answer, but he didn't take his hands away.

"You'll get better."

"How is Gwendolyn?"

"Sulky and bored. I think she misses you. So do I." Suddenly she was very serious. "Can we come live with you again?"

"Oh yes. Please."

At the rustle of passing footsteps, Steve let his hands drop down to her waist—a little admission that this place wasn't their private Eden.

They sat together on the bench for over an hour. He asked how Sam was doing and was surprised to hear that he planned to retire. Eventually, Steve brought up the case. He wanted to know what had been done with his father's body.

"It's still at the morgue."

"Then, when I get out of here, I'd like to bury him." He nodded. "I think I need to bury him."

"Okay. Whenever you're ready. They've long since done with him, and they won't release him except to you."

In the ensuing silence, Ellen made a decision.

"I killed him," she said. "We're never going to be able to pretend I didn't."

"You did what I should have done." His eyes suddenly welled with tears.

For what felt like a very long time but was probably no more than a minute, he seemed in the grip of the most terrible remorse.

"I couldn't have done it," he whispered. "I couldn't . . ."

He wept on her shoulder, without restraint, as if surrendering to his sense of shame. And then finally he stopped, forcibly pulling himself together.

"I'm sorry." He even smiled. "I'm such a coward."

"You saved me. You went in there and shielded me with your own body. You're the bravest man I know."

For a long time they sat there, holding each other wordlessly and then, when they were both in better control, Ellen decided she might as well tell him everything.

"He wasn't dying," she said, her eyes studying his face. "At autopsy they found he had acute pancreatitis, which has a lot of the same symptoms as pancreatic cancer. If he'd put himself under a doctor's care he would have been fine."

Steve shook his head. The irony, of course, was that if Walter hadn't thought he was almost dead he would have gotten away.

"And your last name, by the way, is Brewer. You were named after your grandfather."

"I think I'll stick with Tregear, if it's all the same."

He laughed briefly. Ellen had the sense that he was going to be all right.

"I don't suppose you could spend the night?" he asked. "We could go to a hotel."

"Sure. I've got tomorrow off—and if I didn't I'd call in sick. Will they let you out overnight?"

"Oh, absolutely. I can go anywhere I want. Stockton would probably think it's a great idea."

In another of those shifts of mood to which, Ellen told herself, she would just have to become accustomed, he looked away. God alone knew the terrible things that lived in his memory.

"He would have killed me if you hadn't . . ." He actually flinched, as if he were back in that room, waiting for death.

"He was a monster. And you couldn't kill him, which means that you're not."

She took his head in her hands, almost forcing him to look at her.

"Steve—listen to me—nobody kills because they're a hero. People kill out of fear. I was never so scared in my life as when I shot him. I killed him because I was afraid of losing you. In the end, if you want my opinion, he needed to kill you because he was afraid of you."

"I should have turned him in to the police back in Arkansas."

"If you had, he would have killed you the first chance he got, and then the murders would have just gone on and on."

He shook his head, as if to deny any possibility of an excuse. He started to say something, but Ellen cut him off.

"Listen to me, Steve. I know how these things work. I know how the police handle runaways, and they're used to hearing fantastic stories about how Mom and Dad are cooking babies down in the basement. They wouldn't have believed you, and you would have ended up dead.

"You did the right thing when you were twelve years old. It gave you a chance to grow up and put a stop to all this madness. Nobody else could have done it."

For an instant she saw in Steve's eyes the same anguish she had encountered in countless children during her three years with juvie. She saw the same baffled love, the same willingness to assume all blame, the same longing to be forgiven for sins never committed. *I have failed you,* those eyes said. *Everything is my fault. Please love me again.*

And then it was gone.